Praise for
Alpha Instinct

"Reus has an instinct for what wows in this perfect blend of shifter, suspense, and sexiness. Sexy alphas, kick-ass heroines, and twisted villains will keep you turning the pages in this new shifter series. *Alpha Instinct* is a winner."
—Caridad Piñeiro, *New York Times* bestselling author of *The Lost*

"Reus shows great promise and you'll look forward to visiting this world again soon!"
—*Romantic Times* (4 stars)

"*Alpha Instinct* is a wild, hot ride for readers. The story grabs you and doesn't let go."
—Cynthia Eden, author of *Deadly Heat*

"If you're looking for a new shifter romance to sink your teeth in, then look no further. *Alpha Instinct* is action-packed with a solid romance that will keep the reader on the edge of [her] toes! ... Highly recommended for fans of Rachel Vincent's Were-cat series." —Nocturne R̲o̲m̲a̲n̲c̲e̲ Reads

"*Alpha Instinct* is a strong boo̲k̲ f̲u̲l̲l̲ o̲f̲ m̲y̲s̲t̲e̲ry, intrigue, and a new world t̲o̲ e̲x̲p̲l̲o̲r̲e̲. I̲ h̲i̲g̲hly enjoyed this one, as I̲ h̲a̲v̲e̲ o̲t̲h̲e̲r̲ paranor-mal romance s̲t̲o̲r̲i̲e̲s̲ ... A̲n̲ O̲p̲e̲n̲ Mind

"A well-plotted, emotional and sensual ride that doesn't let go! ....
Ms. Reus delivers suspense, and a romance nothing short of heart pounding."
—Night Owl Reviews

Also in the Moon Shifter Series

Alpha Instinct
Lover's Instinct
(A Penguin e-Special)

PRIMAL POSSESSION

A Moon Shifter Novel

KATIE REUS

A SIGNET ECLIPSE BOOK

SIGNET ECLIPSE
Published by New American Library, a division of
Penguin Group (USA) Inc., 375 Hudson Street,
New York, New York 10014, USA
Penguin Group (Canada), 90 Eglinton Avenue East, Suite 700, Toronto,
Ontario M4P 2Y3, Canada (a division of Pearson Penguin Canada Inc.)
Penguin Books Ltd., 80 Strand, London WC2R 0RL, England
Penguin Ireland, 25 St. Stephen's Green, Dublin 2,
Ireland (a division of Penguin Books Ltd.)
Penguin Group (Australia), 250 Camberwell Road, Camberwell, Victoria 3124,
Australia (a division of Pearson Australia Group Pty. Ltd.)
Penguin Books India Pvt. Ltd., 11 Community Centre, Panchsheel Park,
New Delhi - 110 017, India
Penguin Group (NZ), 67 Apollo Drive, Rosedale, Auckland 0632,
New Zealand (a division of Pearson New Zealand Ltd.)
Penguin Books (South Africa) (Pty.) Ltd., 24 Sturdee Avenue,
Rosebank, Johannesburg 2196, South Africa

Penguin Books Ltd., Registered Offices:
80 Strand, London WC2R 0RL, England

First published by Signet Eclipse, an imprint of New American Library,
a division of Penguin Group (USA) Inc.

First Printing, September 2012
10 9 8 7 6 5 4 3 2 1

ALWAYS LEARNING   PEARSON

For Kari Walker, quite possibly my biggest cheerleader: I cherish our friendship and you. Thank you for always being in my corner and for loving the Moon Shifter world as much as I do.

Chapter 1

December McIntyre managed to smile at her date as he pulled out her chair for her. Her cheeks hurt from all the fake smiles and forced laughter. She should never have agreed to this date when she'd rather be anywhere else. With *someone* else. But she and Liam had no future, and going out with a random guy was the only way to show Liam *and* herself that she was serious about that.

"Have you been here before?" her date—Mike something—asked. As a tourist from the nearby ski lodge, he wasn't a local of her smaller mountain community, so it made sense he'd never eaten at the cozy Italian restaurant.

She nodded. "The *bucatini puttanesca* is really good. So is the *pollo caprese*. Actually, everything on the menu is good." The Russo family had settled in Fontana, North Carolina, decades ago, many years before she'd been born, and Russo Ristorante had become a staple in the mountain community. The locals loved it and so did the tourists. Occasionally they even got tourists from not just

Fontana Mountain but their neighbors, Beech and Sugar mountains.

Almost immediately after they ordered drinks, her date excused himself. He was a broker or something and had to take an important call. Normally that would have bothered her in a date, but she didn't really care about this one. The brief reprieve was fine with her. She wanted to get through the meal, get home, and just go to bed. Going out with this guy had been a colossal mistake no matter how nice he seemed to be. She'd known it the second after she'd said yes. Regret had surged through her, but it had been too late then.

All she could think about was Liam. Liam with his broad shoulders, dark hair, and coffee brown, deep, knowing eyes. When that man looked at her, she got shivers. The good kind. Heat bloomed between her legs when he was around. He didn't have to do *anything* other than train that heated gaze on her and she wanted to melt into his arms. He might be built like a linebacker, but his hands were gentle. At least the few times he'd caressed her face, they had been.

Her image of him was so clear she could almost see him now. In front of her. As she stared into space, she frowned. Then blinked. Good God, he *was* in front of her. Walking straight toward her.

"Crap," she muttered. Tensing, she braced herself. She'd thought if he saw her leaving her bookstore—because she'd seen him watching—with another guy on a Friday night, he'd get the hint and leave her alone. If it was anyone else, she might think he was acting like some sort of creepy stalker, but she knew him better than that. As one of the few lupine shifters who lived in their town, Liam had tried to warn her about some crazy fanatic group that wanted to hurt humans involved with shifters.

At twenty-eight she'd been taking care of herself for a long time—and besides, *they* weren't involved, so there was no reason for some fanatics to come after her.

Should have known Liam wouldn't give up so easily. The maître d' led him and another huge guy directly to the table next to hers. There was a decent amount of space between them, but for the way he was drilling his gaze into her, he might as well have been sitting at the same table.

"Hello, December." Liam's deep, intoxicating voice forced her to acknowledge him.

She flicked a quick look at his dark-haired friend, who cracked a small, almost amused smile until she glared at him—then she focused on Liam. "What are you doing here?" she asked through gritted teeth. It wasn't for the damn food. That much she knew.

He shrugged as if it should be obvious. "Eating."

She narrowed her eyes at him. "You know what I mean. I'm on a *date*, Liam."

At the word "date" those espresso eyes of his got even darker. Under normal circumstances she might have thought it was the light playing tricks on her, but she knew better. She'd seen him enraged once before when a man had tried to mug her. His eyes had changed then. The whites had almost disappeared and she'd found herself staring into not-quite-human eyes. He'd later explained that it sometimes happened when his inner wolf wanted to take over. It had scared her then but not now. She knew he wouldn't hurt her. Not physically. He might be dominating and sometimes too pushy, but he cared for her. In another world she might allow herself to care for him too. But they had no chance and she wasn't going to risk getting her heart broken and losing her only family due to involvement with Liam. Especially when anything that happened between them couldn't last. He barely looked thirty, but she knew he was over a hundred years old.

"Get rid of him." He didn't raise his voice, but there was a razor-sharp edge to it.

Maybe his tone should have made her nervous, but it just infuriated her. *He* infuriated her with all his arrogance. "Or what?"

"Or I'll do it for you."

She balled her hands into fists under the table. "You are so . . . so . . ."

In a fluid, graceful motion that reminded her he was more than human, he stood up and slid into the chair across from her. As if he had every right to do so. He half smiled and her traitorous libido roared to life. Why did the soft candlelight have to play off his features, making him even better looking? "Charming, handsome—"

His smart-ass response annoyed her even more, but it also allowed her to find her voice. "Arrogant and *annoying*," she said in a loud whisper, barely containing the need to shout at him. "Why would you think on any level of normalcy that it was okay to interrupt my date when I've made it perfectly clear nothing is going to happen between you and me?"

His eyes darkened. "I'm not interrupting. I'm just eating. Or don't you think shifters should be allowed in the same restaurants as humans?"

His words were like a slap. Shocked, she jerked back. She had issues with his kind—issues he didn't even know about—but the thought of restricting someone, anyone, access to a public place was horrifying.

Her dismay must have shown because he cursed under his breath. "I didn't mean that, December. I know you don't think like that."

"Then why'd you say it?"

"Because you're driving me crazy, woman. Why are you out with this loser?"

"He's not a loser."

"He's a fu—loser for leaving you all alone. And he's not me. He'll never be able to give you what I can. I can smell how much you want me even now. Just give us a chance, December." His voice dropped slightly, taking on that sensuous quality that made her legs tremble and heat spread across her lower abdomen.

"Liam, we're—"

"Too different. Yeah, that line is getting really old, Red."

A flush hit her cheeks. "Don't call me that."

"Why not?"

"It's too . . . familiar." Unfortunately she very much liked the intimate way the nickname rolled off his tongue. And that was bad.

"I plan to get very familiar with you soon, *Red*." He reached out and fingered one of her bright red curls.

Her stomach muscles clenched with need as his knuckles brushed against her cheek. As his masculine, earthy scent rolled over her, she struggled to remind herself why things would never work between them. When he looked at her with those captivating eyes, it was hard to remember her own name.

The sound of a man clearing his throat jerked her back to reality. Her date stood next to the table, looking between her and Liam with slightly narrowed eyes. "I didn't think I'd been gone that long," he said semijokingly.

"I'm sorry . . ." *Oh God, what was his name?* ". . . Mike. This is a friend of mine. And he's *leaving*."

Liam snorted loudly and glared at her. *"Friend?"*

He wasn't going to make this easy for her. Holding her breath, she waited for him to move.

After what felt like an eternity, he finally stood. Completely ignoring her date, he looked at her. Anyone else would have said a few polite words or excused himself, but not Liam. It wasn't in his DNA. He wouldn't be civil or polite if he didn't mean it. "This isn't over, *Red*."

Mercifully, instead of sitting back down, Liam nodded at the guy he'd arrived with. His friend dropped a bill on the table and they left without even having touched their drinks.

As her date slid back into his seat, she blew out a shaky breath.

"Ex-boyfriend?" Mike asked.

She shook her head. "Not exactly. I'm really sorry that happened."

He shrugged but she could see the annoyance in his expression. Not that she blamed him. In his position she'd be ticked off too. When their server came back to take their order, she knew she couldn't sit through a meal with this guy. Seeing Liam had shaken her to her core and made it clear she wasn't interested in dating anyone else. Until she could purge him from her system, she might not ever be ready. Just knowing he was out there and available made everyone else pale in comparison. After asking their server to give her a few more minutes, she looked at her date. She was ready to bail, but he beat her to the punch.

"You want to leave, don't you?" he asked, his voice wry.

Embarrassment flooded her but not enough that she changed her mind. She nodded and pulled a few bills out of her pants pocket. Removing one, she dropped a twenty on the table. It would more than cover their drinks. "I'm so sorry to have ruined your evening. There's no excuse for my behavior. I know you don't want all the details and I'm just . . . sorry. Would you mind taking me back to my store?" She'd let him pick her up there instead of home mainly because she'd wanted Liam to see them leaving together, but also because she didn't like giving her address out to too many people. Curse of being a cop's sister, she supposed.

"It's no problem and you don't have to pay." He placed a clammy hand over hers. His hands were soft, unlike Liam's callused, roughened ones. She didn't know what it was, but the feel of this guy touching her made her feel ill. He slightly tightened his hold and something akin to fear jumped inside her. Which made no sense. He seemed like a nice man. He'd held open her doors and pulled out her chair and been perfectly polite. But he wasn't Liam.

Somehow Liam had ruined her for anyone else and they'd never even kissed. She wanted to curse his name for that. December stood, using it as an excuse to take her hand back. "I spoiled our date. At least let me pay for the drinks."

Mike hadn't attempted to pull out his wallet, so she figured he didn't actually mind her paying. The walk to the parking lot was quiet. Politely, he held open the passenger door of his BMW.

As they steered out of the parking lot, the need to apologize again overwhelmed her. She'd never been so rude to a date before. "I know I said it already, but I really am sorry for messing up your evening."

Without looking at her, he pulled onto the two-lane highway that led back to the small downtown area. His shoulders hitched slightly in a casual shrug. "It's no problem. That guy obviously upset you."

She started to relax against the leather seat when he continued.

"I don't know why you'd expect anything less when you're associating with animals." The last word dripped with disdain and there was an unexpected rise in the pitch of his voice.

It took a moment for the significance of his words to register. She'd never said anything about Liam being a shifter. And it wasn't as if people could tell what they were by simply looking at them. But the way Mike said "animals," it was obvious he *knew* what Liam was without a doubt. She frowned at the knowledge. "Excuse me—"

She jerked back toward the door when he suddenly brought his right hand up. She saw the flash of the syringe and reacted. Barely had time to think.

Adrenaline swelled through her as he swung the needle at her shoulder. She used her arm to deflect the blow, her wrist jolting as their forearms collided with a solid thud. He still held the small weapon in his strong grip, but he hadn't managed to pierce her.

A bolt of terror splintered through her veins as she stared at the needle. She wasn't sure if it was poison or some sort of sedative, but whatever he planned to do, it wasn't good. If he knocked her out, he could do whatever he wanted. Take her anywhere. The knowledge sent another jolt of fear spiraling through her. Despite the confines of the car, she turned, pressing her back against the door. Then she lifted her leg and kicked out at him. Her winter boots were thick and sturdy and had a two-inch heel that could do some damage. They were still barreling down the highway and he had to keep his eyes on the road, putting him at a huge disadvantage.

"Bitch," he snarled, and tried to stab her leg while keeping the wheel steady.

He missed, so she kicked again. This time she twisted completely and raised both legs. The roads were icy and it was obvious he wasn't used to the snow. If he were, he'd have already gotten chains on his tires. His inexperience was probably why he'd attempted to stab her while driving. *Idiot.*

The vehicle swerved across the road and the syringe flew out of his hand. While he grappled with the wheel, she kicked out at him again, all fury and anger. This time her booted heel slammed against the side of his face and her other foot shoved the wheel wildly to the left. He grunted and expelled a string of nasty curses as the car bucked sideways, but she didn't care.

All the air rushed from her lungs as they fishtailed out of control. Everything slowed. She heard the sound of a horn blaring in the distance, tires screeching, and braced herself for the impact. For the pain.

On instinct she held on tight and crouched low in her seat. Her stomach shot into her throat as they flew off the road onto a snowy, icy embankment. She felt like she was on a roller-coaster ride except she knew the ending was going to be worse. The car spun wildly out of control for what seemed like forever until it skidded to a smooth stop on a bunch of fluffy snow.

Like a miracle, they didn't flip or ram into anything. Mike shook his head and looked around, a dazed expression on his face.

He might be in a state of shock, but December knew it wouldn't last long. She had to get out now, no matter how shaky she felt. She was twisted at an odd angle and sitting low, so she slowly reached behind her with one hand and felt for the handle. As she did, she unsnapped her seat belt with the other.

The door swung open and Mike finally realized what

she was doing. She fell back into the snow and he lunged at her. But his seat belt snapped him back into the seat.

Rolling over, she scrambled to her feet and started running. Or tried to. Her boots pressed into the white thickness as she struggled to make it up the steep embankment to the road, away from the forest they'd almost plowed into.

She heard him shouting behind her, but she kept going. It was dark, but if she could flag down a car before Mike caught her, she knew she'd be okay. She tripped and fell but clawed at the icy ground and pushed herself back up. Her heart hammered against her ribs and her skin crawled as she fought to get away.

Even though she wanted to look behind her, she didn't dare. It would only slow her down. When her boots touched the asphalt, a new burst of energy detonated through her. As fast as she could, she ran along the icy edge of the road. Her coat and jeans were dark, so she prayed any drivers had their lights on.

She'd gone only a few feet when two bright headlights shone in the distance. Waving her arms around like a madwoman, she continued running. She slipped again and tumbled backward. The ground was icy and hard, but she barely felt the impact on her hip.

Her survival instinct told her to haul ass if she didn't want to be killed. Or worse. As she started to push up, strong hands gripped her arms and pulled her to her feet.

A scream tore from her throat. Twisting around, she tried to break free until she suddenly recognized Liam towering over her in the darkness. She stared at him in confusion. *Why is he here?* "What are you—"

"What happened? Are you all right?"

Her heart thumped a staccato beat against her chest as she stared into Liam's dark eyes. "Where did you come from?" She started to involuntarily shake and his grip tightened. He was warm and safe.

"I saw you running down the side of the road. What the hell happened, December?"

She frantically glanced behind her, expecting to see Mike running at them, but no one was there. Turning to Liam, she opened her mouth but no words came out. Instead, the shaking intensified. She didn't know *what* had happened exactly. It had all been so fast. Suddenly she needed more air. It was as if her lungs had shrunk. She sucked in a deep breath, trying to steady herself.

Liam took one of her wrists, concern in his expression. "Your pulse is erratic," he murmured.

Of course it was. Her date had just tried to kill her. Or maybe he hadn't wanted her dead. He might have wanted to . . . "My date," she gasped out. "I told him I wanted to leave the restaurant. He had a syringe. He tried to stab me while he was driving and I kicked him and the wheel. I didn't even think about it. We flew off the road and I escaped. . . ." She shook her head and turned around again. It was too dark to see how far she'd run. "I don't think it was far from here. I just started running."

Still holding on to her wrist, he looked past her into the darkness. "I want you to stay here with Ryan, okay?"

No! She grabbed his arm. "Who's Ryan?" She felt disoriented and a little confused. And she couldn't stop the chills skittering over her skin.

"I won't let her out of my sight." The male voice from behind her made her jump, but when she turned to face the other shifter, all she saw was compassion in his dark eyes.

Liam hated leaving December, but he hurried down the embankment to find the piece of shit that had attacked her. Other than the fresh smells of the forest, he scented slightly burned rubber and December's date. His canines throbbed just from thinking about her out with someone else, but knowing she'd been attacked made his inner wolf almost blind with rage. He'd tried to warn her that members of the Antiparanormal League might target her because of her association with him. Not that he had the kind of "association" he wanted with her. He'd recently discovered that the APL somehow *knew* he cared for her, so they wanted to use that against him or his pack. Or both. It didn't matter that they weren't physically involved—or involved at all really. Which was why he'd been watching her. Even thinking about what might have happened if he hadn't been nearby tonight . . . his inner wolf rattled dangerously, so he shut down those thoughts.

As he neared the car, he saw the passenger's and driver's doors open. December's footprints led back the way he'd just come, but there was another set leading away into the woods. He stared toward the tree line, fighting back the primal growl trying to claw its way out of his throat. The key was still in the ignition, the car still running. Leaning over and careful to take it by the edges, he slipped the key out and dropped it into his jacket pocket. The contents of her purse had been dumped onto her seat. A small makeup bag, a book, and a planner. No wallet. His frown deepened.

His most primal side wanted to hunt this guy down and tear him apart limb from limb. Slowly. But he couldn't leave December. Liam still wasn't sure what had happened, but she'd been close to going into shock. If she hadn't already.

Pushing down the need to hunt and protect what was his, he gathered her stuff and shoved it in her purse. After checking the glove compartment to see if he could find some paperwork with an address on it, he came up empty, so he headed back to the road.

Ryan had already taken her back to the truck. From their silhouettes he could see December sitting in the middle of the bench seat and Ryan in the driver's seat. Normally Liam preferred to drive, but right now all he wanted to do was comfort her.

She kept pushing him away, but he didn't think she would now. She might try to deny she wanted him, but every time she fixed those baby blues on him, he could see lust and confusion battling inside her. He didn't care that she was human and he was a lupine shifter. Differences like that didn't matter. At least not to him. Obviously some people cared enough to want to hurt her.

At the moment she was vulnerable and he knew she might actually let him comfort her. Maybe he should feel guilty about taking advantage of her emotional state, but he didn't. He'd touch and hold her any way he could get her.

As he slid into the seat next to her, she immediately scooted closer to him. Reaching out, he tucked a red curl behind one of her ears. Her ivory skin was soft and slightly flushed, and her breathing was still erratic. Brushing his hand against her cheek, he let one of his fingers stray to her pulse point below her earlobe. Still erratic. Not good.

"Honey, look at me." He waited until her eyes focused on him. "Have you called your brother?" He might not get along with the sheriff, but Parker loved his sister and had more resources than Liam did at the moment.

"No. And I don't want to." Her voice shook but it was still strong.

"Some guy just attacked you. We need to report this."

She stuck her chin out mutinously, but he didn't miss the raw fear that had bled into her eyes. "I'm *not* going down to the station."

He sighed and looked at Ryan over her head. "Go to her store," he murmured. Then he refocused his attention on December. "We're still calling him, Red."

"Don't call me that," she snapped.

The burst of annoyance that rolled off her was exactly what he wanted. She didn't seem to be in actual shock, but after what she'd been through, she'd be coming down from an adrenaline high. She needed to find a balance. And he needed her to answer some questions. "Where did you meet this guy?"

"Uh, my store. He's just a tourist on a short ski vacation—or he told me he was. I'm sure that was a lie. I thought it would be a harmless date and a way to . . ." Her blue eyes widened as she trailed off.

"A way to what?"

"A way to convince you to leave me alone." Her cheeks flushed, staining her ivory cheeks a deeper shade of red.

Her words stung. He didn't want them to, but they did anyway. All he wanted to do was protect her. Yeah, they came from different worlds, but it shouldn't matter. His inner wolf growled at him and in that moment he hated his primal side. The side that told him to just take what he wanted. His human side cared a hell of a lot more about December to ever hurt her and he didn't like the turn his thoughts were taking. Veering the conversation in a different direction, he said, "Your purse had been dumped out and I didn't see a wallet. He probably has your address anyway, but you're going to need to cancel your credit cards."

"I don't carry a wallet. I keep my driver's license, cash

and a credit card on me. Parker drilled that into me years ago. In case I ever got mugged or something. He's really particular about stuff like that." She patted her coat pocket, then stilled, presumably as the rest of his words sank in. "What do you mean he probably has my address? He picked me up from my store."

"You were attacked in your house a few weeks ago." Even thinking about that got his heart racing. If her brother hadn't been there and scared off the guy, anything could have happened.

"Yeah, so?"

"Your date and that guy are probably part of the same organization."

She lifted an eyebrow. "Are you going to start in with that APL stuff again?"

"After tonight I wouldn't think you'd need as much convincing. This is a small town and it's not hard to find out where someone lives anyway." With enough money anything was possible.

She started to say something, then snapped her mouth shut. A frown marred her pretty face as her eyebrows knit together in concentration.

"What is it?"

"He said something about you being an animal. I can't remember exactly what it was, but I never said anything about you being a shifter. Still, he *knew* you were. Right after he said that, he pulled out the syringe. Then everything sort of went crazy." Shuddering, she wrapped her arms around herself and he couldn't help it. He slid an arm around her shoulder and pulled her tight against him. She needed comforting. Whether she admitted it or not. To his utter surprise, she didn't fight him. For a brief moment she stiffened, then melted against him.

Like warm silk, she sank into his side and buried her

head against his neck. Her jasmine scent twined around him, making him dizzy for a moment. The feel of her warm breath on his skin made the ache between his legs impossibly painful. Reaching out his other arm, he pulled her completely against him. The position was awkward for him, but he didn't give a shit.

Liam battled his disappointment as Ryan steered into the parking spot next to December's car. He didn't want to let her go. Wanted to keep holding on to her like this as long as she'd let him. But he needed to get her home.

When she realized they'd stopped, she pulled back and looked at him questioningly.

Sighing, he fished out the car keys from her purse and handed them to his packmate. "Follow me back to her place."

"What do you think you're doing?" she asked.

Liam ignored her as he rounded the vehicle and slid into the driver's seat. He didn't want to move her and he didn't want her driving. She might not be in shock, but she was shaken up pretty bad.

"Liam, what are you doing?"

"What does it look like? We're going back to your place and I'm calling your brother." He'd have already made the call if he hadn't thought it would upset her.

He found it interesting that instead of moving into the free passenger seat, she stayed where she was, in the middle seat. If anything, she actually moved a little closer toward him.

She might try to deny the chemistry they had, but she instinctively knew he'd protect her. December might not even realize it, but her most primal side trusted him. Her desire to be near him proved it. That knowledge soothed his inner wolf. And he would protect her. No matter the cost.

"You think it's safe there?" Her voice was a whisper.

He gripped the wheel tighter. "Hell no, I don't think it's safe, but unless you want to come back to the ranch with me—"

"No!"

"All right, then. We're going back to your place and I'm staying over until we can figure out what the next move is." He knew what *his* next move was. Convince her to move to the ranch with him. Temporarily at least. Then he'd convince her to stay long enough for him to prove to her once and for all that they belonged together. That was the plan anyway.

"What?" Shock laced her voice.

He stole a quick glance at her. She'd gotten most of her color back. "You think I'm leaving you alone tonight?" Not that he actually cared what she said. He was staying with her.

"Maybe we *should* call my brother," she hedged.

He knew what direction she was headed and he didn't like it. "We're going to call him, but I'm still staying over. Someone broke into your house a few weeks ago, then someone tried to kidnap you outside your store a week ago, and now some psycho tried to stab you with God knows what."

"The guy at the store just wanted to rob me. There's not a conspiracy behind every door, Liam. I run a business and it's one of the risks." Her voice was defensive.

Liam snorted at her words. That guy hadn't wanted to rob her. He'd wanted to kidnap her. Liam knew because he'd gotten the piece-of-shit APL member to tell him exactly what he'd been up to. All it had taken to get that information was a broken thumb. Then he'd threatened to do worse if the guy told the cops the real reason he'd been at December's store. Liam and his pack didn't want the cops involved with the APL. Their involvement could scare the extremists into going underground. Liam and his brother, Connor, didn't want that. They wanted to stop the APL before their influence grew and before they hurt anyone else. And they planned to do it their way. Humans and government agencies had too many rules and regulations. Something his pack didn't have to deal with.

As they pulled into her drive, another thought occurred to him. "Do you have your cell?"

"Yeah. I usually keep that on me too."

"Can I see it?"

Frowning, she nodded, but at least she handed it to him.

When their fingers brushed, he cursed himself for the shock that went through him. They barely touched and his entire body reacted. "Will you stay here while I search your house?"

For a moment he thought she might argue, but she finally nodded. "Fine, whatever. You're going to do it anyway."

Damn right he was. "Stay here with her," he said to Ryan as he took her key ring.

The second he stepped inside, he was accosted by her soft jasmine scent. It always subtly lingered on her and in her house it was more potent. Probably not to humans, but with his heightened senses it almost enveloped him with its purity.

As he moved from room to room, it was easy to see December's feminine touches. Most of the rooms had pale earth tones. Soothing and soft, like her. Once he'd checked each room, every window, and all entrances, he allowed himself a small amount of relief. There were no signs of a break-in and he couldn't smell the remnant scent of an intruder.

After the attempted kidnapping at her store Liam had tried to convince her to let him have an alarm installed there and at her house. Even her brother, who basically detested him, had agreed. But December was stubborn. Of course it might have something to do with the fact that he'd *ordered* her to let him take care of it instead of asking her. As second-in-command of his pack—well, technically third now that his brother was mated—he wasn't used to asking for things, though. Especially not when he knew he was right.

December might not have accepted that she was his intended mate, but he knew it with every fiber inside him. He didn't know *how* he knew—he just did. It was as if something inside him flared to life the moment they'd met. A hundred years ago—before his father had turned into a shell of a wolf due to his mate's death and before Liam's pack had been slaughtered—his father had told him he'd likely know his mate on sight. Not all shifters recognized their intended mates right away, but Armstrongs usually did. Just like his brother had recognized Ana as his other half. If only Liam could figure out a smoother approach with December. She didn't come from their world and didn't understand anything about pack law or . . . him. And he wanted to change that.

He might look like he was in his early thirties, but he was over a century old. In all that time Liam and his brother had lived apart from humans. They intermingled with them for business purposes, and as of twenty years ago humans had learned of their existence, thanks to the decision of his Council and a few other shifter Councils around the world. It didn't mean he'd completely embraced his civilized, human side, however. When he wanted something, his wolf side threatened to take over.

The battle between beast and man sometimes seemed never ending.

Sighing, he flipped open her phone and scrolled to her brother's name. Bracing himself for the reaction he'd get, he held it up to his ear.

"Hey, I was just about to call you." Parker's voice was friendly as he answered.

"This is Liam."

Like a switch flipping, he went from friendly to hostile in an instant. "Why do you have December's phone? What the hell is going on? Is she okay?"

"Someone tried to attack your sister. Again."

"What?"

"On the way home tonight her date tried to stab her with a syringe. She doesn't know what was in it or what he wanted, but she managed to stop him. From what I can tell, she got him to run off the road and she escaped. I found her running down the highway."

"Were you following her?"

Liam didn't bother to deny it. "I waited until she left the restaurant with that guy but kept my distance. I wanted to make sure she got home safe, and hell, *someone* needs to protect her."

"Are you saying I can't?" Parker snapped.

"Damn it, man. You know that's not what I'm saying. I only meant I've been keeping an eye on her. After that bullshit with Dr. Graham and those assholes who tried to attack Ana, I just want to make sure December is safe." Over two months ago a local doctor had poisoned the local Cordona pack, killing all the males and pregnant females. Ana Cordona—now his brother's mate— had become leader of an all-female pack by default. Since his brother and Alpha, Connor, had been in love with Ana for over half a century, Liam and the rest of their small pack had recently come to North Carolina and united her pack with theirs. And the poisonings had started up again. That's when they'd discovered that the person trying to poison their pack wasn't their only problem. The APL had targeted any humans associated with shifters or anyone they thought meant something to shifters.

"I know. . . . I appreciate it." The bitter tone of his voice told Liam it had taken a lot for Parker to admit that. "So where is she?"

"We're at her house. She's outside with one of my packmates. I just swept her place and it's clean. The guy she was out with tonight left his car right off the highway. It's about two miles from Russo Ristorante on the west side of the road, down the embankment. It's a BMW." He quickly rattled off the license plate he'd committed to memory.

Parker swore softly. "You're sure she's okay?"

"She's shaken up and I thought she might go into shock, but she's tougher than that. I got the keys out of the ignition and I was careful to pull it out by the edges."

"I'll send a couple of my guys to check out the car and I'll come by to take a statement from her. I'm going to post someone outside her place tonight, but will you be there until someone arrives?"

His mouth pulled into a thin line. Apparently even Parker didn't understand his intentions toward December. That all changed now. "I'll be here and I'm staying the night. Until we figure out what the hell is going on, I'm not leaving her side."

Liam expected a fight but Parker was surprisingly silent. The moment seemed to stretch on forever. Finally he spoke. "All right. I'll see you in a few."

As they disconnected, Liam let his gaze linger on December's bed. The queen-sized bed was a lot smaller than his own, but if he was in it with her, it wouldn't matter. Nothing else would matter other than holding her, sliding his hard length into her hot, tight sheath. Taking care of her. Claiming her. From the moment he'd seen her, it was all he'd been able to think about.

All his life he'd heard about what happened to males when they found their mates, but he'd never bought into that bullshit. The overwhelming need to protect. To mate. To *bond*. He'd never believed it until he met December.

Sighing, he shut her bedroom door behind him. One way or another he was going to find his way between her sheets and into her life. He was going to ingrain himself so deeply into her world she'd never want him to leave. Maybe not tonight, but soon. Very, very soon.

Chapter 2

December knew she should be grateful for Liam's presence. And she was. It was just strange to have him in her house, taking over everything. As he ushered her into the house, she felt some of her earlier tension and fear abate. He wouldn't let her walk into a bad situation and despite the break-in a few weeks ago, her house was one of the only places she felt relatively safe. The break-in had taken some of that away from her, but it was still her haven. She'd put a down payment on the two-story colonial-style brick home a couple years ago when her business had finally taken off. She wouldn't let anyone take away that joy.

"Come on." Liam didn't remove his strong hand from the small of her back as he ushered her into her kitchen.

Despite her desire to keep her distance from him, she found she didn't want him to pull away. "You checked the whole house?" She didn't know why she asked. The question just slipped out.

"Of course," he said absently, and led her to one of the ladder-back chairs at the round table in the corner of the room. It didn't cross her mind to argue or ask what he was doing as he practically forced her to sit, then started rummaging through her refrigerator.

With his back to her she couldn't see his expression, but she was under the impression he was frowning as he stared into the giant stainless steel fridge. It was something about the way his shoulders tensed. "What's wrong?" she asked.

"You have ... chick food in here. There's no meat or ... anything." His voice was incredulous.

"You're looking in my fridge without permission and complaining about what's in there?" She was too frazzled to even be offended. She knew she didn't have much in there. Yogurt, eggs, and some vegetables that probably needed to be thrown out. She lived by herself and ran her own business. Cooking when she got home was not one of her priorities.

He half turned toward her and she was surprised when his expression softened. "Ah, sorry. I wanted to heat something up for you. I doubt you ate at the restaurant and after what happened, I figured it would do some good if you got something warm in you."

Having *him* in her would probably do her good. Her eyes widened as the unexpected thought sliced through her. Embarrassed, she felt her face flush, but thankfully her stomach growled loudly. It sounded like a loud freight train, so she played off her obvious embarrassment at her wayward thoughts. She knew he couldn't read her mind, but she was a terrible poker player and Liam just seemed to know what she was thinking sometimes. "Guess I am hungry. There's some pesto pasta salad in there and you don't even have to heat it up."

By his expression it looked as if it was the last thing he wanted to feed her, but he pulled out the container and filled a bowl. After placing it and a fork in front of her, he proceeded to open a couple cans of soup. The adrenaline that had been racing through her earlier was slowly subsiding and she felt almost sluggish in her movements.

Her hand trembled slightly as she picked up her fork. Frustration surged through her at the action. She didn't know what was wrong with her. At the sound of the humming microwave she looked up to find Liam leaning against the counter staring at her.

And not bothering to cover up his desire.

"Don't look at me like that," she said quietly.

"Like what?" The question was practically a purr.

"Like . . ." He wanted to take her up against the wall. Or on the kitchen table. Or maybe the floor. Hot and hard. She knew he'd be better than anyone she'd ever experienced. The primal pull she felt toward him scared the crap out of her sometimes. Made her feel totally out of her element. ". . . like, you know what," she finished lamely.

When he didn't respond, she cleared her throat. "Did you call my brother?"

He stared at her for a long moment, those dark eyes seeing something he liked. Finally he spoke. "Yeah. He should be by soon. He sent someone to check out the car and he'll be here to pick up the keys. Hopefully he'll get some prints and we'll know if that guy is who he said he was."

"Is Parker . . . did he say if he was staying over?" She stared down at her bowl as she asked the question.

"He can stay over if he wants," Liam said. Not exactly the answer she was hoping for.

She tried a different tactic. "You don't have to stay over if Parker is."

He grunted something incomprehensible as he pulled out a bowl of soup. Normally she'd be more aggravated by his stubbornness, but tonight she *wanted* him to stay over. She wouldn't admit it aloud but the thought of him under her roof made her feel safer than if she had the best security system on the planet.

Liam placed another bowl in front of her, then sat across from her with a bowl of his own. She inhaled and smiled. Chicken noodle. What her brother had always made for her growing up whenever she was sick. Even though this wasn't the homemade kind, it still smelled good. After polishing off the pasta, she normally wouldn't still be hungry, but for some reason she was famished. She felt as if she hadn't eaten for days. Probably had something to do with her earlier adrenaline rush.

"Thank you for doing this," she murmured.

He grunted again. It was something he seemed to do often, but she couldn't figure out his moods or what the grunts meant exactly. Liam did it when he was annoyed, but he also did it when she thanked him for anything. As if her gratitude surprised him. She didn't understand that.

Silence normally didn't bother her, but the stillness that stretched between them tonight did. Maybe it had something to do with the fact that she'd been out with another guy when she'd known it would hurt him. While she hated that part, she desperately needed to keep her distance from Liam. When she was around him, it was difficult to think straight. Tonight it was even worse. She felt wildly off-balance and that spicy, earthy scent of his was driving her crazy.

"Are you sure you can stay away from the ranch tonight?" she finally asked, just to break the tension.

His dark eyes flashed with something she didn't recognize. "I've been doing it the past few days. Why would tonight be any different?"

His words slightly rattled her. "Am I supposed to feel guilty about that?"

"No. I'm just pointing it out. I'm staying here and if you want me to sleep in your car, I will."

"You *are* trying to make me feel guilty."

He grunted and she dropped her fork.

"Enough with the barely monosyllabic answers."

Sighing, he placed his utensil down too. "I don't want to do this tonight."

"Do what?"

"Argue."

"And by talking we'll automatically argue?"

"I didn't say that. I'm just pissed." His words were almost a growl, as if he was trying hard to talk normally.

"At me?"

"The whole situation. I'm pissed you went out with that asshole *and* that he attacked you. If you hadn't re-acted the way you did, this night could have ended a lot differently. Most of all, I hate that you won't let me take care of you. I just want to keep you safe."

"I'm letting you take care of me now."

Her words earned a ghost of a smile from Liam. "Heating up canned soup and serving you cold pasta doesn't count."

She shrugged and took another bite. Other than her brother she'd never had *anyone* take care of her. Her par-ents had died when she was eight and she and her broth-ers had been sent to live with their alcoholic uncle. He hadn't been physically abusive, just horribly neglectful. So they'd always had to fend for themselves with Parker being her only parental figure. When she was old enough, she'd started taking care of herself. Depending on someone wasn't something she wanted to get used to. People left, died, or simply changed. Usually for the worse. She had a lot of friends, but she'd always kept them at a certain distance. It made life easier.

"What are you thinking about?" Liam's deep voice tore her out of her thoughts.

Placing her spoon in her empty bowl, she shook her head. "Just how full and sleepy I am. It's not even that late."

"Your body had a shock tonight. You're lucky you didn't go into actual shock, but the adrenaline you felt earlier has likely waned and now you're feeling tired." He reached out and placed one of his large hands over hers.

Unlike earlier when her date had touched her, she didn't cringe or pull away. She liked the feel of him touching her, however slight. He rubbed a callused thumb over the top of her hand. The action was light, soothing, and totally nonerotic. Still, it made her stomach do little flip-flops.

Almost immediately guilt engulfed her. Her younger brother had died—been killed—because of *her* relationship with a shifter. The pain and weight of it all had nearly killed Parker. If she got involved with another one . . . She tugged her hand back and cleared her throat. "Let me put these in the dishwasher and I'll show you where the guest room is."

He stared at her for a long moment, as if he could read her mind. Then she remembered he could read emotions. *Crap.* Liam wouldn't know why she was feeling guilty, but he'd sense it just the same.

He grabbed her bowls before she could move. "I'll do it. And I know where the guest room is." When he spoke, his voice was remote, distant.

In a weird twist of emotional insanity, she didn't like him pulling away from her. How messed up was that? It was what she wanted, but when he did it, part of her felt lost. She rubbed a hand over her face as she trudged up the stairs. She needed her freaking head examined.

Liam resisted the urge to go after December. She needed to rest and he knew he'd already pushed her enough for one day. Why couldn't females be more like males? She wanted him physically, but for whatever reason she wouldn't let herself be with him. And he'd sensed *guilt* earlier when he touched her. Wasn't sure what that was about.

As he closed the dishwasher, the doorbell rang. With his senses on high alert, he went to answer it. Before he pulled the door open, he was already breathing a sigh of relief. Parker might not like him, but at least December's brother wasn't going to try to kill him.

Parker had a scowl on his face as he strode through the front door. His tan and brown polyester uniform was rumpled and dirty. "Where is she?" he demanded.

Thanks to his extrasensory abilities, Liam could faintly hear water running upstairs. "She's in the shower. What the hell happened to you?"

A small smile played across the sheriff's face. "A drunk tourist thought it would be fun to throw beer cans at some night skiers. When they brought him in, he tried to . . ." He trailed off as if he remembered whom he was talking to. "Never mind. I've got one of my deputies dusting that car for prints. Didn't you say you got the keys?"

Liam pulled out the plastic bag from his pocket. He'd put the keys in there earlier so he wouldn't accidentally touch them.

"December needs to make a statement," Parker said.

"You gonna drag her down to the station now?" From his limited experience with the man, Liam knew the sheriff was a stickler for the rules. Except where his sister was concerned. For her he'd not only bend them—he'd probably break them in two and run over them with a semitruck.

That was probably the only thing the two men had in common. They both cared deeply for the woman upstairs and would do anything to keep her happy and safe.

Parker raked a hand through his dark red hair. "No."

"You think she'll listen about getting that security system now?" Liam asked quietly.

The sheriff shrugged. "Damned if I know. Make the call anyway and send me the bill. They can install it while she's at work. Did you get a good look at her date?" he asked, quickly changing subjects.

Liam clenched his teeth. He'd be the one paying for her security system, but he didn't voice that. As he described what December's date looked like, Parker jotted everything down. He went over everything from what he was wearing right down to the small mole behind his left ear. The man's image had been seared into Liam's memory forever.

Once he was finished, the sheriff flipped his notebook shut. His blue eyes were the same bright shade as December's. They narrowed at Liam. "Where are you sleeping tonight?"

Liam wanted to be offended by the question, but if he had a sister, he wouldn't be showing as much restraint as the sheriff. "The guest room."

Parker was silent for a long moment as he eyed Liam. "If you wanted to hurt her, I know you would and could have by now. I get that you care for her, I really do, but you realize you've brought this on her, don't you?"

Liam fought back a growl at the sheriff's words. "By existing?"

Parker shook his head. "I don't mean this is your fault. The people who want to hurt her . . . well, somehow I doubt they're alone in their thinking. I'm just saying the more you're around her, the more she becomes a target for ignorant assholes."

Liam knew that was true. He also knew that barely half a century ago people of different races would have been ostracized for having a relationship with each other. Racism and hatred never seemed to change and he wouldn't walk away from December because of it. He wasn't a coward and wouldn't let some backwoods idea dictate how he lived. Instead of responding, he stayed silent. There wasn't much of a response to that anyway.

Parker was the one to break the silence. "I've got to get back to work. We're short staffed this week, but I'm going to send a patrol by to keep an eye on the house."

So that was the real reason the sheriff didn't mind Liam staying at December's place. He needed him to protect her. A completely adolescent part of Liam smiled at the thought. It had to be killing Parker that Liam was watching over his sister.

Once the lawman left, he slid the crappy lock into place, then methodically checked the house again. It didn't matter that he'd done it earlier—he was driven with the need to protect December. Someone who truly wanted in wouldn't bother with locks. They'd break a window or smash a door, but Liam wasn't going to make it easy for them. He slept light anyway and tonight he doubted he'd sleep at all.

*   *   *

Edward Adler leaned against the wooden post in the middle of the two-story barn. He hated waiting. Especially for this idiot. But in the war against supernatural abominations, he'd do what he had to. Even if it meant waiting two hours out in the cold for a dumbass pretty boy who'd likely screwed up his first mission. Unfortunately he needed this guy for multiple reasons. He might be the leader of the local group around Fontana Mountain, but he had a boss to report to. And his boss wanted results faster. *Always* faster.

Mike was well past the time he was supposed to check in. They were supposed to meet in the unused barn a couple hours ago. Edward hadn't brought his cell phone. He wasn't exactly worried about the government tracking him, but just in case Big Brother was watching, he didn't want to give them an easy way to keep tabs. Paranoid? Probably. But he couldn't be too careful.

After checking his watch one last time, he shook his head and started to leave. As he reached the door, he heard the sound of boots crunching across the snow outside. Ducking into a nearby stall, he crouched down and waited. The barn door creaked as it opened.

"Edward?" Mike's annoying, nasal voice called out.

"What took you so long?" he asked as he stepped out. When he saw Mike's face, he cringed. Half his face was red and swollen. Soon the markings would turn to a garish bruise. If he lived long enough.

"That bitch did this to me."

"So you *didn't* manage to kidnap her?" He tried to keep the disgust out of his voice. That's what he got for hiring these morons. Unfortunately he needed brainless thugs for the APL's ultimate plan. They were going to be sacrificed for the greater good, even if they didn't know it yet. He couldn't recruit anyone too savvy just yet. Not until the first phase of his plan was complete.

"There were ... complications," Mike said under his breath.

Edward reached into his pocket and idly fingered the handle of his crescent-moon-shaped knife. It was small but deadly. And he'd made it himself. The handle had been carved from a deer horn and the blade was one of a kind. Impossible to trace to any store. "That much is obvious. What happened?"

"I took her to that Italian place, just like you said. I excused myself for a few minutes and when I came back, that fucking animal Liam Armstrong was there. He left but he really shook that bitch up." Mike pressed a hand to the side of his face and winced. "I think she might have knocked a tooth loose."

"What *happened*?" He didn't care about this asshole's tooth.

"I tried to inject her with the ketamine you gave me, but she kicked the shit out of my face."

"How?" Unless she had martial arts training, he couldn't see the curvy redhead kickboxing Mike.

"How do you think? With her fucking steel-toed boots. She kicked at my face and the wheel and—"

"You tried to inject her while you were driving?" Edward tried to rein in his disgust. God, he'd really scraped the bottom of the barrel with this guy.

"Well, yeah. I didn't think she'd freak out like that. Man, she moved fast! And I didn't want to take the chance that once we stopped in town, someone would see me kidnapping her. I thought it'd take one jab and she'd be knocked out, but I didn't even get that far." Mike spread his hands in front of himself in a helpless gesture.

The ketamine wouldn't have knocked her out. That's not what Edward wanted anyway. He'd added medetomidine as an extra sedative. The combination acted as an anesthetic. It would have put her in a semisedated state until they could lock her up. He didn't like his prisoners to be aware of their surroundings. Now they had nothing. And this moron had screwed up. Adler ground his teeth together.

Mike had promised to come through for him and Edward had given him the chance because the guy had begged. He'd wanted him to succeed because Edward wanted that redhead. That giant shifter, Liam Armstrong, was very interested in her, and Adler knew they could use that against the entire Armstrong pack. The APL needed to get shifters on video harming humans and if Adler had the animal's woman, he knew he could send the shifter into a blind rage. In another world Adler could have waltzed into her store and asked her out and taken care of this business himself, but because of his scarred face no woman like her would look twice at him. Women didn't even want to look once at him. No, he'd had to send someone unthreatening. Attractive. A pretty boy. And a giant moron.

Edward took a calming breath. He needed answers before he killed Mike. "So what happened to the car?"

"I had to leave it. She escaped and bolted for the road. I thought I saw that shifter in the parking lot when we left, and I didn't know if he'd been following us. I couldn't get the car out of the snow, so I ran through the woods until I couldn't run anymore."

"Did you wipe down the car?"

His face flushed slightly. "Ah. I wiped down the wheel and handle. Besides it's not like she knows my last name or anything."

Edward's head cocked to the side. "Did you tell her your *first* name?" Christ, killing this guy would be doing the world a favor.

"Well, yeah. It's a common name and I didn't want to worry about having to remember something else."

"You're right. So how'd you get here?" Edward often used the abandoned barn to conduct business. It was on his land but miles south of his home and not many people outside of his circle knew about it. Not even his own boss with the APL.

"I stole a car and parked it at your place. When you weren't home, I figured you'd still be here. I'm really sorry I'm late, man. If you just give me another chance, I'll get her. I'll take her from work or something."

After what had happened, December McIntyre was going to be under lockdown by her brother and probably that filthy animal, Liam Armstrong. They wouldn't be able to get her for a while. This date was supposed to have been their golden opportunity to take her.

He had someone else in mind, though. And his boss would be very pleased if he brought the other bitch in. They'd already tried once with her, but the two men he'd hired had decided to deviate from his orders and gotten themselves killed. But if he could bring her in, it would be an even better score than the McIntyre woman. "We'll figure it out. Cut yourself some slack. It was your first real assignment."

Mike looked surprised by how well Edward was reacting. His shocked expression was priceless. Edward nodded toward the other side of the barn. "Come on. I rode here on a snowmobile. It's parked outside. You can ride back with me."

Edward reached into his pocket and quietly withdrew his knife. The curvature of the blade was perfect for what he planned. As Mike headed toward the other side of the barn, Edward made his move.

"Thanks. I really thought you'd be pissed about—"

From behind, he grabbed the front of Mike's face and head in a tight grasp. He cut deep, hard, and fast. The sound of his knife slicing across Mike's throat was a bare whisper. In a quick, practiced move he cut one carotid artery and the jugular vein. Mike's hand flew to his throat, but it was useless. He gurgled a cry as crimson liquid spurted everywhere. Through his fingers, down his shirt, onto the dirty ground. Edward stepped back to avoid the mess.

He might not like to get dirty, but he loved to watch the life drain from someone. There was something priceless about seeing the fear and knowledge in a dead man's eyes that his life was over.

Once Mike finished twitching, Edward wiped his blade on the back of Mike's coat and went to get his shovel. He'd have preferred not to kill him here, but he couldn't stand listening to him any longer.

A fresh wave of resolve swept through him as he carved the grave into the icy ground. The sheriff's sister might be off-limits for the time being, but he wasn't through with targeting the Armstrong pack. Not by a long shot.

Chapter 3

Through her slat blinds, December could see light starting to peek in. Without looking at her digital clock, she knew it was just barely sunrise. Normally she liked to sleep in on Saturdays, because she opened her shop up an hour later than usual. That so wasn't happening today.

Not with Liam sleeping in her guest room. She should probably be more concerned or scared that some maniac had tried to inject her with God knew what last night, but Liam's dark, dominating presence in her house was much more frightening. Okay, maybe not frightening. But it made her much more aware of . . . everything. Namely, herself and all the sexual feelings he stirred inside her.

She wasn't scared of him. Just scared of her feelings for him. Instead of staring at the ceiling for another hour, she threw off her comforter and headed to the bathroom. After brushing her teeth and washing her face, she stared at herself in the mirror. Her curls stuck out wildly thanks to a rough night of tossing and turning. For a moment she contemplated putting on makeup or taming her hair, then scoffed at herself. Let Liam see her this way. Maybe it would help him get over her.

She opened the bedroom door and jerked to a halt.

Stretched out on the rug covering the hardwood hallway, Liam lay on his back—*shirtless*—directly outside her bedroom.

His dark eyes popped open when she gasped. Something told her he'd already been awake, though. In one quick swoop, he assessed her from head to foot and smiled. Despite her pajamas she felt practically naked under his not-so-subtle evaluation.

As he stared at her, she couldn't help the way her own gaze strayed to his bare chest. His shoulders were impossibly broad and his chest was pure male perfection. All that strength. He wasn't bulky or overmuscled, like those awful-looking bodybuilders. Just firm, but too broad to be called lean. Her gaze helplessly dipped lower and his stomach muscles tightened in response.

The slight action jerked her gaze back to his face.

"Like what you see?" The question was low and sensual and his dark eyes were knowing.

Her mouth dried up and it took a moment before she could speak. She ignored his question and asked one of her own. "What are you doing on the floor?"

"I wanted to be close in case anything happened." Liam moved to his feet with the agility and speed of a jungle animal. Instinctively she stepped back. He didn't advance on her or make a move, but his mere presence invaded all her personal space.

Why did he have to make it so hard for her to keep her distance from him? He might be aggravating with his dominant attitude, but he still wanted to protect her. That made it difficult to get mad at him. Even though she wanted him gone—if only to get back some of her sanity—she also wanted to thank him for staying the night.

"Are you hungry?"

His dark eyes flashed and she knew what he was thinking before he said a word, so she preemptively cut him off.

"For *food*," she continued.

Grinning, he shrugged. "If that's all you're offering, I'll take it."

When he didn't move, she had to turn sideways to shimmy past him. She ignored his soft chuckle. The frustrating man enjoyed making her uncomfortable. As she headed down the stairs, she could feel his eyes burning into her. Mentally stripping her. "Stop doing that," she muttered.

"Doing what?" he asked, his deep voice far too close for comfort.

She resisted the urge to turn around. If she did, she was afraid of what she'd see on his face and afraid she'd like it too much. "You know exactly what. Quit looking at my butt."

"I can't help it, Red."

Changing her mind, she risked a quick glance over her shoulder to find him staring at her appreciatively. The way he looked at her was enough to make any sane woman melt. She definitely shouldn't have given in to the temptation to look. Sighing, she pushed open the swinging door to the kitchen and propped it open with an oversized antique bronze vase.

"I don't have much but I can make scrambled eggs, sausage, and cheese grits if you'd like," she said as he opened her refrigerator door.

"Grits?" His eyebrows pulled slightly together.

"You've never had grits?"

He shook his head.

"Where'd you live before moving here?" She pulled out a carton of eggs. She knew he was originally from Scotland, but he'd hinted that he'd been living in the States for most of his life. And most of that toe-curling Scottish brogue was all but gone. Occasionally it slipped into his speech patterns and when it did, her entire body heated up.

Liam started to fill her coffeepot with water. "All over, really. Upstate New York, Montana, all across the West Coast."

"Well, grits are a Southern thing, but I think you'll like them. They're sort of like polenta but a lot better."

He moved around her kitchen, surprisingly at ease. With the exception of her brother she never had anyone over in the morning. Liam made coffee and set the table while she cooked. Though he was silent, it wasn't an awkward silence. As they moved around the kitchen, it felt familiar. Like they'd done it a thousand times before. A tiny warning bell went off in her head. She wasn't supposed to feel comfortable around him.

He even fixed her coffee the way she liked it. She didn't like that they had the same tastes. As they sat at the table, the doorbell rang. They both froze for an instant, but Liam was quicker than her. She blinked and he was out of the chair and by the kitchen door. "Are you expecting company?" His voice was quiet but there was a deadly edge to it.

December doubted that someone wanting to break into her house would ring the bell, but she didn't say that out loud. He looked like he was in battle mode and she didn't think he'd appreciate the sarcasm. It was barely seven, but her friend Kat had told her she was coming by to pick up a box of books. "I completely forgot my friend was coming by this morning."

"Friend?" Liam's eyes narrowed a fraction.

December's lips pulled into a thin line. "First of all, my friend is female, but second, I'm allowed to have male friends. And I *do*. Plenty of them."

"Why would any male want to be friends with you?"

His words were like a swift punch to her chest. "Excuse me?"

He held his hands up in a defensive gesture. "No, I mean, *just* friends. I mean, I could never be just friends with you. I . . . shit, never mind." His expression was so dejected and out of character she was tempted to smile, but she didn't let him off the hook.

Liam had a possessive streak a mile wide and it annoyed her. She tried to hurry past him, but true to form, he beat her to the door. By the time she'd caught up, he'd opened it. No doubt after looking through the peephole. Or maybe he'd scented her friend. December still didn't understand the animal side of him and what his limitations were.

"Hey, December." Kat's eyes widened as she looked back and forth between Liam and December.

She wrapped her arms around herself at the sudden blast of cold air that trailed in. "Hey, Kat. I didn't realize you'd be here so early." In that moment, December hated the unfamiliar jolt of jealousy she experienced. Especially since it was directed at her friend. The sun was barely up but her friend looked perfect. Her ivory skin practically glowed. Kat was tall and slim, built like a model, but she actually had breasts. With long, dark hair and exotic, almost catlike eyes she was the kind of woman men fantasized about. Now that she thought about it, December was pretty sure her friend had said something about modeling when she was younger. And December felt tiny and small for being jealous of her.

"Sorry, the drive was quicker than I thought in this snow." She looked at Liam questioningly. "Uh, hey, Liam. I didn't know you knew December."

December didn't bother to hide her shock as she turned to him. "You know Kat?"

He took a step back and cleared his throat. "Sort of. I'll let you two do whatever it is you need. . . ." His voice trailed off as he disappeared back toward the kitchen.

December shut the door behind Kat, who was looking at her expectantly. The bottom dropped out of her stomach. Oh God, had they slept together? She shouldn't care since she had no claim on him, but the thought bothered her. Okay, more than bothered her. It made her see red and feel as if claws could sprout at any moment. "The books are in here." She motioned toward her living room where the box of books sat on her coffee table.

Kat trailed after her and flopped down on her brown leather love seat. "So, you and Liam Armstrong, huh? *Very* nice, girl." She was whispering but December had a feeling he could hear them anyway.

December sat next to her but perched on the edge of the couch. "Did you sleep with him?" As soon as the words were out, she wanted to take them back. She couldn't believe she'd asked her friend that.

Kat's pale eyes widened for an instant. Then she laughed as if the thought were hysterical. "Uh, *no*. Not that he's not hot or anything, but, uh, he's not exactly my type. And I'm pretty sure I'm not his either, guessing by the way he was practically devouring you with his eyes."

December hadn't expected the relief that swelled through her. It was like a fast-breaking wave that nearly knocked her off her feet.

Before she could say anything, Kat continued. "So what's up with you two? He's spending the night? When did this happen? I thought you had a date with that tourist last night. He's a stockbroker or something, right? And I've never known you to let a man stay the night. I want details!"

December struggled to compose herself. She'd almost been able to forget about what had happened the night before. Pretend it was a dream. Her friend's question brought reality crashing back on her. She'd tell Kat later what had happened, but if she started talking about it now, she was afraid she'd do something stupid like start crying. "That didn't work out. And Liam and I aren't together. Not like that. We're just friends."

"Friends?" Kat snorted loudly. The sound was so irreverent it made December smile. "Yeah, all my hot male friends have sleepovers with me too. We stay up late and paint each other's toenails. Do *not* hold out on me. I haven't had sex in forever, so give me something juicy."

She didn't bother explaining herself. "How do you know him anyway? He hasn't been in town that long." Liam had moved to the Fontana Mountain community less than a month ago. She still didn't understand all the dynamics of his pack, but his brother was some sort of leader. An Alpha, she thought he was called. Now Connor was leader of the local pack.

Suddenly Kat looked uncomfortable. "Uh, something happened and . . . I don't want to lie, so just ask him about that, okay?"

A thread of unease wormed its way through her, but she ignored it. Apparently they both had secrets. Instead of pressuring her friend, she changed the subject. "I'm sorry I haven't been to the center lately. I promise after the New Year I'll be volunteering again."

Kat shook her head and peered inside the open box

on the table. "You don't have to explain yourself. I just appreciate all these books."

When she gave up teaching and started her own bookstore, December had volunteered her free time at the local literacy center. But when her only two employees had quit within weeks of each other, she was still trying to find at least one decent replacement. Volunteering for anything at the moment was out of the question.

"Well, I've still got a couple more stops to make before my first class, so I'll get out of your hair and let you get back to your *friend*." Kat stood and lifted the box.

"Liam and I aren't—"

"Yeah, yeah. Save it. Why don't you bring him to the party tonight?"

"Party?" She stared at Kat in confusion.

"I can't believe you forgot."

December racked her brain. It sounded vaguely familiar. The past couple weeks she'd had a lot on her mind. Someone had broken into her house, roughed her up, and Tased her, some other jerk had tried to mug her, and then last night . . . She shuddered as she remembered it. Partying wasn't on the top of her to-do list lately.

"We'll be there." Liam's voice jerked her out of her thoughts. She turned to find him walking out of the kitchen. And he now had a sweater on. She hadn't even heard him go upstairs. The man really was stealth personified.

A huge grin broke over Kat's face. "Great. It's at the ski lodge, so just come by my cabin around seven and we'll head there together."

December wanted to argue but knew it was pointless. After the last few weeks maybe she needed to relax anyway. And if Liam was with her, she wouldn't have to worry about anything bad happening.

"So what's this party for?" Liam asked after Kat left.

"I have no idea but it's probably a birthday for some-one Kat works with. It should be fun, though, if it's at the ski lodge."

"I kept a plate warm for you." He motioned toward the kitchen.

She didn't want to be affected by what he'd done, but the gesture was sweet. "Thanks. So, how do you know Kat?" Kat's cryptic answer had piqued her interest.

He shrugged but looked just as uncomfortable as Kat had. "Ah, it's a long story."

She lifted an eyebrow at him as she sat at the table. "I have time."

"I can't tell you and I'm not going to lie to you." He placed her plate in front of her.

"Excuse me?"

"We met under . . . illegal circumstances."

"Illegal? *Kat?*" They hadn't been friends long and she was really private about her past, but her friend volun-teered most of her time when she wasn't working at the ski lodge as an instructor. And once a spot opened up at the local elementary school, Kat planned to start teach-ing again. December couldn't see her engaging in any-thing bad.

"I didn't say *she* did anything illegal. Just that the cir-cumstances were. . . . Listen, I don't want to lie to you and I can't tell you, so let's leave it at that."

Pushing down her annoyance, she speared a piece of sausage with her fork. Did he think his answer made her any less intrigued?

"I didn't sleep with her, if that's what you're worried about."

"I know," she muttered.

"How do you know?"

"Because I asked her." Damn it! Admitting that was as good as telling him she cared.

A wide grin spread across Liam's face. He looked positively smug. At least he didn't respond. The man was smarter than that.

Edward moved closer to the fireplace. The heat in his house had kicked off last night and the place was only now starting to warm up.

"Attempting to take the Saburova woman is crazy. Do you know who her father is?" Joseph asked.

Of course he knew who the criminal was. Years ago Edward had lived in Miami for over a decade. Even though he hadn't run in the same circle, anyone who lived there knew who Dimitri Saburova was. The man was one of the most violent, brutal bastards Edward had ever come across. That was saying something.

Dimitri's daughter had cut ties with her father, but that wasn't why Edward wanted her. Katarina Saburova had been intimately connected with Jayce Kazan, the enforcer for the North American Council of lupine shifters. Katarina and Jayce had dated for many months until she'd moved to North Carolina.

Edward had almost had her captured a few weeks ago. The two idiots he'd enlisted to kidnap her had accomplished that much with relative ease. But then they'd been killed because they hadn't followed his instructions. Instead of bringing her straight to him, they'd apparently locked her up in some cage on their property. Then they'd gotten themselves arrested for going after Connor Armstrong's mate in the middle of the day during a drunken joyride. That had made them a bright shiny target for the Armstrongs. If they hadn't gotten themselves killed, Adler would have done it anyway.

Those fucking Armstrong brothers, Liam and Connor, had interfered. He couldn't prove it but he knew they'd helped Katarina escape. That bitch hadn't killed those two goons on her own. The cops might have bought her story—because they had no reason not to believe her—but he had a video recording of the Armstrong brothers searching Felix's house. The same day and around the same time the woman supposedly killed Edward's two guys all by herself. Unfortunately he didn't have video from the shed where they'd died. It was where they'd taken their victims, and Edward hadn't known about its existence until too late.

Edward straightened. "I *know* who Dimitri Saburova is. She hasn't spoken to her father in a year. He won't be a problem." The heat was nearly suffocating now, so he stepped away from the fire.

"I don't know, man. I knew this guy who went to Coleman Penitentiary instead of flipping on Dimitri. The Feds offered him protection and everything and he *still* chose maximum-security prison." Joseph wiped a hand across his sweaty brow and Edward knew it had nothing to do with the warmth of the room.

"Taking her will be a triumph for us. What do you think the boss will be able to do with her?" They could bring the enforcer to his knees and turn him into a mindless killer.

Joseph looked confused and shrugged. "I dunno."

Edward clenched his jaw. While he appreciated the enthusiasm of these new recruits, they were more or less ignorant thugs. Or wannabe thugs. Which was often worse. They thought they were bad enough to take on anyone. He cleared his throat and tried to keep the disdain out of his voice. "Forget about her father. This bitch dated the enforcer."

"So? They broke up."

He sighed. "It doesn't matter. Those animals are very territorial. He'll come for her. If we take her, he'll trade his life for hers."

Joseph frowned. "You're sure?"

He probably would trade his life for hers, but that's not why they wanted him. If they lured Kazan into a trap where they held Katarina, he'd kill any human in the near vicinity who he thought was involved with her kidnapping. Joseph would likely be one of those humans and if Adler could get it on tape . . . He smiled at the possibilities. Once that happened, the APL could officially launch their media campaign against all these shifter abominations. "Why do you keep questioning me? Haven't I given you a place to stay? Didn't I take you in when you had nowhere else to go?"

Immediately Joseph's eyes dropped. "You're right. I'm sorry."

"Soon that bitch will—"

"Tsk, tsk." Brianna walked into the room carrying a tray of cookies.

Immediately Edward felt like he was a kid again. "Sorry, Brianna."

"If you want to teach these recruits, you also need to teach them manners." Her soft voice was authoritative.

"Of course. I'm sorry." Petite, blond, and damn near perfect, Brianna was the only woman on the planet who got away with talking to him that way.

She was also the only woman he'd ever stand for. Hurrying toward her, he took the tray and laid it on the middle of the coffee table. He desperately wanted to please her and hated himself for it. "These look great."

A slight smile touched her full, pink lips. "I have three more trays of finger foods in the kitchen."

"We'll help you get them." He nodded at Joseph, who immediately disappeared into the other room.

Before he could move, Brianna patted the side of his face. The hideously scarred side of his face. He tensed, as he always did, but she didn't pull back. The disfigurement never seemed to bother her. "You're better than all of these men combined. You just have to act like the leader you are. Cursing is for ignorant thugs and you're not one. Remember that," she whispered.

In response, he nodded. It was difficult to talk around her. He wanted to hate her, but he didn't. He just wanted her approval so much.

"I'm going to shower before the meeting, but you'll make sure everything is laid out properly?" she asked in that genteel voice.

Again, he nodded.

She disappeared up the stairs and only when she was out of eyesight did he breathe again.

"Man, I don't know why that bitch thinks she can tell you what to do," Joseph said as he walked back in carrying a tray of sandwiches.

If he hadn't been carrying food *Brianna* had prepared, Edward would have struck him. "Don't you *ever* talk about her like that. She does a lot for the APL and deserves our respect."

Joseph faltered, likely because of the deadly edge in Edward's voice. "I'm sorry, man. I just don't like to see her treat you that way."

She did so much more than that, but Edward wasn't going to bother explaining that to this nobody. After joining their organization, Brianna had gotten so much intel for them by simply using her innocent appearance. Not her body, though. She had a way of talking to people and getting them to open up. When she'd been evicted from her apartment, he'd offered her a place to live over a month ago. At first he thought he'd made a mistake, but she'd given his life order in a way he hadn't thought possible.

She was like the mother he'd never had. No, she was better. His own mother had abandoned him and his father. Brianna wasn't a whore either. She didn't spread her legs for anyone. She was perfect.

He'd gotten hard once when he accidentally saw her coming out of the shower. It was the only time in his life he'd ever felt shame. But it wasn't her fault. She hadn't been deliberately trying to taunt him. Besides, she *looked* at him. Really, truly looked at him. She never turned away from his scarred face. Which was more than he could say for anyone.

As he felt his body get hot, he inwardly cursed his own thoughts. When he realized Joseph was staring at him with a curious expression, he backhanded him. The kid had to learn not to question him. Brianna was right. If he was going to be a leader, he had to start acting like one.

Chapter 4

Kat smiled at the man who held the door open for her at Gwen's Bakery. Since moving to Fontana, she'd tried to immerse herself like a local. There were only two decent bakeries and while Dee's Doughnuts had good doughnuts, Gwen's had the biggest and best assortment of petits fours she'd ever had. She'd lived in Paris for a few months one summer during college, so that was saying something.

The small mountain town was a far cry from warm and sunny Miami, her last home, but she'd grown up all over the world thanks to her father's business. She could adapt to almost any situation. But she truly liked Fontana. The friendly people, the fresh air, and the tolerant attitude of most of the town.

A pack of shifters lived on the outskirts of town and from what she could tell, most of Fontana had accepted them. There were always exceptions, but moving here had been one of the best decisions she'd ever made. It had allowed her to make a clean break from her father's shady dealings and it was far away from Jayce Kazan.

That man technically didn't have a home. Well, not a permanent one. He was the enforcer for the North American Council of lupine shifters and his job took him everywhere, so he lived out of hotels. Some days she wished she'd never met him, but others . . . she couldn't imagine not having known him. And she hated him for that.

She placed the small white bag of pastries in the passenger seat of her Jeep and steered out of the parking lot. If she didn't hurry, she'd be late to teach her first class. Today she was teaching skiing for beginners. It was mainly kids under ten and she was looking forward to it. As she rounded the last bend before the turnoff to Fontana Lodge, she noticed the same gray truck tailing her that she'd seen as she'd left the literacy center.

Her fingers tightened around the wheel as alarm jumped inside her. It could be nothing, but after she'd been kidnapped a few weeks ago, she paid extra attention to her surroundings. Hell, she still couldn't believe those two monsters had managed to surprise her outside the grocery store. She'd let her guard down since moving to Fontana. In Miami that never would have happened. In Miami she hadn't been allowed to go anywhere without one of her father's bodyguards. Well, until she'd met Jayce. Then she hadn't been allowed to go anywhere without him. Sadness welled in her chest whenever she thought of him. He'd been her first love, her first . . . everything. Her throat tightened and she tried to block out memories of him. She couldn't allow herself to travel down that emotional minefield.

For as long as she could remember, the men in her life had always been so annoyingly protective. She'd never missed that overbearing presence until she'd been at the mercy of two evil assholes. If it hadn't been for Connor and Liam Armstrong...She shuddered and locked those thoughts up too. There was no sense thinking about what might have happened. It would only drive her insane. After the cops had started digging around the shed she'd been held in, they'd discovered "mementos" from other victims. And body parts. So far they'd found at least five female victims, but Kat didn't doubt there would be more on that property.

She swallowed back the bile in her throat. Thanks to two strangers that saved her life, she now had two new friends and an entire pack of shifters she wouldn't hesitate to call on for help. The fact that her friend December was obviously involved with one of them made her feel even better about them.

As she neared the turnoff, the truck behind her sped up even faster. Her unease turned to worry. She gunned the engine and took a sharp turn. Even with the chains on her Jeep her vehicle swerved slightly against the slick, icy asphalt. Keeping her eyes on the road and her rearview mirror was difficult. When she saw the truck continue past the turnoff, she still couldn't allow herself to relax.

Instead of heading for the main parking lot, she zoomed straight for the valet. As an employee she wasn't supposed to use it, but one of the guys had a crush on her and usually let her get away with it. She was probably being paranoid but she didn't care. Better safe than sorry. Especially after what had almost happened to her.

Pulling to a stop, she pushed out a relieved breath. Her heart pounded erratically and she knew she was likely overreacting. The truck hadn't been following her. She was just letting her imagination run wild. As she grabbed her purse and pastry bag, her loud ringtone sliced through the air. She jumped and let out a startled cry.

When she saw the number, all thoughts of gray trucks

and kidnappers dissipated. It was Jayce. She swallowed hard as she stared at the caller ID, a knot forming in her throat.

Kat missed talking to him. So much so that she actually ached to hear him say her name once more in that gravelly, sinfully sexy voice. It was so distinctive she'd know it anywhere. But she knew she shouldn't. After she'd ended things, he'd called her a dozen or so times. She'd been strong eight months ago. She could be strong now.

She silenced her phone and shoved it into her purse. When Randy waved at her from behind the valet stand, she plastered a smile on her face and opened her door. She still had time to scarf down some food before she made it to the bunny slopes.

Shoving thoughts of Jayce's gray, hungry eyes from her mind, she reminded herself *why* she'd walked away. He didn't have a place in her life anymore. He'd given that up when he'd decided she wasn't good enough for him.

December felt Liam glance at her as she steered in front of the lodge's valet. He'd spent all day with her at the bookstore and *still* couldn't take his eyes off her. It might put her a little on edge, but it was incredibly flattering to have such a sexy man like Liam so unequivocally focused on her. And she was grateful he'd unloaded and stocked her new shipments today. While she'd had to get used to his unfamiliar presence, having him around hadn't been that bad.

"We don't have to stay long," she murmured before one of the valet guys opened her door. He'd been quiet on the ride over and she couldn't tell what kind of mood he was in.

As she took the parking ticket, he rounded the vehicle to her side. Something told her that under normal circumstances he would have insisted on driving, but it was almost as if he'd sensed her need to stay in control and had decided not to push.

"We'll stay as long as you want." His voice was low and sensual and even though she tried to fight it, her cheeks heated up as warmth curled through her and settled low in her belly.

Liam wrapped his arm around December's shoulders as they headed into the main lobby of the lodge, almost like he was staking a claim on her. Part of December wanted to pull away from his hold, but she didn't. She loved the feel of his strong arm around her even though it was making her feel off-kilter. As they strode through the lobby, she motioned to their left, since she knew where they were going. Kat had called her earlier and told them to just meet her at the martini bar on the west side of the hotel.

Some guy Kat worked with was having a birthday. December thought she'd met him once or twice. In fact, if she remembered correctly, Kat had tried to set her up with him, but with their conflicting schedules it had never worked out. She hadn't told Liam that, though. He was oddly possessive about stuff. Not creepy or anything, but she was coming to understand that his human and animal sides constantly battled each other.

She'd seen it in his eyes earlier when she'd insisted on driving to the party. He hadn't wanted to let her. Truthfully, she was surprised he'd given in. The small act had allowed her to relax a little. He'd been a big help at the store today, but he'd also been an even bigger distraction.

It was impossible to focus on customers when he was

there. Everything about him was pure male. He practically reeked of testosterone. Normally men like that annoyed her, but with Liam it was hard to keep her hands off him. And after seeing him without a shirt this morning, she kept envisioning what it would be like to run her hands up his muscular chest and down his equally muscular back. Everything else would be just as tight and firm. She absolutely knew it.

When they entered the bar, she was impressed by the changes. A new owner had taken over a year ago and it showed. No more moose heads and garish track lighting adorning the place.

The purple and pink lights created a soft glow around the darkened room and the plush bar stools were definitely an upgrade. It was still early and the place wasn't crowded yet. She immediately spotted Kat sitting on one of the leather couches in one of the corners of the expansive bar. Naturally she was surrounded by four men.

When Kat spotted them, however, she made a beeline in their direction. "Oh my God, I'm so glad you guys are here." She grabbed December's arm, pulling her away from Liam, and dragged them to the bar. "I need a drink."

Kat pulled up a stool and December did the same. She glanced at Liam. "Don't you want to sit?"

"No." He didn't even glance at them. Just took on this warrior-type stance as he surveyed the room. No doubt looking for possible danger.

After everything that had happened the past few weeks, she was actually thankful for his overprotectiveness. Though she wouldn't tell him that. It would be as good as giving him the go-ahead to act like that all the time. And that so wasn't happening.

"You'll never guess who called me today. Twice," Kat said as she motioned for the bartender.

"Your ex?" December asked, even though she was pretty sure she already knew the answer.

Kat looked surprised. "How'd you know?"

"Because you get this crazy pissed-off look every time you mention him." December grinned at her friend. Kat was pretty quiet about why they'd broken up, but a few times when she'd been drunk, she'd opened up to her about how he'd broken her heart and what an asshole he was. "So what did he say?"

"I don't know. I didn't answer the phone."

"Why not?"

Kat shrugged and her scowl deepened. "Because screw him, that's why." She grabbed the mixed drink placed in front of her and downed half of it in one gulp.

"Uh, Kat?" December raised her eyebrows.

"I know, I know. I just need something to take the edge off. He hasn't called in months and now out of the blue he's started up again. He just has that effect on me. I'm so antsy right now and I hate it."

December shifted uncomfortably in her seat and contained the urge to look in Liam's direction. Yeah, she understood how a man could have that effect. And she hadn't even slept with Liam yet. As far as she knew, Kat had actually lost her virginity to her ex-boyfriend. She was one of the few women December knew who'd waited so long to have sex. It was definitely easy to get twisted up over your first. She looked at Liam again and he was still standing soldier straight surveying the bar.

Shaking her head, she smiled at Kat. Maybe tonight they both needed to loosen up. "Want to do a shot?"

Jayce moved through the crowd of yuppie assholes with ease. The loud party in the martini bar of Fontana Lodge was in full swing. Thanks to his extrasensory abilities the scent of alcohol was the most pungent thing here tonight. It was worse than a fucking brewery.

He hated other people touching him and the stench of most humans, shifters, or vampires was enough to make him want to live alone the rest of his life. However long that might be. After five hundred years there weren't many things that could kill him. Not that plenty of supernatural beings and humans alike hadn't tried.

He was broad, but not quite as tall as one might expect for the Council's enforcer. At six feet tall, it didn't seem to matter. Most people were scared of him. Or cautious. With a shaved head and a vicious scar that crisscrossed his left eye, he knew what he looked like. He'd never be called handsome. Hell, he couldn't even pass for marginally good-looking. Which was one of the reasons the crowd automatically parted for him anywhere he went. Most people thought he was a thug.

Everyone except Katarina. She'd seen right through him the instant they'd met. She'd known *what* he was too. For a human she had a rare gift to spot supernatural beings on sight. She was a seer, just like her mother had been. She hadn't known he was the enforcer, but she had known he was a shifter. A lupine shifter. She'd been very specific about that too. She'd told him she could see his wolf perfectly and then she'd had the nerve to tell him he was nothing more than a harmless puppy.

In all his years people rarely surprised him. And women *never* surprised him. Until he'd met Kat. She'd shown no fear when he'd told her all the dirty things he wanted to do to her. He'd intentionally spoken to her crassly, as if she were a common whore and not the most outspoken, intelligent, beautiful woman he'd ever met. He'd needed her to get the hell away from him and thought his rudeness would work. She'd gotten under his skin in the worst way and no matter how rude he'd been to her, she'd simply ignored him or gone toe-to-toe with him instead of slapping the shit out of him like he deserved.

By chance he'd met her when he'd been visiting her father's estate for some "business" dealings. Some members of the Council had wanted him to buy weapons from Dimitri Saburova, her father and one of the most connected weapons dealers on the East Coast. After that first encounter with her he'd gone out of his way to see her any chance he could. It had taken half a year, but in between working various jobs around the country, he'd finally worn her down and she'd agreed to one date with him.

A lunch date.

But that's all it had taken. Some days he wondered what the hell she ever saw in him. The woman was so far out of his league it was painful.

He'd been screwed up ever since she'd left him, but tonight he was going to see her. Had to see her. It had nothing to do with the Council ordering him to come to Fontana to check on the Armstrong-Cordona pack after all their recent troubles. And it had nothing to do with him being on a mission to sniff out members of the APL. He snorted at the acronym. Antiparanormal League. What a dumb fucking name.

As he moved across the dance floor, a blonde with huge, fake tits smiled drunkenly at him, but when he bared his teeth, she jerked in surprise and turned back to her friends.

He couldn't see Kat yet, but he could smell her. In a crowd of a thousand he'd be able to pick her out. She smelled like roses. It was subtle, classic, and didn't fit her personality at all. But that's what her scent was. If he even got a whiff of the stupid flower, visions of her over-took him. Not that he needed to smell roses to think of her. She'd overtaken his every waking thought since she'd gone. He'd even tried to fuck other women, but he couldn't. His cock wouldn't obey him. Just absolutely fucking refused to listen. It wanted Kat and only Kat, and after eight months of celibacy, he was horny as hell and desperate to see her again.

When the crowd shifted to the left, he saw her sitting on a bar stool talking to a short, cute redhead and—holy shit, Liam Armstrong. Hadn't seen that tall bastard in a few years.

Liam knew he was there. Had probably known since he walked in. Jayce should have scented him too. But he'd been so focused on Kat that nothing else had pen-etrated his thick skull. He cursed himself. Whenever she was near, he was distracted. And that could get him killed if he wasn't careful.

Liam made eye contact with Jayce as he continued moving through the crowd. The move was casual, but the tall wolf shifted his position and stood so that he was half blocking both women.

Part of Jayce wanted to pummel Liam for covering his view of Kat, but his most primal side gave Liam credit for protecting the females. Most males, even hardened warriors, were scared of Jayce. A trickle of unease rolled off Liam, but he wasn't shitting-his-pants afraid like so many other wolves. And he was ready to fight if need be. Jayce wouldn't admit it out loud, but that wolf's stock had just gone up in his opinion.

Kat still hadn't noticed him, so he paused by an empty high-top table near the edge of the small dance floor far enough away from the bar. He pulled out his cell phone. Liam was staring him down with a mix of curiosity and aggression, but Jayce ignored the other wolf for the moment. He hit speed dial one, then waited and watched.

Kat laughed at something the redhead said, then glanced at her purse sitting on the bar. She fished out her phone. When she spotted his number, she glared at the phone, then tossed it back into her purse. The redhead asked something, but Kat just shook her head and waved a dismissive hand in the air with those long, elegant fingers of hers. Fingers that had raked over every inch of him.

It shouldn't matter. He'd known the kind of reception he'd get from her. But seeing her outright reject him pierced him worse than any injury he'd suffered in battle.

Kat tucked a strand of her long, dark hair behind her ear and nodded at the redhead. For a moment her glance flicked away and that's when she spotted him. He pushed away from the table and didn't pause in his determined stride.

For a fraction of a second her eyes widened in shock, but just as quickly she glared at him. She jumped off her bar stool, elbowed Liam out of her way, and marched toward him. Placing well-manicured hands on jean-clad hips, she covered the last few feet between them, mindless of the loser wearing an ascot who tried to get her attention.

"What the hell are you doing here?" Those pale blue eyes of hers held him captive. They flashed angrily and his entire body went on red alert. He loved it when she looked at him like that. Maybe he was messed up in the head, but he loved her angry. That anger usually translated to heat in the bedroom. Their makeup sex had always been off the charts.

He fought to breathe until she punched her finger in the middle of his chest and he realized she was still talking.

"When someone doesn't return your calls, that means they don't want to talk to you. Get it? I do not want to see you or talk to you." Her words were practically a growl.

"I'm not here for you," he said, keeping his voice intentionally devoid of emotion. His statement was sort of the truth. He wasn't *solely* there for her. Well, tonight he'd come to the lodge for her specifically. He'd planned to visit the Armstrong-Cordona ranch in the morning. Since Liam was here, he lied in an attempt to salvage some of his pride. Pathetic.

"What?"

"I'm here to see Liam."

"Oh." She faltered slightly but she was still pissed. "Well, good, then. I see the man I plan to fuck tonight, so I'll just see you later. Or better yet, *never*." Without pause she stomped away.

Fuck? Kat never talked like that. She rarely said the word, even when she was turned on. Hell, she rarely cursed at all. Blood rushed wildly in his ears. He turned to find her sashaying toward some pretty boy with a popped collar. His inner beast roared to the surface.

Jayce quickly looked at Liam as he forced himself to control his breathing. The urge to shift forms was powerful, but he shoved his inner beast back. "I've got to take care of something, but I'll talk to you later. Tell your brother I'll be at the ranch tomorrow morning around eight." Jayce noticed that the redhead's eyes widened in fear as she backed away toward the bar, no doubt because his eyes had likely changed from their normal gray to black, but he didn't care.

Liam nodded in what almost looked like understanding.

Jayce didn't waste time. He stalked up to Kat and Mr.

Preppy. The guy's jaw dropped open and Kat opened her mouth, no doubt to blast him again.

"We need to talk." He grabbed her arm, not hard, and he was surprised when she didn't struggle.

She just glared at him for a long moment. Then she nodded. "You're right—we do."

Keeping his hold on her elbow, he continued out of the bar and made a sharp left. He'd seen a utility room down one of the halls when he'd done some earlier reconnaissance. It was unlocked, so he steered them both inside the small room.

Kat yanked her arm out of his grasp. "What the hell do you want?"

Ignoring her, he shut the door behind them. She rolled her eyes and plopped down on an overturned bucket. He flipped on the light. That's when he realized she was drunk. More than tipsy and definitely on her way to getting tanked. Something she'd rarely done before.

Her eyes were glassy as she stared at him. "I'm waiting, Mr. Bossy." She hiccuped and swayed on her seat.

The drunkenness explained why she wasn't tearing him a new asshole for manhandling her. "You planned to *fuck* that guy tonight?"

She shrugged. "Maybe, maybe not. Depends how drunk I get. What's it matter to you?"

"You matter to me." It was one of the most real things he'd ever said to anyone. Especially a woman.

She laughed at him. "I matter? You're so full of shit, Jayce. You like me well enough in the bedroom, but that's all you want from me. I don't know why you're here and I don't care." Pushing up, she swayed again but clutched on to the metal rack against the wall. "It might surprise you, but men find me attractive and smart and plenty of them would like to warm my bed at night. Unlike you, they don't view me as some dirty secret." She hiccuped again. This time louder, but her voice cracked on the last word.

Dirty secret? What the hell was she talking about?

"Big, stupid enforcer can't bondmate with his pathetic little human. Well, fuck you, Jayce! I'll screw whomever I want, whenever I want. I've had plenty of lovers since we broke up and there's nothing you can do about it."

No she hadn't. He'd have been able to scent someone if she had. She was still untouched by anyone but him. But the hurt and pain in her pale blue eyes were crystal clear. He didn't understand it and he didn't have the heart to contradict her. She was the one who'd walked away from him. She'd broken things off, then left town as if what they'd had together meant nothing. He'd called her so many times afterward it was embarrassing.

"Katarina." He reached for her, but she swatted his hand away.

"Don't touch me!" Her voice rose with each word as she sidestepped him toward the door. The agony she projected tore at his gut. He didn't understand it but he wanted to take it away.

Kat had never hidden her emotions from him when they'd been together. Anger, lust, heat, passion, love — she'd projected everything freely. But never hurt. Not like this. She yanked open the door and practically sprinted away from him.

He pressed a hand to his chest. Something foreign and uncomfortable made his chest ache. For months he'd waited for her to reach out, to explain why she'd left. He'd thought she'd finally woken up and realized she was too good for him. If he hadn't been so busy with Council matters, he'd have tracked her down long ago.

He knew they didn't have a future together because he couldn't bond with her, but that didn't mean they couldn't spend more time together. Just a few more years. That's all he wanted with her. *A little more time.* He snorted to himself. He sounded fucking pathetic. No wonder she'd left him.

Chapter 5

"We should go after her." December slid her nearly full vodka tonic away and stood up.

Liam shook his head. Even if Kat had been sucking drinks down faster than December and was likely buzzing, he knew Jayce wouldn't take advantage of her. "No. Jayce won't hurt her. He . . . cares for her."

"Who is that guy? He's scary." She shuddered.

That was an understatement. When Jayce's eyes had changed color, Liam knew December would have had no doubt he was also a shifter. She'd seen it happen to him after he'd stopped that guy from trying to kidnap her from her store, so he'd explained that he'd been trying to control his wolf. From the confusion he'd witnessed on her face, he guessed she still didn't understand what he meant, but he had plenty of time to introduce her to his world.

As December started to go after them, Liam placed a hand on her forearm, stopping her. She kept fidgeting in her seat and playing with her straw as she stared in the direction Kat had gone. "This is stupid. Kat's my friend and I want to go after her."

He scrubbed a hand over his face. It had been obvious Kat and Jayce needed to clear the air about some things and Liam didn't want to get in the way of that. "He's the enforcer."

She frowned. "What does that mean?"

Liam shifted uncomfortably, trying to find the right words. "He's sort of, ah . . . He quells any problems that packs can't handle on their own."

"Problems?"

"If one pack encroaches on another pack's territory or if a pack is into illegal activities and it's affecting our relationship with humans, Jayce comes in and cleans house."

"Why does that sound bad?"

"Because it is."

"And he's here to 'clean house' for your pack?" He could see the pulse point in her neck jump and even above the din of noise he could hear her heart rate increase.

"No. His visit isn't about that. After the poisonings on our ranch and after Taggart's death—"

"He's dead?"

Damn it. Liam hadn't meant to let that information slip. His brother, Connor, hadn't told the sheriff yet that he'd killed Sean Taggart, their old neighboring Alpha, in a sanctioned *nex pugna*. A death fight. Liam figured the sheriff probably already knew Taggart was gone, but even so, Connor hadn't told anyone except the Council. And it wasn't Liam's place to tell anyone, even if December was his mate. Or intended mate, as it were. Pack business stayed pack business unless the humans got curious.

The Council and the human government were still trying to find a way to integrate their laws. So far, the humans let shifters take care of problems internally. If shifters died or were murdered by other shifters, the human government saw fit to let them handle things on their own unless it directly affected humans. And that wasn't often. Shifters and humans didn't exactly run in the same circles.

"Ah, yes, but it's not common knowledge."

"Meaning my brother doesn't know." It wasn't a question.

This was what hanging around females did to males. Now he understood why his brother got so distracted around his own mate sometimes. "No, he doesn't."

"Well, I'm not going to say anything, if that's what you're worried about." She started to say something else when her eyes widened.

Liam turned and tracked her gaze. Kat was hurrying toward them with tears streaking down her face and from the way she stumbled, he guessed she'd had more to drink than he'd realized. They hadn't even been there that long.

"Shit." He didn't know Jayce well enough, but if he and Kat were fighting, that was not a good thing. Jayce's eyes had started to change earlier and if he was near his breaking point . . . Well, a pissed-off enforcer in a room full of humans was bad for everyone.

"Are you okay? Did that bastard hurt you?" December asked as Kat stopped in front of them.

"I'm fine. I'm going home but wanted to let you know so you wouldn't worry." She grabbed her purse from the bar.

"Why don't you stay with me tonight?" December asked softly.

Kat shook her head. "No. I just want to get out of here and sleep in my own bed, but you two should stay and enjoy yourselves."

December looked at Liam and he shook his head. It was obvious December wasn't letting Kat leave on her own, and he didn't plan to let her go by herself either. He wrapped one arm around December's shoulders and the other around Kat's—mainly because he was afraid she'd trip and fall. "Come on. We'll walk you back to your cabin."

She tried to shrug off his arm but tripped and re-thought her plan. "This is stupid. I'm perfectly capable of—"

"We're not letting you go by yourself, so just deal, Kat." December's voice was surprisingly haughty.

"You sound like me," Kat said, a slight slur in her voice.

December chuckled lightly. "Not so fun when the roles are reversed, is it?"

As they exited the bar, Jayce was walking back in. When he saw the three of them, his gunmetal gray eyes flashed dangerously dark.

If Liam didn't understand the primal need to protect what was his, he might have rolled his eyes at the glare Jayce shot him. "We're taking Kat home."

"You don't have to explain yourself to him," Kat snapped, all rage and anger bubbling to the surface.

Liam sighed. Getting in between a male—who also happened to be the enforcer—and his female ranked right up there with the top five dumbest things Liam had ever done. But he didn't exactly have a choice. Kat was December's friend and she was a female. It was in his nature to look out for her.

"Damn it, Kat. We need to talk." Jayce took a step toward them.

Instinctively Liam dropped his arms from December's and Kat's shoulders and stood in between them and Jayce. "Not tonight, Jayce. She's upset and—"

"Not tonight and not ever. I already told you I don't

have a fucking thing to say to you," Kat interrupted from behind him.

"Good Lord, girl, how much have you had to drink?" December asked, her soft voice a soothing balm that almost made Liam forget the situation he was in.

Liam didn't turn around but instead kept his focus on Jayce. "She's obviously upset. Do you really want to do this here?"

Jayce's jaw clenched furiously. Finally he shook his head and took a step back. "I'll see you tomorrow, Liam. And . . . thanks."

It appeared to actually pain Jayce to say the word, but Liam nodded and turned back to the two ladies. December had her arm wrapped around Kat's waist, steadying her. Liam motioned toward the front lobby. "Come on."

Barely ten minutes later Liam stood on the front porch of Kat's cabin with December, who was leaning against the railing of the porch. The small cabin was clustered among at least a dozen others just like it. From what Kat had told them, most of the ski instructors and other staff lived on-site during the winter months.

"I don't like leaving her by herself," December said.

Liam fished her car keys out of his pocket. They'd picked up her car from the valet to drive Kat to her place and now he was ready to go. All he could think about was peeling off December's knee-high boots and form-fitting sweater dress. Her coat might be covering it, but he remembered what it looked like and he wanted to see more of her. A lot more. "She said she'd set the alarm after we left."

"So?"

"So, I heard her set it."

"You heard . . . Oh. I forgot you can do that."

His extrasensory abilities allowed him certain advantages. Like hearing the alarm code being punched in from *outside* Kat's house.

"Still, what if that weirdo comes by to harass her?"

Liam sighed. December's protectiveness of her friend was admirable, but all he wanted to do was get her back to her place and work on convincing her that sleeping in the same bed was a very good idea. Especially since he knew Jayce would be watching Kat's place tonight and she'd be more than safe. "He's not a weirdo, December. If I had to guess, I'd say he loves her."

"I still don't like it. I've never seen Kat so upset before. And I don't think I've *ever* heard her curse before." December crossed her arms over her chest and shivered. Despite her wearing a thick, fitted jacket with a fur-lined hood over her sweater dress, the cold temperature had to be bothering her.

Liam had a naturally higher body temperature, so it didn't faze him. His protective nature kicked in, though. He wanted to bundle her up and force her to go home. "It probably won't make you feel better, but he's going to watch her place tonight and keep an eye out for her."

Her brow wrinkled in confusion. "How do you know?"

"I can smell him."

Her cold breath curled in front of her as she looked around. All the cabins were quiet, probably because almost everybody was still at the party. The nearby slopes were empty and the surrounding trees barely rustled with the wind. "I don't see anyone."

"He's here. Trust me. I don't know him well, but I know he'd never do anything to physically hurt her."

"You can't know—"

"Yes, I can. Shifters act a certain way around their mates. They might not be officially together, but he feels for her the way I feel for you. I saw it on his face."

"Oh." At his words her cheeks flushed a deeper shade of red and it had nothing to do with the cold. At least she understood his meaning.

When she still didn't move, he gestured toward her car. "You gonna make me freeze my ass off out here all night or are we gonna go?" he asked jokingly.

Her blue eyes narrowed. "I know you're not cold, but you're right. Let's get out of here."

Once in the car he turned the heat all the way up. At least she hadn't fought him about driving home. Not that he would have listened. She'd had a couple drinks and he hadn't had any. There were some things he'd compromise on and others he wouldn't. Letting her drive with alcohol in her system wasn't something she'd ever win.

After they'd made it halfway back to town, she uncrossed her arms and flipped the heat down a couple notches. "I never said thank you, so . . . thanks."

"For what?" He kept an eye on the rearview mirror as he drove. After everything that had been going on lately, he wanted to make sure they weren't being followed.

"I don't know, for not being a jerk about Kat, I guess."

His eyebrows drew together. "I don't follow."

Her shoulders lifted slightly. "We had to leave the party early and you didn't make a big deal about it. Plus you defused what could have been a drama-filled situation. I just appreciate it, that's all."

Liam still didn't understand why she was thanking him, so he mumbled a nonresponse. Maybe the males she'd known in the past were different, but he couldn't comprehend why she thought he'd care about leaving a party. He'd only gone to be with her in the first place.

The sooner they left meant the more time he got to spend with her alone. He'd barely had any time with her all day. Her store had been packed with holiday shoppers and as soon as they'd gotten to her house, she'd spent the next hour in her room getting ready for tonight. Part of him wondered if she'd been intentionally avoiding him, but right now he didn't care.

Right now it was just the two of them. And he planned to take full advantage of it.

Edward leaned against the door frame as he listened to Greg, one of his APL recruits, talk. It was late and almost everyone had left. The small meeting had gone well and if they pulled off taking Katarina Saburova, his boss would be very pleased. Edward was in charge of the new recruits in the Fontana area and so far his track record was shit.

The two recent failed kidnapping attempts from his group were garish blights and he planned to rectify that soon. He'd joined the APL because he was tired of the blasé attitude of most people and even the government where supernatural beings were concerned. They walked around freely like they had every right to. It was wrong and nauseating. His own mother—whore that she'd been—had left his father for one of those abominations almost as soon as shifters had come out to the world twenty years ago. Edward might be close to forty now, but it didn't alleviate the pain when he thought about her and that lupine shifter. She'd not only left his father but cut contact with him too. She'd become nothing more than a pathetic groupie overnight for those animals. It was like the woman who'd raised him had never existed. She'd broken his father's heart when she'd left, but she hadn't cared. She'd said she wanted a different life. To this day he had no clue where she'd ended up or if she was still alive. The male she'd shacked up with hadn't been part of a pack, just some lone wolf, making it impossible to track her down.

". . . Once I get Katarina's new work schedule, I think we'll have something solid to work with," Greg finished.

Edward nodded absently. He hated being distracted but Brianna was in the kitchen with Tony. He hated that pretty boy and it had been hard to miss the looks he'd been giving her all night. Edward cleared his throat and stepped back inside the house. "Call me with any updates."

Greg nodded and fished his keys out of his jacket pocket. "Will do. Talk to you soon."

As he shut the front door behind him, Edward slipped off his coat and hung it on the rack. The house was quiet. Too quiet. "Brianna?"

No answer.

He hurried down the hallway toward the living room. Empty mugs, glasses, and a few small plates were still strewn on the coffee table. He found the kitchen empty also. His heart pounded erratically against his ribs. What if Brianna was just like all those other whores? He felt his face heat up as he thought about her and Tony.

They were probably up in her room right now. His hands clenched into fists. He didn't have to put up with that shit in his own house. She could pack her shit and leave with Tony if that's what she wanted.

As he started for the stairs, he heard a loud thump outside. Pausing, he waited and heard it again. This time louder. When he pushed back the sliding glass door, he stepped onto the back deck. His boots were silent as he crossed to the stairs.

Once he stood on the snow, he paused again.

"Get off me," Brianna gasped.

Rage snaked through him. Grabbing a small shovel he'd left leaning against the stairs, he hurried toward the east side of his house.

With his back facing Edward, Tony had Brianna pressed up against the side of the house. He had one hand around her slim throat and the other was shoved down her jeans. Brianna's eyes were wide and frightened. She struggled against him, but with her small frame she was no match for Tony's linebacker build.

"Quit struggling, you stupid whore. You think you're too good for me, huh? You're gonna like everything I do to you." Tony's words were a low growl as he leaned toward her terrified face.

Edward was going to kill him. That was a fact. He didn't announce his presence or make a sound. Creeping up behind Tony, he lifted the shovel and slammed it down on his head full force. The cracking sound split the night air with a violent rush.

Blood spurted from his skull as he fell into the snow. It created a crimson river that made Edward's body heat up.

Clutching her throat, Brianna fell to the snow next to him. Coughing and sputtering, she tried to catch her breath. In that moment he felt shame for thinking she'd betrayed him by fucking Tony. He dropped the shovel and fell to his knees.

"Are you okay?"

She nodded and tried to suck in air. "Thanks . . . to you."

That's when he noticed her sweater had been torn and the side of her face was already showing a purple bruise. A dark rage threatened to overtake him. "He hit you."

"He would have done worse if it hadn't been for you." That's when she surprised him. She threw herself against him and wrapped her arms around him. When she buried her face against his neck, he realized she was crying.

It was weird to have a woman come to him for comfort. Most women—and sometimes men—turned away from him in disgust. He patted her back, hoping she'd let go, but she just held on tighter. As she gripped him tighter, something strange surged through him. She needed him. It was so obvious. He might hate that he needed her approval, but she wanted his comfort.

He tightened his arms around her slight body, but as he felt himself start to get hard, he jerked back in horror. He couldn't touch Brianna like that. Not her. She was perfect.

Disentangling her arms, he stood and held out a hand for her. "We need to get rid of the body."

Sniffling, she nodded as she stood. "Isn't he your boss's son? What's going to happen to me now?"

"No one will ever know what happened tonight." Edward picked up the shovel from the ground and looked at the body as a plan formed. Joseph had left to take care of some business down in Georgia and wouldn't be back for a couple days, so they didn't have to worry about him coming back. And Greg wouldn't question him.

"What are we going to do?" she asked as she wrapped her arms around her trembling body.

"I keep some dogs nearby. I think we can use this to our advantage." Edward checked Tony's pulse to make sure he was dead. Yep. Now all he had to do was let his dogs maul the body. Once he'd been ripped to shreds, they could dump Tony somewhere in town along with his truck.

It would look like shifters had done it. Hot damn. He was sorry Brianna had been hurt, but this was the best thing that had happened to him in a while. This would bring heat from the local government and from the APL's national office. Tony might have been a piece of shit, but his father was very important.

Edward smiled to himself. This was going to work out just fine.

Chapter 6

It was close to midnight by the time Liam and December got back to her place. He'd been very quiet on the drive back and she wasn't sure why that unnerved her. After checking her house for potential intruders, he finally came back downstairs to meet her in the foyer.

She wished she could think it was crazy or overboard for him to do a full-service sweep of her house after a simple night out, but she knew it wasn't. The different scenarios of what could have happened to her last night had been running through her head over and over. It was like the scenes were stuck on auto replay. On the way back to her house tonight, she'd had a flashback of that maniac trying to stab her with the needle and she'd actually jerked away in response. She'd been helpless to stop her physical reaction and she hated that. If Liam hadn't been with her in the truck, she was afraid she'd have completely freaked out. She'd never tell him but she was so thankful he'd been driving. Her reaction had taken her completely by surprise.

"What are you thinking about?" Liam asked as he reached the bottom stair.

Yeah, like she was going to admit to him she was afraid she was on the verge of a minibreakdown. "Uh, nothing. Is the house free of bad guys?"

He nodded, his expression slightly concerned.

Her hand shook when she tucked her hair behind her ear. "I was thinking maybe getting a security system isn't such a bad idea. Didn't you say you had a friend who could help me out with that?"

"I already made the call. He'll be by Monday. I tried to get him here earlier, but he couldn't swing it."

Even though she was grateful, she was still annoyed he'd made plans behind her back. She held on to that annoyance. Anything was better than the fear that had latched on to her insides and was threatening to suffocate her. "You *already* called?"

Liam shrugged, then took off his coat and hooked it on the rack. Looked like he planned to stay another night. Her heart rate increased at the thought.

She wanted to tell him to leave and that she'd be fine, but she knew having Liam under the same roof was the only way she'd get a decent night's sleep. The thought of depending on anyone for peace of mind made her want to scream. She hated the feeling of powerlessness she'd experienced the past few weeks. Even though she'd defended herself against Mike—if that was even his real name— she'd nearly gotten the crap beaten out of her before by that other asshole who'd Tased her. The thought of being in her own home by herself shouldn't make her scared.

"You've got to stop doing stuff like that." She couldn't even inject any anger into the comment as she stripped off her coat. Not this time. She wanted that security system in her home so when she closed her eyes at night, she wasn't terrified and imagining masked men breaking into her bedroom.

Liam's dark eyes flared to life as he looked her over from head to toe. For the hundredth time that night. "And you've got to stop dressing like this." His voice was soft, sensual, hungry.

"Don't change the subject." Despite her desire to stay annoyed at him, a tingling warmth spread through her all the way to her toes as he looked at her. No one had ever made her feel that way. Treasured and desired as if she were perfect. When he looked at her like that, like she was the only thing in the world that existed, she melted.

He didn't respond. Just continued staring. Her heartbeat quickened. It was as if he couldn't tear his gaze away from her. As if he'd never leave her. It was hard to think straight.

His breathing turned uneven, mirroring her own. He took a step closer to her, crowding her in, mowing down all her much-needed personal space. She moved back until she was flat against the front door, but he didn't stop his advance.

Caging her in with his hands on either side of her face, he bent his head toward her until they were mere inches apart. For a brief moment, his eyes flicked a shade darker and she knew it wasn't the light playing tricks on her. Apparently they could change when he was turned on too.

Putting a hand up against his chest, she meant to push him back. She really did. Instead, she fisted his shirt and tugged him closer.

In the instant before their mouths fused, she saw something in his expression she didn't recognize. Almost like triumph, but it was gone so fast, and then his mouth was on hers. Claiming her. Then she didn't think at all.

Dominating.

Invading.

Encompassing.

Liam seemed to take over everything as he kissed her. His tongue flicked against hers in slow, sensuous strokes. She could feel the urgency humming through him, but he was gentle in his caresses. And he still hadn't made a move to touch her with anything but his lips.

His hands were firmly planted on the door. She wanted those big hands on her body. More than she'd admit. The thought of him pushing up her dress and touching her most intimate area made her tremble.

As if they had a mind of their own, her hands wound their way around his neck and she pressed her body flush with his. Her breasts rubbed against his hard chest and she wished there were nothing separating them. No clothes, no bra, nothing. She wanted skin on skin.

When one of his hands cupped her head in a tight grip, she moaned into his mouth.

The sound seemed to affect him. His body jerked unsteadily—then lightning fast he fisted her hips and lifted her up. Her breath caught on the show of male power. She wound her legs around his waist as he pressed her against the door.

Her entire body felt on fire. The ache between her legs was too much. Yet not enough. She needed more. Feeling absolutely possessed, like an animal in heat, she moved against his hard-on. Even with his jeans and her underwear as a barrier it was obvious how turned on he was. His erection was rock hard and she wanted it inside her. Her inner walls clenched with the need.

Holding her up with the weight of his body, he reached between them and cupped her mound through her panties. His hand covering her made her moan even louder. Gently, he rubbed the base of his palm over her. The rhythmic motion was the perfect amount of pressure. Moving against his hand, she encouraged him with her body to do more, to touch her deeper. As he started to peel the thin scrap of material away, a loud bang interrupted them.

Her eyes flew open. Breathing hard, she stared at him. He still didn't remove his hand.

Before she could think to say anything, the knock came again. She felt the vibration go through her entire body. That's when she realized someone was banging on the front door. The door she was propped up against.

"December? It's me. I forgot my key." Parker's voice was slightly muffled through the solid wood door.

"Shit," Liam muttered. He paused but finally he let her go and stepped back.

Disentangling herself from him, she felt despondent when her boots hit the hardwood floor. Her nipples strained painfully against her bra and the ache between her legs wasn't going away anytime soon. Not unless Liam did something about it. She quickly straightened her dress and smoothed a hand down her hair, though she doubted it would do much good. Her face had to be bright red and her lips likely swollen, but there wasn't a lot she could do about that.

She tugged the door open to find her brother wearing his uniform under a thick coat, and carrying a stack of folders.

Parker's eyes narrowed as he glanced past her at Liam. "Didn't know you'd still be here." His voice wasn't exactly unfriendly, but it wasn't warm either.

"My truck is outside," Liam said flatly, stating the obvious.

The two men stared at each other in annoyance.

Trying to forget what she'd just been doing with Liam,

December stepped back and let her brother in. "Why are you here so late? Is everything okay?"

"We managed to get a few partial prints from that BMW. Got a name too. I want you to look at his file and see if it's the same guy. If it is, I've also got a couple files with his known associates. I want to know if you've seen them around." For a moment he looked at Liam, and December knew her brother wanted to tell him to leave, but in the end Parker just shook his head tightly, as if he knew it would be a fruitless endeavor.

"Okay." She nodded toward the living room and both men followed.

Parker dropped the files onto her coffee table and spread out some pictures. The first photograph she recognized instantly. Tiny dull knives jabbed against her insides. The pain was instantaneous and unstoppable. Simply the sight of that monster's face made her jerk back and fight to breathe.

"I take it that's him?" Parker asked, watching her carefully.

She nodded because she was afraid her vocal cords wouldn't work. All she could do was stare. He looked harmless enough. Nice even. He had defined, angular features, making him handsome in an almost feminine sort of way. Blond hair and dark eyes. Yep, it was him. Mr. Perfectly Harmless. How could she have been so wrong about him?

"Are you okay?" Liam's concerned voice caused her head to snap up. He reached out and put a comforting hand on her back. The action was subtle and in no way inappropriate, but he was staking a claim.

She could feel it in the way his fingers slightly tightened against her.

When she focused on him, she could feel herself being sucked out of her trance. Liam alone had the power to ground her. To make her feel safe. She nodded again but this time found her voice. "I'm fine."

"His name is Mike Taylor according to his arrest record," Parker said.

"Taylor? He told me his last name was . . . I can't remember, but that wasn't it." Why was the memory so fuzzy? It was on the tip of her tongue. She supposed it didn't really matter anyway. Her brother had found out his real name. That's what was important.

"Well, we know who he is now. He did a short stint in prison for fraud, but while inside he apparently got involved with a group called the Antiparanormal League. They're not as big as the Aryan Brotherhood but they're growing in numbers in the prison system. Do you recognize any of these guys?" Parker slid a few more pictures in front of her.

She concentrated and racked her brain, trying to remember if she'd ever seen the men in her store or loitering outside it. None of them looked remotely familiar. "No, I'm sorry."

Parker sighed and put them back in a folder. "I'm actually relieved you don't recognize them."

"Did you find out anything else about this guy? Where he lives?" The edge in Liam's last question was unmistakable.

Parker's eyes narrowed and December knew it was because he didn't like Liam's presence. No matter what Liam did, Parker was going to be annoyed. "We found an old address, but he doesn't live there anymore and you know I can't tell you what it is anyway. This is *our* investigation, Liam. I don't want you or any of your pack getting involved in this. We're going to find this guy and prosecute him."

Liam grunted.

Parker shook his head. "I'm serious. This all has to be done legally."

"*You* do what you have to do, Sheriff. *I'll* do what I have to." Liam leaned back against the couch casually, but every line in his body was tense. He was like a coiled snake, ready to strike.

December fought off an unexpected shiver, drawing Liam's attention to her again. "You okay?"

She didn't like the feeling of being under a microscope and she really hated that he read her so well. It made her defenses go up without warning. "Fine," she said through gritted teeth.

Parker started gathering his folders and stacking them into a neat pile. "Liam, you can clear out of here. I'll be staying the night." His voice was dismissive.

Her brother's words hung heavy in the air. December wasn't going to fight him if he wanted to stay. Parker had been looking out for her since they were kids. He was her one constant in life. Her family. She loved him more than anything. The thought of telling Liam to leave, however, punched a hole in her chest. She didn't like imagining the hurt look on his face.

Sometimes he was hard to read, but other times he let her see exactly what he was feeling, and it was usually when she'd said something to reject him. If she told him to leave now, he'd take it as a personal affront. It was simply the way he was hardwired. From the overprotective way he'd been acting the past few weeks, she had no doubt he wanted to stay with her and protect her. Just like he'd done last night. If she chose her brother over him, it would hurt him. Even if she didn't exactly understand why, she knew it deep in her core.

Before she could think how to formulate a response, Liam stood. "I'll call you tomorrow, December."

Her eyebrows pulled together as she looked at Liam. She searched his face trying to see what was going on in his head, but she got nothing. His expression was blank.

She flicked a quick glance at her brother. "I'm going to walk him out."

Once they were at her front door, Liam grabbed his coat but didn't make a move to leave. Instead he reached out and gently cupped her jaw.

Her heart pounded wildly against her chest. After the kiss they'd just shared, she desperately wanted a repeat even if the voice inside her told her it was stupid.

Instead of kissing her the way her body craved, Liam leaned forward and lightly pressed his lips to her forehead. "I'll be thinking about you all night," he murmured.

His words sent a ribbon of awareness curling through her, straight to the ache between her legs. By his knowing smile, she had no doubt he could smell her desire. *Stupid extrasensory abilities.*

"I . . ." She didn't want to return the sentiment. Didn't want to let him know how much she was beginning to care for him. "I will too," she whispered.

His dark eyes glinted under the foyer light as a half smile formed on his lips. And then he was gone. Taking all his warmth with him. Closing her eyes, she sagged against the front door. She shouldn't miss him. She'd wanted him gone. Had wanted her house and her life back to herself. Now that he wasn't under the same roof, she wished he were. Hell, she wished he were in her bed right now and that instead of just kissing, they were making love. Hot, wild sex that would leave them both panting and begging for more.

"What kind of future do you possibly think you have with him?" Parker's voice caused her eyes to snap open.

He leaned against the entryway, his arms crossed over his chest.

Feeling self-conscious under his scrutiny, she shrugged. "I don't know what you're talking about."

"Don't lie to me."

She started to protest when he cut her off.

"I don't know what's going on between you two, but I'm not stupid. I see the way you look at him, so I'm telling you this now so there's no misunderstanding later. If you mate—or bond, or whatever the hell they call it—with him, I'm out of your life. I won't stand by and watch you bind yourself to someone who will only bring you heartache and violence."

Her brother's words were like a slap. She straightened against the door. "What?"

"I'm not saying Liam's a bad guy, but getting involved with one of them is stupid. There are some things I can't . . ." His jaw clenched and he got this faraway look that was all too familiar.

Parker was thinking about Brandon, their dead brother. A balloon of guilt rose, then popped inside her, every time she thought about their younger brother. How her stupidity and naïveté had gotten him killed. If she'd never made friends with Allison, a shifter who had attended her high school, her friend's drugged-out feral brother would never have latched on to December's scent and followed her home. And her brother wouldn't have died trying to protect her. She pressed a hand to her stomach to quell the nausea. She wanted to snap at Parker and tell him he was being stupid, unreasonable. But it was her fault Brandon was dead, and Parker had looked out for her their whole lives. He was her only family. "I understand, Parker." Without another glance at him she hurried up the stairs.

Once inside her room she didn't bother with washing off her makeup. She took off her boots and climbed into bed wearing her clothes. It was stupid but she could smell Liam on her and didn't want to lose that scent. That knowledge scared her. Her brother would never accept him. Something she'd known deep down inside her, but now she had no doubt in her mind.

When it came down to it, family was family. After everything her brother had sacrificed for her, she owed him. Fighting back tears, she closed her eyes and pulled her comforter over her head. Getting tangled up with Liam would break her heart in too many ways to count. Staying away from him seemed to hurt just as bad. She didn't want to have to choose between her only brother and the man she was falling for.

Liam hated the sense of loss he experienced at having to leave December's house. But he'd seen that look in her eyes. The one that said, "Don't make me choose between you and my brother." Yeah, he'd have lost that one. That much was clear. And she hadn't wanted to cause Liam pain. He wasn't sure if that made him feel better or worse.

Thankfully Ryan and one of his other packmates had dropped his truck off at December's earlier. Otherwise he'd have been walking because he sure as hell wasn't asking her brother to take him home. The drive wasn't long but it seemed to stretch on forever. All he could think about was that kiss.

What it had felt like to have December plastered to him as he tasted her. He'd been so close to sinking his fingers inside her heat. She hadn't made a move to stop him either. She'd been urging him on with those hot little moans and the way her body had moved against him. If

her brother hadn't shown up, he had no doubt that tonight he'd have sunk more than his fingers inside her.

He slammed his fist against the steering wheel as he
reached the gate to the ranch. After unlocking it and
steering inside, he quickly relocked the gate before parking in the building next to the main barn. He could scent
a few of his packmates out patrolling the land, but other
than the normal ranch smells, everyone else was in for
the night.

Instead of heading to the cabin he shared with four
other male warriors, he walked toward the main house.
Connor lived there with his mate, Ana; her sister Noel;
Erin; and Vivian, a jaguar cub they'd adopted. Liam
frowned as he realized that Jayce might be coming to the
ranch because of Vivian's presence in addition to everything else. Lupine shifters' adopting feline shifters was
unheard of. Apart from the species' differences, lupine,
coyote, and ursine shifters lived in North America and
most feline shifter packs were located in South America.
There were always exceptions to the rule, but it didn't
happen often. As enforcer, it would make sense for Jayce
to check on the new feline shifter living on lupine land.
But if he or the Council had a problem with her, Liam
knew his entire pack would go to war for the adorable
little cub.

After stomping the snow off his boots and without
bothering to knock, he opened the front door. Voices
trailed from the kitchen. According to his nose, it was
Ana and Connor.

Liam found Connor sitting at the table and Ana was
in his lap, nuzzling his neck. The sight was nauseating. He
didn't like the spike of jealousy that ran through his
chest. It made him feel small and petty because he truly
was happy for his brother. Connor had walked away

from Ana fifty years ago as pure self-sacrifice. If anyone deserved love, it was his brother.

Ana glanced up and smiled. "Hey, Liam."

He grunted.

"Uh-oh. Lady problems? Didn't you take my advice and chill on the possessive crap?" she asked.

Next to her, Connor tightened his grasp and pulled Ana even closer to his side. "What's wrong with a little possessiveness?" Connor murmured against Ana's neck.

She playfully elbowed him and the pain inside Liam intensified as he watched their interaction. His brother had pined over Ana for so long. To see them finally together as bondmates made Liam happy, but at the same time it was like a dagger embedded in his chest. He wanted that same thing with December so much he ached for it. And he wouldn't ever settle for just mates. He wanted to be bonded with her. If she let him make love to her under the full moon and sink his canines into her neck, bonding them for life, it would link them telepathically and give her the same longevity as him.

"That's not it." He grabbed a beer from the fridge and downed half of it, wishing it would take the edge off but knowing it wouldn't. Nothing could do that except maybe a fifth of whiskey.

While he was guzzling his beer, he heard Ana murmur something about waiting for Connor upstairs.

Once Ana was gone, he slammed the bottle down on the counter and turned to face his brother.

Connor raised his dark eyebrows. "What's going on?"

He didn't feel like explaining to his brother how close he'd been to making love to December before they'd been interrupted. "Just frustrated, that's all. Did you tell everyone that Jayce will be here tomorrow?" He'd texted Connor earlier to let him know about Jayce. After the poisonings at the ranch, their neighboring Alpha's recent death from Connor, and the possible issues with the APL, they'd been expecting his visit, just not so soon. The Council liked to take their sweet time unless problems directly involved shifter relations with humans. With the APL's recent attacks on them maybe that's exactly why Jayce was there early. Then again, maybe not.

"Yeah. Did he say why he's in Fontana early?"

"No, but I think it has more to do with Kat Saburova than us."

Connor's eyebrows hiked even higher. "Probably should have seen that coming."

Liam and Connor had saved Kat from two asshole kidnappers/would-be rapists a few weeks ago. Since then, they'd kept in touch and looked out for her when they could. Even though Jayce was her ex, male shifters were very territorial about their females. They had a burning need to protect females. It made sense that he was here now a week earlier than he'd told their pack he'd be arriving.

Liam cleared his throat and broached a subject he wasn't looking forward to. "You think he knows Ana jumped into the middle of the *nex pugna*?"

During the sanctioned death fight between his brother and their old neighboring Alpha, Ana had tried to attack the other wolf. While it was stupid and she'd done no harm to the dead wolf, she'd simply acted on instinct. She'd thought her mate was injured and the animal inside her had reacted. Still, interfering in a *nex pugna* was punishable by the Council.

"No." Connor shook his head, but a frown carved deep into his face.

Liam didn't envy his brother being Alpha. Connor had all the responsibility of taking care of not only his newly blended pack but also the welfare and happiness of his new bondmate. Finding a balance between everything had to be hard. Hell, Liam could barely balance his own responsibilities. He wanted to be here for his brother, but lately he'd been consumed with the need to protect December, and he'd been shirking his duties. He'd been a virtual ghost at the ranch, but so far no one had a problem covering for him. Probably because most males understood what he was going through.

December was almost like an addiction. Finding a mate was bad news for a male in that sense. The need to protect a mate was overwhelming. For him, it felt even worse because of her resistance to what he was and the type of relationship they could have. If she'd been a shifter, she'd have felt the pull like he did. He knew she was attracted to him, but he didn't know what the effect was for humans. Not to mention she was female. No matter the species, they were so damn different and confusing. He shook his head. He had more important things to worry about. "December's brother stopped by her place earlier. They lifted some prints from the BMW."

Connor's expression darkened. "Did they find that asshole who tried to hurt her?"

He shook his head. "No, but I got a name. Mike Taylor. It's common enough but he did some time in prison and he's got ties to the APL."

"I'll see what Ryan can dig up," Connor said.

Ryan, their oldest packmate, could hack almost any system. The rough-looking cowboy didn't seem like the type, but computers were his thing.

"The sheriff made it clear we're to stay away from him."

Connor's lips curved into a hard smile. "Right. Just like we'll steer clear of the APL."

Good, at least his brother wanted the same thing he did. Not that he'd been worried about his response. The human who'd tried to hurt December was going to pay. "I'm gonna get some shut-eye, but I'll be here for the meeting in the morning." At Connor's nod, he let himself out and headed back to the cabin even though it was one of the last places he wanted to be.

Right now all he wanted was to be wrapped up in December's arms.

Chapter 7

Edward was careful to stick to the speed limit as he drove into town. The sun was peeking over one of the mountains, but it was still mostly gray outside. Since it was Sunday, the roads were quiet.

He glanced in the rearview mirror. Brianna was right behind him, driving his truck because he was driving Tony's. As he passed the sheriff's station, he automatically slowed so that he was a mile under the limit. With a dead body in the back he couldn't afford to get stopped now. It was covered with a tarp, but if a cop got suspicious enough, it was easily discoverable. And killing a cop brought too much heat.

Edward steered into one of the main gas stations in town but was careful to avoid the video camera pointed at the front door. Instead he parked on the side of the building and Brianna did the same.

As he got out, he glanced around, but the streets were empty. He glanced at Brianna through the windshield and motioned for her to stay put. Then he quickly removed the tarp and shoved it into the nearby Dumpster, but left the body right where it was in the back of the truck. Since it was cold out, he likely wouldn't begin to smell too soon and Edward needed him visible sooner than later.

He looked at the body one last time and smiled. The son of a bitch had been ripped to shreds by his dogs. His face was gone but he'd be easily identifiable by his dental records and prints. Dumb fucker had a record. For sexual assault or some shit. After he'd recruited those other two morons who couldn't keep it in their pants, he'd made a point not to recruit any sexual deviants with records. Unfortunately Tony's father had wanted him down here working with Adler. And Adler wanted to keep his boss happy for now.

"That's it?" Brianna asked as he slid into the passenger seat. Clutching the steering wheel, her knuckles were stark white.

She must be worried. "It'll never be traced back to us."

"What about Tony's father?" she persisted.

"Once the cops run his dental records or fingerprints, they'll notify the family. I'll probably get a call from his father. Or they might even send someone down to speak to us. We just have to act surprised and stick to the story. He left after the meeting and that's the last time we saw him." Lying was easy for him but he worried Brianna might break under the pressure.

Surprisingly his words seemed to have a calming effect. Her shoulders loosened as they continued driving. "Do you think his father will come see you himself?"

Edward hoped not, but he shrugged. "Maybe."

She bit her bottom lip but kept her eyes on the road. He stared hard at her for a moment. She was edgy, nervous. He didn't like it, but she wasn't used to getting her hands dirty. Not this way. It explained her behavior.

When she glanced at him, he quickly looked away. No sense in getting her more upset by his scrutiny. Not when things were finally starting to fall into place.

Kat opened her eyes and groaned in misery. It tasted like something had died in her mouth. She'd had beer, vodka, and shots of . . . something sweet last night. What had she been thinking?

Struggling to sit upright, she tried to clear her mind. She hadn't been thinking and that was the problem. She'd been pissed at seeing Jayce in the flesh. Well, hurt more than anything. She glanced down and realized she wore a pair of Jayce's old jogging pants. She'd snagged them when she left Miami. His smell wasn't on them anymore, but she still liked to wear them. Pathetic.

Once she made it to her bathroom, she brushed her teeth and washed her face. The cool water splashing against her skin did little to make her feel better, but at least she'd gotten rid of the foul taste in her mouth.

When she opened her bedroom door, she paused. The scent of rich coffee lingered in the air. She knew she hadn't preset the pot the night before. Maybe December had done it before she'd left.

Kat froze in the entrance of the kitchen. With his back to her, Jayce stood by the stove. A jug of orange juice, two cups, and two plates sat on the center island.

"About time you woke up," he said without turning around.

She glared at his back as she strode into the room. "What are you doing here? And how did you even get in? I know I set the alarm."

"You have the same code you did in Miami." He shook his head and finally turned to face her. When he did, she could see the scrambled eggs in the pan.

Her place was warm enough, but with Jayce in the same room, her nipples instantly hardened. God, she felt like Pavlov's dog or something. The man just brought out a certain response in her no matter how much she wanted to deny it. Her body simply came alive when he was near. She crossed her arms over her chest. "That still doesn't explain what you're doing here."

"I'm cooking for you." His explanation was so matter-of-fact, as if that should explain why he was at her place completely uninvited. As if this were a normal occurrence.

Pain throbbed in her head and his presence only made it worse. It was a little after seven, though, and she didn't want to argue. Not before her coffee. Bypassing the orange juice, she went straight for the near-full pot of coffee. After adding a little cream, she took a sip and sighed. Perfect.

"I love seeing that smile on your face." She looked up to find Jayce staring at her. He never said anything he didn't mean and hearing those words on his lips was too much.

His dark, penetrating gaze was also too much to take this early in the morning. He was trying to ambush her. That was the only explanation for him being in her home. Feeling her knees weaken, she hurried to the other side of the center island and sat on one of the stools. "I thought you said you were here to see Liam. So why are you at my place?"

"I have business with the Armstrong-Cordona pack, but I arrived early to see you . . . to spend time with you."

Her spine stiffened. "I can't imagine why."

"Oh, can't you?" More than sarcasm, there was a deadlier edge to his voice. Not directed at her exactly, but she knew his moods well enough.

"I've moved on, so I don't know that we have anything else to say to each other." When he didn't respond,
she sighed and pushed her mug away. The hot liquid sat
heavy in her stomach. "What do you want, Jayce?"

"To have breakfast with you." He turned the stove off
and moved the pan off the burner.

She relaxed a little at his words. Breakfast she could
deal with. Anything else, not so much.

"And to figure out why the hell you left. I thought we
were . . ." He trailed off in an uncharacteristic manner.
Jayce never had a problem saying what was on his mind.

Her stomach tightened. Struggling to remain calm,
she tried to shrug casually. Instead her shoulders jerked
unsteadily. "You know why I left."

His jaw clenched. "No, I don't. You told me we had no
future, then disappeared. Just like that."

His words put a match to her temper. "And you told
me humans didn't undergo the change well." When she'd
asked him about how well humans transformed to shifters, he'd told her it was a rare occurrence and most humans didn't survive the transition. Only one percent.

He frowned. "Yes, I did. And?"

"You failed to mention that when shifters bond with
their lovers, turning them into bondmates, the chance of
survival increases *substantially*." To a hundred percent. If
he'd loved her enough and wanted to mate and bond
with her, then she'd have turned just fine. It would have
been a hot, very pleasurable experience. If she'd let him
sink his canines into her neck while they made love under a full moon, it would have been an instantaneous
transformation for her. But she'd had to learn that from
someone else. Jayce had lied to her and fed her some
bullshit line about how she might not undergo the transition.

He still held the spatula in his hand. The only evident giveaway that he'd understood her words was the whitening of his knuckles as he clenched the utensil. But she could also see his inner wolf clawing at him from the insides. Thanks to her seer abilities, she could see a person's true nature. She'd known exactly what he was the moment they'd met. Unlike a lot of shifters, his wolf was always at the surface, making him much closer to his beast side than his human one. If she hadn't grown up with this ability, it might have freaked her out a little more than it did now. She didn't understand why his animal seemed to be agitated that she knew the truth.

"You know about that?" A quiet question.

Hot tears pricked her eyes, but she angrily blinked them away. He wasn't even denying it. "I'm not stupid. You had to know I'd find out eventually." When she'd found out the truth, she'd realized he didn't love her and never would. He wanted her as a bedmate, but that was it. She wasn't good enough to bond with, wasn't good enough to turn into a shifter. She was only good for sex. Unless he bonded with her, Kat would grow old while he wouldn't, and eventually he'd grow tired of her.

There had been only one option. She'd had to cut her losses before it was impossible to walk away from him. Not that walking away had been easy. It had been the hardest thing she'd ever had to do. Still he didn't answer, so she continued. "You're not even denying you don't want me as your bondmate. Is it because I'm human?" She hated that her voice cracked, but too many emotions were pushing at the surface, trying to get free. Her entire life she'd always felt like a bit of a freak because of her abilities. Having a criminal for a father hadn't helped her to fit in anywhere. She'd been nothing but an outsider until she'd met Jayce. She'd thought he'd wanted the same things she had. That he'd cared for her as much as she'd cared for him.

Instead of responding he just stared at her. She couldn't read anything in his eyes. They were completely devoid of emotion. But his wolf was going crazy inside him. It looked like it wanted out and she wasn't sure why.

Last night's liquor and the coffee from this morning sloshed around wickedly in her stomach.

Finally he tore his gaze away and set the spatula down. He wouldn't look at her and that was worse than anything else he could have said or done. "I've got to get to a meeting. I'll let myself out, but make sure you reset the alarm." His voice was quiet, unemotional.

And that was it. Now he knew why she'd left him, and couldn't even deny he'd been lying to her. A hollow, sick feeling welled up inside her. When she'd walked away from him before, it had given her some sense of control, knowing she'd been the one to cut ties. Now that he was here, in her kitchen, validating everything she'd known the past few months, it cut like a sharp razor.

Once she heard the front door shut, she turned off the coffeemaker and dumped the food he'd cooked. Even looking at it made her want to puke. Though she hated doing anything Jayce said, she reset the alarm and headed back to bed with tears streaming down her cheeks. Getting up had clearly been a mistake this morning. As she pulled up her cover, her cell phone rang. For one insane moment hope flared inside her that it was Jayce. Which was stupid. When she saw December's number, she brushed her tears away and pressed the talk button. If anyone could make her feel better, it was her friend.

*   *   *

Jayce had never loathed himself more than he did at that moment. Kat deserved more than him. So much more. And she deserved an explanation. But he couldn't explain to her why he was leaving, because she wouldn't understand. She was too young, too innocent. She might have grown up on the outskirts of a violent environment, but her father, bastard that he was, had always protected Kat.

As the enforcer, Jayce had too many enemies. Violent, vicious, sadistic enemies he'd racked up over the years. And they were powerful. By keeping Kat simply a human he slept with, she wasn't a target. But if he bonded with her, turned her into a shifter, she would become a walking bull's-eye overnight. The perception others had of her would change in an instant. She'd no longer be Kat Saburova. She'd be Jayce's woman, the enforcer's mate. With that tag she'd be hunted. Maybe not at first, but eventually someone would come for her.

With his job he couldn't protect her all the time. Almost five hundred years ago his father had attempted a relationship with a human a few years after Jayce's own mother had died giving birth to him. While the human had been making her decision about whether to turn, she'd been killed by one of his father's enemies. Then a couple hundred years later, Jayce's older brother had gone bat-shit crazy after his mate was killed. That was two hundred years ago. And he was still torn up over it as far as Jayce knew. Hell, he didn't even know where his brother was now.

Jayce had known the time would eventually come when Kat would find out about the bonding process. He'd just been trying to figure out how the hell to walk away from her before that happened. When she'd done it instead, he'd felt as if she'd punched through the middle of his chest and ripped his heart out with her bare hands. If it hadn't been for his job, he'd have gone insane. Now she knew the truth and there wasn't a damn thing he could do about it.

It was better to let her think he didn't want to take her as his bondmate because she was human. If she knew the truth about how much power she wielded over him . . . He shuddered as he started the engine to his truck. She knew all his buttons and if she pressed the right ones hard enough, he'd eventually turn her. He had the will-power to keep her safe now, but the animal inside him was selfish. So fucking selfish it scared the shit out of him. His beast didn't care about the dangers that Kat would face. It just knew that whenever she was around, it needed to be near her, to touch her, to get wrapped up in her sweet scent. Walking out of that kitchen had taken all his self-control. Only one thing had driven him out: fear. He shook his head, hating the weak emotion that clawed at him.

It took a lot to scare Jayce. He wanted Kat by his side, in his bed, under him, on top of him, all the time. Right now he was barely hanging on to his humanity. The lon-ger he was around her, the more he wanted to claim her. To mark and bond with her. To bring her directly into his world, consequences be damned. Somehow he closed the lid on his thoughts and focused on the road in front of him.

After the turnoff to the Armstrong-Cordona ranch, he followed the single-lane paved road until he reached a dirt road. It wasn't long until he reached the main gates. The wooden sign above the already open gates read COR-DONA RANCH, but he knew that Connor Armstrong hadn't been mated long enough to Ana Cordona for them to have made a change. Hell, it was probably the last thing on Connor's mind right now. Mated males usually didn't think of much else during the first year other than their mates. Alpha leaders were exceptions, but the draw to be near their mate at all times was overwhelming. Jayce had seen his fair share of males go mad when their females strayed or died.

He wasn't sure where to park, so he pulled through the gates and stopped by a giant oak tree. It sat in the middle of an expanse of houses. The houses and cabins formed a huge circle with just enough space for privacy, but it was a tight-knit pack. If he had to guess, the two-story brick house that was just a little larger than everyone else's was Connor and Ana's.

Out of habit, he checked his two daggers and his Springfield .45. As a rule he preferred any blade to a gun, but he wasn't stupid. His job demanded he be prepared at all times. As he approached the house, he scented Liam behind him. The other wolf's boots crunched on the fallen snow, but his scent was distinctive.

Instead of stopping completely, Jayce slowed and waited for him to join him. "You didn't stay with your female last night?"

Liam flicked him an annoyed glance. "No. I didn't sleep out in the cold watching her all night either."

Damn. He hated that the other wolf could see through him. Another strike against being mated. Females made a wolf crazy and predictable. Jayce had slept out all night in the cold watching Kat's place, and the messed-up thing was, he'd do it again.

Liam surprised him by continuing. "But I have in the past couple weeks. More than once. Females are fucking complicated," he muttered.

The admission surprised Jayce. It was the kind of thing he'd expect his brother to say to him but not anyone else.

Even if he wouldn't acknowledge it to anyone, he missed that family connection. As enforcer for the Council he didn't have ties anywhere. He couldn't afford to. His father was dead and his brother was living God knew where. Being with Kat was the closest he'd ever come to having a real connection with someone. A real family. Maybe on a different planet in a different lifetime he'd have had a shot at happiness with a woman like her.

But not here. Not now.

Not ever.

"After this meeting I'm heading to December's store. I just talked to her and Kat's gonna be there helping out later today." Liam threw the last bit in quickly and didn't make a big deal about it.

His heart jumped. Like a randy cub, he couldn't wait to see her. Instead of commenting, Jayce changed the subject. "Where are we having the meeting?"

Liam nodded at the house they were headed toward. "Right here. Connor, Ana, Ryan, Noah, and Erin are already there. Most of the warriors are out patrolling right now, which is why it's so small."

Jayce nodded. The smaller the better. The only person he was really interested in talking to was Connor anyway. He was the Alpha and had the final say. As pack leader, Connor had the alpha temperament times ten. It was what made him the leader, the *Alpha*, not simply alpha in nature. This pack was unique in that all the males were warriors as opposed to simply alphas, and he didn't need all that extra testosterone in the room right now. Warriors were alpha in nature but not all alphas were warriors. The warrior class were simply born fighters. They were bigger and badder than the rest of the shifter population and didn't make apologies for embracing their animal side. Something Jayce could appreciate. His animal side was more prevalent than even that of warriors. It was a constant battle inside him. His beast saw the world in black and white and made no apologies for being a predator. It was why he fought in his human form. He was just as fast and dangerous as a human. As an animal, a shifter often overlooked human reasoning because it didn't factor into the animal's decision making. So even though he was a different breed altogether, he usually connected better with his warrior brethren. Didn't mean he wanted to be in a room full of them right now, though.

Liam opened the door and entered first, out of respect. If he'd been human, it might have seemed odd, but in the shifter world, entering a room first meant taking on the possibility that an ambush was waiting. By going first he was showing Jayce there was no harm waiting in the house. Even though he was the enforcer and there on official business, he was still a guest of their pack. Liam hadn't expected to like Jayce so much, but after seeing the issues he was having with Kat, he felt an odd connection. They both had female problems.

Liam had stomped the snow and dirt off his shoes before entering and Jayce did the same. A low hum of voices trailed from the dining room. As they entered the room, everyone quieted. Connor sat at the head of the long, rectangular table and Ana sat next to him.

Connor stood and nodded. "Jayce."

"Connor." Jayce stood stiffly as he glanced around the table at everyone. When his eyes landed on Erin, the petite redhead Liam and his brother had found naked, beaten, and bloody behind a Dumpster over a year ago, they lingered longer than on the others.

Connor had never reported they'd found Erin, because

she'd begged them not to. She also wouldn't tell them where she'd come from or who had hurt her. If she had, Liam and Connor and probably the rest of the pack would have lined up for a chance to kill the bastard or bastards who had dared hurt her. Violence against females in the shifter world was rare and by the abuse she'd suffered, it had been obvious shifters had hurt her. Humans wouldn't have had the strength to. But when she hadn't wanted to do anything about her attack, they hadn't pushed her. They'd taken her in and made her part of their pack and protected her the only way they could.

It was clear to anyone in the room that Jayce's assessment of her wasn't sexual, but it was curious. "You're Erin Flynn." It was not a question but a statement.

Her back went ramrod straight and Noah, who sat next to her, moved a few inches closer in a proprietary manner. "Yes."

"Did you used to belong to the Murphy pack?"

Her face paled and after flicking a nervous glance at Connor, she looked back at Jayce and nodded.

"They listed you as dead at the last Council meeting."

At his words, Erin's gray eyes flashed angrily. "Well, they were wrong," she said through gritted teeth.

Jayce continued to stare at her, as if searching for something. The room was eerily silent as they met each other's gazes. When Erin didn't flinch away, Jayce finally nodded slightly. "After this meeting, we need to talk."

Erin swallowed hard but nodded.

Liam watched as Noah's canines started to extend, so he cleared his throat loudly and took the empty chair next to him. The other wolf looked at him and when he did, his breathing began to even out. Noah and Erin weren't mated or bondmates or even intimate as far as

Liam knew, but Noah didn't care. He'd been protecting her since they'd found her.

Jayce focused his attention on Connor as he sat at the opposite end of the table. "Before we start this meeting, you should know that the Council cleared you in the death of Taggart."

Connor's nod was barely perceptible. "I wasn't worried."

Liam knew his brother hadn't been worried about the ruling of the actual killing. That had definitely been justified. Considering Taggart had kidnapped a defenseless cub and tried to rape Ana *twice*, that bastard deserved everything he'd gotten.

"That's not the reason you're here, though, is it?" Connor spoke again.

Jayce shook his head. "The APL problem is growing. Right now it's a small group of angry humans, but if we don't do something to ferret out their leaders, we'll have a problem."

"We have the names of six known members. Three are dead, one we haven't managed to dig up anything on, one is in jail, and the other has gone missing," Liam said. The man missing was the asshole who had attacked December. *Mike Taylor.* They'd been trying to track his movements, but it was as if he'd fallen off the face of the earth.

"How do you know about the dead men? Did you kill them?" Jayce asked.

Liam looked at his brother. Connor nodded and took the lead. "We tracked down two APL members after they tried to kill my mate." His voice heated up as he continued. "When we found them, they'd kidnapped another woman. They planned to rape her, but we got there before they could." He paused a moment. "It was Katarina Saburova."

Jayce's eyes widened and the muscles in his neck corded tightly as they tensed. A thick, overpowering haze of potent rage flooded the air.

Liam and his brother hadn't told the Council about Kat's kidnapping and her subsequent involvement in killing one of the men or even their own involvement in the killings. At the time, involving the human had seemed like more trouble than it was worth. But with Jayce in town and with his connection to her, it seemed smarter to tell him about it now instead of letting him find out later.

"That's how you know Kat?" Jayce looked at Liam almost accusingly.

Liam nodded. "It happened a few weeks ago."

"I didn't know. . . . Was she hurt?" His voice was raspy.

Liam knew that asking about this in a room full of strangers was a blow to Jayce's tough-guy image, but it was obvious he didn't care. "She was roughed up but she wasn't raped."

"I didn't see any reports about this." Now Jayce was back in control of himself. His voice was even, monotone.

"She killed one of the men and we killed the other. We left before the police showed up, because she insisted on it. Said that she didn't want shifters involved because she worried we'd somehow get blamed even though they were rapist bastards. We've kept in contact with her since," Connor said.

"Was she targeted because of her involvement with . . . shifters?" Or one shifter in particular. Jayce didn't say it, but everyone in the room knew what he meant.

Connor nodded. "We think so. They called her a shifter whore more than once and from what we've gathered, they're loosely connected to the man who tried to hurt December a few days ago."

Jayce's gaze narrowed slightly. "That's only two men. You said you knew of three dead APL members."

"A couple weeks ago I found a guy trying to kidnap December outside her store—he's the one in jail and the police only think he wanted to rob her—and he mentioned that a guy named Chuck was killed by an Edward Adler, who sounds like their boss, for failing to complete a couple APL missions."

"Chuck?" Jayce asked.

"I don't have a last name, but apparently Chuck was responsible for the first attack on December weeks ago— in her *house*—and for the attack on another woman we're friends with. Apparently his boss wasn't happy with his failures." Liam sure as hell wouldn't lose any sleep over his death.

Jayce frowned. "They ever find a body?"

"Nothing's been reported. At least not here or in any of the surrounding areas." This time Ryan spoke up. He'd been monitoring every agency and news report online.

"What about this Adler guy, then? What's his deal?" Jayce asked.

"So far we haven't been able to dig up anything concrete on him, but whoever he is, he sounds like the leader of the APL in this area. The man I questioned was scared of him. Almost more terrified of him than he was of me." Liam had been able to smell the terror rolling off that asshole who'd wanted to take December. Even though he wasn't in jail for attempting to kidnap her, he'd copped to a few other crimes just to get himself locked up. The guy had been smarter than he looked. In jail he was protected from Liam and his boss.

Jayce was silent for a while and no one else said

anything. He was the one who'd been sent by the Council, and while Connor was Alpha of this pack, Jayce had a broader scope of how powerful the APL was. The past few weeks the only thing Connor had been concerned with was keeping his pack safe and Liam didn't blame him. But if they could drive the APL from the Fontana region, they would.

Finally Jayce spoke. "What I'm about to say stays in this room." When everyone nodded, he continued. "The Council has been in contact with the Tuatha. They've sent someone in to infiltrate the APL branch in this region. I don't know who their spy is or how much progress they've made, but I'll see if I can get in contact with them and work out a plan to bring down their leaders. It might be possible to work together."

"The Tuatha told our Council all this?" Connor sounded surprised.

Liam didn't blame his brother. The Tuatha were the royal branch of the fae, and their headquarters were located in Ireland. Unlike his kind, which had a semidemocratic set of rules, the fae were completely draconian. And they weren't exactly known for their diplomacy. Most supernatural beings stuck to their own kind, but the fae were positively brutal in their rulings and in their separation from all others. Everyone knew that their laws were black-and-white, and if someone did something they perceived as wrong, they struck hard and fast and asked questions later. Death seemed to be the usual punishment. And as far as Liam knew, there weren't many fae living in the United States. They tended to stay in Ireland and Scotland.

Jayce nodded. "We're not the only ones who have been targeted by radical groups. Apparently the APL is trying to branch out overseas and the fae aren't taking any chances. They want to stop this group before they have a chance to spread. And they're the ones who reached out to us. Maybe to see what we had planned. I'm not totally sure. Even though I'd rather keep this in-house, if they have knowledge we don't, I want to capitalize on it."

"Agreed," Connor said, then glanced at Ana. His mate had been unusually quiet, but Liam knew they were likely communicating telepathically. Another perk between bondmates. When Connor turned back to Jayce and spoke, Liam knew he'd been right. "You haven't said where you're staying, but we have an extra guesthouse. You'd have plenty of privacy if you want to use it."

Yeah, that definitely came from Ana, not his brother.

Jayce nodded. "Thanks. My bags are in my truck." He looked at Liam, then back at Connor. "I'm heading to town to talk to December McIntyre after this. I didn't realize the extent of her involvement and attacks. I'm going to question her to see if she remembers anything important. I'd like to take Liam—unless you object?"

The question surprised Liam, but he figured Jayce was just being respectful of Connor's territory. And Liam would have gone anyway. December had been scared of Jayce last night and he wouldn't let the other shifter meet with her alone.

Connor nodded without pause. "Of course."

Once the meeting dispersed, Jayce spoke to Connor for a few minutes in private, then excused himself and went to find Erin. It was a little rude not talking to Connor longer, but he'd make up for it later. So far he actually liked this pack. They didn't reek of fear around him and they were honest. At least what he could scent.

As he strode across the yard, he spotted the redhead

and the other male who'd been glued to her side at the table—Noah—entering the barn. He trailed after their voices and scent. The male was angry at something and she was pissed at having the same argument again. He found them by one of the stables. It appeared as if the redhead planned to take one of the horses out, but the male had pinned her up against one of the open doors with his body.

For a moment Jayce's instinct to fight flared to life. He calmed when he realized the redhead wasn't pushing him away. Her hand was on the male's chest, but she was grasping his shirt. Her other one wrapped around the back of his neck in a tight grip. Jayce knew she could defend herself, because he understood *what* she was.

He wanted to talk to her about that but decided to wait. The lust emanating from both of them was overpowering and if he was honest, he was fucking jealous. Jealous of two virtual strangers. Christ, he needed to get laid. No, he needed to get some more time with Kat. But that wasn't happening anytime soon. Now that she knew the truth about him—or a version of it anyway—she likely wouldn't stay in the same room as him. Too bad for her he had to talk to her about that kidnapping. Even thinking about her at the mercy of two monsters made his canines throb. He preferred to fight in his human form—all enforcers did—but his inner wolf wanted blood at the thought of Kat in danger.

If it wasn't for his job, he'd steer clear of her for the rest of this trip, but he couldn't. Unfortunately the longer he was around her, the more he felt his resolve stripping away. If she pushed him hard enough, he might be driven to claim her, to mark her. And if that happened, she'd eventually hate him. Hate living with the knowledge that she was marked for death every single day.

Chapter 8

"You want to grab breakfast? December's store won't be open for another hour and I don't think ambushing her as soon as she opens is a good idea," Liam said to Jayce as he steered down the long driveway. Judging her reaction to Jayce yesterday, he wanted to tread lightly. Keeping his intended mate happy was the most important thing to him.

"That's fine." As he settled against the seat, Jayce unzipped his coat, revealing two blades strapped across his chest in a crisscross fashion.

"The humans ever give you grief about your weapons?" Liam asked.

Jayce shrugged. "They're usually concealed, but yeah, sometimes I get hassled. I've got a permit, though, so fuck 'em."

"What are those things made of, silver?" The intricate carvings along the blade were unique and had obviously taken time.

"It's a mix of what humans today would consider titanium and pure silver, but they're . . . different."

"You gonna expand on that?"

"They were blessed by the fae about a thousand years ago."

"Holy shit." Liam knew his brother's mate had a dagger blessed by the fae passed on from her father, but they were very rare. The magic made them damn near indestructible. How a blade was blessed made a difference in what the exact purpose of it would be. Ana's dagger could put feral shifters into comalike states, making them easily disposable, but Jayce's could have completely different powers. It just depended on who had blessed it and why.

Liam started to ask another question when Jayce slammed his fist against the center console. "I can't believe Kat was kidnapped and didn't call me." The small outburst surprised Liam. Jayce's words were laced with anger and something else Liam recognized.

Fear.

"She's a strong female." Liam knew he'd feel differently if it were *his* female, but Kat was unique compared with women—and humans in general—that he knew. She had a fuck-all attitude when she needed to and seemed to bounce back easily.

"I know. I . . ." He looked sharply at Liam as if he was surprised he was even talking to him about her. Jayce shook his head, the action almost imperceptible. Then he changed the subject. "You ever worry about mating with your human?" The question was asked cautiously.

Hell yeah, he did. Every second he was awake. Not mating with her wasn't an option, though. "December is mine." Liam said the only thing that made sense to him.

"She'll become a target."

He ignored the thread of fear that curled through him at the statement. "She's already a target." Liam hated that, but he also knew that if she was bonded to him, she'd be stronger and they'd be linked telepathically. He'd be able to communicate with her anywhere in the world. Be better able to protect her.

Jayce grunted and Liam figured the conversation was over. It surprised him that Jayce had even opened up as much as he had. The man had a reputation for kicking ass and asking questions later. As the enforcer he had little room for diplomacy. But he was still a male and at the moment, he was seriously messed up over a female. That put them on even footing.

Even though he was the enforcer, a female could still wreak havoc on him. The knowledge made Liam perversely happy.

As they continued down the two-lane highway, a strange euphoric sensation rolled over him. His hands went numb as he gripped the steering wheel.

"Shit," Jayce muttered.

"What?" Liam blinked a couple times.

"You feel that?"

He nodded because he couldn't talk. It was as if he were floating on a cloud. Everything around him was light and airy, like he was in a giant bubble. Then his truck started to sputter. It gurgled and made deathly choking sounds. *What the hell?*

"Pull over," Jayce ordered.

They were on a deserted stretch of highway, surrounded by trees on either side. With numb hands, Liam did as Jayce ordered.

"Fight it," Jayce said as Liam put the truck in park. Then he punched him. Hard, across the face.

The sharp, abrupt action across his jaw jerked him back to reality. His jaw stung but it was better than that woozy shit. He glared at Jayce. "What the fuck is going on?"

"You feel that energy? It's the Fianna."

"Fianna?" Liam's head snapped back against the seat. The Fianna were legendary fae soldiers descended from the warriors of Ireland hundreds—maybe thousands— of years ago. "I thought they were just a myth."

Jayce snorted. "No myth. They're real and those fuckers are here. Get out."

Liam might not know exactly what was going on, but he did as Jayce said. As soon as his feet hit the ground, that strange energy intensified.

"Fight that feeling. They don't want you lucid. It's easier for them to kill you that way."

It felt as if his heart started to slow as he stood there. He shook his head but it was no use. The sluggishness was starting to take over.

"Fight it!" Jayce snarled.

Before he could respond, Liam's inner wolf took over. It was so fast, so unexpected, he didn't have time to think about it. It rarely happened that he couldn't control his beast, but something deep in his core knew there was danger nearby and made the decision for him.

He bit back a cry as his bones broke and realigned. His clothes and shoes shredded to ribbons as he shifted to his animal form. The pain hit with the intensity of a sledgehammer throughout his entire body. The intensification of the agony was because the change was not his choice. His animal was taking over.

Fast and hard.

And his inner wolf wanted blood for taking away that control of power. As always, the pain was fleeting. Once his bones slid into place, he growled deep in his throat.

Now that he was shifted, that euphoric sensation from earlier was completely gone. His wolf was ready to fight. Liam glanced at Jayce, who'd stripped off his jacket and unleashed his blades. He held one in each hand. They gleamed in the sunlight.

For a moment Liam wondered why he hadn't shifted, but then he remembered that enforcers preferred to fight in their human form. They were faster and deadlier that way.

Jayce nodded at him and they headed deeper into the woods. The Fianna weren't hard to track now that he was in his wolf form. There were two of them if he scented correctly. The distinctive fresh-rain scent of the fae was unique to their kind.

"Go for their throats. They have the same weaknesses as us," Jayce murmured as they continued stalking over snow and dried, dead underbrush.

Yeah, Liam already knew that. Regular fae had killed his pack a hundred years ago in a battle for land. Killing them would be no sweat. Liam's paws barely felt the cold underneath him. His entire body was primed to attack. The blood running through him was hot and fiery. As the trees grew thicker, he spotted two very tall men. They were dressed in all black, were lean, and each wielded a short sword. One had long blond hair, the other red, but other than that, they looked like brothers.

Liam silently advanced on the blond. Whatever the two warriors had done to him earlier, it had worn off and now he was just pissed.

He reined in the impulse to spring. Losing control was something he rarely did. Except around December of course.

"We just want to talk," the redhead said while gripping his sword tightly.

He spoke the same time the blond wielded his sword in Liam's direction. Talk? *I don't fucking think so.* Liam lunged for the blond's legs, careful to avoid the sword slicing through the air toward his neck. He rammed into his shin but didn't take the warrior down.

He wanted to knock this guy off balance. Liam rolled onto the ground and jumped back to his feet. In his peripheral vision he watched Jayce fighting the redhead. The sounds of their blades clashing against each other rang out through the air like a violent song.

Liam bared his teeth but was careful to keep his neck protected as he began to circle the tall warrior. The man handled his blade with ease, but Liam noticed he favored his left hand.

He started to circle the man faster, hoping to wear him down and maybe trip him up. The faster he went, the more the man's annoyance grew. And the tighter Liam enclosed his circle. When he saw an opening, he lunged at him. Using all the strength of his hind legs, he hurtled himself through the air, full force, and slammed against the fae warrior's chest.

The blond cried out but didn't let go of his sword. Liam felt the blade dig into his side. Not deep, but enough to piss him off and make his vision blur for an instant. The ache was excruciating as it ripped through skin and muscle. Instead of moving away, Liam grabbed on to the sword-wielding arm with his teeth and ripped through the man's tendons and muscles.

The warrior cried out again, though it was more of a guttural growl, and he dropped the sword.

"Son of a bitch," he shouted.

Bleeding and snarling, Liam backed off but only because the warrior had dropped his weapon. Taking the life of another supernatural being could have dire consequences. If he could avoid the bloodshed, he would. Not that he'd sacrifice himself for this asshole. Especially not since he was fae.

Keeping half his attention on the blond, he glanced at Jayce.

Jayce had his two blades crisscrossed against the redhead's neck, ready to lop his head off in a second. Unfortunately for him, the redhead had his own sword stuck directly against Jayce's chest, right over his heart. Neither man moved.

"I'll drop mine if you drop yours," the redhead said.

Jayce looked at Liam and nodded slightly. He slowly withdrew one of his blades as the other man did the same. Once the Fianna warrior had completely removed his weapon, Jayce sheathed both his.

The blond dusted himself off and stood. He glared at Liam. "Stupid mutt."

Liam took a menacing step toward him.

"Enough!" The redhead sliced a hard look at the blond. Clearing his throat, he looked back and forth between Jayce and Liam. He placed a hand on his chest. "I'm Rory. This is my brother Eoghan. We're—"

"Fianna warriors." Jayce's voice was dry.

Rory nodded. "We just want to talk."

Jayce's eyes narrowed. "You have a hell of a way of showing it."

"I apologize for our tactics. We needed to talk to you privately." The redhead kept his attention on Jayce.

"About what?"

"One of our . . . warriors is missing."

Jayce frowned. "And that's our problem why?"

"We were able to infiltrate the local APL group in Fontana but lost contact recently. This group—no matter how insignificant—is everyone's problem. They have been making plans to expand to our shores of Ireland."

Jayce nodded and Liam growled his agreement. Even though the APL were humans and their ability to hurt them one-on-one was small, if they were allowed to keep gaining followers and spread their hate, it could be a problem for every supernatural being.

"So why not contact us like a normal . . . person?" Jayce asked.

"You never know who's watching and we don't want our presence in Fontana known."

Jayce shrugged, seemingly content with the answer. Then he rattled off a phone number. "That's my cell. Think you can remember it?"

Rory's dark eyes slightly narrowed, but he nodded.

"Good. Next time *call* me if you need something."

"So you haven't heard anything about a Fianna warrior going missing around these parts?"

Jayce shook his head. "No, but there's been a decent amount of movement from the APL around here lately. Attacks against humans."

"Why would they bother with their own kind?"

"They're targeting humans known to have affiliation with shifters."

"You associate with humans?" This time the blond, Eoghan, spoke. His voice dripped with disdain.

Liam bared his teeth as a low growl started in his throat. He really didn't like this guy and he better not see him in town near December.

The blond's gaze quickly snapped back toward him. He held up a hand in defense. "I meant no offense by it."

"We'll keep an ear to the ground." Jayce looked at Liam and nodded back toward the way they'd entered the woods.

Without turning his back to the two warriors, Liam slowly crept backward. His blood trail thinned the farther he walked. His body was already healing, but he still ached. Once they were out of sight and near the truck, he shifted form. The change was quicker this time as his bones quickly realigned and slid back into place. He was also a hell of a lot colder.

The icy wind bit into him bone deep without his fur or clothes as protection. He might have a naturally higher body temperature than humans, but the winter had turned chilling in the past week. And he'd lost blood. Not a lot, but his wound was still gaping and crimson spilled down his side, pooling onto the snow and dirt. At least he'd been stabbed below his ribs. He groaned as they reached the truck.

Jayce waited while he grabbed his duffel bag from the extended cab. As a shifter, Liam always carried an extra set of clothes.

"You need help bandaging that?" Jayce asked.

Liam snorted. He'd done this more times than he could count and he was sure Jayce had too. "No thanks."

Jayce was silent as Liam cleaned off his wound and quickly covered it with a bandage. Then he managed to wrap gauze around his waist a couple times to secure it. By dinner he'd be healed, but since he'd been cut with a fae's blade, it would take longer than normal. Once he was finished, he put on a fresh set of clothes. "You think the APL figured out who their spy is?" Liam asked as he slid on his boots.

Jayce shrugged, his expression devoid of emotion. "I doubt it. The Fianna are trained well and master chameleons when they want to be. I think they might have been trying to see how much we knew."

"Hell of a way to ask." Liam's shoulders were tense as he pulled back onto the highway. His truck was magically working again. Not that he cared much about his vehicle. All he wanted to do was see December again. The need to claim her was growing stronger. Almost overwhelming. He wasn't sure if it was because she was actively resisting him or because he'd finally tasted her last night. Now he knew what he'd been missing and he wanted more of it.

Parker slipped on a pair of latex gloves as he entered the morgue. It was one of the last places he wanted to be, but after the morning he'd had, it was unfortunately necessary.

Bonnie lifted her gaze from the dead body on the metal table. "Hey, Sheriff. I was just going to call you."

Under the harsh lights the body looked somehow worse than it had when they'd found it at the gas station. He knew the victim was male, but there hadn't been any identification on him, so he'd run his prints through AFIS. He'd struck gold with a name.

Tony Mayfield.

The guy had a short rap sheet but he was a violent criminal. Assault with a deadly weapon, aggravated sexual assault, as well as a few petty crimes. This guy was a Grade A loser, but Parker still had to investigate his death. "You know the time of death?"

She shrugged. "About twelve hours ago. Give or take."

"Find anything interesting?"

The petite blond medical examiner nodded. "I know what you were worried about earlier, but this wasn't a shifter attack."

He let out a breath he hadn't realized he'd been holding on to. He might not trust most shifters, but he didn't want to deal with the fallout from having a shifter attack a human. Humans had been living in harmony with the Cordona pack for decades, and after the Cordonas had assimilated into the Armstrong-Cordona pack about a month ago, he knew a lot of people in town were worried about newcomers. Especially *male* newcomers. "So what happened to him?"

"All these wounds happened after death. Since I'm sure you don't want all the details, I'll just tell you that this"—she lifted his head and turned it to the side—"was what killed him."

Parker could see the indentation and bruising pattern on the skull. "Someone hit him."

"That's right. One blow with a flat, hard object. To kill a man like that would take considerable strength. Given the trajectory of the blow, the assailant is a couple inches shorter."

"What about . . . ?" He motioned to the rest of the body. Strips of skin were missing, making him look like a human chew toy.

"This was all postmortem. I'm taking saliva samples and dental impressions, but my guess is this was two dogs at the most. If it had been any more, I don't think we'd have even this much of the body left. The teeth marks are from regular dogs. Much too small to be from a shifter. Besides, I doubt a shifter would . . ." She trailed off and shrugged.

She didn't have to finish. He knew what she meant. Shifters were hunters by nature, but they weren't stupid. From what Parker understood, unless they were feral and out of their mind with rage, they wouldn't leave a body in plain sight. And this body had definitely been moved. Parker was sure of that much. There was no blood spatter in the back of the truck where they'd found the guy. The fact that he'd been left in plain sight for anyone to discover told him it was a calculated move. Someone had not only wanted them to find this body but made sure it was very public. Which left a whole mess of other questions. Someone killed this guy, then had let dogs maul the body before moving it. It didn't make a lot of sense. "Find anything else on the body?"

Bonnie nodded. "A blond hair. Long enough that I'm guessing it's female. Also some fibers which are probably part of his clothes. I won't know more until I've had more time with the body. I'll send everything to the lab once I've finished."

"Good work." He stripped off his gloves and tossed them in the trash before exiting the room.

His shoes squeaked against the floor as he headed down the hallway. Once he made it outside, he sucked in the crisp, cold air. Anything was better than the sterile atmosphere of the morgue. He didn't know how Bonnie handled being in there all the time.

As he reached his truck, his cell buzzed in his pocket. He inwardly groaned when he saw the number. "Hey, Julia." His voice was cautious. He doubted this was a social call.

"Sheriff. How's your sister doing?" She sounded sincere, but he knew better.

The nosy reporter for the only newspaper in Fontana was a bulldog most of the time. When December had been attacked in her home, Julia hadn't reported it. Now he knew why. She was holding on to that favor for a favor of her own. Hadn't taken her long to call it in. "She's fine. What do you want?"

"No small talk?"

"You really want to waste your time?"

"Not really. I heard a human was killed by a shifter last night. Can you confirm this?"

Parker held a tight lid on his annoyance. They'd kept the crime scene locked down tight. Abel, the owner of the gas station where the body had been found—and the one who'd discovered it—sure as hell wouldn't have told Julia. "Where'd you hear this?"

"You know I can't reveal my sources." Her voice was haughty.

He snorted. "Then I can't confirm or deny anything."

She let out a frustrated growl. "Fine. I got an anonymous call."

"Your cell or at work?"

"I'm supposed to be the one asking you questions."

He was silent.

Finally she spoke again. "Work. Satisfied? Now, what's going on?"

"I can only tell you that, yes, we found a body, but it wasn't a shifter attack."

"Do you know the identity of the victim?"

Parker shook his head at her persistence. He knew but he wasn't telling her. "Even if I did, I couldn't tell you until we notify next of kin. You know that."

"So you *do* know who it is. At least tell me if it's a man or woman."

He sighed and scrubbed a hand over his face. "The victim is male."

"Thanks, Sheriff. You're a doll. Are you going to the Chocolate Ball next month? I heard they're doing a bachelor auction. If you're on the auction block, you better get ready for—"

"*Good-bye*, Julia." He disconnected and slipped his phone back in his pocket. The tall, leggy brunette was hot, but she'd been after him since he'd moved to town almost a decade ago and she wasn't his type. Hell, he didn't know what that was, but it wasn't a bulldog in high heels who'd use him more than anything else.

As he headed back to the station, he mulled over the

phone call. It was too early for her to have gotten an anonymous call about the body. If it had been discovered later in the day, he'd have understood, but Abel had found it before anyone else and he wasn't known for gossiping. No one at the station would have tipped her off. And he doubted anyone in town even knew about it yet. Fontana might be small but news didn't spread *that* fast. The best possibility he could think of was that someone connected to the victim called. Now he had even more questions.

Someone obviously wanted Julia to think a shifter had attacked a human. The motive could be as simple as someone hating paranormal beings, but it was a hell of a risk to take, dumping a body in the middle of town like that. Unfortunately he wouldn't know more about the DNA found on the body until they got results back from the lab. Since they were a small town, they had to send everything out. It would be a few days until he knew more.

At least he could still contact the family. If he could find them. He'd done a brief search before heading to the morgue and hadn't come up with anything concrete. He'd found names but no addresses. That in itself was odd. A dull headache started at the back of his skull. Something told him there was more to this case than a simple murder.

Chapter 9

After driving around for a few hours, Liam and Jayce parked on Avalon Street a few blocks down from December's store. After leaving the fae, Liam hadn't wanted to come directly to see December. He wasn't exactly concerned they'd have any interest in her, but he didn't like the idea of them even knowing of her existence or her importance in his life. Their opinions of humans had been perfectly clear. The driving time hadn't been a waste, though. It had given Jayce a chance to scout out the rest of Fontana and get a feel for the layout of the town. Liam understood that looking at maps could help someone only so much. Sometimes being on the ground was the only way to do reconnaissance. Now it was well past lunchtime as Liam opened the front door to December's store.

Immediately he was accosted by the scents of the candles that lined the window. Butterscotch cookies and vanilla. Nothing could overpower her scent, though. The jasmine was probably too subtle or even missed by most people, but everything about her called to his most primal side.

She glanced up from the cash register and half smiled when she saw him. When her gaze trailed past him, her face filled with concern. Liam bit back a sigh, hating that she was uncomfortable. At least Jayce had his jacket zipped up, covering his blades. He could only imagine her reaction to those.

There were four women waiting in line and Kat was busy helping another. He realized she must be helping December out since she was short staffed. And Kat had almost the same reaction as December when she spotted them. A smile for Liam and a glare for Jayce. Next to him, Jayce gave a low, almost inaudible growl in his throat. She couldn't hear him, but Liam could. It was a strained, almost distressed sound. Liam was careful not to look at him. He didn't know what was keeping them apart, but it was obvious Jayce was messed up over her. The sexual tension in the air was so thick it was nauseating.

"Quit looking at her like that and at least pretend to be browsing or something," Liam said under his breath.

Jayce shot him an annoyed look before stalking down one of the aisles.

A steady stream of customers flowed in and out for the next hour, but finally the place cleared out. The second the last woman left, Jayce tossed down the book he'd been looking at and riveted his attention on Kat.

"You were fucking kidnapped and didn't tell me?" His low-slung words were directed at Kat, as if he'd been holding it in the entire time they'd been waiting.

"Shit." Liam tried to place himself in between them.

Kat's eyes narrowed dangerously. "I didn't tell you because it's none of your business," she shot back, her voice just as low as his.

Both of them completely ignored Liam's attempt to come between them.

"I had to find out weeks after the fact. What the hell, Kat?" He took a step toward her.

Liam tensed as December shot out from behind the cash register, her eyes ablaze. "Don't talk to her like that. She doesn't owe you anything."

When Jayce turned his angry stare on December, a warning growl started deep in Liam's throat. Before it had a chance to escape, Jayce relaxed and took a step back as he focused on Kat. "Can I talk to you in private?"

Kat sighed and glanced at December. "I know you haven't had a break today. If you want to grab a late lunch with Liam, I'm fine here at the store."

December glared at Jayce as she spoke to Kat. "You sure?"

"Yes. I'll be fine, I promise. And so will your store. Take a break."

She glanced between the two of them for a few long moments before nodding. "Okay. We won't be gone long." Once December agreed, Liam let out a relieved breath.

After she slipped on her coat, he hooked his arm around her shoulder as they exited. She stiffened but didn't pull away. Considering the kiss they'd shared last night, he didn't understand why she was acting as if he were a stranger. Like she hadn't been ready to let him take her up against her front door. His body instantly hardened at the thought, but he forced his mind to the present. "Is Big Earl's okay?" He motioned to the local diner at the end of the block.

"It's fine. Liam . . ." She tried to extricate herself from his hold.

Even though he wanted to pull her tighter, he loosened his grip. He felt more than heard her sigh of relief. His inner wolf howled as he felt her put those walls back up, blocking him out. The signs she put off were physical *and* emotional. "Damn it," he muttered. If she was pushing him out again, he was back to square one. An ache started in the middle of his chest at the thought.

When they reached the diner, he held open the door for her. He wanted to enter ahead of her, like his inner wolf demanded. Human males had a strange custom of letting females walk into buildings ahead of them. It was supposed to be civilized or something, but it was stupid. Letting a female walk into an unknown situation made no sense. He knew December wouldn't understand that, and since the doors and windows were glass, he forced his protective instincts back down. He could see they weren't walking into an ambush.

Regardless, he instinctively scanned the diner for any possible threats. They received a few curious stares, but he didn't sense any overtly hostile vibes. He'd been seen in town enough times that he was sure most people knew exactly who and *what* he was. Being seen with December might hurt her reputation and while he cared about that, he wouldn't stay away from her because of it. The most dominant side of him wouldn't let him. Not being near December wasn't an option.

He chose the booth closest to the back exit. When December slid into the seat, he immediately sat next to her and positioned himself so that he had a view of the entire room. He could tell she was annoyed that he'd sat next to her instead of across from her, but his position served two purposes. No way anyone could ambush him, and he got to press up against her. The latter was the only excuse he needed.

She shifted away and put a few inches between them, avoiding his gaze. "Why does that guy keep bothering Kat?" The heat in December's words was unmistakable.

"It's complicated."

She shook her head. "No, it's not. I've never seen her so upset."

He shrugged, not wanting to talk about them. "They're exes. And I don't care about their issues. I care about you, December. What the hell changed between us from last night to now?"

Nervously she tucked a strand of red hair behind her ear as she glanced out the window. "I have no idea what you're talking about." Her voice held no conviction.

For a moment he stared at the tense line of her jaw and the long, smooth arch of her neck. "You mean you don't remember how your body pressed against mine, how you wrapped your legs around my waist? I could feel your heat, December. Could smell your desire. Hell, I can smell it now." He leaned in closer. "You. Want. Me."

Her ivory skin flushed crimson, but at least she turned to face him. "I've never denied wanting you, but it's just physical. Why can't you let this go, Liam?"

"Only because you keep pushing me away." He started to say more when a waitress came to take their drink order. The busty blonde eyed him curiously and the blatant interest in her gaze was hard to miss. When he smelled her lust, almost immediately he sensed December's jealousy. The spike in the air was sharp and strong.

It soothed his inner wolf. She wasn't as unaffected as she'd like him to believe. Once the woman left them, he shifted slightly in his seat so he faced December. Wordlessly, he placed a hand on her thigh.

She tensed under his touch. "What are you doing?" she asked.

His chest tightened as he gently squeezed her leg. What he wouldn't give to tease and trace his fingers up her bare skin. He wanted to memorize every inch of her body with his tongue, hands, and mouth.

He ignored her question. "Why are you pushing me away?"

"We just got carried away last night, Liam. I don't see why we have to make a big deal of it."

"I'm not making a big deal. I want you to give us a chance." He could practically hear the no on her lips so he hurried on. "Come out to the ranch with me tomorrow after work. I want you to meet my pack and I'll take you horseback riding if there's enough daylight left."

At the suggestion, her eyes lit up, but her lips pulled into a thin line. "I . . . don't know."

"Why not?"

"I don't want to lead you on."

He frowned at her words, but she continued. "Just because I agree to spend time with you, I don't want you to assume this means anything about mating or bonding or a future for us."

She could say whatever she wanted, but he knew that if they spent enough time together, he could prove to her they had a shot at a long-term relationship. If she had been a shifter, she wouldn't fight her attraction to him. She'd simply accept that they were suited for each other. He wasn't sure if the fact that she was human added to his attraction to her. Her constant struggle to pull away from him made him crazy, but it also turned him on in a way he didn't understand. His inner wolf wanted her submission, but the predator in him also loved the hunt. Something told him that once he'd finally claimed her—and he planned to do that soon—things would never get old between them. The sexy redhead would always keep him on his toes.

Slowly, he moved his hand up her leg a couple inches. "You like horseback riding?"

Her blue eyes glazed over for a moment as he trailed his fingertips higher. Even though she wore jeans, he could feel the heat and energy flowing through her muscles. Her body temperature had risen in the short time since he'd been touching her. While he might not be able to see them, he would bet her nipples were hard and aroused against her bra cups. The thought of what color they'd be made his cock strain against his pants and he had to bite back a groan.

Leaning closer, he started to tell her what he'd like to do to her, but the waitress returned. Sighing, he waited while she ran through the specials. Even after they'd given their order, she lingered for a moment to stare at him. He wanted to growl at her to leave them alone but knew it wouldn't do him any good to alienate citizens of the town. So he pushed down his impatience and gritted his teeth while she stood there staring at him hungrily.

"We don't need anything else, Betsy." December's annoyed voice sliced through the air and jerked the woman out of her trance.

The blonde mumbled something under her breath and hurried away.

"Seems like you have an admirer." December inched away from him, closer to the window by their booth.

Instead of giving her space, he moved with her and kept his leg lined up with hers. He just wanted to touch her, maintain that simple connection. "Do you care?"

She shrugged instead of answering. But at least she didn't deny it.

"So, horseback riding this week?"

"Um . . ."

"Tomorrow when you get off work."

"Is that a question?" There was a slight trace of amusement in her voice. That was a good sign.

"Tomorrow?"

December shook her head slightly and sighed. "I can't tomorrow, but how about Tuesday? And I'm only agreeing because it's been months since I've been riding, so don't get any ideas."

"Why can't you go tomorrow?" It came out harsher than he intended.

Her eyebrows rose at his abrupt question. "I have plans."

"With who?" he demanded.

"Not that it's any of your business but I volunteer at the local high school on Monday nights as a literacy tutor."

He instantly relaxed at her words. "Oh."

Her pretty mouth pulled into a thin line. "See? This is another reason we'd never work out. You can't grill me about where I go and what I do." When he started to respond, she cut him off. "And don't give me some bullshit line about how you're worried about my safety. You're ridiculously territorial, Liam. The only reason I've let it slide so far is because of everything that's been happening."

His first instinct was to deny her accusation, but he *was* territorial. He was an alpha *and* a warrior, so it was ingrained into the very fiber of his being. Unlike the betas of his pack, who depended on alphas and warriors alike to protect them, he protected what was his, including her. It was the pack way. The animal way. Unfortunately for his inner wolf, she might be beta in the physical sense but she sure as hell wasn't submissive. If she had been a shifter, she'd be alpha to the bone. Always butting heads with him. She didn't care about his protective instincts or understand them and he had no response for her. Anything he said was guaranteed to annoy her, but he couldn't change who he was. As she stared at him, waiting for a response, her brother walked through the front door of the diner.

Potent relief surged through him at the interruption. Something Liam had never thought would happen at the sheriff's presence.

Without waiting for an invitation, Parker took off his hat and slid into the seat across from them. "I'm glad you're together."

That's a first. Liam lifted an eyebrow.

"What's wrong?" December asked.

The sheriff glanced behind him, presumably to make sure they weren't being overheard, then looked back at them. "This is all off the record, Liam. I want you to pass this information on to your brother."

He nodded, all his muscles tensing. "Okay."

"Found a body early this morning. Male, Caucasian, early thirties. He'd been ripped to shreds by a couple dogs, but that's not what killed him. A blow to the head did."

Liam glanced at December, who looked as confused as he felt. "And?"

"The body was moved and dumped at Abel's Gas Station. There aren't a lot of reasons to dump a body in plain sight. It's only a theory, but it's possible whoever did it wanted this death blamed on shifters."

"That seems like a stretch." But it didn't. Liam just didn't want December to worry about anything else right now.

Parker shrugged. "Maybe. Maybe not. There's more to it than that, but that's all I'm willing to tell you."

"Why *are* you telling me all this?"

Parker's eyes darkened. "With all the bullshit happening

around here and rumors of the APL, I can't afford not to. This is a peaceful town and if some assholes think they can start anything here, they're dead wrong."

Liam nodded slowly as Parker's words sank in. If the APL members couldn't exterminate them all, going after their reputation was a good way to get the rest of the town to hate them. It didn't take much to get people riled up, and he'd seen firsthand how quickly humans could turn on shifters if they had enough fear in their hearts. Not to him personally, but he watched the news enough and he had friends who'd been driven from towns because of simple human fear. "I'll tell Connor."

"Good. And make sure everyone in your pack stays out of trouble."

Liam bit back a sharp retort, mainly because Parker was December's brother. It's not as if his pack had gotten into any trouble since they'd moved to Fontana. Connor was a good Alpha and he looked out for all of them. Anything that was pack business stayed that way. They didn't involve the humans in anything they didn't have to. He cleared his throat. "Of course."

"Listen, I've got to work late tonight—"

Liam knew where he was headed, so he cut him off. "I'm staying at her place."

December cleared her throat. "Excuse me. 'Her' is sitting right here."

"December, not now," Parker said absently as he grabbed his hat. He kept his attention on Liam and nodded once.

Liam knew Parker hated depending on him for anything. Mild distrust rolled off him in both his scent and his expression. But the man obviously knew Liam would never hurt December and would do anything to keep her safe.

As the sheriff left the diner, December elbowed him in the side. "I hate when you do that. I'm sitting *right* here. I think he's just as bad as you."

Under normal circumstances it wouldn't have hurt, but she hit him directly where he'd been stabbed. He gritted his teeth. For such a small woman she had some serious strength behind her. Or maybe he'd just been stabbed deeper than he realized.

Her gaze narrowed on his face. "Tell me that didn't hurt."

"It didn't."

"Then why'd you flinch?"

"I didn't."

"Don't lie to me."

"I didn't flinch, but . . . I might have gotten stabbed earlier."

Immediately her eyes widened and she reached for him. "*Stabbed?* Are you okay? What happened? Why didn't you go to a hospital?"

As she took his hand in her smaller one, his entire body warmed. Shit, he wasn't above playing the sympathy card. Not if it made her want to touch him. "There's nothing anyone at a hospital can do and I'm fine. I'll be healed completely by tonight."

Her expression was still worried. "Who stabbed you?"

If he told her, she'd tell her brother there were fae warriors in town, and that was the last thing they needed. More involvement from law enforcement. "It's not important."

"Was it one of those APL members?"

"No."

"Are you going to tell me who it was?"

"No."

Her ivory cheeks flushed an angry red. Even if he

couldn't scent the changes in her, he was coming to learn the small nuances of her body and expressions. Plus she wore her emotions right out in the open. Those blue eyes of hers gave away everything. "You just expect me to accept everything you say without asking any questions." Her voice was heated but at least she hadn't pulled away.

Slowly, he rubbed his thumb over her open palm. He needed to change the subject. Fast. "Did you wear that sweater to drive me crazy?"

The abrupt switch in topic made her blink. "What?"

He let his gaze travel down over her breasts. She wore a green sweater that wrapped around her waist with some sort of tie thing. All he'd have to do was pull the bow free and it would fall open. Just a hint of cleavage peeked through the V-neck cut. "You know how fast I could take that thing off you?" he whispered.

Her breathing became shallower as he continued rubbing small circles against her skin. "You can't use sex to distract me." Her voice came out raspy and sinfully low.

"I'm not doing anything." He was touching her in a completely nonsexual spot, but it was obviously affecting her.

Her mouth slightly parted and her eyes filled with undeniable heat. When her tongue moistened her lips, it took all his restraint not to crush his mouth over hers.

Slowly, he started to lean closer to her. He was fully aware there were eyes on them, but he didn't give a shit. Apparently she didn't either. As she leaned toward him, her eyes started to drift shut. And his cell rang in his jacket pocket. "Son of a bitch." Even though he wanted to ignore it, when he heard his brother's unique ring, he simply couldn't. Brother or not, Connor was his Alpha and he always had to be on call for him.

December's cheeks flushed a deeper crimson this

time and it was definitely because she was turned on. And embarrassed. She stared at her glass while he fished out his phone.

"Yeah?" he practically barked at Connor.

"Is Jayce with you?" his brother asked.

"No, but he's not far."

"Ryan got a hit on a possible address for a Mike Taylor. Could be nothing." Connor's voice was cautious.

"But it could be that asshole." If Liam got the chance to kill the bastard who'd dared to touch December, he was taking it.

"I need you and Jayce to check it out."

"Text me the info. We'll head over there now." At his words December's head snapped up, but he ignored her curious stare.

As soon as he disconnected, December asked, "What's going on?"

"I've got to take care of some pack business. I'll have the waitress wrap up your food."

"Oh, will you?"

Shit, what had he said? Her tone had gone from concerned to annoyed in seconds. "Uh, yes?"

"Just because you're leaving doesn't mean I'm not going to stay and finish my meal. And if you give me some line about walking me back to my store for my protection, I swear, I'll scream." Her chin jutted out mutinously.

She was right. He knew it. Even if he didn't want to admit it. The walk back to her bookstore was less than thirty seconds. Barely a block down the road. But his inner wolf didn't care. *Pick your battles.* His sister-in-law's voice sounded loudly in his head. This was one of those times he needed to restrain his protective nature. If he didn't, he was going to drive an even bigger wedge between him and December. "You're right." He grabbed a few bills from his wallet and laid them on the table. "Will you get my food to go and I'll meet you after work to take you home?"

For a moment, she looked shocked. Then concerned. "Where are you going so suddenly?"

"I . . . I can't say."

"You just got *stabbed* today. What's the matter with you? Is this something dangerous?"

He couldn't be sure, but he wasn't going to tell her that. "No."

Apparently he paused too long for her liking because she glared at him. "You're so full of it."

"Okay, I don't *know* if this will be dangerous." He shifted uncomfortably in his seat. Answering to someone about his daily business wasn't something he was sure he could get used to.

"And you're not going to tell me what 'this' is?"

"I'm sorry, December."

Her lips pursed as she looked away. "Fine, do whatever it is you're going to do. Just don't think you can keep pushing me out of your life and think we have a future together."

"I thought you said we *didn't* have a future. Are you saying if I open up more, we will?"

She opened her mouth, then snapped it shut. Seeing that combination of confusion and annoyance on her face soothed every part of him. He wasn't sure why, but it did. Before he could stop himself, he leaned forward and brushed his lips over hers. A soft, almost chaste kiss that made him want to turn off his phone, forget about what he needed to do, and find a secluded place where they wouldn't come up for air for days.

Without glancing back at her, he hurried from the restaurant and tried to catch his breath. While he wanted to dominate and make love to her every way possible, the woman had such a stranglehold on him it scared the shit out of him. Mated males could turn into fools because of their females, and he and December weren't mated or even bondmates yet.

Liam zipped his jacket up higher as he and Jayce strode up the walk to the place his brother had sent him. It was a run-down mobile home in a trailer park on the outskirts of Fontana. The bottom half of the home was rusted and pieces of siding were completely missing. The entire park was quiet and Liam didn't scent too many people around.

As they neared the blue and white structure, he didn't sense that anyone was inside, but he didn't plan to take any chances. "I'll take the back door," he said quietly to Jayce, who only nodded.

Without pause he veered to the left and rounded the home. Keeping an eye on his surroundings, he noticed the curtain in a neighboring trailer flutter. The movement was slight, but if the people here were nosy, they'd have to get in and out fast before someone called the cops.

If he'd been seen, it was too late to worry about hiding now. At least they'd parked off the side of the road in the trees about a mile down the dirt road leading to the trailer park.

Pressing his back against the side of the structure, he peered around the corner to the rear. The grass was wildly overgrown and there weren't any neighbors to the back of the place. Just woods.

Good to know in case they needed to make a hasty exit. With his gloved hand, he tested the handle to the door. Locked.

Putting his weight into it, he rammed the door with his shoulder. The flimsy lock easily broke under the pressure. As he stepped inside, there was a bedroom to his right and a hallway leading to what looked like a kitchen/living room combination.

The instant he stepped into the bedroom, he heard the front door jerk open. He paused. "Jayce?" Anyone else wouldn't have been able to hear him.

"Yeah," he said just as quietly.

"I'm going to check the bedroom."

"All right. I've got the kitchen and living room. Smells like something died in here," Jayce said in disgust.

Liam nodded in agreement even though the other wolf couldn't see him. The place was colder inside than out and the stench of mold and rotting food accosted him. He eased open the fiberboard door and quickly took in the room. A huge wet stain on the carpet in the corner was the source of the moldy smell. Looked like the guy had a leak and hadn't bothered to fix it.

A few papers and bills were strewn across the desk by the window. Liam gathered them together and shoved them in his jacket pocket. After finding the desk drawers empty, he checked the closet, under the bed, and any place he could think of.

Nothing.

If this guy was hiding something, it likely wasn't in his room. And they didn't have time to do a full-scale search. When he was done, Liam found Jayce searching the cabinets in the kitchen. "Find anything?"

"Lots of porn, ammunition, and a couple handguns," Jayce said without turning around.

Liam opened the refrigerator but there wasn't much there. He lifted a few of the condiment containers and when he lifted a mustard bottle, something inside it rattled. He quickly opened it and found a flash drive wrapped in a plastic bag. "Interesting." He shoved it in his pocket and paused at the same time Jayce did.

Sirens sounded in the distance. Too far away for the human ear, but if they were coming for them, he had to guess they had five minutes to get out of there.

"You ready?" Liam asked.

Jayce nodded and shut the cabinet.

Glancing around, Liam did another visual sweep. It was doubtful this guy had cameras set up, but he didn't want to take the chance.

Liam opened the front door but fell back as a bullet whizzed by his head and smacked into the wall. "Shit!" Falling onto his back, he kicked the door shut. He'd seen two guys holding pistols, but there could be more.

The loud slam of the door was drowned out by the staccato pops of gunfire. Bursts of noise surrounded them as the front windows exploded. Glass shattered and splintered, covering the dingy furniture of the living room.

"Stupid fuckers," Jayce growled as he crouched low and crawled away from the door.

Two more huge holes ripped through the wall above their heads. Plastic and old insulation exploded in a burst, filling the room with a cloud of pink dust particles.

"Did you get a look at them?"

"Three men wearing masks," Jayce said, his tone even.

"I'll take the kitchen and keep an eye on the back hallway." Liam began crawling as he spoke.

The two rooms were separated, but only by the flooring. The living room had the kind of thin carpet used in industrial buildings and the kitchen had cheap linoleum flooring.

As the trailer rattled and shook from the gunfire,

Liam slowly inched his way toward the window. His heart rate picked up, but he'd been in worse situations. Unless the bullets were lined with silver, he wasn't too worried. Still, if he got hit, he'd be weaker and these humans would have a better chance of gaining ground against them. Hell, they'd managed to catch them off guard. Something that wasn't going to happen again.

When the shooting suddenly stopped, Liam pulled out his 9mm semiautomatic pistol from the back of his pants. He didn't like to open fire on anyone, especially in the middle of a housing area, but these assholes deserved what they got. He slowly stood up and grasped the bottom of the curtain. Moving it to the side a fraction of an inch, he peered out. One guy wearing a black mask was hunkered down beside a car with no wheels. Looked like he was reloading.

Liam couldn't see the other two but had no doubt they were there. It was possible one of the men had rounded to the back of the house, but he hadn't heard the door open or scented anyone.

There were about twenty yards between him and the guy and it was a crappy angle. But he had to take the shot.

Without waiting, he aimed and fired. After Liam let off a burst of gunfire, the man cried out as he flew back into the dirt. Liam smiled as the man howled and clutched his shoulder.

As Liam started to duck back down, a sharp pain ripped through his arm. Biting back a cry, he slid down the lower cabinets and clutched his upper arm.

"You all right?" Jayce asked.

"Fine," he said through gritted teeth. "Got hit, though."

"Well, you hit one of those douches too."

Jayce cursed. "I can't see the others. . . . Wait . . ." He fired off a couple shots.

Liam heard another startled cry followed by a string of curses. Sounded like he'd hit another one. That left one more guy.

The sirens in the distance were a lot closer now. Close enough for anyone in the trailer park to hear. Liam tore open one of the drawers and grabbed a rag. As he wrapped it around his arm, Jayce hurried into the room.

He opened the cabinet under the sink and pulled out a bottle of bleach. "Those guys heard the sirens. They're on the run, but we don't have much time." Jayce poured the bleach on the small stream of blood forming around Liam's feet.

Liam was careful not to wipe his gloved, blood-covered hand on anything as he stood. A brief wave of nausea bubbled up, but he shook his head. Getting out of there was more important than anything. He could dispose of his clothes later. "We can leave through the back woods and double back to the truck."

"I'll meet you by the back door." Jayce flipped open a lighter and set the kitchen curtains on fire.

Liam started to protest but knew it wouldn't matter. Even if they had a chance to come back, the cops would have combed over the place. Better to destroy all evidence that they'd been there. Holding on to his arm in an attempt to keep any more blood from leaking through the makeshift bandage, he headed to the back.

He checked outside. No one was waiting to ambush them. "We're clear."

When he heard Jayce close behind, he hurried out the door and sprinted for the woods. The sirens were so loud now it would be a miracle if the cops didn't see them. He didn't risk a backward glance as he ran. His inner wolf howled at him, begging him to shift to his animal form, but that would leave his clothes and gun behind as evidence—not to mention it would give away what they were.

Once they'd made it into the thick cover of trees, they both paused and turned around. Thick, orange flames licked into the sky and a few cops surrounded the home. When one of them turned and looked in the direction of the woods, he and Jayce both started running.

Liam wasn't hurt too badly, but by the scorching sting traveling down his arm, he knew the bullet had been lined or tipped with silver. The skin around the wound had turned slightly gray. Whoever had shot at them knew what they were and obviously weren't afraid to go after them in a semipublic area.

Whatever these assholes had planned, it wasn't good and it only reinforced Liam's need to convince December to move to the ranch with him. At least temporarily. He wanted her safe and under his protection.

First he had to clean his wound. If he'd been shot by regular bullets, he'd have already started healing. Since this one had silver on it, he needed to get it out quickly.

He grunted from the spreading pain as they ran. He could feel it in his shoulder now and the agony wasn't letting up. It was getting worse.

"You okay?" Jayce asked.

"Yeah. We've got to get to the ranch, though." His brother wasn't a doctor by a long shot, but he'd extracted bullets from him before. If the silver was allowed to spread through his system, it could weaken him for days and eventually kill him.

Chapter 10

Stretched out on the floor in Ana and Connor's kitchen, Liam gritted his teeth against the probing surgical tool. His arm wasn't gushing blood, but they needed to get the rest of the bullet out so his wound could start healing. Due to the blood loss he was weaker than normal, and if he'd been human, he'd have passed out by now.

His body was working overtime and the wound was fighting to close itself. The remnants of silver on his skin wouldn't let it.

"This is it," Connor said.

He grunted in pain as his brother finished pulling the last bullet fragment out.

"Quit being such a baby and stay still." Ana held Liam's arm straight as he tried to jerk away.

He glared at his brother and Ana. "Next time you get shot, I'll see how you feel."

"I thought male wolves were supposed to be tough." Vivian, the little jaguar cub Ana and Connor had adopted, sat at the kitchen table with her chin propped between her hands. Her eyebrows drew together in curiosity as she watched him.

"Damn it, Ana. Why are you letting her watch this?" This was tough enough without a ten-year-old cub questioning his masculinity.

"Ooh, you said a bad word, Uncle Liam!" Vivian looked expectantly at Ana and pressed her lips together.

Ana shrugged as she began cleaning his wound. "She wanted to, and besides, she needs to understand why we're so different from humans. And do *not* curse in front of her."

"Don't feel bad, Uncle Liam. I fell off my horse last week and cried for an hour. It's okay if you want to cry." Vivian stared at him with those big brown eyes as if she expected him to do just that.

"Yeah. Go ahead and cry, little brother." Connor dropped the last shard into the metal pan he'd set next to Liam's head. His lips twitched as he fought back a laugh.

"F— Screw you." Lying there, he tried to picture December's face while Ana sanitized and bandaged him. Anything to distract him. Unfortunately it didn't work. The adrenaline had worn off and after being stabbed this morning, he felt as if he could sleep for a couple days straight. He'd tried calling her at work, but she must have left already. And she hadn't answered her cell. Though he wanted to jump up right then and call again, he'd try her once he was sitting up and dressed.

As Ana continued to bandage him, he could already feel himself getting stronger. Since the foreign object was gone, his body would naturally push out any remnants of silver, but it might take a day or two until he was completely back to normal. The silver slowed the healing process and even though most of it was gone, he knew he wouldn't be at a hundred percent.

"So when are we going to meet your girlfriend? Ana says you're just like Connor and don't know how to—"

Ana cleared her throat loudly. "All right, little one. Let's leave Uncle Liam and Connor alone." She dropped the bloody towels into the trash bag she'd laid out and scooped Vivian up into her arms.

"But I don't want to leave," Vivian pouted.

"Too bad. You need a bath before dinner."

Vivian grumbled under her breath, but she wrapped her arms around Ana's neck and laid her head on her shoulder as she did.

Once they were out of sight, Liam sat up. More than pain, annoying discomfort pitched through his arm. He ignored it. "So how is it being newly mated and living here with the extra females?" One of Ana's sisters had died, so they'd moved back into the main house with her other sister, Noel, along with Erin and had also adopted Vivian.

Connor grinned slightly as he started wiping up the blood on the tile. "Sometimes we have to get . . . creative, but it's good for Ana being near Noel all the time."

Liam bit back another groan as he pushed off the ground with his good arm and slid onto one of the chairs. "What about Vivian? How's she adjusting to living with a bunch of wolves?"

"I don't think she cares one way or another, but she has been having a lot of fun shifting in the middle of the barn and scaring the shit out of the horses." His brother shook his head. "You going to see December after this?"

He nodded.

"How are you going to explain that?" He gestured to the bandage.

"I'm not." Considering the walls she'd been erecting at lunch, he doubted they'd get to the part where clothes came off, so he wasn't worried about having to explain anything. Not wanting to talk about it anymore, he switched subjects. "You think Ryan will be able to figure out what's on that flash drive?"

Connor lifted his shoulders noncommittally as he tied shut the garbage bag full of rags and Liam's bloody clothes. "Hell if I know. If anyone can get past that encryption, it's him."

Liam picked up the sweater Ana had left for him and slipped it on. As he lifted his arms, his muscles strained against the movement.

"So . . . how are things with December?" Connor looked at him with an expression that said he knew *exactly* how things were with her.

Liam's shoulders automatically tensed as he thought about earlier. "Fine."

His brother was silent for a long moment. Finally he spoke. "A couple weeks ago I had Ryan run a background check on December and the sheriff—"

Liam shot out of his chair. "What the fuck?"

Connor took a menacing step forward and slightly bared his already protruding teeth. "Sit and *listen*." The words were spoken so low, but the underlying authority in them jolted Liam straight to his core.

The anger flowing through him didn't subside, but the subtle reminder that Connor wasn't only his brother but his Alpha wasn't lost on him. So Liam did as he said. He might be an alpha in nature, but his brother was pack Alpha for a reason.

Connor's canines retracted as he stepped back and leaned against the counter. "Have you talked to December about her past? Her family history?"

Liam shook his head. Talking was the last thing on his mind when he was around her.

"You should."

"What's that supposed to mean?"

His brother sighed in the way only a big brother could. "Damn it, Liam. I know you're pulled to her like nothing you've ever felt. Believe me, I get it. But you need to get to know her before you mate and bond with her."

Liam snorted. Mating and bonding? All he'd done was kiss December. As his brother's words sank in, a sliver of concern wedged its way inside him. "What do you know about her that I should?"

Connor shrugged and shook his head. "Ask her yourself."

Liam understood him well enough that he knew his brother was through answering questions. And he really hated that Connor was right. What *did* he know about her? He knew that she smelled like jasmine and that her breasts were soft and fit perfectly against him. He also knew that when he finally stripped her naked and had his way with her, it still wouldn't be enough. But the truth was, he *didn't* know much about her. Her likes and dislikes. No wonder she kept pushing him away. Ignoring the fresh pain in his upper arm and the fading discomfort in his side, he grabbed his keys. It was time to take her on a real date and treat her the way she deserved.

Joseph tossed his cigarette onto the icy sidewalk and stubbed it out under his boot. Even wearing a thick down jacket, he was still chilled. The sun was setting and taking the limited warmth with it. Pausing by a light pole across the street, he bent down and retied the laces as he watched December's Book Nook. It was a few minutes until five. She should be leaving soon.

When his phone buzzed in his pocket, he glanced at it,

then silenced it. Edward thought he could tell him what to do, but that bastard had turned into such a pussy lately. Whatever that blond slut Brianna said, he did. Joseph wasn't even sure where she'd come from, but he didn't trust her. She hadn't been part of the APL long enough, yet Edward still deferred to her. Not overtly, but it was so obvious he cared what she thought.

It was disgusting.

Concentrating on the task at hand was the most important thing. The two women inside the bookstore talked and laughed as they started shutting off the lights and blowing out the candles.

Edward wanted him to tail Katarina back to the ski lodge, but that was some *stupid* shit. He didn't care what his boss or even what Edward's boss ordered. Going after her was like asking to bring all the heat of her father down on their organization.

Edward talked to him like he was some stupid thug, but he didn't have a death wish. Katarina Saburova's father was far more terrifying than any shifter or vampire ever would be. No, he'd take the sheriff's sister. Edward might be pissed at first that he'd disobeyed orders, but he'd get over it. And if he didn't, fuck him.

The sheriff's sister was a good bargaining chip. The local pack leader's brother was all into her, so they could use that against the Armstrongs. Edward had told him that getting that pack out of Fontana and the region was their number one priority right now. Doing it this way made more sense. If they tried it Edward's way, it would just bring more violence into the area and more heat on the APL.

That was the last thing he wanted. When he'd joined the APL, it wasn't to bring violence to humans. It wasn't like he was a terrorist. He just wanted the shifters gone.

His brother had been killed by one of those animals in a bar fight. Over a stupid table. And the judge had let the shifter off on some sort of technicality. His brother might have run his mouth from time to time, but no one deserved to die like that. It wasn't fair.

Joseph's breath quickened as the women exited the store. The redhead looked around as if searching for someone. Not wanting to get caught staring, he slowly headed down the street away from them and toward his parked truck.

But she didn't pay any attention to him anyway. He slid into his vehicle and turned around to watch them through his tinted back window. A few people carrying colorful shopping bags walked past him on the sidewalk, but no one noticed him.

Katarina stood there waiting with December. Finally the redhead shook her head and shooed the other woman to her car. Looked like she didn't plan to wait around for her man.

Joseph smiled and kicked his truck into gear. He already knew where she lived, so he didn't plan to follow her. He'd simply wait for her to come to him.

Taking side streets, he reached her block quickly. The neighborhood had quaint, historic-looking homes and was exceptionally quiet. A far cry from where he'd grown up in a crowded city in a loud, run-down apartment building where his family had been the only whites.

He parked a few houses down from December's place and scanned the neighborhood as he got out. No blinds open and no kids playing in the front yard. He slipped on his gloves and zipped up his coat as he hurried across the street.

His opportunity to strike would be limited, but getting her out of the house should be easy. He needed to subdue her, tie her up, then pull his truck into her drive and deposit her into the backseat. He could risk trying to drag her to his parked truck, but then he wouldn't be able to bind her without taking a huge risk. And that left more opportunity for her to fight back or make a scene, or for someone to notice them.

Glancing around once more as he strode up the stone walk toward her front door, he breathed a sigh of relief that no one was watching. Unless she'd stopped somewhere, she should be home soon.

Instead of going all the way up to her front door, he ducked behind one of the bushes by the entrance and withdrew his gun. Not perfect cover, but with dusk falling it was good enough. Just as he got into position, he watched her steer past the house. Without standing, he couldn't see, but he could hear when her car door slammed.

When he heard her boots clacking against the walk, he tensed, ready to spring. With his gun ready, he knew he'd have only one shot at this.

As she neared the small step before the covered entrance, she jerked back as she noticed him. Before she could scream, he brandished his gun high enough for her to see.

"Say a word and I'll shoot you in the gut. You'll bleed out before the cops arrive." He wasn't actually going to shoot her, but she didn't know that.

Color drained from her already pale face. She dropped the plastic bag she was carrying.

He cursed under his breath. "Pick it up and act natural and unlock your damn door."

A battle waged in her head. He could see it in those pretty blue eyes. He guessed she was trying to figure out if she could make a run for it.

"I'll empty my gun into you before you've taken three steps."

She swallowed hard. Her keys were clutched tightly in her hand, but she still hadn't made a move to do as he said. "What do you want from me?"

"I don't want to hurt you, but if you make me, I will."

"That's not an answer." Her voice shook and her entire body began to tremble as she stared at his gun.

The longer they stood out there, the bigger chance he had of getting caught. He went for semihonesty. He didn't want to hurt a human, even if she was seeing a shifter. "Listen, I don't want to hurt you. My boss just wants to talk to your boyfriend and taking you is the only way. You're just a bargaining chip. You won't be hurt if you cooperate."

She shook her head. "I don't have a boyfriend."

Being nice obviously wasn't going to work either. Standing, he jabbed the gun into her side. She cried out but he ignored it. "Open the fucking door. Now."

With trembling hands she eventually opened the door. As soon as they were inside, he bolted it shut. "Sit." From the foyer, he motioned toward one of the couches in the living room.

Still clutching her purse and keys, she did as he said. "If you take me, you have to realize he'll kill you." She didn't say who, but it didn't take a genius to figure out whom she meant.

"I thought you said you didn't have a boyfriend." He pulled out the flex-cuffs he'd brought and tossed them to her. "Put these on."

She dropped her purse to catch them. "He's not my boyfriend, but that doesn't matter to him. You take me, you're dead. You haven't done anything wrong yet. If you walk away now, no one has to know about this."

At her condescending voice, something inside him snapped. He lifted the gun at her again. "I'm not some fucking child. Put. Those. On."

A surge of adrenaline rushed through him as she obeyed him. He was tired of taking orders from everyone. Once she'd secured her wrists in front of her, he tucked his gun in the back of his pants, then pulled out the tape he'd brought.

"Wait, what are you—"

He secured a piece over her mouth. "I'm sorry I have to do this."

For a moment she looked confused; then she started to struggle. When she kicked out at him, he cursed and did what needed to be done. Clocking her hard across the jaw did the trick. Her head lolled to the side as she slumped against the couch.

Now all he had to do was carry her to his truck. He could move it to her driveway, then quickly load her in. So fucking easy.

"Who's fucking smart now?" He smiled to himself as he slipped out her front door. As he hurried across the street toward his truck, he nearly stumbled when he spotted that shifter driving down the road. The giant hulking bastard eyed him briefly, then dismissed him.

Joseph watched as he pulled into December's driveway. His heart beat a staccato drumbeat and a flash of cold fear snaked down his spine. He'd been so close. It was too late to attempt anything now. He didn't have any silver bullets and he didn't have enough training to take him on. And he sure as hell didn't have a death wish.

Unlike most APL members, he didn't think of himself as some invincible badass. Hurrying, he jumped in his truck and sped away. At least no one would know about his failure. There was no way he was telling Edward about this. He'd just make up some bullshit story about how Katarina had been protected and he hadn't been able to get close to her. No one ever needed to know about this blunder.

As he glanced in the rearview mirror, the last thing he saw as he turned the corner was the shifter walking toward the front door. He certainly had a surprise waiting for him.

Liam knocked on December's door for the second time. He'd tried calling her a couple times, but she wasn't answering. Her car was in the driveway, so maybe she didn't want to talk to him. His brother was right. He'd been going about everything all wrong. Pushing himself on her and not bothering to get to know her.

He'd been so driven with the desire to mate he kept forgetting she was human. Sighing, he tried again. "December?"

When she didn't answer, he pulled out his cell. She knew he'd planned to stay tonight. As the phone rang, he heard the jingle of her phone from inside. Then he heard something that sounded like a soft moan.

A surge of alarm shot through him like lightning. Snapping the phone shut, he tried the handle. When the door swung open, he cautiously stepped inside. He'd already been ambushed once today. This could be another trap.

As he moved farther inside, he realized she was the only person there, but he faintly scented something— someone else had been there recently. A male. The mix of cigarette and whatever cologne the man wore lingered. An icy fist clasped around his heart. "December?" he called again as he stepped farther inside.

Following her scent, he started for the living room, then froze. Tied up and with tape across her mouth, December had a bruise forming across her face. Her eyes were closed and she was softly moaning. And he could hear her light breathing. She was alive. A red, burning rage started deep inside him.

He didn't even realize he'd moved, but suddenly he was kneeling by her side. With one quick pull he snapped the plastic bands off her wrists, then slowly eased the tape off her mouth. His throat seized as he checked her pulse. It was strong.

"December?" Her name was barely a whisper on his lips. What the hell had happened to her? *I should have been here.* The thought reverberated loudly inside him.

As he cupped the back of her head, her eyes fluttered open. In confusion she stared at him for a moment before lashing out. Her hand struck his face, but her scream died on her lips as her eyes focused on him.

"Liam?" She tried to push up farther, so he helped her to a sitting position. "Where . . . ?" She looked around at her surroundings before staring at him. When she did, she touched the side of her face and winced.

"Who did this to you?" To his own ears his voice was guttural, more animal than man. His inner wolf tore at him with sharp razor's-edge claws, begging to be set free.

When she flinched, his human side took over dominance. His body shook with the need to draw blood. Whoever had done this would die. The scent that lingered in the air would be forever cauterized in his mind. "Are you hurt? Physically?"

"No." The word was scratchy. Then more started flowing. "He had a gun. He said he was going to use me as a bargaining chip against you. I should have fought harder, but he had a gun." Her voice cracked on the last word. Taking him completely by surprise, she lunged at him and threw her arms around his neck.

For once in his life he felt useless. Absolutely. Fucking. Useless.

December cried silently against his neck. No big wails or sobs from her. Just heartbreaking little gasps as her slim shoulders shook and she trembled in his arms. She buried her face against his neck and the wet tears streamed down his back.

He wanted to take away her pain. To ask her more questions. To find out who'd done this so he could hunt him down. But he knew now wasn't the time. She needed to cry.

So, he held her. Wrapping his arms around her waist, he pulled her until she was sitting in his lap and let her cry.

He wasn't sure how much time had passed, but after what felt like an eternity, she lifted her head to stare at him. Her eyelashes were thick and clumped with tears. She blinked a few times and shook her head as if clearing cobwebs. "I can't stay here tonight."

He wiped away her tears with his fingertips, hating that she was crying at all. "December, we need to talk about what happened."

"I'm not staying here!" He almost jerked back at her shout.

But he understood what was happening. Her body shook wildly and she was likely close to hyperventilating. He needed to get her the hell out of there. Standing, he lifted her and hurried up the stairs.

"What are you doing?" She stared at him in confusion as he placed her on her feet in her room.

"Pack a bag. Bring whatever you need to last a couple weeks." When she frowned, he hurried on. "I'm not saying that's how long you'll be gone. Just make sure you have everything you need."

"Okay." With shaking hands she opened her closet door and rolled out a suitcase.

While she packed, he texted his brother, then Jayce to fill them in on what had just happened. He'd eventually call them, but he didn't want her overhearing any of this. Even though he could have sent out a telepathic message to Connor, he didn't because right now all his focus was on December. And this was his fight, no one else's. His brother might be his Alpha, but some things a male needed to take care of on his own. He hadn't gone truly hunting in a long time, but now that he had this guy's scent, his days were limited.

For a moment Liam was sorely tempted to contact her brother, but December was in a state of shock and not thinking clearly and the last thing he wanted to do was involve the police. Parker might want to put her under lockdown and no one could protect her better than Liam. And more than anything, he just didn't want the cops to know about it. He'd take care of this his way.

Chapter 11

"**T**his is bullshit." Liam slammed his fist on the sturdy dining room table.

Connor's dark eyes narrowed and Ana just shook her head. Everyone else at the table was silent as Liam and Connor stared at each other.

Finally Connor spoke. "We're not going to go off half-cocked hunting this guy down. I understand why you're angry, but we have to be smart about this. Can you kill this guy? Sure. But what will it do for the pack? We need to find the leader and cut off the head of this organization. If we kill this guy, someone else will replace him. This isn't just about you. It's about all of us."

Liam forced himself to take steady, even breaths. His inner wolf wanted blood and he didn't care what his Alpha said. That knowledge terrified him. Thankfully December hadn't been hurt. Not really. Shaken up and scared, but not truly injured. He'd never felt so out of control in his life. Had never wanted to defy his Alpha—his blood—with the intensity he did now.

Right now he wanted to tell his brother to go fuck

himself and hunt down the bastard who'd tried to take December. Beast and man had never been so unified about anything before. A loyalty to his brother that ran bone deep was the only thing keeping him grounded.

"What do you plan to do anyway, Liam? Leave December here all alone while you go off hunting?" Ana raised a dark eyebrow and gave him a look that made him feel like a cub being scolded.

Next to her, Erin snorted loudly. "Your woman is so scared out of her mind that she's staying on a ranch with a pack of shifters and you're gonna *leave* her? Yeah, real genius idea."

Ana nudged her and shook her head. "It doesn't matter the species, they're all clueless," she murmured.

Liam clenched his teeth together so he wouldn't say something he'd regret. Right now December was taking a bath at the guesthouse. He'd called ahead and asked Jayce to move his stuff into the males' cabin, into Liam's room. He didn't care if it was rude. December needed this right now.

She'd told him she wanted some time to herself, and he knew his time was limited before she got out. He'd planned to ask Ana to stay with her while he went after the guy who hurt her, but now he was reconsidering.

Connor looked away from Liam and nodded at Ryan. "Continue with what you were saying."

Ryan cleared his throat and looked around the table. "I still haven't managed to decrypt that flash drive, but we might have good news. The guy who tried to mug December a couple weeks ago is getting out of jail Tuesday morning. It's because of the nature of the crime and overcrowding or something."

"How is that a good thing?" Liam asked. Another asshole APL member with a vendetta against them would be walking free.

This time Connor spoke, his attention on Liam. "He's afraid of us—you specifically. You want to do something useful? I need you to talk to this guy."

"Talk?" He'd broken the guy's thumb before and that had gotten him plenty of answers.

His brother nodded tightly. "Yes. *Talk*. We know his boss's name is Edward Adler, but so far we can't find out much about him. That guy, William, was scared enough of you to admit to his crimes and go to jail without a fight. And he gave up Adler's name. We might be able to use him if you can play on his fear of you."

Liam liked where this was going. If he couldn't hunt down the man from tonight, this was second-best. Nodding at his brother, he stood. "Fine. I need to check on December." Out of respect he knew he should be asking permission to leave the meeting, but he didn't care at this point. All he wanted was to see December. The females were right. Leaving her now would be worse in the long run. She needed to know he'd be there for her, and if he was honest, he desperately wanted to comfort her. To convince himself she was unharmed.

Sighing, Connor nodded and dismissed him.

Liam barely felt the cold night air as he crossed the ranch. A few females were out walking and he could scent some of the males out patrolling the grounds, but all he could focus on was getting to December.

She'd been unusually quiet the entire drive to the ranch and when he'd left her to take a bath, she'd barely said two words to him. He'd rather have her calling him arrogant and annoying and yelling at him instead of this subdued version of her.

He'd left Aiden guarding the house and though he couldn't see him, he knew he was in the shadows watching and would leave once he saw Liam. Once inside, he locked the door even though he'd be able to scent anyone who entered the house. He did it because he knew it would make her feel better. Hurrying up the stairs, he followed that sweet, jasmine scent. The bedroom door was open, letting light spill out into the hallway. He could hear her moving around inside the room and when he reached the door, he froze.

Sitting on the edge of the bed wearing some kind of blue, sheer nightgown thing that barely fell to midthigh, December was smoothing lotion on one of her legs. Her damp, red hair spilled down her back and covered her face as she bent lower to rub the lotion onto her calves.

His cock hardened in an instant as he watched her. He must have made a sound, because her head jerked up.

She smiled softly as she sat up and turned to face him. "Hey."

"Hey." He tried not to focus on the way her nipples peaked so tightly against the silk or how the soft curve of her breasts molded perfectly against the thin material. While he wanted to run his hands all over her body, more than anything he wanted to just hold her. "How are you feeling?"

She shrugged and put the small bottle on the nightstand. "The bath helped but I'm still kind of freaked-out. That guy wanted me as a way to get to you and it was so obvious he saw nothing wrong with what he was doing. I still don't know what I'm supposed to be feeling, but I guess I'm just pissed he was there in the first place and that I didn't react better. I should have fought him." Breaking his gaze, she stared at the gold duvet and traced over the intricate design with her fingertip.

He hated the fear and loathing he heard in her voice, but was thankful she was talking again. It was the most she'd said since they'd left her house. Careful to keep his movements slow, he walked to the edge of the bed and sat next to her. Even though he knew touching her would be torture, he lightly cupped her jaw until she looked at him. "There was nothing you could have done. You're not a trained soldier and that guy had a gun."

Her eyes were red-rimmed from crying. The sight brought up a new wave of anger, but he shoved it away. He needed to keep himself under control or she'd sense the change in the air.

Her wide blue eyes searched his. "Will you stay with me tonight?"

Like she even had to ask. "I'll be right outside all night."

Her cheeks flushed. "No. I mean . . . with me?"

He felt as if his heart skipped a beat. Pausing, he tried to catch his breath. He'd been waiting to hear this for what felt like forever, but never under these circumstances. "Of course," he rasped out.

The tinge of pink covering her cheeks darkened to crimson and the wave of desire that rolled off her was unmistakable. She wanted him and he definitely wanted her, but he didn't trust himself to be gentle. And that's what she'd need tonight.

She wouldn't need a randy shifter ready to rock the bed for hours. If he let himself sink deep into her, he knew that's exactly what would happen. He cared for her too much to do that.

Forcing himself to stay immobile when all he wanted to do was jump her, he said, "Are you hungry? Do you want anything before we go to bed?"

She shook her head and scooted along the edge of the

bed until their thighs touched. He could practically feel
the electricity arc between them, sharp and potent. She
swallowed hard, then leaned forward.

No, she did *not* want anything to eat. Except maybe him.
December knew that taking this next step would come
back to bite her in the ass later, but she didn't care. She
desperately wanted to feel all Liam's warmth and strength
covering her. After the day she'd had, she wasn't afraid
to admit she needed him. Wanted to feel him push deep
into her and bring her such exquisite pleasure she could
forget all the craziness going on around her.

So there was no mistaking what she wanted, she
reached over and held on to his shoulders, then straddled him. As her knees sank into the soft bed, his rigid
cock pressed against her.

Liam's dark eyes widened as he froze, making her
wonder if she'd made a mistake. "What are you doing?"

"You really need me to explain it?" Lifting up slightly,
she rubbed herself over his hard length. Teasing him like
this was wildly erotic. And being on top of him gave her
a welcome sense of control.

For a brief moment, his eyes glazed over. He fisted
her hips and before she could react, he flipped her onto
her back and pinned her against the bed. She should
have known he wouldn't let her be on top very long.
Maybe that should have annoyed her, but the feel of his
firm, muscular body on hers gave her an unexpected
sense of safety. Which was a little ridiculous considering
he was more or less the big bad wolf in the flesh.

The silky duvet was soft and soothing against her exposed skin, but the heat in his dark eyes was enough to
scorch her. Spreading her thighs wider, she let him sink
against her. Even with the small barrier of clothing be-

tween them, she could feel his heat. When she rolled her hips, his eyes flashed dangerously darker. A reminder that this man was a lethal predator. But he'd never hurt her.

He might drive her crazy, but she knew the only thing he'd ever bring her in bed was pure pleasure. Right now that's all she wanted.

"Hold on to the headboard." His words weren't exactly a whisper, but he spoke so low it came out as a rumble.

Even though she wanted to thread her fingers through his dark hair and hold him close, she did as he said. Stretching her arms up, she clutched on to the vintage iron headboard. When she did, his mouth captured hers.

The urgency humming through him was unmistakable, but his kisses were slow and sensuous. His tongue rasped over hers in lazy strokes, as if he had all the time in the world. She felt as if she'd combust from the heat surging through her, and he wanted to take his time?

Frustration built inside her until his hands found their way to her outer thighs. Clutching her bare skin in a dominating grip, he paused a moment before he pushed her flimsy nightgown up. His large, callused hands slid up her hips, her waist, and the sides of her breasts until he'd pulled the gown completely off her.

She'd removed her hands from the headboard while he stripped her, only to have him guide them back. As she held on to the iron posts once again, he pushed up and stared down at her mostly naked body.

He always said how much he wanted her, but now that she was splayed out in front of him, she worried that he didn't like what he saw. She wasn't stick thin and definitely had her share of curves. Instinctively, she started to cover herself, but he stopped her with one word.

"Don't." He seared her with a hot, penetrating gaze before lowering his head over one of her breasts.

Her nipples were already hard from his intense scrutiny, but when he tugged one into his mouth, she felt the sweeping action of his tongue all the way to her toes. It was a shock to her senses, electrifying and erotic.

As he kissed a moist path around her nipple, then made his way to the underside of her breast, she tore her hands from the headboard. She didn't care what he said. She wanted to touch him. To feel all that masculine power under her fingertips.

Tunneling her fingers into his dark hair, she held his head as he continued his delicious assault. So intent on what he was doing, he didn't seem to notice. Continuing the trail with her hands, she rubbed them down his back, savoring all that raw strength.

Unable to stop herself, she wrapped her legs around his waist and began rubbing herself against him. His jeans and her underwear weren't much of an obstruction. His cock pressed so insistently against her, all she could imagine was what it would feel like to have him slide into her. Everything about him was big and she had no doubt he'd be no different down there. Her inner walls clenched involuntarily.

Liam lifted his head, causing her eyes to open. In a daze, she stared at him. Why was he stopping? He was so talented with his tongue she thought she might actually climax from his teasing alone. Her entire body was that primed for release.

"You are so fucking perfect, woman." His voice was gravelly and rough and the words turned her on more than she could have imagined.

She wasn't sure how to respond. If there even was a

response. The intense look on his face took her breath away, making speech or coherent thought impossible.

"I want to kiss you here." He reached between them and cupped her mound. The feel of his large hand covering her made her abdomen clench and sent a shiver of desire curling through her.

Knowing how dominating he was, she was touched he'd asked first. "I want that too."

And she did. Very much.

Smiling, he dropped a lazy kiss on her mouth before he pushed off her. In doing so, she loosened her grip around him and let her thighs fall open.

As he leaned back, he grasped the thin straps of her bikini-cut panties and pulled them down her legs in a quick, almost jerky motion. His hands shook slightly and something told her that was a rare thing for him.

Spread out like this for Liam, December looked like a gift one of his ancestors might have offered to their gods. But she was his alone. Even though his most primal side wanted to flip her onto her stomach, take her from behind, and mark her so that everyone would know she belonged to him, he held fast to his control.

His body ached with the need to sink into her, but he cared for her too much to take her so roughly. Especially now. Not after what she'd been through tonight. She deserved gentleness and care. Her desire was potent and damn near overwhelming, but he sensed how fragile she was and he just wanted to take care of her.

When he stared at her like this, it was hard to breathe. A thin strip of trimmed, light red hair covered her mound. The arousing scent she gave off was something that would forever be embedded in his memory.

When she went to cover herself, he realized he'd been staring too hard. He'd finally gotten her where he wanted her and he refused to screw this up. As gentle as he could, he placed his hands on her inner thighs and lightly pressed them open farther. Bending down, he swiped his tongue along her wet slit in one fluid motion. She tasted just as sweet as she smelled.

Her hips jerked erratically at his first lick, but he didn't stop. Increasing the pressure, he continued teasing her until her thighs clamped around his head and she fisted the sheet beneath her. She was so close he could scent it. Even if he couldn't, the panting sounds and moans she made got louder with each stroke. And it was written in every tense line of her body.

With one finger, he slowly inserted it into her tight sheath. She was so wet he couldn't help the satisfaction that curled through him. This reaction was because of him. She was turned on because of him. She might want to deny their connection, but her body couldn't.

Slowly, he pulled out, then pushed back in with another finger. When he did, her inner walls clamped around him. He could feel the small contractions starting the faster he moved his fingers, so he increased his pace.

The moans that tore from her throat were in unison with each unsteady roll of her hips. His balls pulled up so tight at those sounds he was afraid he wouldn't be able to control himself.

Finally, her back arched as the orgasm ripped through her. Clutching the sheet beneath her, she moaned and writhed as she found that release. His name fell from her lips as her body finally stilled against the bed. Her erratic breathing and the blood rushing in his ears were the only things he could hear.

Looking up, he found her staring at him with wide,

blue eyes and a faint smile on her lips. "Wow," she murmured.

If he could put that look of satisfaction on her face every day, she'd never want to leave his bed. Or him. Smiling, he covered the distance between them and stretched out on top of her. He'd never been great with words, but especially not in the bedroom. His partners had all been shifters and talking wasn't usually on the menu.

When she wrapped her arms and legs around him and molded to him, he relaxed. This was exactly where he'd wanted her and now that he had her naked and underneath him, he couldn't imagine letting her walk away from him. Something tightened around his chest when she increased her grip. After what she'd been through tonight, she trusted him enough with her body to completely open herself to him. Considering the invisible walls she'd been putting up for him, this act of submission touched him on a level he didn't quite understand.

When she started to tug at his shirt, he tensed. Reaching between them, he covered her hands, stilling her.

"What are you doing?" She frowned at him.

"If I take off my clothes, I'll forget all my good intentions." It was hard to remember why he was being so noble when she had her hot, naked body wrapped around his.

Withdrawing her hands from his, she smoothed them up and down his back. The action was surprisingly soothing. "And what good intentions would those be?"

"Not to take advantage of you," he managed to rasp out.

She smiled seductively. "I don't think it's taking advantage when I'm offering myself."

Liam knew he could strip and be inside her in seconds.

Seconds.

But he held back. When they finally took that next step, he didn't plan to let her go. He'd mark and claim her then. He wouldn't risk her throwing it back in his face later that this was a mistake or that she regretted it. That she'd been weak or needy or some excuse. When they took that step, he wanted it to mean something to both of them. No doubts and no barriers between them.

He placed a light kiss on her lips, then pulled the covers back and slid in next to her. "I want tonight to be only about you," he murmured against her hair as he pulled her back against his chest. She tried to protest, but he just tugged her tighter and kissed the top of her head as she settled against the pillow. "Tell me something about yourself." He kept his voice a low whisper and his grip around her firm.

"Like what?" Her question was asked just as quietly.

"Anything. Something I don't know." He didn't care what she told him as long as he learned more about her.

She paused for only a moment. "When I was about five, a German shepherd adopted me."

His eyebrows drew together at her statement. "Adopted you?"

"Mm-hmm. Before my parents died, we lived in a giant house in South Carolina. Lots of land. Easy to get lost on. Parker was supposed to be watching me, but I was a handful and managed to escape his watchful eyes. Long story short, I got lost and was close to hysterics until I stumbled on an adorable puppy who I thought was just as lost as me."

"So he adopted you?"

"Pretty much. He decided I was his owner and led me home. My mom wasn't an animal person, but there was no way she could deny me or his cute little face."

Liam could feel her smile against the pillow. Hell, he could practically feel her entire body smile as she spoke. "What was his name?"

She chuckled, the sound low and husky and sexy as hell. "Bubblegum. Parker tried to tell me it was a dumb name for a dog, but I was five and that was that. No one could change my mind. I haven't thought about him in years." There was a wistful note in her voice before she continued. "What about you? Did you ever have any pets?"

He couldn't help it. A sharp bark of laughter escaped. "Sweetheart, wolves don't have pets."

"Oh, right . . . smart-ass." She nudged his leg with her foot as she snuggled deeper against him.

"Get some sleep, Red." He kissed her head again.

She didn't try to fight him and minutes later the sound of her steady, rhythmic breathing filled the air.

Rock-hard and sexually primed, he knew it would be impossible to sleep anytime soon, but holding December this way was worth it. As she snuggled closer into his embrace, a light movement by the window made him tense. A black raven landed on the ledge. Pausing, it stared at him for a moment, then just as quickly flew away.

A trickle of unease curled through him like scorching, slow-moving lava at the odd sight. It was said that the goddess Morrigan took the shape of a raven when she visited her warriors. In that form she supposedly revealed that death was close. Neither he nor his brother believed in or followed her, but his parents had. They'd been devout worshipers of the goddess they'd believed had created them.

He cursed his sudden unease. He wasn't some impressionable cub. Worrying about the bird's appearance was stupid and he wasn't sure why it bothered him. Death had surrounded him his entire life. Something he'd never thought about until he met December. Now that he had someone to protect, things had changed. So had his priorities.

Shoving the ludicrous thoughts aside, he tightened his grip on her and closed his eyes. He'd rather focus on December's soft curves and delectable body than some bullshit mythological sign.

Chapter 12

Edward's hand tightened around his coffee cup as he heard the front door open, then shut. Brianna glanced over her shoulder from where she stood at the stove but quickly looked away. He'd been in a dark mood all morning and had been very close to taking it out on her.

Something he had no doubt she knew, because she'd been unusually quiet and stayed out of his way.

"Hello?" Joseph called from the front of the house.

Edward didn't shout out for him. If Joseph wanted to find them, he could damn well look, like a normal human being.

Wearing a thick down coat and the same jeans and boots from yesterday, Joseph walked into the kitchen. He paused in the entrance and froze, probably because of the glare Edward gave him. "What's going on?"

"Where were you all night?" he asked calmly.

He shrugged and stepped into the room. As he did, he pulled off his gloves. "I did what you said. I followed Katarina Saburova and tried to stake out her place, but I got a bad feeling, so I left."

"Bad feeling?"

"Yeah, man. Like her place was already being watched by someone else or something. You said the enforcer wants her, so I didn't want to hang around too late and get killed if that dude was there."

"So where have you been all night?" The story sounded like bullshit, but lately everything out of Joseph's mouth did.

He shrugged again in that maddening disrespectful manner and headed for the stove. "Something smells good." When he tried to take a piece of the bacon, Brianna whacked his hand with a wooden spoon.

Edward inwardly smiled, but something about Joseph's attitude was off. "So where were you, then?" He hated repeating himself, but he wanted an answer.

"I met a chick and stayed the night at her place. You're not my fucking father. I tried to do the job and couldn't, so I got laid. It's none of your damn business what I do in my off time."

He hated his attitude, but that sounded more like the Joseph he knew. Sighing, he pushed his mug away from him. He was just being paranoid. Joseph sure as hell wasn't a mole in the APL and he had no reason to lie. The guy was too fucking stupid, so it didn't surprise him he'd been thinking with his dick last night. He could reprimand him, but it likely wouldn't do any good and he didn't have the energy this morning. "There's a fresh pot of coffee on if you want some."

Visibly relaxing, the young man shrugged off his coat and laid it on the back of one of the chairs. "I'll grab some in a minute. I need to shower and wash that bitch's stank off me."

After he disappeared from the room, Brianna shook

her head. "He's so disgusting. I don't know why you put up with him."

He depended on these recruits and she knew it, even if she wouldn't admit it out loud. Thanks to his scarred face, he was likely to be remembered everywhere he went. Before his accident he'd been a normal-looking guy. Good-looking enough to get laid on a regular basis anyway. It had been so easy for him to fly under the radar everywhere he'd gone. He'd had the kind of face people forgot.

Not anymore. Now he couldn't get close enough to either of the women his boss wanted him to take. Pretty women steered clear of him. Some wouldn't even step into an elevator with him. Well, except Brianna, but she was different.

To take either of the women associated with those animals, they had to do it without causing a stir. They needed to get in and out fast. Unfortunately finding good help was damn near impossible. Most of his recruits had no training or had washed out of various military branches during boot camp.

"I don't know if I can use him anymore." He stood and helped Brianna bring the plate of bacon and scrambled eggs to the table.

She brought their plates over and sat. "It's only a minor setback. He might be disgusting, but he probably made the right choice last night. If the woman was being watched, he'd have been killed and our plan exposed."

Edward still wasn't sure he believed Joseph's story. Something about his tone had been off. Nervous. But maybe he'd just been nervous of him. "He's an idiot."

Her blond eyebrows rose curiously, but she didn't deny his words. "So what should we do?"

"I want you to befriend Katarina."

Her eyes widened for a fraction of a second. "What?"

"Befriend her, gain her trust, then we'll take her."

Brianna shook her head. The movement was slight but firm. "I don't know. I don't even know how I'd meet her."

"She's a ski instructor."

"So? I already know how to ski." She stabbed a cluster of the fluffy eggs with her fork and avoided his gaze.

"She doesn't know that."

Brianna thoughtfully chewed for a moment before setting her fork down. "I don't know. It's risky."

"If we get her, the boss will visit and I guarantee there will be a bonus in it for both of us." If the APL knew how to do one thing right, they knew what people liked. Cold, hard cash. There was room to move up in the organization, and for a job well-done they received more than a pathetic pat on the back.

She bit her bottom lip but finally nodded. "Okay. I'll do it."

Liam nudged open the bedroom door with his foot. Even though he'd heard the steady sound of her breathing from outside the door, he needed to see with his eyes that December was still asleep. He'd gotten up early to call Kat and ask her to watch December's store during the morning before her afternoon ski classes. She was pissed he'd woken her up until he'd explained what happened to December. And he trusted Kat not to say anything to the sheriff about December's attack. The more he thought about it, the more he realized that the police had no business involved in what had happened to her. If they found the guy, they'd want to prosecute him, and jail was the last place Liam wanted him.

After calling Kat, he'd woken Erin up and asked her to work with Kat today, then watch the store once Kat headed to the ski lodge. The she-wolf had given him a lot of grief for having to spend time in town and he probably owed her a favor, but it was worth it. He figured she'd also be pissed once she saw Noah hanging around the store, but Connor had ordered him to shadow Kat for the next few days as a precaution, so Erin would just have to deal with his presence for a few hours. Liam didn't care how much he owed the she-wolf after this.

December needed a day off, especially after what happened yesterday, and he planned to make sure she enjoyed herself.

He hated sleeping in his clothes, but last night he'd made an exception. It went against every instinct he possessed, especially when the sexy redhead in his bed was wearing nothing. Since his gunshot and knife wounds were healed, there was nothing holding him back from taking her the way he wanted. Quietly, he pulled back the cover and slipped in behind December. As soon as he did, she turned toward him and wrapped her arm around his waist.

Groaning, he did the same and smoothed his hand down her bare back until he cupped her butt.

When he did, her eyes fluttered open. For a moment she looked slightly disoriented; then she blushed. "Morning."

Okay, she didn't seem freaked-out by the fact that she'd woken up naked in the same bed as him. Just nervous. That he could live with. "Morning, yourself."

Though he tried to keep his gaze on her face, he strayed. Those perfect pink nipples were hard and rosy this morning. He didn't bother to bite back a groan. Smiling, she reached between them and cupped his hardness. The bold action shocked the hell out of him.

"You wake up like this every morning?" she murmured silkily.

He'd gone to bed hard and woken up hard, but he didn't tell her that. "Only when pretty redheads are with me."

Her smile widened as she continued rubbing over his covered erection. He wanted to tell her to stop, but what she was doing felt too good. But when she went to undo his button, he moved so that he was on top of her. He grabbed her wrists and held them above her head.

Settling in between her thighs, he had to force himself to breathe normally, to control his primal urges. "December—"

Arching her back, she rubbed her breasts against him like an animal in heat. Even though he had a shirt on, it didn't matter. His cock surged at the intimate contact. That's when he realized her eyes were slightly dilated. He stared at her for a long moment. She nipped at his mouth and playfully tugged his bottom lip between her teeth.

He managed to pull back. "How do you feel this morning?" he asked quietly.

She smiled seductively and rolled her hips against his. "Not as good as you could make me feel."

His throat seized as he realized what was going on. The scent that rolled off her was subtle yet distinctive. She was ovulating or something equivalent to what shifter females went through when they went into heat. Shifters went through their cycles only twice a year, but December was human. From what he could tell, she wasn't going through the mating frenzy lupine shifters went through, but she was incredibly turned on. More so than usual. It was the only thing that could explain her sudden change of heart. Last night he hadn't scented anything, but this morning, it teased his nostrils, taunting him. Telling him to mark and claim her. Even if there wasn't a full moon out, he could still mark her. They wouldn't be bonded, but it would let other shifters know she was his.

Right now she'd no doubt let him do any damn thing he wanted. Self-loathing rose up inside him at the thought.

"December, you need to take a cold shower and I'm going to make some coffee." Somehow he forced the words out. He definitely deserved a medal for this. A really big one.

Her brow wrinkled and she tugged against his grasp on her wrists. "For weeks you've been trying to get me into bed with you and now you don't want me?"

He wanted her more than he wanted his next breath, but it wouldn't be fair to her. "I think . . ." He struggled to find words that wouldn't freak her out but came up short, so he plunged ahead. "I think you're in heat."

She went rigid. "I'm not a freaking animal—" Her eyes widened immediately. "I didn't mean it like that."

He knew she didn't, which was why it didn't bother him. "I know you didn't. I don't know the right words or the human equivalent to what our females go through, but you're . . . affected by my presence right now. I can see it in your eyes. You feel different this morning, don't you?"

Her eyebrows furrowed together for a moment. "I am really . . . horny, I guess." Her face flushed at the admission.

It wasn't as if she were drugged. He wouldn't be taking advantage of her. On one level he knew that, but his human side didn't want to take her just yet. Not like this.

He wanted her levelheaded and he wanted to know her better. Last night was a start but it wasn't enough. "Trust me on this and just take a cold shower. I want to spend the day with you, Red. Just the two of us, no interruptions."

She shook her head, making her hair swish against the pillow. "I've got work and—"

"I called Kat. She's watching the store this morning. Then one of the females from my pack will take over for her this afternoon."

She gave her head a slight shake. "What about the alarm system? Didn't you say someone was installing it at my house today? It is *Monday*, right?"

He nodded. "One of my pack members will be overseeing the installation."

Smiling, she rubbed against him again. "Then why do we need to leave this room?" she whispered.

Using restraint he didn't know he possessed, he released her wrists and pushed off her. Lightning fast, he was off the bed and grabbed a change of clothes from the bag he'd brought. "I'll be in the kitchen." Without a backward glance he hurried from the room. Behind him he heard her mumble something about him being a jackass, but he ignored it.

His brother's advice telling him to talk to December about her past rang in his head. He'd planned to talk to her yesterday, but getting shot and then the shit that had happened at her house had blown his plans to hell. And he wanted her clearheaded the first time they made love. That thought brought him to an abrupt halt at the end of the stairs. "Making love" wasn't a term he was accustomed to, but he knew that's exactly what he and December would be doing.

*   *   *

December let the warm, pulsing water rush over her body as she scrubbed herself with a loofah. She wasn't sure what had come over her this morning. Waking up naked in Liam's arms, she'd felt positively possessed with the need to feel him inside her. Last night she'd wanted to take things to the next level, consequences be damned, but this morning had been . . . different. She'd been almost overcome with a hunger.

Now that she was by herself, she felt more in control of her lust. Not that it took away from her burning desire for Liam. After being attacked in her home yesterday, she'd been terrified and sure she was going to die. But Liam had been there for her. Just like before. It didn't matter how much she told herself she needed to stay away from him—Liam always came through for her.

She knew she needed to tell him about her past. About her younger brother's death. The longer she was around him, the more she realized she owed him that much. She understood why her older brother mistrusted shifters, but she couldn't lump them all together. Not after all the kindness she'd seen from Liam.

As she rubbed the sudsy loofah between her legs, an image of his head between her open thighs flashed in her mind. Even though she was alone, she felt herself blush. The way he'd pleasured her last night had been amazing. Unexpected. He'd been so giving and he hadn't wanted anything in return, even though she'd have willingly given back to him.

Her thoughts started to take a much hotter turn, so she twisted the shower knob to cold. The icy blast jolted her out of her fantasies. Quickly, she finished showering, dried her hair, and got dressed. She wasn't sure what Liam had planned for the day, but she was relieved not to be going in to work. She felt bad that Kat was covering for her when she wasn't even technically an employee, but for the first time in what felt like forever, December wanted to enjoy herself. After last night, she figured she deserved a little break.

She found Liam downstairs in the kitchen with his back to her, pouring a cup of coffee. The rich aroma made her stomach growl, but it was hard to care as she stared at him. Today he wore a pair of faded jeans that hugged his butt so perfectly, her abdomen tightened with pent-up need. She wanted to grab him and pull him close.

When he turned to face her, his knowing expression said he could read her thoughts. Which was ludicrous. Though he could probably scent her desire. *Damn it.* She really hated that sometimes.

"How are you feeling?" He stayed where he was, leaning against the counter, so she remained in the entryway.

"Fine. And I am *not* in heat." She might feel a little loopy and a lot more turned on than usual, but she wasn't in heat. She was human. That idea was crazy.

His eyebrows rose as if he didn't believe her. "Hmm."

She glared at him. "Don't 'hmm' me. You said you called Kat. Are you sure she's okay working at the store today?"

He nodded quickly. "When I told her what happened last night, she had no problem."

December cringed at his words. She hadn't thought to call the police last night and since Liam hadn't brought it up, she figured he hadn't called either. Which didn't surprise her. If he didn't have to involve the law in something, she knew he wouldn't. Part of her wondered if she should tell Parker, but she knew it would upset him, and worse, he'd probably try to get her to leave town or something.

She might not feel safe in her own home at the moment, but she did feel safe with Liam and she wasn't going to give those assholes who'd been harassing her the right to make her flee like a coward. This was her town and she wouldn't walk away from her friends or her job. And on a primal level she wasn't sure she wanted to acknowledge, she trusted Liam to take care of the man who'd come after her. "Did you tell her not to tell anyone?"

"No, but I don't think you have to worry about her. She knows how to keep a secret."

"How do you know?"

He shrugged, which infuriated her. The man kept so many secrets it was nauseating. She didn't bother trying to grill him. It was too early, she hadn't had any coffee, and she was unusually turned on. Rolling her shoulders to ease some of the tension, she eyed him suspiciously as a new thought occurred. "Did you do something to me?"

"Like what?"

"I don't know. Put a spell on me or something?"

A bark of laughter escaped. "I'm not a witch or a faerie, so no spells, I promise. Why?"

Ignoring his question, she made a beeline for the coffee. If he hadn't done anything to her, she figured ignoring her raging libido was the best thing. As she brushed past him, their arms made contact and a zing of awareness shot straight to the hot ache between her legs. And he'd only touched her *arm*. She refused to look at him, because she didn't want him to see the truth in her eyes. The truth being that if he asked, she'd strip right there and let him take her up on the counter. As she poured herself a cup of coffee, he moved to the side, but didn't give her much space.

She could feel his gaze on her, intense and scorching hot. If he kept looking at her like that, she had a feeling they weren't going to make it out of the kitchen with their clothes on.

"So why a bookstore?" His deep voice always had such an erotic effect on her senses, but the question surprised her and managed to jerk her out of thoughts of nakedness.

Cup in hand, she turned to face Liam, still barely a foot from her. Her cup acted as a small barrier between them, but she savored using it as a shield. "I enjoyed teaching, but I wanted something that was all mine." She paused as she contemplated opening up to him, but finally continued. "I can teach anywhere, but buying my store gave me roots the same way buying my home did. I volunteer at the literacy center and have story time for the younger kids once a week so I still get that interaction, but I love owning my own business and I love books, so it was a perfect choice."

He was silent for a moment before he slightly nodded. "It suits you."

"What about you? I know you've lived all over, but what exactly do you do?"

He took a sip of his coffee as he shrugged. "I'm Connor's second-in-command, so I help him with any pack business, but for the last couple decades I've handled most of our real estate dealings."

"Real estate?" That surprised her.

He nodded. "I even have my license."

Her eyebrows rose at that. Somehow she couldn't see him as a real estate agent. He must have read her expression, because he grinned, his lips pulling up in that sexy way that made her knees weak and erotic heat burn in low places.

"I just got my license so I'd have access to better listings."

"So what kind of real estate do you purchase?"

"Commercial and residential. Some properties are long-term investments, others we've bought just to flip for a fast profit, and others . . ."

As he trailed off, she set her cup down. "Others what?"

He looked at her for a long moment, as if debating something, but finally he spoke. "We have some places set aside as safe houses of sorts. No one knows about them except pack members."

Her throat tightened as she digested what he'd told her. If he was telling her this, it meant he was starting to truly trust her. And trust implied a whole mess of things she wasn't sure she wanted to face. If he started opening himself up, things wouldn't just be about the physical. Not that their relationship was. It was just easy to tell herself that's all she wanted from him. An alarm bell went off inside her head, warning her not to let him too close. Glancing down, she stared at the cup she'd set on the counter.

"Are you all right?" His voice was low and concerned as he placed a gentle hand on her forearm. When his fingers lightly stroked her skin, she had to fight off a shudder.

Turning from him, she opened the oak cabinet above the coffeepot and found a travel mug. "Didn't you say you had plans for us today or something?" she asked as she poured the coffee from her cup into it.

He let his hand drop, but her hands still shook. If he noticed, at least he didn't let on.

"I'd like to show you around the ranch and introduce you to everyone if you feel up to it."

Since he didn't seem to have any inclinations of going back to the bedroom and she didn't want to stay cooped up in here all day, she nodded. "Sounds good."

*   *   *

Jayce put the truck in park and glanced at Erin. "You okay?" She'd been exceptionally quiet on the ride over and he hadn't missed the way she was practically plastered against the passenger door, as far away from him as possible.

The redhead's gray eyes flashed warily. "Why did you want to bring me with you? Are you here to kill me?"

The bold question made him jerk back. "Why would you ask that?"

"Uh, you're the enforcer and I'm nobody. I thought you wanted to talk to me after that meeting, but you never did, so ... why'd you ask Connor if I could ride with you today?" She unsnapped her seat belt and kept her position close to the door.

Everyone always assumed the worst when he was around. As if he went around killing random pack members. It annoyed the shit out of him. His fearsome reputation was justified, but it had gotten blown out of proportion if she actually thought he had a reason to kill her. "For backup."

She snorted loudly in a manner that reminded him of Kat. "Yeah, right."

He bit back a smile. "Why did the Murphy pack report you as dead? Did you run away?"

It was so brief he might have missed it if he hadn't been staring at her intently, but a flash of raw fear sparked in her bright eyes, then disappeared. "They probably reported me dead because they think I am."

He'd talked to Connor about the petite she-wolf and he knew how they'd found her. Behind a Dumpster, beaten, bloody, naked, likely raped, and obviously left for dead. Humans wouldn't have been able to hurt her that way, so he guessed shifters had hurt her. The thought of his own kind hurting any females made him see red.

Shifter violence against females or those weaker was rare. If she'd been abused, he couldn't understand why she hadn't reported it. He'd have wiped them all out. "Should I eliminate the Murphy pack?"

Her eyes widened at the question and for the first time since she'd gotten in the truck with him, the tenseness in her shoulders loosened. "Wait, *what*?"

"Do they deserve to be judged?"

She swallowed hard. "I . . . don't want to talk about them. They think I'm dead and that's fine with me." Her voice sounded so small in the truck cabin and pulled at his most protective side. Yeah, the Murphy pack was going to get a visit from him after this shit was over. "So if you don't want to kill me, why'd you want me along?"

He gave her a searching look. She really had no clue what she was. At their first meeting he'd immediately noticed something different about her. All enforcers, regardless of race or location, had similar qualities about them and he'd picked up on some of hers. "I think you're a born enforcer."

She laughed wryly. "I'm so not in the mood to be messed with and I don't care who you are. Cut the shit and—"

He growled at her dismissive tone. "I'm serious, shewolf. You prefer to fight in your human form, don't you?"

"Not always, but . . . yeah."

"Why?" He figured he knew the answer but wanted to hear her response anyway.

Her shoulders lifted slightly. "It's been that way since I was a cub. Once I let my wolf out, it can be difficult to rein her back in. Like, I'm not quite in control of my wolf. Not always."

He understood that more than most. "And you prefer blades as your weapon of choice." This time it wasn't a question. Though her jacket was zipped up, he knew she carried two blades strapped to her chest. Hers weren't ancient or blessed by the fae like his, but they got the job done.

She nodded. "So?"

"All traits of an enforcer. Just like your eyes. Gray with a barely perceptible ring of amber around them." Those unique eyes narrowed and she started to talk, but he cut her off. "It's subtle, underlying your own scent, but you have a distinctive cedar aroma you exude." The sharp and sweet smell was barely noticeable, easily missed in a room full of other shifters. But even before her eyes, it was why he'd noticed her. Indiscernible as it was, he scented it every damn day on himself, so it had stuck out to him, making her a bright beacon. Then he'd seen her blades and wondered if he'd stumbled on another like himself. Neither his Council nor other enforcers around the globe broadcasted the unique qualities of enforcers. They didn't want to deal with warriors or wannabe warriors coming out of the woodwork convinced they had what it took to be an enforcer.

Before the still fairly newly formed Councils around the world had decided to come out to humans, enforcers hadn't had a designated name. He'd always been distinctively different from his father and brother in the way he'd fought. Being a shifter who preferred to fight as a human was a rare thing. Thanks to the open communication between shifters across the globe, he'd learned there were others like him. And they all had similar qualities. Despite all that, their deadly fighting abilities were the only reason the various Councils had decided to use his kind as enforcers for the general population. It was probably a good thing there weren't many like him around. In the not so distant past, packs hadn't been as linked to one another as they were now and had still governed themselves. Which they more or less did now. He was always a last resort for serious problems that pack Alphas couldn't handle on their own. Or if a pack was causing other shifters or humans trouble on a visible scale.

"I don't know what you're smoking, but—"

He bared his teeth and lightning fast, he grabbed her by the throat and pinned her head against the window. "I'm sorry for whatever you've been through, but if you speak to me like that again . . ." Jayce trailed off as he felt the prick of her blade pressing against his chest, through his jacket.

"Get your fucking hand off me," she rasped out, anger lacing every word.

He didn't want to be impressed, but she'd managed to pull a small dagger from—somewhere on her person and take him off guard. And she wasn't afraid to die. He could sense it clearly. "I could snap your neck." It wouldn't kill her, but it would incapacitate her long enough for him to do so.

"And I could ram this blade into your heart."

"Withdraw," he growled low in his throat.

Finally she pulled it back and he let go of her. She coughed a couple times and glared at him.

Jayce shook his head. "You're definitely an enforcer. I've seen trained warriors practically piss their pants when I get too close."

She rolled her eyes and tucked the small blade in her jacket pocket, likely into a sheathed covering. "I'm not afraid of you."

He chose to ignore her statement because it wasn't entirely true. "I wasn't kidding about why I wanted you here. I want to see you in action if these guys get rowdy."

She stared at him, as if she wasn't quite sure she

believed him. There was wariness in her gaze impossible to miss. "Your eyes don't have any amber around them — they're just gray."

"True." His were much paler than hers and completely one color, but the distinctive gray was still exclusive to his kind, few though there were. "I don't know that you are what I suspect; I just want the chance to find out."

Instead of responding, Erin flicked a glance at the one-story biker bar on the outskirts of town. The small building with no windows wasn't much to look at. Technically it was in the next town's district, but it was close to Fontana, and Ryan had found some information that APL members liked to hang out here. Specifically the two dead fuckers who'd kidnapped Kat. If their friends frequented this place, Jayce was going to find them.

It was eight in the morning and the parking lot was half-full. "What kind of losers are at a bar this early?" Erin asked.

"A lot of these guys probably live here and some are probably sleeping off a hangover from last night."

She shook her head. "You *so* don't need me. You could probably stare these guys down. You definitely look scary enough."

He didn't want to, but he half smiled at her ballsy attitude. No one ever talked to him like that. Well, except Kat. Thinking of her made his chest ache, though. He opened his door. "Let's get this over with."

As he opened the heavy wooden door covered with peeling bumper stickers, Erin pointed at one in disgust. It was of two stick figures, one male standing and a female kneeling in front of him with her head by the male's crotch. The saying under it read "You belong here." "I *really* hope we get to kick some ass today," she said low enough for only him.

"Me too," he murmured.

The door shut behind them with a loud bang. The stench of cigarette smoke, sex, marijuana, booze, and body odor was stale and overpowering. A few men sat at the bar sipping beers, a man and woman were naked and passed out on a pool table, a few men wearing leather jackets and pants were playing pool, and a bored-looking woman with tattoos covering her arms and neck stood behind the bar. After a quick glance around, he noted ten possible threats. Nothing they couldn't handle.

With his shaved head and scarred face, Jayce knew he'd normally fit into a place like this. He also knew if this bar was owned by a local biker gang, they wouldn't like outsiders. And Erin might be strong but she looked innocent and out of place. Something they could use to their advantage.

He strode to the bar with Erin next to him. Instead of pulling up a seat, he leaned against the bar. Erin sat on a stool and swiveled it around so she faced everyone.

"Never seen you two before," the dark-haired bartender said, her voice mistrustful.

Normally Jayce would try to infiltrate a place to get information, but he didn't have that luxury at the moment. The Armstrong pack and the Council wanted answers about the APL. Busting heads was the only way to get it fast.

Steeling himself for what he knew was about to happen, he leaned forward and spoke loudly. "Looking for anyone who knew those two shitheads Felix and Bennett who got killed a few weeks ago."

Watching the giant mirror behind the bar, he waited to see who reacted first. Whoever did, he was going to have words with.

The older men in the worn jackets sitting at the bar

didn't move. Just kept drinking. The bartender glared at him. "No idea what you're talking about, but I think you're in the wrong place, buddy."

The two beefed-up guys playing pool immediately set their sticks down and started to reach inside their jackets—likely for a weapon.

"Bingo. Jackass one and jackass two have stepped up," Erin murmured.

Ignoring the bartender and the men at the bar, Jayce turned. Before he took a step, Erin unzipped her jacket. Moving faster than most trained warriors, she withdrew her blades and flew at the two men.

The expression of surprise on their faces was almost comical. Using the butt of one of her blades, she slammed it across one man's face and kicked the other in the groin. As soon as she did, they groaned and crumpled.

Almost immediately the rest of the bar jumped into action. Even the naked guy on the other pool table managed to get up. Turning away from Erin because it was obvious she could handle herself, Jayce squared off against three men. Two middle-aged bikers who looked like they'd done steroids at one time and a small wiry guy who knew how to handle a blade. Definitely the most skilled of the three.

Jayce went for the smaller guy first but didn't bother to take out his weapons. For a human, the man was fast. He ducked low and tried to knife Jayce in the stomach while the other two came at him from both sides.

Kicking out, he slammed his boot into the guy's sternum. At the same time he struck out with his elbow at the man on his left. The crunching sound when he connected with the man's nose was like music to his ears.

The third guy wrapped his arms around him like a moron. Slamming his head back, Jayce connected with this guy's nose too. The crunching sound was quickly followed by a curse. His adrenaline spiked at the scent of everyone's fear. Some of these bastards had known the men who'd taken Kat. They would suffer for that alone.

Minutes later almost everyone in the bar was subdued. The bartender still stood behind the bar and from what he could tell, she hadn't made an attempt to call the police. Made sense. They probably dealt in more than one illegal enterprise.

When Jayce spotted Erin, she had two men facedown on the ground with her knees digging into their backs and her blades digging into the sides of their throats. Everyone else around her was either knocked out or cowering in fear.

He noticed one of the first men who'd tried to stand up to them had pissed his pants. Perfect. That was who they were taking for a ride. Jayce pointed to the one on Erin's right. "That guy."

She nodded and grabbed him by the collar before yanking him to his feet. Wordlessly, they left the bar. Jayce didn't bother with his weapons. This guy was so scared it was pathetic. "We're just going for a short ride and if you tell me what I want to know, I'll let you go. Got it?"

The tall, dark-haired man nodded. "Yeah," he whispered, barely audible enough for them to hear.

Jayce didn't like playing games or torturing people to get information, but he would if he had to. Technically he was here for a job, but this was about so much more. He owed Kat this. The stench of fear rolling off this guy was so potent, Jayce knew that very soon he was going to have all the information he needed.

Chapter 13

December watched as Liam readied her horse. She knew how to saddle her own horse, but she didn't tell him that because she didn't want to get too close to him. She felt really off-kilter today. All he had to do was lightly touch her and her entire body lit on fire.

A low burning in her belly had started and the ache between her legs was acute. The cold shower had helped a little but not much. And Liam definitely wasn't helping. As he'd introduced her to what seemed like dozens of shifters, he'd kept his big, strong hand at the small of her back the entire time.

Barely touching her.

Yet purposely reminding her of what her body craved. *Him.*

All over her. Inside her. If she closed her eyes, she could imagine what it would be like to have his big, muscular body moving over hers as pushed deep inside her. Could just imagine what he'd feel like.

Liam held out the reins for her and stared at her questioningly. "You sure you're all right?"

"Ask me that again and I'll scream," she said only half jokingly. Maybe he had been on to something with that whole "in heat" thing. Not technically of course, but she couldn't deny that she felt weird today.

Liam's eyebrows rose but he didn't respond. While he got his horse, she slid onto the saddle of the palomino Liam's sister-in-law was letting her ride. It had been months since she'd been riding, but once they left the barn, she was able to clear her head for the first time in weeks. The feel of the cold wind rushing over her was somehow soothing. Liam was surprisingly quiet as he led them to a well-traveled trail. It was big enough for only one horse at a time, so she stayed behind him and enjoyed the view.

She'd bundled up in a heavy down coat, a knit cap, and thick leather gloves. In contrast, Liam wore no jacket, a fairly thin long-sleeved T-shirt, worn jeans, and boots. The thin shirt gave her a nice view of all those rippling muscles. As she watched his back muscles flex, she shifted against her saddle. The rubbing action soothed her aching a little, but she was immediately embarrassed by what she was doing.

As if he could read her mind, Liam turned around. The positively wicked smile he shot her annoyed and turned her on at the same time. "We're almost there," he said.

She started to ask where when he turned back around. She didn't have to wait long, though. Moments later he directed his horse to the left down another very short trail that opened into a clearing.

A small pond was frozen over and most of the oak trees had lost the majority of their leaves, but it was a quiet little oasis. Liam slid off his horse and before she could do the same, he held on to her waist and was helping her down.

For a moment he stood there, gripping her and just staring like he wanted to take her right there on the ground. And she was afraid she might let him. God help her, this man was quicksand. Only days before, she'd been keeping him at arm's length. Now she wanted him to wrap those big arms around her and never let go. What was wrong with her?

Liam suddenly cleared his throat and dropped his hands as if she'd burned him. He tilted his head toward a large, fallen tree. "Will you tether the horses to that log?"

Mouth full of cotton, she nodded and swallowed while he grabbed a backpack off his horse. After securing the two animals, she found Liam by the frozen pond laying out a purple and white quilt that looked handmade.

Fallen leaves and dried grass crunched beneath her boots as she neared him, but he didn't look up as he pulled a thermos and two mugs out of the backpack.

"You can sit if you want," Liam mumbled, barely loud enough for her to hear.

Crossing her legs, she sat on the edge of the quilt as Liam zipped his pack up. She frowned when he wouldn't look at her until she realized he was nervous.

He wiped his hands on his jeans and finally met her gaze. "I hope this is okay."

Smiling, she scooted closer so that their knees touched. "This is really sweet, Liam." And totally unexpected.

He blew out a long sigh. "Ana said you'd like this. . . . Not that I didn't want to do it," he rushed on.

She bit back a smile as he fumbled around with opening the thermos. The scent of hot chocolate teased her nose and made her stomach rumble. He poured her a cupful and practically shoved the mug into her hands.

"Why are you being so weird?" December asked before blowing on the hot liquid.

He nervously rubbed a hand over his head, ruffling his dark hair. "I . . . I've never done this before."

"Done what?"

"Tried to . . ." Liam shook his head. "I've never really tried to impress a woman."

She jerked back at his bold admission. The stark honesty touched her. "Like ever?"

He was silent for a moment before he shook his head. "I've never been with a human and when she-wolves are attracted to males, they don't need, uh . . . never mind."

She had an idea where he was headed and she didn't want to talk about *that* any more than he seemed to want to. Time for a subject change. "Okay, then, you're one hundred and . . ."

"Eight," he supplied, looking relieved she'd turned topics.

"One hundred and eight, and you've never been on a date. I don't know how I feel about being your guinea pig." She gave him a playful smile before taking a sip of her hot chocolate.

When December smiled at him like that, Liam forgot to breathe. He felt like a jackass admitting he'd never tried to impress a woman before, but he figured if he screwed up, maybe she'd be more forgiving if she knew he was trying.

He'd always thought human traditions were stupid until now. His inner wolf still wanted to claim and mark her more than he wanted his next breath, but he wanted to get to know her better first. His brother had been right. Hearing her story last night about a dog named Bubblegum still made him smile. Though his canines ached even now to sink into December's soft flesh, she deserved to be courted and treated right. As he tried to think of something semi-intelligent to say, she beat him to it.

"How come your pack is called the Armstrong-Cordona pack but some of the men you introduced me to today have different last names?" She asked the question so fast, as if she'd been practicing it for a while.

He eyed her curiously. "Is this normal date talk?"

Her cheeks flushed. "Nothing between us has been normal, so why start now? Besides, I'm curious."

He shrugged. "There's no big secret. It's true that most packs are families—like Ana and her sisters and cousins—so they usually carry the same family name, but that's not always the case, like with our pack. My brother and I decided to form one with other lone wolves, but joining a pack doesn't mean you lose your identity. And having an Alpha means you always have someone to protect you."

"So you're not an alpha too? Could've fooled me," she murmured. Her breath curled in front of her, mixing with the rising heat of the hot drink.

"I'm an alpha in nature but not pack Alpha. There's a difference. I might disagree with my brother sometimes, but Connor is my leader and he's one of the best Alphas I've known."

She thoughtfully chewed her bottom lip for a moment. "So, what about betas and warriors . . . and the enforcer? 'The enforcer' is a new term, but I've heard the others before. What do they mean?"

"Betas are simply weaker shifters in their animal form. They're not as big as everyone else and they depend on alphas and warriors to protect them. Warriors, on the other hand, are guardians for everyone. Born fighters."

"You're a warrior, right?"

Smiling, he nodded. "Yeah."

"So you're an alpha but you're also a warrior?"

Again he nodded.

"So all warriors are alpha in nature, but not all alphas are warriors?"

"You got it."

"Then what about Kat's ex? The . . . enforcer? What's his deal? Or what is he?"

That was an interesting question and not one Liam was sure he had the answer to. "Ah, enforcers are . . . sort of a different breed altogether. Each shifter Council around the world—whether ursine or feline or whatever—has the equivalent of an enforcer working for them. Some have more than one—and in Australia, the lupine Council has two—but here in North America all we have is Jayce. They're similar to warriors but tougher, harder to kill, and born to that role. I don't know all the science behind it or even how he gained his title, but I do know that he's at least five hundred years old and really hard to kill."

Her brow furrowed slightly. "I see."

He figured she didn't completely understand what he was saying and he didn't want to talk about himself anyway. He wanted to know about her. "How long have you lived in Fontana?"

Her head tilted slightly to the side at his question, sending a waterfall of her thick, red hair tumbling over her shoulder. "Since I was seventeen."

"Why'd you move here?"

She dropped his gaze as she answered. "Because my brother got a job here."

There was more to it than that and he wanted to know exactly what. "Where'd you move from?"

A subtle mask slid into place, making her expression completely unreadable. "I don't want to talk about it. Tell me more about your family. What happened to your parents?"

Something dark settled in his chest. He didn't like talking about the past and it was obvious she didn't want to talk about hers, but if he wanted her to open up to him, he needed to give her a reason to trust him. Give and take, he reminded himself. "My father died when I was eight. If it wasn't for Connor, I wouldn't have survived."

Now her face was an open book. He hated pity, but that wasn't what he saw on hers; it was sadness and ... understanding. "I didn't think your brother was that much older than you."

"He's two years older."

"And he took care of you? Didn't you have any other family?"

"Our entire pack was killed." He managed to keep any inflection out of his voice, but he could tell she wasn't fooled. The pain of losing his father and the rest of his pack still tore at his insides. Time might have healed most of the wound, but the scar was still there.

She set her cup down and scooted a few inches closer. Placing her hand on his, she didn't say anything. Didn't ask how they died. But her touch was exactly what he needed. His inner wolf craved the soothing contact. Her silence made him want to open up. "Connor and I were out playing. We lived in the Highlands at the time and as the cubs of the pack Alpha, we had freedom to run and play as long as we stayed within a couple miles of our home. My mother ... died a year before and it broke our father's heart. It's like he lost sight of protecting his pack and when a group of fae decided they wanted our territory, the pack was too weak to defend itself. Everyone there was slaughtered." If they hadn't been out playing that day and if their father hadn't telepathically warned them to stay away, they'd be dead too. Some days Liam hated his father for turning so weak after their mother died. He'd emotionally abandoned them a year before his death, but actually losing him had ripped Liam's heart out. But he didn't tell her any of that. Some things he couldn't bear to say out loud.

December's hands suddenly squeezed his, the action a soothing balm over emotions he thought he'd buried long ago. "I lost my parents when I was eight too. Car accident, nothing as violent as what happened to your pack, but I actually do understand what it's like to feel so alone at such a young age."

His own heart twisted for her loss. He didn't know much about her family life, but she'd only ever mentioned Parker and it was obvious they depended on each other. "At least you had your brother."

She paused, then nodded. "I did. He's the best big brother." He was under the impression she was going to say something else, but instead she pursed her lips together, as if forcing herself not to speak.

For a while neither of them spoke. He wasn't sure how much time had passed. It was hard to care when she stared at him with those intoxicating blue eyes that seemed to darken each second that ticked by.

It started out as a trickle, but as time stretched out between them, her lust was almost a live thing as it wrapped around him, strong and seductive. Everything male inside him flared to life at the scent.

He fought to breathe and to contain his inner wolf. This wasn't how today was supposed to go. "December—"

With surprising speed, she cut him off as she leaned forward and brushed her lips over his. For only a brief second he thought about pulling away, but when her tongue teased his lips, he buried that idea fast. After what he'd just shared with her, he felt raw and exposed and the feel of her kissing and touching him soothed his most primal side.

He cupped the back of her head tightly, letting his fingers tangle in that thick mass of hair. Her tongue invaded his mouth with surprising insistency. Damn, the spicy scent of her need was so potent it enveloped all of him and seeped into his pores. It made him burn with the desire to touch all of her.

Her hands clutched his shoulders and she slid onto his lap, straddling him where he sat. Normally he needed to be on top, to assert his dominance, but the feel of her writhing over him like this was more than he'd fantasized about. He liked this side of December, but he had to know he wasn't taking advantage of her.

Somehow he pulled his head back but kept his hand on the back of her head. "I don't want you to regret what you're doing, Red."

Her expression softened at the use of his nickname for her. "I won't," she said simply.

"I was serious earlier. I think . . . you're ovulating, which basically means you're in heat for my kind."

"I think you're right." Her quiet answer surprised him.

He needed her to understand exactly where he stood on this. "When I take you, I'm not letting you go. Do you understand?"

A blend of anticipation and uncertainty clear in her eyes, she nodded shakily. He knew she didn't completely comprehend what he was saying, but the most selfish part of him didn't care. December was his. Now he was going to show her exactly what he meant.

When she began moving over his erection, his grip on her head tightened. The need to claim her was overwhelming, but he fought back his inner wolf. He was the one in control, not it. With one hand, he reached for the zipper of her jacket and tugged it down. Once it was free, he slid a hand under her thick sweater.

The feel of her soft skin made him groan and as he reached one of her breasts, she moaned into his mouth. Her fingers twisted wildly in his hair as she held on to him with equal urgency. As he pulled one of her bra cups down and tweaked her nipple with his thumb and forefinger, she jerked against him.

After last night he shouldn't be surprised, but it still awed him how reactive she was to everything. He barely touched her and she was panting for more. Not that he was any better. His cock pressed mercilessly against his jeans, demanding to be unleashed.

But first she needed to be naked. He quickly shoved her jacket all the way off. As he started to lift her sweater, she shivered. There wasn't snow on the ground, but the sky was overcast and the weather was right for snowfall. Pausing, he held his hands still on her waist.

Her blue eyes flashed hungrily. "Why are you stopping?" With flushed cheeks and swollen lips, she looked good enough to eat. He wouldn't even have to take her sweater off. He could just push her jeans down and slide into her. He could use his body heat to keep her warm.

But she deserved better than that and he didn't want their first time to be rushed and on the ground. "Your teeth are practically chattering." He tugged her sweater fully back in place.

She started to shake her head when she shivered

again. This time it was more pronounced and she leaned closer into his embrace. "Maybe you're right," she murmured. "But if we hurry, we can be back to the ranch soon."

His cock jumped at her words. Reaching behind her, he grabbed her jacket and helped her into it. Wordlessly, she zipped it up, then headed for the horses while he packed up. No more words were necessary. Once they made it to a warm place, he was going to sink inside her and stay that way for hours.

We need to talk. Connor's voice sounded loudly in Liam's head as he and December arrived back at the ranch. Not all shifters, even related ones, could communicate in telepathic form, but he and Connor could. But they didn't do it all the time. If they could call or text each other, they often chose that option. Liam was especially careful about that now that his brother was mated. He didn't want to interrupt Connor if he was getting busy with his mate.

I'm with December. We're about to put the horses back in the stable. Can it wait?

No. Meet me at the main house.

Liam bit back a sigh. "I've got to talk to my brother for a few minutes. Do you mind heading back to the house by yourself?" he asked as December closed the stable door.

She shook her head and her cheeks tinged red. He couldn't tell what she was thinking, but whatever it was, it was good for him. The woman was so turned on right now and the lust coming off her was so potent, she was practically combustible. Once he got her naked and underneath him, there'd be no turning back for either of them.

Leaning down, he brushed his lips over hers but stopped himself from fully claiming her mouth. If he did, he knew he'd throw her over his shoulder and forget about talking to his brother. Liam watched as December strode toward the guesthouse and once he saw her reach the front porch, he headed across the yard to the main house.

As soon as he stepped inside, he scented that it was a full house. From what he could tell, Ana and her sister Noel were upstairs with Vivian. He found Connor in the living room standing by the stone fireplace waiting for him.

"Everything all right?" He didn't bother sitting on one of the couches because he didn't plan to stay long.

"Just got off the phone with Jayce. He took Erin with him to a biker bar on the outskirts of town to follow up on a lead and—"

"What?" Why hadn't his brother told him about it?

Connor set his jaw firmly. "Liam, your woman needs you right now and I'm not sending you off for something Jayce can easily handle. He's in town to investigate the APL, so I'm letting him do his job."

His brother was right but he didn't like being kept out of the loop. Not for anything that involved him or, more important, December. "What did they find?"

"Unfortunately not much. They questioned one of the guys who knew the men who took Kat a few weeks ago, but he's not part of the APL. Just a local biker. He admitted that some APL members hang out at the bar and he's heard that something big might be going down soon, but he didn't have any details."

"And they believed him?"

Connor lifted his shoulders noncommittally. "The guy was terrified and Jayce took down his address from his driver's license to prove a point, so I'd say yeah, he was probably telling the truth."

"Thanks for letting me know."

Connor nodded. "Why don't you bring December by here for dinner tonight? Let her get to know Ana and some of the other women a little more."

Liam smiled at the offer. If they left the bedroom, he would. "Okay, thanks."

When he entered the guesthouse and caught December's unique scent, his entire body tensed. Everything was about to change between them. Without waiting a second longer, he took the stairs two at a time. Natural light spilled out from the open door to their room.

He found December sitting on the edge of the bed without her jacket or boots, but she still had clothes on. Way too many.

"Is everything okay with your brother?" Her voice shook slightly.

He nodded, unwilling to talk about any of that, and took a few steps into the room. She didn't need anything extra to worry about right now. "Having second thoughts?"

"Not exactly."

He stopped dead in his tracks at her words. "What's not exactly?"

"I want to ask you to do something for me."

"Anything." He didn't even have to think.

She twisted her hands together in her lap and finally continued. "Will you shift for me?"

He frowned, surprised at her question. "You mean now?"

She nodded tightly.

"That's all you want?" He wasn't sure why she was so nervous. By her tone he'd figured her request was something a hell of a lot worse than this.

"Yes."

"Okay." He stripped off his shirt and boots, then started with his jeans when she stopped him.

She crossed her arms over her chest. "I didn't say get naked."

He bit back a smile at her confusion. "And I don't want to rip my clothes."

"You can't . . . Oh, okay." She scooted back on the bed a few inches and stared at him expectantly.

Keeping his gaze on her, he shoved his pants down and stepped out of them. His cock sprang free, already hard, but there wasn't much he could do about that with her in the same room.

Preparing himself for the pain, he closed his eyes and let the transformation come over him. His bones shifted and broke, then realigned with lightning speed. It always happened fast, but it still hurt like hell. As fur replaced skin, and paws replaced hands and feet, he enjoyed the pleasure that rushed over him once in his animal form.

His senses were more acute in this form and December's fear was off the charts. It shouldn't piss him off, but it did. She'd asked him to do this. Why the hell was she afraid? Maybe it was because he was so big. On all fours he was about five feet and hulking. Wanting to ease her fears, he lay down on his belly, then turned over to bare his neck and stomach to her.

As soon as he did, she slid off the bed and took a few steps toward him. Kneeling, she reached out and gently stroked the side of his face. At first she looked curious, but then her expression gave way to awe.

Leaning into her, he nuzzled her hand. The feel of her rubbing his fur was soothing on so many levels. It wasn't sensual, like when in his human form, but it made him happy. She laughed under her breath and he could almost feel the tension leave the room.

"Okay, you can change back," she murmured as she stood.

So he did. It didn't hurt as much shifting to his human form. Seconds later he was standing next to December by the foot of the bed. "Did I pass your test?" he asked, smiling.

Her lips curved up at the corners. "No test. I just wanted to see all of you."

Making himself vulnerable to anyone went against his animal nature, but he couldn't seem to help himself around December. There wasn't much she could ask of him that he'd refuse to do.

She sucked in a short breath as her gaze tracked over him. It was almost imperceptible, but he was watching her closely. Her eyes darkened with lust and her mouth parted a fraction.

As she licked her lips in a maddeningly erotic manner, he wondered if she did it to drive him crazy. But when her eyes clashed with his, he saw insecurity there. That shocked the hell out of him. Everything about this woman called out to his most primal side. Nothing she did could turn him off.

"Do you want this, Red?" He had to ask before they went any further. His heartbeat was an erratic drumbeat against his chest as he watched uncertainty cross her face.

Chapter 14

December was still unsure about a lot of things where she and Liam were concerned, but there was something about his entire body that just softened when he called her Red. It made her feel special. So while she was uncertain about the future, one thing she knew for sure—she wanted him in her bed. "I want this and I want you."

She just wasn't sure what would happen to her afterward. Getting involved with him was crazy, even if the man had saved her life so many times. That's not why she wanted him, though. He'd been part of her fantasies for the past month and it was hard to deny the attraction between them. How much she was drawn to him. And knowing he'd dealt with the same losses as she had—and at the same young age—made her feel connected to him in a way she hadn't thought possible.

He covered the short distance between them with a determined look in his eyes. No one had ever looked at her like that before. With a mix of hunger and desire that was practically smoldering.

She wanted—needed to run her hands up his bare chest. To feel his body against hers. After what he'd done for her last night, she wanted him to experience as much pleasure as he'd given her.

As their lips molded together, she slid her hands up his chest and linked her fingers around the back of his neck.

When he clutched her hips, she automatically lifted and wrapped her legs around his waist. The action was so smooth, so natural. She ground her hips against his, savoring the feel of his hard length. Soon they wouldn't have any barrier between them. Maybe that should have scared her, but it didn't. Everything about this day was right. She felt it straight to her core.

She tightened her legs around him as he worked her sweater and bra off. They barely pulled their mouths apart before their lips once again sought each other out.

Now it was skin on skin. As she rubbed her chest against his, she let out a small moan. Where she was soft, he was all hard muscles. There couldn't be an inch of fat on him. He was pure muscle, strength, and raw power. The sensation of her nipples rubbing against his chest brought another rush of heat between her legs.

Suddenly her back hit the bed. Her eyes flew open. December had been so focused on kissing him that she hadn't felt them move.

As he stretched out on top of her, he stared at her for a moment with an almost vulnerable expression. Before she could contemplate it, he once again devoured her mouth and began grinding his hips against her. She might still have some clothes on, but it didn't matter. He was moving right over her clit. She shouldn't be so sensitive, but whenever Liam touched her, it was like something inside her flared to life, begging to be released. She could probably climax just like this. The knowledge floored her.

She clutched his shoulders, knew she was digging her nails into his skin, but he didn't seem to mind. If anything, the harder she held him, the more unsteady his movements became.

In an abrupt, jerky movement, he pulled his head back. "I need to be inside you now." It sounded as if he had gravel in his throat.

Through heavy-lidded eyes she watched him. He grabbed a condom from the dresser so fast it amazed her. He tugged her pants and underwear down her legs in a quick, precise movement.

When he ripped open the foil packet, his hands shook slightly. She reached out to take it from him, wanting to feel his erection in her hands, but he shook his head. He didn't say a word as he sheathed himself.

Her mouth fell open slightly as she looked at him completely naked. She barely had time to appreciate all that raw, masculine power and all those taut, toned muscles before he covered her again.

This time nothing separated them.

He pushed into her without pause. The action wasn't hard but it wasn't exactly gentle either. It was unsteady and what she wanted. Feeling that thick, hard length push deep inside her pulled a shaky groan from her. She couldn't bite it back even if she wanted to.

She wrapped her legs around him tighter. Both of their movements were a little out of control and she'd probably be sore later, but it didn't matter. All that mattered was this moment. "Oh, God." She wasn't sure how thick the walls of the house were and at that moment she didn't care if the entire ranch heard her. She'd never been very vocal during sex, but right now she had to restrain herself from crying out louder.

As he moved in and out of her, her inner walls clenched tighter and tighter. Her entire body was primed. She was so close to release, she knew it wouldn't be much longer until he gave her exactly what she was craving. When he reached between them and thumbed her clit, she let go. The stimulation was perfect. Her back arched and she gripped him harder. The orgasm tore through her with a wild intensity and she freely let the pleasure rip through her.

Liam nipped her neck as he continued thrusting. The scrape of his teeth over her skin only spurred her on. She felt as if she could break apart at that moment.

Still holding on to him, she leaned close so that her mouth was close to his ear. His breathing was erratic and she knew he was close, but she wanted to him to come right then. Needed him to experience what she was feeling.

"Come for me," she whispered. The words drew a wild, raw cry from him.

He thrust into her again, this time harder and faster. He kept thrusting until he came. Shudders racked his body as his hips moved against hers until finally he stilled and buried his head in the crook of her neck. The only sound coming from him was his erratic breathing. He lightly nuzzled the sensitive area behind her ear, feathering her skin with soft kisses.

Stroking her fingers down his back, she kept her legs wrapped around him until he finally pushed up on his elbows. As he stared down at her, a shiver rolled through her at the heated look in his eyes. He still had that hungry look. And she knew she was the only thing on the menu.

Wordlessly he pulled out of her and instantly her entire body mourned it. She wanted to wrap her body around his and just hold him. But maybe that's not the way he was hardwired. He was definitely more in touch with his animal side than most and he might not be into postcoital cuddling. The thought made her chest ache. She wanted to feel that closeness with him.

Her eyes widened when she realized what he was doing. He disposed of the condom before opening a new packet. She watched in fascination as he rolled another one on his already growing cock.

"What—"

He didn't let her finish. Grabbing her hips, he hauled her toward him as he rolled onto his back. He continued pulling her until she straddled his hips. "I should have given you more foreplay, but we'll go slower this time," he murmured.

She smiled as he slid into her once again. His hips rolled up and her open body welcomed him easily. This time she was ready for him and she liked that he was letting her control the situation. There was nothing remotely painful about his strokes. Her body was slick with her own juices and heat. They fit like two puzzle pieces. Lifting up on her knees, she watched the hard lines of his face as she took him inside her again and again.

Without warning, something warm pricked her eyes. Tears? Leaning down, she kissed him, hoping he wouldn't notice. He'd gotten under her skin fast and she cared so much about him it scared her more than anything ever had.

December stared at the huge, mangy beast. The red, glowing eyes had to belong to a demon. It was the only explanation for this creature. But where had it come from? The thing didn't seem to see her. It was looking past her, to the left.

She took a small step back. Her uncle's farm wasn't that big. If she could just make it to the barn, she'd be safe.

When it didn't move, she took another step back. Her heart pounded wildly in her ears. So loud she was sure it could hear the sound. But the beast hadn't moved.

She took another, bigger step. Then another. Almost home free now. She just needed to get to cover.

"December!" It was her younger brother, Brandon.

She didn't turn around to see where the shout had come from. She already knew. Her brother was coming from the barn. Had no doubt seen her.

Why had he shouted? He mustn't have seen the animal yet.

The animal turned its gaze on her now, all its attention honed and focused. It was so big and much taller than her on all fours.

She tried to scream but the sound lodged in her throat. All she could do was squeak out a "Help."

"Run!" Her younger brother's shout loosened the vise around her legs.

Turning, she sprinted back toward the barn. Her brother had a pitchfork in his hands, but he was too small. Bigger than her, but still no match for the animal.

"Brandon, run!" She swore she could feel the hot breath of the beast on her neck. She grabbed his arm, but he shrugged her off.

His gaze stayed fixed behind her. "Get Parker."

"No, I—"

"Now!" He was only fifteen but at that moment he seemed a lot older.

She jumped into action. If she could get a weapon, she

could help him. As she ran through the barn doors, she turned and nearly fell over.

Brandon was on the ground, stabbing the animal, but he was no match for it. Its jaws were open wide—

"No!"

"December?" She opened her eyes to find Liam staring down at her. One of his big hands lay across her bare stomach as he looked at her, concern in every line on his face. She glanced around the room in confusion, then remembered where they were. Sunlight still streamed in through the wooden blinds. They'd only dozed for a little while if it was still daytime.

"Are you okay?"

"I'm fine." Reaching up, she wiped a bead of sweat off her forehead.

Liam's dark eyes seemed to see right through her. "You sure?"

"I . . . had a nightmare." She didn't want to talk about it but knew she needed to. Liam needed to know about her past. She'd already jumped in feetfirst with this relationship or whatever was going on between them, so now it was time to come clean.

"About what?"

She didn't want to tell him. Didn't even like thinking about it. After her brother had been killed, Parker wouldn't even say his name for the longest time. They'd moved to Fontana and it was almost like they'd swept the past and memories under the rug. Swallowing hard, she stared at a spot on Liam's shoulder. "My brother."

"Parker?"

She shook her head. "No. My younger brother, Brandon. He was . . . he died." Liam's grip tightened and she tensed against his hold. "He was killed by a shifter. He was trying to protect me. I was young but he was even younger. And so brave." Her voice cracked on the last word. She didn't know what to say after that.

"Honey, I'm so sorry." He slid his arm around her waist and pulled her so that she had no choice but to lean into him.

After seeing him in his shifted form, she knew he looked nothing like the crazed animal that had killed her brother, but thinking about it still hurt. Even though her breasts were pressed against his chest and his erection pushed insistently against her abdomen, there was nothing sexual about his hold. He was simply comforting her.

"Do you want to talk about it?"

No. "Maybe. Not really, but I miss him so much sometimes. It's been almost eleven years. I feel like I should be over it."

Liam snorted softly. "You should never have to get over losing family."

Stupid tears sprang up but she ignored them. And thankfully Liam didn't lessen his grip on her to wipe them away.

"I was friends with this girl Allison. *Best friends.* Shifters had come out to the world less than a decade before, but she'd only moved to town with her family—pack—a year before that. I didn't know what she was at first, but I didn't care. A lot of people at school treated her and her brothers differently, but we just clicked. I knew what it was like not to fit in, so maybe that's why we became such fast friends." She swallowed again, trying to push back the inevitable pain that came with talking about it.

"To make a long story short, one of her brothers got really heavy into drugs. Heroin, I think, but I don't know. Doesn't matter anyway. I guess he turned . . . feral. . . . Is that the right word?"

When he nodded, she continued. "I still don't know

what happened, but he must have liked something about me or my scent, because he followed me home. We lived with my uncle at the time. . . ." She trailed off as her thoughts took another turn. The man did not need to know her entire family history. She'd already opened up to him enough as it was. "Anyway, my brother died trying to save me from being attacked. It's why Parker doesn't like shifters."

Liam stroked his hand down her back in a soothing gesture. "I'm surprised you even talked to me when you realized what I was," he murmured.

She cupped the side of his face. It was only midafternoon and he already had stubble covering his jaw. "It was part of the reason I was freaked-out when we met, but I don't want there to be any more secrets between us. I'm not ready to bond or mate or whatever it's called, but I only want to be with you. I don't want to date or see anyone else." She figured if what they'd just shared didn't make her intentions clear, telling him would.

"Can I kiss you?" His voice was low and sensual, and increased the ache between her thighs.

She slightly shook her head. "I can't believe you're asking."

As he leaned forward, her phone rang. "Ignore it."

She did. He invaded her mouth with his tongue and the hand that had been caressing her back cupped one of her breasts and gently squeezed. She moaned into his mouth when her cell rang again.

They both pulled back at the same time. He slid out of bed and grabbed her purse off the rocking chair in the corner of the room. After he handed it to her, she fished around until her fingers grasped her phone.

She paused when she saw the number. "It's the police station. . . . Hello?"

"December. Thank God." It was Parker.

She mouthed it to Liam, who nodded and sat on the edge of the bed.

"Are you okay?"

"I'm fine." She didn't want to get into anything with Liam so close. With his supersonic hearing she had no doubt he could hear every word her brother said.

"Why are you staying at the Armstrong ranch? I stopped by the store today and Kat said you'd been hurt."

She cringed. Hopefully her friend hadn't said anything else. "I'm not hurt. I just needed a day off."

"Don't lie to me. Why are you at their ranch?" The way he said "their" dripped with disdain.

She motioned to Liam that she wanted privacy and, without bothering to put on clothes, hurried to the attached bathroom. "What I do with my private life is my business. I like Liam. A lot. I know you don't like it, but you're going to have to get used to it. He's already done so much for me—something you know. If you'd just give him a chance, you'd see he's not like the shifter who killed—"

"Don't fucking say his name," he growled.

"Why not? He was our brother and he deserves to be remembered."

Parker swore under his breath. "I know that. Why the hell are you staying at the ranch—and don't give me a bullshit story about wanting a day off. Did something happen?"

She bit her bottom lip. She and Liam hadn't talked about it, but neither of them had mentioned contacting the police. It was sort of like they had an unspoken agreement about the whole thing. The guy had worn gloves and the cops couldn't do anything anyway. Mainly she didn't want to involve her brother because she knew he'd want to put her under lockdown and she'd rather stay with Liam. And strangely enough, she trusted Liam to figure out what was going on. "I already told you. I wanted to spend some time with Liam. A lot has happened in the past couple weeks and I needed a break."

"So that's it? You're shutting me out over some shifter? A fucking stranger?"

"Don't do this," she begged.

"Do what? Make you choose? I won't, little sister. Have your fun with him, but don't come crying to me when he hurts you." The phone line went dead.

Fighting back tears, she sagged against the counter. The tile floor was cold under her feet, but she barely felt it. An acute ache pushed at the middle of her chest with the force of sharp daggers. She'd known Parker would have a problem with her and Liam, but she hadn't expected that vehement reaction. He'd always been there for her. The one person she could count on. But she couldn't continue to live her life for him.

Staring blindly at the floor, she tried to catch her breath. Parker would get over this. He had to.

Chapter 15

Parker glared at his phone. As if that would do any good. What the hell was his sister thinking? He shouldn't have been such an asshole, but she was being an idiot. He'd already fielded calls from a few citizens concerned about December's association with the Armstrong pack. Not that he gave a shit about some small-town busybodies.

Anything could happen to her out on that ranch and he'd be helpless to stop it. Pushing back from his desk, he grabbed his hat and shoved his phone into his pocket. He was going to give them a visit right now. He and Liam could finally hash this thing out once and for all. While Parker appreciated all the help Liam had been giving him in watching December, it was time to draw some clear boundaries. He'd convince December to temporarily move in with him. Or maybe get her to take a vacation. Anything to get her away from here.

A quiet knock on his half-open door caused him to look up. Natasha, his receptionist, tucked a dark strand of hair behind her ear. "Hey, Parker. Uh, got a call from Edith Hopper, but if you're leaving—"

He shook his head. "Is her husband smacking her around?"

Natasha's mouth pulled into a thin line. "Sounds like it. And she seemed really scared this time."

"I'm on my way." He palmed the keys to his cruiser and shook his head as he left the building. He'd been to their house so many times over the past year, but Edith kept refusing to press charges. Maybe she'd finally come around this time, though he doubted it. Parker wasn't sure where they'd moved from, but he hated dealing with Stephen Hopper. Wife beaters were the absolute worst. Fucking cowards. He'd arrested him a few times for resisting arrest and for battery against a law enforcement officer, but the state kept letting him out. And he kept using his wife as a punching bag.

When he pulled into the driveway, he assessed the house and the ones surrounding it. A few neighbors stood on their porches watching, which likely meant the Hoppers had been fighting out in the front yard earlier.

The neighborhood was typical middle-class and their two-story brick house was immaculate outside. In the winter, Edith covered all her rosebushes and other plants and kept everything neat and trimmed.

The blinds were shut on all the windows and the house was dark. As he got out of his car, he unsnapped the strap over his gun. Stephen Hopper had gotten violent too many times for him not to be careful.

As he strode up the sidewalk, he braced himself for a heated confrontation. He knocked once and when he didn't get a response, he banged on the heavy wood door again. "Police. Open up."

He heard shuffling sounds inside, so he stood off to the side and knocked again. "I can hear you. Open the door, Stephen. We need to talk."

"We ain't got nothing to talk about. Get the hell off my property."

"I can't do that and you know it."

"Why're you here? I didn't call. Did that bitch wife of mine call?" he shouted.

A pained, female cry sounded but was quickly silenced.

Parker's muscles tensed. What he wouldn't give to clock this guy across the face. "I got a call from one of the neighbors. You know I've got to check up on it. Why don't you come out here so we can talk face-to-face?"

"Why don't you go fuck yourself?"

Parker keyed his radio, intending to call for backup. This definitely wasn't going to be easy. Stephen was likely drunk and Edith's face probably already sported multiple bruises as evidence.

As he spoke into the radio, a huge hole exploded through the door. Wood fragments flew everywhere, dusting the front porch in splinters. The loud blast was definitely gunfire.

"Shit." Parker dove over the pristine white porch railing into a cluster of bushes. Another explosion sounded and a sudden, gripping pain fractured through Parker's shoulder.

Looking down, he stared at his body as if it weren't his own. As if he were somehow detached from it. A crimson stain spread across his tan shirt as quickly as the pain lapped across his arm and spread down his chest. Holy shit, he hurt. Even though he wore a vest, the bullet had slammed into the nonprotected part of his upper shoulder and the blood was gushing. Clutching his wound, he crouched lower and crawled to the edge of the house.

He drew his gun and held it tight as he crawled away. Sirens blared in the background. Either a neighbor had called or the dispatch had heard the blasts through the radio. He didn't care which. He just wanted to take this son of a bitch down.

As he finally reached the edge of the house, two strong hands grabbed him. He started to struggle when he realized it was Ed Dean, the Hoppers' neighbor.

"The bastard went back inside. Help's on the way. Come on," he whispered. Pulling him to his feet, Ed looped his arm under Parker's shoulder and assisted him across the yard. Once they crossed the thick line of bushes separating their properties, Parker couldn't fight the dizziness anymore.

As he swayed, Ed helped him to his knees. Parker knew he was saying something because his mouth was moving, but he couldn't make out the words. Everything was getting dark. He couldn't tell if it was because the sun was setting or if he was losing consciousness. Before he could dwell on it, blackness engulfed him.

Edward's heart rate increased as he listened to the scanner he'd bought a year ago to eavesdrop on the local police. So far he hadn't been able to use any of the information he'd gleaned, but today Christmas had come early.

Shutting it off, he stood and hurried down the stairs. Greg had stopped by to talk to him about some difficulty in getting Katarina Saburova's work schedule. Though he hadn't wanted to see him tonight, now he was pleased for his presence.

He found Joseph and Greg downstairs in the living

room talking quietly. Brianna wasn't there, but he smelled something like spaghetti coming from the kitchen. Annoyed, he held his anger in check. The woman could bake, but she only knew how to make three meals and they all had red sauce. How hard was it to look up a recipe? He was giving her a place to live after all. Lately she was starting to grate on his nerves. He wasn't sure what it was, but it was like a fog being lifted from his eyes.

"Hey, Edward." Greg actually stood, but Joseph just stayed where he was lounging against the couch.

"I need you two to get to Fontana Hospital. Park near the ER and be on the lookout for either the Saburova woman or the sheriff's sister."

Joseph raised a mocking eyebrow. "How do you know they'll be there?"

"Sheriff McIntyre has been shot, so I guarantee his sister will be there. If you see any opportunity, take it. If any of those animals are there, don't do anything stupid, though. All I ask is that you look for an opening. If there isn't one, don't force it. Just leave." Without waiting for a response, he hurried toward the closet in the hallway that led to the front door.

Edward pulled out a bag he'd packed a while ago. Rope, flex-cuffs, a hood, and a Taser. A small but effective kidnapping kit. As he turned, he found them both waiting. Ignoring Joseph, he handed the bag to Greg. "Don't fuck this up. And hurry."

As he shut the door, he heard Brianna coming toward him. When he turned to face her, his anger rose sharp and fast. She had that disapproving look on her face he was coming to hate.

It was too much like his mother.

He'd thought she was perfect, but lately everything

she did had him clenching his fists and straining not to hit her. He wasn't sure what it was, but it was almost like she'd cast some sort of spell on him and it was wearing off. The very idea was bullshit, but he felt clearheaded for the first time in a while.

"Is that really smart? Sending them out there? What if they get caught? If the sheriff was shot, then it stands to reason the place will be crawling with cops." Her eyebrows were raised condescendingly.

Unable to restrain himself, he grabbed her by the shoulder and slammed her against the wall. She flinched and cried out, but he shoved a hand over her mouth. Whatever she had to say she could keep to herself.

"All the cops will be in the waiting room. And not that I need to explain myself, but if they sense any heat, those two idiots will leave. Don't question me again," he growled.

With wide eyes she nodded, so he let her go. Gasping for breath, she scurried away from him. For the first time in a while he felt in control of himself. Smiling, he clenched and unclenched his fists. Maybe tonight they'd get lucky after all.

Liam helped December take off her jacket, then hooked it on the coatrack by the door. She'd been quiet all through dinner. He knew it had something to do with the phone call she'd gotten from her brother and even though he'd wanted to eavesdrop, he'd gone downstairs and given her privacy. It went against all his instincts, but damn if he'd start their relationship that way. He might not know shit about women and relationships, but trust was a human condition.

When she was turned on, he knew what to do. Hell, when she was angry, he still knew how to act around her.

This quietness was different. He didn't like it. "You want a glass of wine or something?"

She shook her head and slightly swayed on her feet. "I think I had too much at dinner. I really just want to go to bed."

Alone? He didn't ask but he thought it. As if she read his thoughts, she shook her head. "You better be joining me."

It was a subtle trickle, but the lust she emanated wrapped around him like a soft, warm embrace. Not wanting to waste time, he scooped her into his arms and headed up the stairs. She let out a tiny yelp, but as he moved, she began working her sweater off. The move surprised him.

He couldn't help but stare at the purple bra she revealed. It was lacy, feminine, and incredibly hot. Her pink nipples were visible through the sheer material. "Did you wear that for me?"

She smiled seductively and nodded. "I'm wearing a matching thong too."

His cock jerked at the mental image. So far she'd worn utilitarian stuff. Not that he cared. He didn't understand why she bothered with any undergarments anyway. But this . . . was damn sexy.

As they reached the bed, he covered one of her breasts with his hand as he kissed her. He wanted to see what she had on underneath her jeans, but he wanted inside her more.

Her fingers tunneled through his hair, pulling him close. They fell onto the bed, shoes and all. Liam started to push the lace cup down when the familiar sound of her ringtone filled the air. She stiffened. He lifted his head back and stared down at her. Her breathing was erratic and her heart pounded out of control, but he could see the indecision in her eyes. She wanted to finish what they'd started, but she also wanted to answer her phone.

Groaning, he pushed off her and found her purse on the ground.

"I'm really sorry—"

He shook his head. "You don't need to apologize."

A few seconds after she answered, her face had turned ghostly pale. She asked short questions and grunted responses until finally she hung up the phone.

"Is everything okay?" He wanted to reach out for her, but it was like she'd erected an invisible wall between them. Shutting him out. It drove him crazy.

She shook her head and blindly stared at him. Her normally bright eyes were dull. "My brother's been shot. He's in the hospital. . . ." She slid off the bed and tugged her sweater on. "I have to go."

Shit. "I'll drive you."

"No. I need to do this by myself."

"December—"

"This isn't a personal affront. I don't have any details and you're the last person he'll want to see."

Ouch. He understood but it still hurt. "Fine, I get it, but you're not driving alone. You've had too much to drink and there are still people out there who want to hurt you." When she started to argue again, he held up a hand. He considered telling her Connor would take her, but knew that would earn him another argument. "Ana will drive you."

For a moment it appeared as if she might argue, but she nodded. "Okay."

Liam mentally projected to his brother what was going on and that he needed help taking December to the hospital. He was going to head over there after her, though he wouldn't tell her that. She'd only protest and he didn't want her wasting the energy.

She was silent as they left the house and trekked across the ranch toward the main house. Connor and Ana stood on the porch. His dark-haired sister-in-law had dealt with so much death recently, he knew she'd understand more than most what December was going through. Not that December's brother had died or would die, but Ana was strong and for that he was grateful.

Liam had his arm slung over December's shoulders as they approached. Before she joined Ana, he pulled her into his arms and kissed the top of her head. Every instinct inside him wanted to take over the situation and just drive her there, but he couldn't put that divide between them. If he tried to steamroller her, he'd just push her further away.

She swallowed hard and looked up at him. "I'll call you, okay?"

Clenching his jaw, he nodded. Seeing tears shine in her eyes was too much. He could handle a lot of shit, but seeing her like this and knowing he couldn't do a damn thing was torture.

Immediately Ana linked her arm through December's. It was out of character for her to be so open with a human, and Liam was grateful she was being so kind to December. "Come on. We'll take my truck."

"Thanks for going with me," December murmured, and let Ana guide her.

Once they were out of earshot, Connor looked at him questioningly. "You want to drive?"

It was rare for his older brother to let him drive, but Liam knew what he was doing. Trying to give him some sort of control in a situation where he had absolutely none. He shook his head. "No, I'll probably crash."

"All right. We wait sixty seconds, then follow." It was a statement, not a question.

Even though the thought of letting December out of his sight for even seconds tore through him like shards of glass, he knew Ana would telepathically communicate with Connor if anything was wrong. Not to mention Ana was pretty tough herself.

Sighing, he fell in line with Connor and headed to his parked Bronco. He hoped December's brother was okay and he really hoped his getting hurt had nothing to do with shifters. Knowing what he did now about December's past, he couldn't bear the thought of her losing another family member.

December sipped a crappy cup of coffee as she sat in the waiting room with Ana. They hadn't been there long and the doctors had assured her that Parker was going to be fine. The bullet had missed any major arteries, but he was in surgery.

Surgery.

Anything could go wrong. And after the last conversation she'd had with him, she couldn't help but worry the universe was seriously messing with her. If he died after the things she'd said to him, she'd never forgive herself. The thought of life without Parker was unimaginable. He might be overbearing, but from the time she was eight, he'd taken over the parenting role for both her and Brandon.

When their parents had died, they'd gone to live with an uncle, and while he hadn't been physically abusive, he'd simply been nonexistent in their lives. He'd been the town drunk and always on a bender. At least he hadn't been violent. Just a jackass unfit to care for three kids. Or himself really. He'd certainly taken advantage of their inheritance, though. Barely eleven, Parker had stepped up and taken on a role no one so young should ever have to worry about.

Her throat tightened as morbid thoughts assailed her. If she lost him—

"He's going to be fine." Ana's soft voice cut through the haze of her mind.

Jerking to look at the other woman, she frowned. "Are you a mind reader?"

She shook her head. "I don't have to be. Your brother is in surgery. You heard what the doctor said. If he made it through in the first half hour, he's going to come through this fine."

Not trusting her voice, she nodded. Her mind knew that, but in her heart she was still terrified.

"December?" She looked up at the sound of Kat's voice and stood. A tall man with jet-black hair who looked vaguely familiar hung back a few feet, as if he'd followed her friend.

Some of the aching in December's chest loosened at the sight of her friend. For a brief moment she thought about asking who the man was, but he said something to Ana as he took a seat next to the brunette and December realized he was a shifter. Probably shadowing Kat. Not that any of that mattered right now. "What are you doing here?"

"Everyone in town heard about what happened. I knew you'd be here, so I hurried right over." Panic laced Kat's voice.

Having her friend here helped more than Kat probably realized. "I'm so glad you're here." Immediately she threw her arms around Kat's neck, needing her friend's support. Ana had been perfectly nice and a calming influence, but December didn't know her well enough to let her guard down around her.

Kat tightly returned her hug. "Have you heard any news?"

She nodded stiffly as she stepped back. "He should be out of surgery soon, but I don't know if he'll even want to see me." As the words escaped, she realized it was true. After that last conversation she was terrified bone deep that he wouldn't want anything to do with her.

Kat brushed her words away with a wave of her hand. "Don't be stupid. For all his stubbornness, your brother loves you." She grabbed the cup from her hand and sniffed. "This is cold and gross. You want a refill?"

Nodding, she glanced at Ana, who still sat in the plastic chair. "You want some coffee or tea?"

Ana shook her head. "I'll stick around in case the doctor comes back." Then she nodded at the man sitting next to her.

It was a slight movement but December noticed it. On cue, the man stood, as if he was going to follow them. Her entire body tensed, but she kept her mouth shut. Arguing with this stranger was pointless and she didn't have the energy.

But Kat did. "*Sit.* You've been shadowing me all day and we need some privacy right now. I swear, if you follow us, I'll scream and call security on you." From her almost haughty tone, December wasn't sure if her friend was bluffing or not.

Ana placed a light hand on the tall shifter's arm. He hadn't said a word, but it was obvious he was fighting a battle. When Ana squeezed and murmured something, he slowly lowered himself back into the seat. Ana focused on both of them. "Just . . . don't go anywhere else, okay?" Even though it was phrased as a question, it almost sounded like an order.

December nodded. She understood the other woman's concern and there was no way in hell she'd be going anywhere right now anyway. Not unless someone held a gun to her head. Probably not even then.

After getting more coffee from the only food station open so late in the hospital, they headed back to the waiting room.

"So where's Liam?" Kat asked after taking a long sip of her latte.

"I told him not to come. I . . ." She shrugged as she trailed off.

"No, I get it. He and Parker are like oil and water."

If only that were the case. The two men were so much alike, but they couldn't see it. And despite her recent argument with Parker, she knew how much he cared for her. "Not really. They're so much alike. Parker's just—"

Kat's dark eyebrows rose. "Got issues?"

December snorted. "Don't we all?"

As they headed back down the maze of hallways, their boots squeaked along the linoleum floors.

When they passed the emergency room doors, Kat stopped and patted her jacket pocket. "Crap. I forgot my phone in the car. I need it in case . . ." She trailed off as her cheeks reddened. "Never mind."

In case Jayce called. Even if her friend didn't answer the phone and even if she'd never admit it out loud, December guessed she liked that he'd been calling her so much lately. "Go get it."

Kat shook her head. "No. It's fine. I'm being stupid."

December glanced around. A security guard sat behind the information desk and a couple nurses stood by the check-in area. Even though it was late, doctors and other staff milled around. She turned back to her friend. There were a ton of people around, but she'd promised Ana she wouldn't go anywhere. Not to mention Liam would freak.

Her indecision must have shown on her face because Kat half smiled. "Just wait here and I'll go grab it. I got a spot right in the main parking lot, so it'll only take me a minute. You can *see* my car from the door."

"I'll go with you."

Kat shook her head. "Uh-uh. I'm not getting you in trouble with Ana *or* Liam."

"Fine. I'll wait by the doors." December walked with her to the exit doors and waited for the security guy to buzz them out.

She stood next to the doors and peered through the glass pane. An ambulance with flashing red lights tore into the parking lot. The siren was silent and as soon as they pulled to a stop, the EMTs jumped out and began removing a stretcher with practiced precision.

December stared at the scene and swallowed hard. That had been Parker a few hours ago. Wiping away a few hot tears that sprang up, she averted her gaze and glanced back at Kat as she strode up from the parking lot. Her hand was clutched around something, no doubt her phone, as she jogged toward the ER entrance.

The doors swung open as the EMTs rolled in the stretcher, so December stood back. As she did, she noticed a white van with tinted windows roll up behind the ambulance. She froze for a split second as a man in a ski mask jumped out.

Her heart seized as she realized what was happening. As if in slow motion, she watched the man withdraw something. He aimed it at Kat's back.

December screamed so loud it hurt her own ears. She

could feel people staring at her, but she pointed as she screamed. Kat turned around, then started to run, but he jolted her with a Taser. December started for her when the security guard grabbed her arm.

"Ma'am! What—"

She struggled against him, trying to tear her arm out of his grip. When he wouldn't let her go, she pointed. "They're taking my friend!"

He followed her gaze and immediately jumped into action. "Shit." He withdrew his gun and sprinted toward the already moving van. December followed not far behind. Her leg muscles strained as she tried to will herself to move faster. It seemed longer but everything had happened in the span of seconds.

She was too far away to reach Kat. In horror, she watched as the man threw Kat's limp body into the open side door and jumped in after her. She kept running after the vehicle until the security guy grabbed her around the waist and yanked her to a stop.

"I've called in backup and I got the license plate number. We're going to get your friend back." He continued talking into his radio, but she tuned him out and pulled her cell out of her jacket pocket.

"Please answer," she murmured as she dialed Liam's number.

He picked up on the first ring. "December."

"They took Kat," she croaked.

"What?"

"At the hospital. She just went to get her cell from her car. A white van pulled up. They Tased her or something. I tried to get to her, but they were too fast." Her breaths were coming out shallow and disjointed as she struggled to get the words out. "I—"

"Where are you right now?"

"By the ER entrance. I—"

He cursed low, then said, "I'll be there in sixty seconds. Stay put and stay inside."

He disconnected before she could respond. She wasn't sure how he could get there so fast, but she didn't much care. All that was important was finding her friend.

Chapter 16

"Fuck, fuck, fuck," Liam muttered loud enough for everyone around them to hear.

"Cool it." Connor pointed toward the next hallway. "Left here."

But Liam couldn't. He should have trusted his gut. He shouldn't have let December out of his sight. They'd followed Ana and December, but it had taken a while to find parking. Finally they'd gotten a spot on the top floor of the garage.

As they rounded the last corner, he spotted December talking to a security guard and two police officers. When she saw him, she darted away from the men and rushed toward him and Connor.

"The cops have the license plate number, but they're so slow," she growled out under her breath. "It was a white van. The man who grabbed her had on a mask, but there's obviously a second person because someone had to be driving."

"Where'd they take her from?" Connor asked.

"Right outside the ER." She pointed over her shoulder. Her blue eyes were wide and frightened.

"Show us exactly where." Liam knew what his brother intended to do.

December gave a quick excuse to the police officer—obviously someone she knew—and darted outside with them. She kept going until they were near the edge of the stone overhang that covered the ER entrance. "Right here. They briefly parked behind an ambulance."

Liam deeply inhaled and knew his brother was doing the same. They hadn't left long ago, so chances were their scents were the strongest. Kat's scent intertwined with someone else's. A male. He looked at his brother. "You got it?"

Grim faced, Connor nodded. "Let's go."

December grabbed his arm. "What are you going to do?"

"Track her using her scent."

For a moment she looked as if she might say more, but she snapped her mouth shut and stepped back. "Please find her," she whispered.

Even if she'd never looked more sad and lost, now wasn't the time to comfort her. Every second counted. Liam and Connor took off across the parking lot. As soon as they were out of sight, they'd shift to their animal form. They could track better that way and they were a hell of a lot faster than most humans realized. Especially his brother. As an Alpha, Connor was stronger and faster than regular alpha or even warrior shifters.

They were both silent until they reached the edge of the parking lot. Kat's scent was strong near the exit, but they both knew the farther the men got with her, the more her scent would fade. Using a couple cars for cover, they shifted to their animal form. They'd just have to leave their shredded clothes and shoes.

Lose me if you have to, Liam projected to him, unwilling to let his own speed slow his brother down.

I will.

As they exited onto the two-lane highway they kept to the side of the road in the shadows as best they could. Luckily there weren't many cars on the road and it was dark anyway. His paws pounded against the icy ground, but he barely felt it. The lack of cars and people would help with their tracking.

He homed in on the subtle scent of roses. Kat's scent. Finding her was the most important thing for all of them. Jayce would rip this town apart trying to find her. Not that Liam would blame him.

He'd do the same for December.

Five miles out of town the scent petered out, but it was still faint once they reached a four-way intersection. Then it disappeared.

You got anything? he projected to Connor.

Damn it, no. His brother looked east, then west, as if trying to pick a direction.

West there's just a lot of land and a few farmhouses, Liam said.

And east there was a bunch of subdivisions and the ski lodge. They'd be bound to pick up on her scent at the ski lodge eventually, considering she worked and lived there.

We split up. I'll go east, you go west, Connor said.

Unfortunately that still left everything to the north, but there were only two of them and they couldn't communicate telepathically with the entire pack. *I'll meet you back at the ranch if I don't find her.*

Check in with me periodically anyway.

Will do. Liam began running down the narrower road and sent up a prayer that one of them found her before it was too late.

December felt as if she could crawl out of her skin. She'd just seen her closest friend kidnapped, her brother was in the hospital, and there wasn't a thing she could do about either. She wanted to scream. Or *help* in some way.

Instead, she'd been questioned by the police for the last hour answering the same questions a dozen different ways. They'd finally left and if she hadn't been the sheriff's sister, she had no doubt they'd have taken her down to the station for further questioning. Instead they'd let her stay at the hospital to wait for her brother to come out of surgery.

When Parker's doctor strode into the waiting room, she jumped out of her seat and Ana did the same. The shifter who'd been there earlier had long since left, to help look for Kat, December guessed. The older doctor had a half smile on his face as he approached. That had to be a good sign. Her heart leapt but she refused to get excited.

"How is he?" she asked.

"He's going to be fine. Right now he's resting but—"

"When can I see him?"

The gray-haired man's smile faltered. "I don't think that's such a good idea right now."

"Why? I thought you said he was going to be okay."

"He doesn't want to see anyone."

"But I'm his sister."

He nervously cleared his throat. "I don't know what's going on between you two, but he was specific in that he didn't want to see *you.* I'm so sorry, December. I—"

She turned away and strode out of the room. She didn't need to hear pity or sympathy from a virtual stranger. Maybe she should have expected it. But she'd thought they could work past anything. Especially since he'd just been injured. What was an argument in the face of something like this?

As she strode down the hallway Ana easily caught up with her. "He'll come around," she murmured.

"Yeah, sure." But she didn't believe it. Probably not any more than Ana did. The woman was very nice and a surprisingly calming influence, but she didn't know her family or anything about her history. She shook her head in an effort to shove those thoughts free. "Have you heard from Connor?" She knew Ana and her mate communicated telepathically. Liam had explained it had something to do with being bondmates.

Ana nodded. "They're still looking."

"Just the two of them?"

"No, while you were talking to the police, I called the house. Noah, the man who was here earlier, is out with everyone too. I couldn't get hold of Jayce, though." For the first time since she'd met her, Ana looked nervous.

While December might not understand Kat and Jayce's relationship, even she knew he wasn't going to handle what had happened well. Suppressing a shudder, she pulled her mittens out of her pocket and slid them on as they stepped outside.

Two uniformed officers were talking to one of the EMTs but hurried over when they spotted them. "Are you leaving?" one of them asked. At one time she'd known all the officers' names, but Parker had hired a few new guys in the past year.

She glanced at Ana, then nodded. "Yes."

"We'll be escorting you home," the same one said.

December wasn't sure if they knew she was staying at the Armstrong ranch, but she didn't say anything. They'd figure it out once they started following them.

The drive back was quiet, leaving her wrapped up and suffocating in her own thoughts. She'd never thought of herself as a morbid person, but visions of Kat helpless and hurt somewhere assaulted her mind. December clearly remembered what it had felt like to have that monster pin her to the floor of her bedroom and use a Taser on her. Then weeks later another stranger had punched her in the face, knocking her out in her own living room. She might not be sure exactly who had taken Kat, but she knew they were part of the same group as the men who'd come after her. A shudder rolled through her and she sent up a silent prayer for her friend.

Once they reached the turnoff from the two-lane highway onto the long, winding road that led to the ranch, the police car fell back and turned around.

After Ana pulled through the gate, she turned to her. "Why don't you head to the main house while I park? We can wait for news together."

Grateful, she nodded. She hadn't wanted to go to the guesthouse by herself and simply wait for Liam to return. She might not know Ana well, but it would help to be in the other female's presence. Grabbing her purse, she got out of the vehicle and hurried toward the house. As she made her way across the icy ground, the sound of a man clearing his throat made her jump.

She swiveled to find Jayce walking across the yard. It appeared as if the hulking shifter had appeared out of nowhere. He blended into the darkness as if he were part of it.

"I didn't want to scare you," he said softly, and kept a few feet between them. "Where's Liam?"

It hit her with startling intensity. He didn't know what had happened. For a moment, she racked her brain trying to think of a way to tell him. Nothing sounded right, so she plunged ahead. "He's out looking for Kat. God, I'm so sorry. She was . . . kidnapped at the hospital. Two men in a van pulled up and took her. I tried to run after them—"

"How long ago?" His expression darkened, his eyes taking on a supernatural glow, and the deadly edge to his question sent a shiver snaking through her. If he found who'd done this, she had no doubt he'd rip them to shreds.

"A couple hours. The police have the license plate, and Connor and Liam went after her scent. I think Ana tried to call you."

His jaw twitched once and his gray eyes turned to an inky black. She knew it wasn't the light playing tricks on her either. "Did you notice anything else about the men who took her?" His voice was ragged and it appeared as if he was visibly trying to control himself.

She shook her head. "They wore masks and the van was white. They used a Taser to stun her."

Rage seemed to flow off him in waves. "Do you know what direction they went?"

"No, I'm sorry." And she was. Even thinking about what could be happening to Kat right now made her sick. The bastard who'd tried to take December from her own house had no problems punching a woman. She only prayed Kat was okay.

Wordlessly, he turned and ran in the other direction. Through the darkness she heard the sound of bones breaking and knew he'd shifted. There was a loud, animalistic roar that reverberated off the trees, almost making them shake. The air seemed to crackle with electricity for a moment.

Then a dead silence descended in the air.

*   *   *

Kat tried to open her eyes, but it was difficult. Blinking a few times, she shook her head until her vision cleared somewhat. When she tried to move, she realized her hands were bound above her head.

What the hell?

An icy fist clasped around her chest as she took in her surroundings. It was apparent she was in some sort of barn or shed. A removable wooden ladder leaned against a loft directly across from her. A few old saddles and some other riding gear lay in the corner of the small building. Hay and straw littered underneath her feet—she realized someone had taken her boots—and it was cold. Damn cold. The structure wasn't big and it definitely wasn't insulated. Wind whistled through trees outside and she could see the moon peeking through a hole in the ceiling.

She desperately tried to remember what had happened or where she was. She'd been at the hospital. She remembered December screaming, alerting her; then a man shot her with something—maybe a Taser; then blackness. Looking up, she realized her hands were bound with some kind of plastic ties and linked to a hook. Raw fear snaked through her straight to her toes, but she knew if she let her panic take over, she wouldn't do herself any good. This wasn't the first time some asshole had taken her. She had to keep a level head if she wanted to survive. As she started to struggle against the bindings, the sound of something rolling stopped her.

"Good. You're finally awake." She turned at the sound of a cold, male voice.

The rolling sound had been a large wooden exterior door. As she stared at him, confusion settled over her. "Greg? What's going on?" She occasionally worked with the blond-haired ski instructor.

As his dark gaze raked over her, she felt as if she were naked. Exposed. The look of lust in his eyes made her want to puke. She swallowed hard. "What are you doing?"

Finally he looked her in the eyes. "I'm just supposed to watch you until the boss shows up, but we're going to have some fun."

The way he said "fun" made her gut roil. "You're one of those APL members." It wasn't a question.

"And you're a shifter-loving whore," he spat.

As he came toward her, she kicked out at him with her socked foot. She missed him, but the gleam in his eyes told her he didn't care. He wanted her to fight.

When he came at her again, she managed to kick his shoulder. He grunted in annoyance and cursed under his breath, but it didn't faze him.

He just kept coming. Without her hands it was hard to defend herself. No matter how many times she kicked at him, she didn't have much strength behind the blows. He'd strung her up so she was poised on the tips of her toes. Her shoulders felt as if they were about to pop out of their sockets. Arched like that, she didn't have a good position and the more she tried to kick, the more she hurt and the more out of breath she became.

As she kicked out at him again, he grabbed her calf and used it as leverage to get closer. His viselike grip didn't lessen on her leg as he slammed his body against hers. She tried to use her other leg as a weapon, but he pinned her against the wall with the full force of his weight.

"If you don't fight, I'll go easy on you," he whispered in her ear. His unmistakable erection pressed against her abdomen.

She dry heaved at his words. Her reaction evidently

pissed him off. He punched her hard in the stomach. She coughed and tried to catch her breath, but it was impossible because he hauled off and punched her again.

It was as if someone had slammed a two-by-four across her middle. She tried to bite it back but the cry escaped regardless. Tears rolled down her cheeks when he slapped her across the face.

When he grabbed the front of her sweater and ripped it fully open, she managed to kick out again, but it was useless. Using his weight again, he pinned her back against the wall as he unbuttoned her jeans and shoved them down.

Kat screamed as loud as she could, even though instinct told her they were alone in the woods somewhere. When she did, he slapped her again, but she didn't stop. She couldn't stop. She lashed out again and this time managed to clip him in the groin.

"I told you I'd go easy on you!" he shouted at her. "Now you're going to pay," he growled, sounding angrier with each word.

The pain in her stomach had lessened, or maybe she was becoming numb, but her face still throbbed as she watched him. He strode to the other side of the barn and picked up something. When he turned to face her, she realized he was holding a whip of some sort.

The long, brown cord uncoiled and hit the hay-covered dirt with a soft thud. He lifted it and cracked it once against the ground.

She flinched at the slapping sound it made, because she knew what he planned to do. She could see the coldness in his soulless eyes. When he lifted the whip and struck out at her, she tried to turn away the best she could.

The end sliced into her outstretched arm and down

the side of her rib cage. As her skin tore away, she screamed again. She might not beg for her life, but she couldn't stop the screams. She managed to twist around even more, but he just continued beating her. The edge of the whip sliced across her back and legs. Over and over. A merciless torture without end.

With each blow she screamed until she realized she was screaming Jayce's name. But he never came for her.

Chapter 17

Liam watched the barely perceptible rise and fall of December's chest. Sleep hadn't come easy for either of them last night and after he and the rest of the pack had returned home, he'd gotten only a couple hours.

The thought of Kat out there, at the mercy of a bunch of crazy radicals . . . He didn't know how Jayce was dealing with it. December had told him the enforcer had left to hunt for her. He still wasn't back as far as Liam knew.

Reaching out, he gently pushed back a curl that had fallen across her face. She stirred but didn't wake up. She looked so peaceful with her bright red hair pillowed around her face and her pink lips slightly parted.

His throat constricted as he stared at her. Last night it could just as easily have been her. The knowledge shredded his insides with razor wire. If he'd never walked into her store, never pursued her so insistently, she'd still be safe. The APL wouldn't have a reason to target her. This was his damn fault. She'd told him she didn't want anything to do with him and he hadn't listened. Instead he'd listened to his most primal side and now she was on the radar of some crazy assholes. The threat to her before had seemed manageable somehow. Now it just felt insurmountable. What if these maniacs *never* stopped coming for her? His pack was making some progress in ferreting out the local group's intentions, but that might not be enough.

He and December hadn't talked much about a future. Sure, they'd made a big step in their relationship, but she'd never said she wanted to become his bondmate. If she did that, she'd turn into a shifter and have the same longevity as him. But if she decided to stay human, she'd always be weaker. If someone else decided to come after her again, who was to say he could stop it? Despite the fact that he'd like to be her permanent shadow, he knew he couldn't always be there for her. Not every second of the day. And neither of them would want to live like that anyway.

No wonder Jayce had questioned him if he'd ever worried about his involvement with a human. Bringing a human into their world was insane. Now Kat was paying the price. He would never forgive himself if something else happened to December.

How could he have been so stupid? So blind? For the first time ever, he finally understood why his brother had walked away from Ana half a century ago. He'd done it because he loved her and had wanted to protect her. That was real love.

What Liam had done had been selfish. By barreling his way into her life, he'd put December in mortal danger. Last night was proof enough he couldn't protect her all the time.

Once they killed these APL bastards—and he had to believe they would—there would be someone else filled with rage and hate ready to take the place of them and hurt anyone he cared about.

"What's wrong?" December's soft voice sliced through the quiet room.

His head jerked at the direction of her question. She stared at him with heavy-lidded eyes, as if she hadn't quite woken up yet. He hadn't even realized she'd stirred. Clearing his throat, he shook his head. He wouldn't voice his fears to her. "Nothing. I'm going to be leaving soon."

She sat up and clutched the sheet to her chest. "Are you going to look for Kat? Take me with you," she said before he could answer her first question.

He shook his head. "I can't. The APL guy I caught behind the Dumpster of your store a while ago is getting out of jail. He was very cooperative before. I want to see if I can get him to open up again." And if he didn't, the guy would pay. Worse than last time. A broken thumb would be the least of his worries.

"I can't just do nothing all day. Kat's my friend and I feel so helpless. Let me help." Desperation laced her words.

He understood the feeling. They all did. Whoever had taken her had been smart enough to mask their trail. Or maybe they'd just driven around in so many circles it had masked her scent anyway. Even though he and his brother had been on the hunt, it was as if Kat had fallen off the face of the earth. "Believe me, I understand. I talked to Connor about it and we think you should open your shop today."

Her eyes widened in horror. "What?"

"Whoever took Kat still likely wants you. Erin is going to be inside the store with you and I've got another pack member who will be right out front the entire time. If they get a hint of either of the male scents from last night, it could give us a lead." Sending December out in public was the last thing he wanted to do right now, but with Kat's life at stake, this might be the only lead they got. They could do nothing and hope for the best, but eventually someone would come after December again. He wanted to stop that before it ever happened. And no one's guard would be down right now. The pack was primed and ready for action. If anyone tried *anything*, that person would be answering to any number of the Armstrong pack members.

Without hesitation, she nodded. "I'll do it." Some part of him had wanted her to say no. That she was too afraid to go in to work. It would have given him an excuse to tell his brother she wouldn't be going into town. But when she stuck her chin out, almost mutinously determined, he knew she'd do anything to get her friend back. There was no way he'd let her go to work without his pack's protection. Even letting her go without him made his canines ache. Especially with Kat's kidnapping so fresh in his mind.

He wanted to lean over and kiss her until neither of them could think straight. But he didn't. Thinking about letting her deeper into his life made him crazy. He couldn't let what happened to Kat happen to December. If pushing her away was the only way to accomplish that, he'd do it. No matter how much it tore him up. Turning his back to her, he slid out of bed and began getting dressed.

After he laced up his boots, he headed for the door.

"Uh, Liam?" December still sat on the bed clutching the sheet, looking a little lost.

And it was his fault. He knew he was pulling away from her. If he didn't do it now, he didn't know how the hell he could walk away from her. From what they had together. But if he didn't, she'd be a target the rest of her life. How could he do that to her? Ask that of her? His inner wolf screamed at him to walk over and kiss her. Soothe her. Hold her in his arms. Tell her everything would be all right.

But he couldn't.

In the doorway he turned to look at her but kept his expression devoid of emotion. "I'll have my phone on me all day if you need me. Once I'm done, I'll stop by the store."

With confusion and more than a hint of pain in her blue eyes, she nodded. "Okay."

His chest ached with the need to comfort her, but he ordered his legs to move. Hurrying out of the house, he didn't breathe until he was outside. Even the small distance didn't help. He could still see the hurt on her face. Knowing he'd put it there made it worse.

"Fuck me," he muttered. He knew he was being an asshole—he just didn't know another way to keep December safe.

"No thanks." Jayce appeared from behind one of the trees, looking haggard and tense.

Dressed in all black, the other wolf had a look that said someone was going to die today. *Just fucking great,* Liam thought. He needed to question that guy William Braun and he didn't need Jayce tagging along, freaking the guy out before he got the information they needed.

As they strode across the yard, he cleared his throat, not sure how to broach the subject. "When did you get back?"

"Half an hour ago. I'm going with you to question that asshole." A statement, not a question.

"I don't think—"

"I don't give a shit what you think. I'm going with or without you." The threatening note in his voice wasn't exactly subtle.

Liam shook his head. "You're not thinking clearly—"

"I've never been clearer headed in my life. And if you try to stop me, I'll rip your throat out," he growled without looking at him.

Liam wasn't sure if he'd actually do it or not. He wasn't exactly scared of the guy, but a male terrified for his female was a scary thing. The potent scent of rage and pain rolling off Jayce was stifling. And he and Kat weren't even mated. Hadn't been together for months. Sighing, Liam projected to his brother that he was taking Jayce with him.

Connor wasn't happy but he didn't argue the point. Probably because, as a mated male, he understood more than most the kind of pain Jayce was dealing with. If Ana were out there right now, Liam had no doubt that Connor would have ripped apart the town trying to find her.

As they reached his Bronco, Jayce slid into the passenger seat. The silence was tense and uncomfortable as Liam steered through the gate. Normally he didn't mind the quiet, but today it felt as if one wrong word would crack the very air around them.

"We're going to find her," Liam finally said. For himself or Jayce, he wasn't sure.

Jayce grunted something incomprehensible.

Kat was a strong female. Stronger than any human he'd ever met. "They took her for a reason. They're *not* going to kill her. From what we've gathered, they want to use our females against us."

"They might not kill her, but they're all dead. I've pissed off a lot of people in the last five hundred years, long before I became the enforcer. We don't even know if this was the APL." His voice was remote yet pained.

It was them. Liam could feel it to his core. He hesitated a moment longer before asking what was really on his mind. "If you could go back . . . would you do things differently with her?" He wasn't sure why Jayce had never bonded with Kat when it was obvious he loved her.

Jayce was silent so long Liam wasn't sure he'd answer. Still staring out the window, he finally spoke, his voice hoarse. "Yeah. I'd have run fast and far the fucking *moment* I met her if I'd known this could happen."

Liam was quiet after that. Knowing what he knew now, he wished he'd done the same thing. There wasn't anything else to say. The drive through town was short. Following the directions Ryan had given him last night, he kept going until he found himself in the middle of a quiet, upper-middle-class neighborhood downtown.

American flags were displayed proudly from most houses, the fallen leaves were all raked, and all the houses were neat and tidy. No chipping paint jobs or rusty cars in any driveways. A far cry from the trailer park the other APL member they'd hunted down lived at. Guess social status didn't matter as long as these assholes had a common goal.

"You sure this is it?" Jayce asked as they pulled into the driveway of a two-story farmhouse-style home.

"This is his last known address. According to Ryan, his wife and two kids still live here."

"This bastard has kids?" Jayce growled.

Liam nodded. "Two little girls, so try to tread lightly. We want information, but we don't want this guy so shitting-his-pants afraid he'll tell us anything to make us go away."

"Don't tell me how to do my job."

Liam rolled his eyes and ignored him as he got out of the vehicle. Jayce wasn't thinking like a trained warrior or an enforcer right now. He wasn't thinking at all. If he couldn't keep a level head, they'd be screwed. Stepping around a fallen pink bike, they strode up the walkway. Liam rang the doorbell once.

A few moments later the door opened and a pretty blond woman stood before them. She eyed Liam curiously and Jayce with blatant fear. Probably because Jayce looked like a hardened biker or gang member with the scar on his face and shaved head. The fact that he was staring unblinking at her with those scary gunmetal gray eyes definitely wasn't helping their cause.

"Uh . . . h-hi?" she stammered.

"Hi, we're here to speak with your husband." Liam tried to keep his voice soothing.

She glanced over her shoulder, then back at them. "Um . . ."

"Honey, who is it?" A male voice called out.

"Some men here to see you." There was fear in her voice and he wasn't sure if it was because she knew what they were, or because her husband had just gotten out of prison and now had two big strangers showing up to see him.

He rounded a corner and when he saw them, his face paled to a deathly white. He faltered for a moment but quickly hurried down the tiled hallway and expertly blocked his wife with his body. Liam might not like the guy, but he could respect him for protecting his family. "Honey, this'll just be a second."

"But—"

"I've got to talk to these guys outside. Go finish making breakfast for the girls." Without waiting for a response, he stepped out onto the porch and pulled the door shut behind him. With his gaze on Liam, he held up both his hands in a defensive gesture. "I just got out of prison. I don't want any trouble."

"And you won't get any if you tell us what we want to know." Jayce's voice was low and threatening and held more animal in it than human.

Liam wanted to punch him for being such a dumbass. They couldn't have this guy so scared he wouldn't talk. Or worse, tell them whatever he thought they wanted to hear.

"Who are you?" William asked Jayce cautiously.

"He's a friend of mine," Liam said. "We're not here to cause problems for you, but we need some information."

He glanced over his shoulder even though the door was shut. "I'm done with the APL. After I got sent away, I thought my wife was going to leave me. Hell, if I hadn't got out so quickly, I think she would have. I'm done with all that shit and I don't want any more trouble."

"You have information we need."

He shrugged, the action jerky and nervous. "I already told you everything I knew last time, remember?" The man held up his crooked thumb, which hadn't healed properly.

"Yeah, you told me your boss's name, but that's it."

"I don't know any more than that. Everything is really compartmentalized with them. They don't trust outsiders and I hadn't been a member very long."

"What about safe houses?" Liam asked.

The man gave a confused look, but Liam didn't buy it. "What?"

"You'd planned to take December for your boss. Do I need to refresh your memory? Where did they plan to keep her?" Even thinking about that day he'd caught this guy behind her store made Liam see red. Maybe he wasn't the only one who needed to calm down. He clenched his fists at his sides and took measured breaths. He was in control, not his inner wolf.

"Fine, they have safe houses. I've never been to any of them, but I heard rumors that Adler has a couple for hostages. I kinda figured it out anyway, since no one would want to keep hostages at their own homes."

Jayce took a menacing step forward and Liam had to throw his arm out to block him. Killing this guy wouldn't do them any good. Especially not in such a public place and in front of his family. "Where are these houses?" He ground the words out, hating that he had to deal with such scum.

"I don't know, I swear. I went to Adler's house for a meeting once, but I was blindfolded for the drive since I was so new. From what I could tell, his house isn't in town but just past it to the east. There weren't a lot of lights out there either. Just farmland. I didn't see any other buildings near the house, though, so I don't know of any landmarks."

"Anything else you can think of?"

"I don't know, man. Half his face is burned and he hates anything paranormal and he hates women. Well, except for one woman. There's this lady, Brianna—she seemed pretty new to the group too, but he was different around her. Almost like she—I don't know—had a controlling effect on him or something. I can't . . . be associated with those people anymore. I don't know what I was thinking," he said, almost to himself. "Can you just leave now? I don't know anything else!"

Liam looked at Jayce, who nodded. This guy was scared and from what Liam could sense, he was telling the truth. Lies often had a distinctive, almost metallic tang to them and this guy wasn't exuding that. But he still wanted to instill fear in him. "If I find out you know more than you're telling, I'll come back and break more than your thumb."

With wide eyes, William paled even more. "Shit, man! I don't know anything else, I swear. I just want to live in peace with my family." Beads of sweat rolled down the side of his face as he looked back and forth between them.

Nodding, Liam turned and strode back to the vehicle. Once they were inside, he started the engine, then headed back to the ranch. "We lost the trail at a cross-roads last night, but what he's saying might be true. There's a lot of farmland and mountainous terrain to the east. Good place to hide just about anything or anyone."

Liam started to say more when Connor's voice sounded in his head. *Get back to the ranch. Ryan finally cracked the encryption. We might have something.*

On our way, he projected back.

He quickly relayed the message to Jayce and was almost surprised by the sudden burst of undisguised hope that rolled off the other wolf. The sweet, pure scent was completely at odds with the tough-looking shifter. It didn't matter that he'd had half a millennium learning to cover his emotions. His feelings for Kat were obviously stronger than any of that.

Silently Liam prayed they'd find Kat soon. They didn't know nearly enough about the APL, and the fact that they had no issues targeting women was terrifying. And after what William had just told them . . . he fought back the thoughts.

They would find her. They had to.

December closed the register and handed change back to her twentieth customer of the morning. They'd been unusually busy and she shouldn't have had time to think about anything, but unfortunately that's all she could do. She was lost in her head.

Worried about Parker. Scared out of her mind for Kat. And confused about Liam. She knew that should be the last thing on her mind, but after the way he'd acted this morning, she wasn't sure what was going on. The cold, distant side of Liam wasn't something she ever wanted to get used to.

While she understood they were both stressed, she wanted to lean on him. And she wanted him to do the same with her. If they were going to take the next step in this relationship, she couldn't deal with someone who didn't see her as an equal. As the bell above the door jingled behind the last customer, she strode toward the front door and locked it.

Then she turned the OPEN sign to CLOSED.

"What are you doing?" Erin came out from behind one of the aisles. Her red hair was pulled back into a tight ponytail and December couldn't be sure, but she thought the petite she-wolf had some kind of weapons underneath her thick down jacket. She hadn't taken her coat off all morning and December knew that shifters weren't as affected by the cold as humans.

She lifted an eyebrow at the she-wolf. "What does it look like?"

Erin's eyes narrowed. "You're supposed to keep your shop open."

She began turning off the front lights. "Yeah, well, things change. I can't stay here working while my brother is in the hospital and my best friend is missing. This is insane." She'd already gotten more than a few comments from locals who'd stopped by to see why she had her shop open. And they were right. She shouldn't be here. Her brother was recovering from a gunshot wound and everyone now knew that Kat had been taken. Of course no one knew by whom or why except Liam's pack. The cops were doing all they could, but they had no leads either.

"Liam's going to be pissed." Erin's voice was wary.

"I don't really care. He's not here." And he'd seen fit to keep her in the dark about a lot of stuff.

Erin shrugged, then sighed. "What do you need to do to close up?"

She nodded to the line of lights on the far wall. "Turn those off and I'm going to run my daily report."

The shifter who had been watching the store all morning from outside knocked on the front door, so Erin let him in. December glanced up from the cash register but ignored the curious look he gave her and Erin. Let the she-wolf explain it.

As December finished running her report, she vaguely heard Erin telling the other shifter what was going on. When she finished, she set the alarm and locked up. The moment she slid into the passenger seat of Erin's truck, she called Liam.

"What's wrong?" His deep voice was concerned.

"Nothing, but we're coming back to the ranch."

"Why?"

"Because being here is stupid. Whoever took Kat got what they want. They're not going to be hanging around town. I want to help. And if I can't, I'm going back to the hospital. I'll just wait around until Parker decides to pull his head out of his ass." The words spilled from her like a waterfall.

Liam cursed but quickly acquiesced. Probably because he knew he had no choice. "Fine, but I won't be here when you get back."

"Where are you going?"

He hesitated, then said, "I can't tell you."

"Why not?" This whole secrecy stuff would never fly with her. Not with important stuff.

"It's better that you don't know. We might have a lead on where they took Kat."

"I can help *search* at least." She might not have his capabilities, but she wasn't helpless. And more than once she'd helped in county searches for missing kids who'd simply gotten lost in the woods or mountains.

"This isn't up for discussion. As soon as we leave, we're going dark. No communication. Nothing. I don't know how long we'll be gone." He sounded so matter-of-fact it was maddening.

"Liam—"

"I'm sorry, December, but I've got to go." Then he disconnected.

She seethed as she stared at her silent cell phone. For a moment she thought about calling him back but knew it was pointless.

"He's just trying to protect you." Erin's soft voice cut through the quiet interior of the vehicle.

December waited a moment to see if the male shifter sitting in the back would finally speak, but he was wisely silent. "Yeah, well, he has a dumb way of showing it."

She snorted softly. "Don't they all."

Liam hated the way he'd ended the phone conversation with December, but he didn't have time to explain anything. Ryan had finally cracked part of the flash drive and they had to take immediate action. So far they had two pages of names and addresses of active APL members. Including active safe houses.

He wasn't sure why the Taylor guy living in the trailer park had this information, but if he had to guess, he'd probably planned to use it as blackmail. He was likely dead now, though. Liam hoped he was. It would save him the trouble later. Since that bastard had tried to attack December after their date, he'd fallen off the radar. No credit card activity whatsoever. He might have another alias, but so far Ryan hadn't been able to find one.

Connor zipped up his coat as he stepped out onto the front porch, where Liam and Jayce waited. "Are your phones off?" he asked.

Liam nodded. "And batteries taken out."

"Same here," Jayce said.

His brother nodded approvingly. "Good."

When they went on a mission of this sort, it was standard practice to disable their phones. They weren't so naive to think the government didn't keep tabs on them. Not always of course, and probably not even that often, since their pack didn't get into trouble, but right now they couldn't take the chance of being tracked. Today they were likely going to kill some APL members. There didn't need to be any proof they were in the same vicinity at the time.

Connor pulled out the keys to his truck as they strode across the yard. "I've sent Noah and Jacob to check out the houses in town."

When Jayce started to interrupt, Connor cut him off. "They've got Kat's scent and they're trained. They know what they're looking for. I think it's unlikely they're keeping her at a house in town anyway, but we have to check it."

Which was why they were checking out a farmhouse a few miles on the outskirts of Fontana. It was listed under the name of a man who'd died twenty years ago and there had been two asterisks next to the address. But nothing else. They might not know what that meant, but they all thought it was important.

And it lined up with what the guy William had told them that morning. The place was to the east of town and surrounded by about a hundred acres.

As they headed there, a light dusting of snow began to fall. It would hurt their abilities to track people, but it would also cover their tracks if necessary. They were all silent until they neared the designated turnoff on the two-lane highway.

A small wooden sign on a post said DOGWOOD HOUSE. If they hadn't been looking for it, they'd have definitely missed it. The dirt road was full of potholes, but from the recent tire tracks in the snow, someone was home.

The road was lined with dogwood and pine trees and when they neared an opening, Connor backed into the small gap as far as he could go.

Quietly, they got out and covered most of the truck with underbrush. It wasn't completely hidden, but if someone was driving by and not looking for it, he wouldn't be likely to see it. And the falling snow would hurt anyone's visibility. According to the information on the flash drive, they had less than a mile to trek to the house.

Sticking to the cover of the trees, they paralleled the dirt road until they reached a clearing. A combination wire and wood fence surrounded a two-story brick house. Despite the unpaved, bumpy driving path, the house itself was in good shape and all the bushes surrounding it were neat and trimmed. Smoke drifted from the chimney and two trucks and one car sat in the paved driveway. Someone was definitely home.

From their side view, they could see a balcony on the second story that likely led to a bedroom. And the light was on.

"I'll go in through the balcony. Liam, you and Jayce

figure out how to take the downstairs." Connor's voice was quiet even though they were about forty yards from the house.

Liam nodded in agreement and Jayce did the same. The falling snow gave them some cover, but there were a few brief moments where they were all exposed. Luckily, they were a hell of a lot faster than humans and made it to the house unseen.

As Connor climbed the side of the house toward the balcony, Liam and Jayce split up, each taking different sides of the house. When Liam spotted a man through the kitchen window, his heart rate sped up. The guy was making what looked like a grilled cheese sandwich on the stove. A gun was tucked into the back of his pants, but that looked like his only weapon.

Testing the side door, Liam was surprised when it opened. Picking the lock would have been child's play, but leaving it unlocked was stupid practice for anyone. As he stepped inside, he tried to home in on Kat's presence but couldn't get anything. No subtle roses.

As a rule he preferred to fight in animal form, but it didn't make sense right now. He didn't feel threatened and if he didn't have to kill this guy, he wasn't going to. Withdrawing his pistol, he crossed the kitchen in complete silence.

The guy still stood at the sizzling stove humming a Christmas song. Liam pressed the gun to the back of his skull and withdrew the man's weapon with his free hand. "How many people are in the house?" he murmured.

"Fuck you," the blond-haired man said, his voice just as low.

A burst of fear exploded off him, so Liam took a step back. "Keep your hands up and turn around slowly."

When he did as he said, Liam motioned with his gun

for him to move toward the small round table in the corner of the room. As the guy moved, he flipped off the stove and moved the pan off the hot burner. Now Liam scented two other distinctive males in the house along with Connor and Jayce. There were traces of other people, but they weren't as strong, as if they'd left recently. "Where's the girl?"

Awareness flared in his eyes and a slight metal tang flowed off him, but the man shook his head. "I don't know what you're talking about."

"I can smell the lie coming off you. Where. Is. The. Girl." Not a question.

He shrugged. "Probably dead by now."

Liam could tell he was lying again. He took another step forward. "Don't be stupid. We both know your little group doesn't want her dead. They need her alive as a bargaining chip. If you tell me where she is, I'll let you live."

"I'm not going to tell you one thing, you fucking animal," he spat.

Liam tucked his own gun away and bared his teeth. Unlike vampires', all his teeth could protract on command, not just his canines. He knew it was a frightening sight. Right now he was in control of his inner wolf, but the beast was threatening to take over each second that passed. As he snarled at the man, the fear that rolled off him fed his wolf. He liked the scent and he wanted more of it.

"I'd rather die than tell you anything!" The man lunged up, grabbed one of the chairs, and threw it at him.

Liam easily ducked as it sailed toward his head. When he did, the human withdrew a gun from under the table.

Instead of shifting, he kicked out at the man. The other gun flew through the air, but that didn't stop the human. He threw a punch meant to hit him in the face, but Liam ducked. Liam knew his own strength and knew this wasn't going to be a fair fight.

Right now he didn't care much about fair. He only cared about finding Kat. As he dodged to the side, he threw a punch of his own.

When his fist connected with the guy's jaw, he grunted in satisfaction. The man stumbled back but didn't lose his footing.

Cursing, he came at Liam again, but this time he protected his face. Kicking out, he connected with Liam's inner thigh.

As Liam struck him in the stomach, the man punched his face. The pain was minimal but pissed Liam off. He growled low, and using his leg and upper-body strength, he threw a hard left hook.

The instant he connected with the man's jaw, he knew he'd broken it.

The man cried out as he fell back to the table. His body sprawled onto it, then slid to the tile floor. As Liam bent to check for a pulse, a movement behind him had him drawing his gun.

He stopped when he saw Connor and Jayce. "What did you find?"

"No Kat," Jayce's voice was low and filled with anger.

"I sensed two other guys. Where are they?"

Stone-faced, Connor flicked a quick glance at Jayce, then back to Liam. "Both dead."

Jayce killed them both before I could stop him. Broke their necks, Connor projected to him.

"Did you get any information from either of them?" Liam asked.

Jayce and Connor both shook their heads; then Jayce spoke. "I spotted snowmobile tracks leading away from the house when I came in through the garage. They're fresh, but if we don't hurry, the snow will cover them."

"We'll follow them, but we don't indiscriminately kill anyone." Connor's attention was solely on Jayce as he spoke.

Jayce just shrugged, but the raw rage in his eyes gave him away. "You've got your rules, I've got mine. They're APL, they die. My orders from the Council are clear."

Liam knew his brother well enough to know that this conversation wasn't over—and he somehow doubted the Council had ordered Jayce to kill all APL members—but now wasn't the time to argue with him. If there were fresh tracks, it could lead them to a safe house.

That could lead them to Kat.

Chapter 18

December tried to blend into the background as Ryan clicked away on his computer. He'd said she wasn't bugging him and she believed him, but she also didn't know him well enough to know for sure.

The cabin was apparently where most of the males lived, including Liam when he wasn't with her. It was a complete bachelor's pad. The expansive first floor was basically one room with the living room and kitchen connected.

Stacked dirty plates and cups looked as if they'd been sitting in the sink for a week, and it was beyond disgusting. They hadn't even soaked some of the plates. So, she'd decided to do their dishes. Anything to keep her hands busy. To make her feel like she was helping in some way. Not that it did much to distract her mentally.

Aiden, the shifter who'd accompanied her and Erin to and from her store earlier, lounged on the couch in the living room with his eyes shut. A couple other pack members were out patrolling and she'd seen a few females around the ranch, but it was really cold outside and it seemed almost everyone was staying indoors.

Erin sat on the love seat across from Aiden, reading a book. December wasn't entirely sure, but she had a feeling both of them had been ordered to watch her all day no matter what happened or where she went.

"You don't have to do that, you know. These guys are pigs and should learn to clean up after themselves," Erin said without looking up.

December half smiled. "I know. I just hate not being able to do anything. Shouldn't we be out looking for Kat?"

Erin glanced up from her book. "If anyone will find her, it's Connor, Liam, and Jayce."

That might be so, but it didn't lessen December's fear any. She'd even tried calling the hospital as a way to distract herself, but after being told five times that Parker wasn't taking her calls, she felt even worse.

"Oh, shit," Ryan said almost absently.

The first words he'd spoken in the last half hour. December shut off the sink and wiped her hands on a dishrag as Erin and Aiden stood up.

"What is it?" Erin asked.

"It might be nothing, but I've been pulling up various satellite images of Fontana and cross-referencing them with the remote addresses we've got so far...." He trailed off as he continued clacking away on the keyboard.

"And?" Erin persisted when he didn't continue.

He pulled up a couple maps and pointed at what looked like the top of a building in the middle of the woods. "This is on the property Connor and the others are headed to, but it's not listed as a safe house anywhere. Or if it is, I haven't cracked that part yet. And see this?" He traced his finger along the screen, highlighting what looked like a faint trail. "This could be an access road. The trees cover most of it, but it looks like it connects to the highway miles out of the way from where they're looking."

December's heart rate increased. What if this was where Kat was? "Can you call Liam and tell him about this?"

Ryan glanced at her before shaking his head. "They've gone dark. None of them have their cells activated."

She wasn't exactly sure why, but she could guess. "What if they miss this area? What if it's where Kat is? And what if they move her?"

"Wait, we can let Ana know and she can communicate with Connor." Aiden spoke up for the first time.

"I thought you said their phones were turned off," December said.

Erin glanced between the men, then looked at her. "Connor and Ana can communicate telepathically."

"Oh, right." Liam had told her about that. It was just hard to fathom. Before she could say anything else, Erin continued as she pulled out her cell phone.

"She's not here and I don't know if she has her cell on." They were all silent as Erin called. Moments later she snapped her phone shut and shook her head. "Straight to voice mail."

"Why isn't she at the ranch?" Ryan asked what December was thinking.

Erin cut her another inscrutable look as she answered the question. "At the hospital trying to talk to Parker. And before you ask why, Liam asked her to go. He knows how important your brother is to you and thought maybe Ana could talk some sense into him."

December's throat clenched impossibly tight. Even with everything going on, Liam was still thinking about her happiness. It was tempting to focus on that, but she knew they had more important things to worry about.

She motioned to the screen, diverting everyone's attention. "How old is this image?"

Ryan shrugged nervously. "Six months, give or take. They update these images once or twice a year."

December looked at Erin and Aiden questioningly. They all stood there, as if they weren't going to do a thing. Gritting her teeth, she turned on her heel and headed for the front door. She wasn't a hostage and if she wanted to leave, she damn well would. It wasn't as if these APL members had superstrength. If she could get her hands on a weapon, she could defend herself. No one would be sneaking up on her this time.

"What are you doing?" Erin demanded as she strode after her.

"What do you think? If you guys can't get hold of Liam, then what else can we do? Do you plan to just sit here and do nothing? If this turns out to be where Kat's being held and they move her in the meantime . . ." She didn't finish because it was pointless. She didn't care what they said.

She was going.

Erin touched her arm lightly as she grabbed her coat from the rack. "Hold on a sec," she murmured, and looked at the other wolves. "Noah and Jacob are checking out other leads in town and we can't ask the others to leave the ranch unprotected . . . but we can go."

Aiden nodded and motioned to December. "Just leave her at the main house."

December glared at the tall shifter who spoke as if she weren't even in the room. "Kat is my best friend and unless you plan on tying me up and knocking me out, I'm going." The three of them stared at her, but she held her ground. "My brother's a cop. I don't own a gun, but I know how to use one. Give me a weapon and I promise to stay out of the way. Besides, if you don't take me, I'm following anyway."

Erin and Aiden both cursed, but the she-wolf nodded tightly. "You stay out of the way or I *will* knock you out."

"Deal. Now can we leave?" Every second they spent here was a second wasted. Her heart pounded mercilessly, the blood rushing loudly in her ears. Kat might not have much time left and if this was where she was being held, they had to help her.

December wiped clammy palms on her jeans as they drove down the barely formed trail. Snow had fallen hard earlier, making the road thick and slushy, but Aiden didn't seem to notice as he drove. She sat in the backseat with Erin and so far everyone had been quiet.

They'd missed the turnoff the first time, but Ryan figured it out by calculating the longitude and latitude. Or something like that. She didn't really understand or care how he'd figured out where they were going. She just wanted to find her friend.

"We should be there soon," Ryan murmured.

They'd been driving through the forest down the dirt trail for a while, though it probably seemed longer than it actually was.

A few moments later, Aiden slowed the truck and killed the engine in the middle of the trail. He glanced back at them. "We go on foot from here. I don't like you being here," he said to her, "so stick close and keep your weapon on hand at all times."

She nodded, unable to get rid of the nervousness threading through her. "Okay."

When she stepped out into the snow, she sank nearly a foot into the powdery softness.

Instantly Aiden knelt in front of her and turned so

that his back was facing her. He glanced over his shoulder at her. "Liam will probably kill me for touching you, but I'm going to carry you. We can move faster that way."

She didn't care one way or another how they got there. Quickly, she slid onto his back and held on as they began the trek down the trail. He was a little taller than Liam and she was thankful for his added warmth. Even with her thick coat her face was already frozen. The farther they went, the thicker the trees got, but there was still a distinct—if smaller—trail that was probably used for snowmobiles.

After a few minutes all three shifters slowed in unison. December had no idea why but figured maybe they scented something or someone.

"We're close," Aiden said as if he read her mind. Stopping completely, he bent down and let her off his back.

Adrenaline pumped through her wildly. They were close to finding Kat. She didn't know how she knew, but she did. This was it. It *had* to be. Kat was likely scared out of her mind.

Suddenly, the trail thinned and opened to a small clearing. What they'd seen from the satellite images was a small, dilapidated barn. Not for animals exactly, but probably for storage, though whoever owned it hadn't kept it up well.

Erin sniffed the air and glanced at them. "You smell that?"

"Dead bodies. Really old ones," Aiden said.

December didn't smell anything, but her throat clenched at their words. "Kat?"

Erin shook her head. "No, these bodies have been here weeks at least. The scent is really faint, which means they're likely buried nearby. Not deep enough, though."

December started to say something when the sound

of multiple engines silenced her. They all moved back toward the trees and watched.

Two men and an ethereal-looking blond woman drove up on sleek black snowmobiles. When they turned them off and headed for the barn, Aiden motioned to her. "Stay put. If anything happens to us, turn on your phone and call the cops," he whispered.

Nodding, she crouched down behind one of the trees and withdrew her gun. In her other hand, she held on to her cell phone. She'd kept it off like they'd instructed, but at the first sign of trouble she was ready to take action.

Kat heard the distant sound of engines but kept her eyes closed. She'd feigned being passed out a while ago just to make the pain stop. Somehow she tried to think of what her captor had done to her in detached terms. The colder she got, the easier it was. And she *knew* she was dying.

Knew it bone deep. It wouldn't be much longer. When blood had trickled out of her mouth and nose, it hadn't been hard to guess she had internal bleeding. With no one here to help, it was only a matter of time.

Only a vague sense of triumph remained. After all his abuse the bastard hadn't been able to get it up, so at least he hadn't raped her. As she tried to take another ragged breath, she closed her mind off. She wasn't here and she couldn't give him any more power. When she died, she wasn't going to be thinking of him. No, she'd be focused on something much more pleasant.

She was in Miami. On the beach. The warm Atlantic water lapped around her feet as she dug her toes into the white sand. Jayce was next to her, holding her hand, telling her all the things she'd ever wanted to hear from him but he'd never said.

The sound of the large exterior door rolling open jerked her out of her thoughts. More tormentors arriving? She almost dry heaved at the thought. Her heart clenched on a fresh wave of terror as she tried not to stir or alert them to her consciousness.

"Oh my God! What the hell have you done?" a female voice shrieked.

Kat decided to open her eyes. Everything was hazy, but she spotted two new men and a woman entering the building.

The petite blond woman glowed supernaturally. The humans wouldn't be able to see it, but thanks to her seer abilities, Kat could. The female wasn't human, but she couldn't tell exactly what she was. Not a vampire and not a shifter, that was for sure. There was no underlying animal at the blonde's surface. She was unique in a way Kat had never seen. The thought was clear in her head. But what was she? And why was she with these men? Her mind briefly struggled to put together what she was seeing, but just as quickly she gave up even worrying about it. Didn't matter. Kat was dead anyway.

Deep down she didn't want to die, but she didn't want to live if this pain was all that was left for her. If they were going to keep torturing her pointlessly, *then* she'd rather be dead. She wanted to cry but it was too painful, especially since she could barely breathe. The tape was so restrictive it only added to her misery.

"I was trying to get information out of her," Greg, her tormentor, said casually.

"Then why is her mouth taped shut?" a man with a scarred face asked. "If you're going to torture someone, you have to do it right. Don't fucking lie to me. She's our ticket to bringing down the enforcer, but if she's dead, she won't be of any use to us."

"You're all monsters," the blond woman breathed out, horror lacing every word.

The man with the scar turned and backhanded her. The sound of the blow ricocheted around the small space. "This is a war. If you can't handle this, then leave." As if she meant nothing to him, he turned from her and back toward the men.

"Listen, I didn't sign up for this shit. I thought we were just holding her hostage. No one said anything about . . . *this*."

"Shut up, Joseph. You're such a fucking pussy," Greg, her tormentor, said, his voice full of venom.

The three males continued to argue. The man with the scarred face was angry because Greg had beaten her so thoroughly. He made it clear he couldn't use her as a bargaining chip if she was dead. Apparently enough time had passed and she'd been missing long enough that the scarred man—Kat guessed he was the boss—was ready to contact the enforcer and see what they could get in exchange for Kat's safe return. But now they would have to wait until she healed a little—if she recovered at all. She must look pretty bad if they thought she might not recover. Her most animal side knew this was it. She wanted to scream out in anger—if her mouth weren't taped and if she had the energy—at how short her life had been. There was so much she still wanted to do.

As she stared at the three men, Kat watched in horror and fascination as the blond woman smoothly pushed to her feet and started to glow incandescently. Instead of being fearful, the woman looked angry. Her entire body lit up and her blue eyes flashed darkly, almost evilly. Kat couldn't tear her gaze away from the sight. By their expressions, it was obvious the males could see her glowing too. She wasn't visible just to Kat's seer senses.

"You arrogant bastard," the woman breathed out, her voice eerily dark and unnatural. All her focus was on the scarred man. "For months I've put up with all of you, but *you* are the worst. Controlling your sick, twisted mind has drained my powers on a daily basis, but no more. Finding out who your boss is isn't worth *this*." Her voice deepened even more, sending a chill snaking through Kat's entire body.

Out of the corner of her eye, Kat watched Greg inch toward the door. She wanted to cry out, to alert the woman that he was trying to escape, but her mouth was taped shut. The other man, the scarred one, hadn't moved, though. He just stood frozen, staring, as if he were a marble statue. Transfixed by the vision before him.

A burst of light shot from the woman's right hand. It glowed as bright blue as her eyes. The stream of energy split through the air directly at the scarred man.

He tried to run but it was useless. The bolt of light slammed into his head, ripping it clear from his body. Kat gagged as his lifeless body fell to the floor with a thud. Blood and gore spilled out of him as his entire body began splitting apart as if he were a rag doll. It was like his skin just fell apart, losing all its elasticity.

The woman turned to face Kat and fixed that eerie, unearthly blue gaze on her. Her eyes were haunted, full of regret. "I'm so sorry. I didn't know he'd done this to you. I thought they were just holding you hostage or I'd have come sooner." Now her voice was ragged and tired and no longer deeply unnatural. She held out her hand toward Kat and this time a soft, green burst of light flowed from her hand.

Kat flinched but a warmth spread through her chest, and the pulsing, ripping pain she'd felt moments before began to fade. As energy seeped back into her, two giant, snarling wolves and a redheaded woman carrying two blades burst through the door.

The blonde turned at the noise and, when she did, broke contact with Kat. Immediately the blonde slumped to the hay-covered dirt ground.

The abrupt removal of the blonde's energy made Kat cry out against her taped mouth. Fresh pain shot through Kat's limbs. Whatever the woman had been doing wasn't working now. The muted sounds of her cries pushed the man who'd been frozen into action.

He reached for his gun, but the fight was over before it started. The gray and white wolf lunged at him and tore his throat out in one clean swipe.

Kat closed her eyes to block out the pain, their presence, and the new violence. She knew what she looked like and couldn't bear the shame of anyone seeing her like this. If these two wolves were here, she knew Jayce wasn't far behind. The thought of him seeing what had been done to her made bile rise in her throat.

When she felt soft hands touch her bound, outstretched arms, her eyes flew open and she instinctively started to struggle until she realized the redheaded woman was cutting her down.

Gently, she laid her on the ground and removed the tape from her mouth. Kat tried to cover her exposed breasts, but her arms wouldn't work. The other woman slid off her coat and laid it over her.

"I'm dying," she gurgled out, blood dripping down her chin. She didn't know why she'd said it. The words just escaped.

The redhead glanced over her shoulder at something. There was a breaking, ripping sound, but Kat couldn't move to see what it was. "Where's Ryan?"

"He went after that other human," a male voice said. When the man appeared in Kat's line of sight, she flinched at the sight of him. He was naked and big and scary looking.

He held up his hands in a defensive motion as he knelt down. "I'm not going to hurt you. We're here to save you."

"She's not going to make it to a hospital," the redhead murmured.

One look at the other shifter's face and Kat knew she'd been right. She was dead. "Where's Jayce?" Maybe she could at least say good-bye to him.

"Out looking for you," the woman said soothingly.

So he wasn't there. And she wouldn't get to say anything to him. Hot, burning tears sprang up and rolled down her cheeks, mixing with blood and dirt. A sob wanted to break free, but even that small action hurt. But she was powerless to stop them.

The sound of pounding footsteps, then a gasp, greeted her ears. Through her hazy vision she saw December bending toward her. Kat couldn't tell for sure, but it looked like her friend was crying too.

December slid a hand under her head and gripped one of her hands. "It's going to be okay," she whispered as she tightened her grip on Kat.

It wasn't, but Kat appreciated the lie.

The man said something to the redhead, but Kat couldn't understand him. Her vision was getting darker as the seconds ticked by. Too many memories rushed through her mind and she really wished she'd gotten to say good-bye to her father. They might live by different moral compasses, but he was still her dad and he'd always loved her. And she really wanted to say good-bye to Jayce. The image of him wouldn't leave her alone, even as she was dying. She used to love running her fingers over his shaved head and even his scarred cheek. He never let anyone touch her the way he'd let her. She'd been free to do whatever she wanted because he'd been hers. Just for a little while. Everyone had always been so afraid of him, but with her he'd always been gentle. Even if he hadn't wanted to bond with her, he'd shown her a softer side she knew no one else had seen. She'd take that small knowledge to her grave and savor it.

"Just do it!" December shouted at the man. The other redhead began yelling at him too with the same intensity as her friend.

Kat tried to block them all out. She didn't understand what was going on and she didn't care. Whatever they were fighting about wouldn't matter soon. She just wanted the pain to stop.

Suddenly her world rocked on its axis and she stared in confusion as the male shifter leaned toward her. "I'm sorry. If I don't at least *try* this, Jayce will kill me." Before she could even think about what he meant, his canines protracted and he sank his teeth into her neck. The pain was sharp and acute and it extended from his bite to all her nerve endings.

It was as if her bones were shattering, then slowly being pieced back together. A sudden, hot burning sensation surged through her and a harsh screaming filled the air. It took a moment for her to realize she was the one screaming.

Her back arched and she shoved off the ground as the pain dulled and a new sense of life and energy flowed through her. Trying to catch her breath, she sat up, still clutching the jacket to cover her body. Blinking rapidly, she looked at the three of them.

"What did you do?" Her voice sounded normal, not

hoarse and scratchy. And ... she moved both her legs against the dirt. They both worked. Gingerly, she pressed a hand to her ribs. No pain. No trouble breathing.

"You were going to die. I know I had no right, but ... I bit you." The huge male looked stricken as he stared at her.

"He saved your life," December said softly.

She frowned as reality began to set in. A lupine shifter had *bitten* her. Since she wasn't dead and she wasn't a feral wolf, that meant only one thing. She was now a shifter. "I thought there was only a one percent chance the change would work if we aren't bondmates. And I thought I could turn feral or something if it didn't work."

The man nodded. "We had nothing to lose. You were dead either way. If you'd turned feral ... I'd have had to kill you."

Kat looked down at herself and stared blindly. She couldn't believe she'd survived his bite. She had more knowledge of shifters than most, so she understood the chance of her successfully changing after a shifter bite was very small. That was why they didn't go around turning humans. The chance of death or turning mad was too great to risk. She briefly wondered if the fact that she was a seer with naturally higher psychic abilities had made a difference.

As another man walked back into the barn carrying clothes, the male shifter in front of her stood and strode toward him. When he started getting dressed, a new rush of emotions surged through Kat.

A dam burst as tears and pain exploded from her. Not physical pain. Emotional pain. It was like a free-falling wave that wouldn't crest. It went on and on. The tears streaming down her cheeks just wouldn't stop.

December helped her slip on the coat and zip it up.

When Kat stood on shaky legs, it fell to midthigh, covering her, but it didn't matter. She still felt exposed.

Naked.

Violated.

She couldn't stop crying or shaking. When the male who'd bitten her lifted her into his arms, she didn't protest. It wasn't an attraction, but she felt linked somehow to him. She needed his touch and as she wrapped her arms around his neck, an odd soothing pulse flowed through her. It didn't last long, but his touch helped ease her pain and fear. "Where's the man who got away?" she managed to gasp out through her tears. As she thought about what he'd done to her, fresh tears escaped.

"Dead," the man who'd brought the clothes said in a guttural growl. She realized he must be the other wolf from earlier.

She also wished she could feel some relief to know that Greg, her tormentor, was dead. Instead, she felt nothing.

"We need to get out of here," the redhead with the blades murmured.

"What about her?" December pointed to the blond woman still lying lifeless on the ground.

The question jerked Kat back to her senses and dried up her tears. "I don't know what she is, but she's not human. She tried to save me. We need to bring her with us."

The other male nodded and scooped her off the ground as if she weighed nothing.

As they started to leave, the shifters stopped suddenly. December glanced around nervously. "What is it?" she whispered.

Kat had no fear left inside her. Only pain.

"Connor, Liam, and Jayce. They're here," the redhead said quietly.

Kat buried her face against the male's chest. "Don't tell them how you found me," she whispered.

He didn't respond. Just stroked his hand down her hair and murmured soft soothing sounds. He was going to tell them. She knew it. Fresh pain and tears—she didn't know how she could have any left—welled up inside her. The thought of Jayce knowing what had happened to her made her sick. Bile rose in her throat, but she managed to control it.

She heard when they entered the room and the collective murmur of curses and demands for an explanation. Liam was angry December was there and Connor was ranting about something else.

But she refused to look at any of them. Like a coward she just kept her head buried against the chest of the shifter holding her. She didn't even know his name, but letting him hold her was better than having to look at Jayce.

To see pity in his gray eyes. She might want to feel his arms around her, but it wasn't going to happen. Biting back another sob, she tried to block everything out.

Jayce stared at Aiden holding Kat tightly in his arms and thought his heart would shatter. She wore only a coat and with her long, elegant legs dangling and completely bare, he wanted to go over there and cover her. He wanted to rip her from the other male's arms and cradle her up against his chest, just so he could feel her warmth and reassure himself she was truly going to be all right.

But he didn't.

She kept her face turned away from everyone while Connor and Liam were trying to figure out what happened. If Kat knew he was there, she gave no indication. It nearly killed him.

Fighting to hold it together, he tuned everyone else out and kept his gaze on her.

While he might not know what happened, the smell of her blood was fresh. And there was a lot of it. She'd been hurt. If he had to guess, probably tortured.

The thought made his inner wolf howl with the need for vengeance. He preferred to fight in his human form because once he let his wolf out, people often died. He was in control, but his wolf was old and powerful and right now it wanted out.

It wanted blood. And it really wanted death.

As he listened to the conversations around him, he gathered that Ryan had gotten a lead on this place and they'd all rushed over.

A low growl started in his throat as the truth of what happened came out. It was Kat's blood on the ground and wall. Aiden had bitten her to save her from sure death.

And she'd survived. Physically anyway. After a shifter bite, the transition from human to shifter was always quick. Either the human body survived or it didn't. Which was why shifters rarely bit humans. And if they did, the possible repercussions and rules of pack life were fully explained to them. Becoming a shifter was a life-altering decision, one never taken lightly. Often humans turned feral and the changed human would have to be put down. But not Kat. She'd obviously been strong enough to withstand the change. He guessed her strong psychic mind had something to do with it, but they'd never know for sure. There wasn't a science behind who survived a bite and who didn't. The only ones who survived one hundred percent of the time were bondmates.

Jayce had never been so consumed with the desire to hunt and kill as he was now. He hated himself for wanting to kill the man who'd saved Kat, but he did none-theless.

Aiden was now his enemy. Linked to Kat. To his woman.

As he listened to the conversations around him, he gathered that the men who'd hurt Kat were dead. One in the woods by Ryan's hands. One killed by Aiden. And one had been killed by the unconscious blond female in Ryan's arms.

Jayce should have been here sooner.

Then he could have avenged what had happened to Kat. No one had come out and said how they'd found her. Just that she'd been near death and Aiden had bitten her to save her.

For a moment his gaze strayed to the still unconscious petite blonde. She wasn't tall like most Fianna warriors, but he knew that's what she was. He could scent it on her. She must be the missing warrior the others had been looking for.

"Everyone needs to shut the hell up!" Connor finally roared.

Silence descended on the small group. Jayce couldn't tear his gaze away from Kat. She clutched on to Aiden tighter and the other wolf did the same. When he leaned down and murmured something in her ear, pain screamed through Jayce's lungs as if he'd been shot with pure silver. His muscles began to tremble. For a moment he couldn't breathe.

The possessive rage flowing through him burned like acid. He should be the one holding her. Not some stranger. Clenching his fists tightly, he tore his gaze away from them and turned to Connor. If he stared longer, he'd do something he'd regret.

Like kill Aiden.

*   *   *

December stared at Liam's brother in trepidation. His dark eyes had turned even darker and his canines had protracted slightly. She didn't think he'd hurt any of them, but he looked seriously pissed. And all she cared about was getting Kat out of there. Her friend might be healed, but after seeing her so bruised, so bloody, she could only imagine what she'd been through.

Connor looked pointedly at the enforcer. "There's a body just outside. Dispose of it." Jayce took a step forward, as if to defy him, but Connor shook his head sharply. "You can't help her now," he murmured.

It was obvious Connor meant Kat. December's heart cracked for the other wolf. He'd been staring at Kat since the moment he'd entered the barn, and the pain on his face was so raw, so real, it made her want to cry for him too.

Next, Connor looked at Erin as he pointed to one of the decapitated males. "You go with him and dispose of that one."

Once they both moved into action, he looked at Liam. "You and I have some digging to do."

December looked up at Liam in confusion. "What's he talking about?"

"There are bodies buried underneath here." He stomped once with his foot. "Not killed by us and we don't know who they belong to. We're going to uncover them, then anonymously call the cops once we've disposed of the men we've killed."

"What about . . ." She glanced at her friend.

"We don't want anyone to know she was here. We've come up with a cover story, which we'll go over with her later. We need to destroy any of her blood evidence too. Go back to the ranch with them." He looked at Kat, then at the dried blood on the wall and ground. "She's going to need you right now," he murmured.

Liam reached out for a moment as if to cup her cheek, then jerked his hand back as if he thought she'd burn him.

She looked at Aiden and Ryan. "I'll be right behind you."

When the two men started to leave the barn, she grabbed Liam's arm as he started pulling a shovel down from one of the racks. "We need to talk first."

"Now isn't the time." He didn't look at her as he slammed the end of the shovel into the hard earth.

"What the hell is wrong with you? You're acting like we're strangers. Like you can barely stand to touch me. Or even look at me." She hated that her voice cracked on the last word.

After everything she'd been through the past couple days, she needed him now more than ever and she wasn't afraid to admit it. The fact that he kept pulling back burned a giant hole in her chest. He'd been concerned when he'd entered the barn, but he hadn't made a move to hold her, console her. It ripped her heart out.

He held the shovel still and looked at her with those dark, penetrating eyes, but he wouldn't respond. When he turned away from her again, she gritted her teeth and hurried after the others. Now wasn't the time to push him, but she sure as hell wasn't going to let things go on like this.

Chapter 19

"Are you sure you're up for this?" December held Kat's hand as they sat on the couch in the living room of the ranch's main house.

Kat's normally bright blue eyes were dull as she nodded. "I just want to get this over with. Whatever cover story they've come up with, it's better than what really happened to me."

It was the most Kat had said since they'd returned to the ranch. They'd been back a few hours, but she hadn't slept or wanted to take a shower or anything. She'd just changed into some of December's clothes even though they didn't fit well, then curled up in a ball on the bed December had been sleeping on. And December hadn't left her side.

Having long since returned from the hospital, Ana had been their communication link with the others still not back yet. Once she received word from Connor that the males and Erin were on their way back from disposing of those bodies, she'd come to get December and Kat to let them know that if Kat was up to it, Connor and Liam wanted to talk to her.

"Kat, I'm so sorry—"

"Please don't say anything. It'll just make it worse." Kat's voice was so low December almost didn't hear her.

Tears pricked her eyes but she fought them back. She hated this feeling of helplessness and could only imagine what Kat had gone through. And she wouldn't make it worse by crying when her friend was being so strong. If Kat wanted to talk about it, she'd listen, but December would never push. Instead of trying to say anything else, she squeezed Kat's hand tighter. Even though her friend was taller and leaner—and now a lot physically stronger—her hand felt delicate and almost fragile. As if she might break at any moment.

Kat scooted closer to December as Connor and Liam entered the room. For a moment, December felt her stiffen—probably because she was waiting for Jayce to enter—but when it was just the two of them, some of the tension ebbed from Kat's shoulders.

Connor and Liam sat on the longer couch across from them. Connor spoke first. "Kat, I can't tell you how sorry we all are—"

Kat shook her head sharply. "Just get to the point, *please*."

Liam and Connor exchanged a quick look; then Connor nodded sharply. "Okay. Normally humans aren't turned into shifters without fully understanding the ramifications of their decision. In this case, however, I understand there was no other decision. I'm sure you have a lot of questions and I'll answer anything you want, but right now we have to act quickly. We've disposed of the six men from the property where we found you and destroyed all your blood evidence there. As far as we know, Adler was the local leader of this group and he was among the bodies."

Kat's face paled as she nodded. She squeezed December's hand tighter. "I know. I saw him die."

Connor's jaw flexed. "We combed the house for records or anything we can use against the APL, but at this point we don't know who Adler answered to or how much they know about your kidnapping. If you want to tell the police you were taken by the APL, then—"

"No!" Kat's answer was sharp and clear.

For a moment, her nails protracted and slightly dug into December's palm.

December bit back a startled cry at the same moment Kat dropped her hand and stared at her, horrified.

"I'm sorry," Kat whispered.

December shook her head and reached for her hand again. A ghost of a grateful smile played across Kat's lips before she focused on Connor again.

"It sounds like we're on the same page, then," he said. "We don't want the local cops involved any more than you seem to want them. We killed five—technically six—humans tonight and no matter that we were trying to save you, it will look bad that they're all dead, especially the ones at the main house. We broke into that house and it's obvious two weren't killed in self-defense...." His voice trailed off as he looked at December. "Are you going to tell your brother about any of this?"

She was surprised by the bluntness of his question, but maybe she shouldn't have been. Lying to the police or her brother specifically wasn't something she'd ever thought she'd do. Of course she'd never thought to be targeted by crazy radical hatemongers either. December shook her head. "I'll never speak about what happened tonight to *anyone*."

Connor looked at her for a long moment and must have been convinced of her sincerity, because he nodded once. Then his attention turned to Kat again. "If you're willing, I'd like you to go with Aiden to the police station tonight. No offense, but you look like shit and if you come in with a story of how you escaped two kidnappers and were found in the woods by one of our pack members, it'll be more believable now than if you come in fresh faced a day or two from now. And the longer you're here, the bigger chance someone has of finding out you're not currently being held anywhere."

Kat nodded. "What's the story, then? Why did these two men kidnap me and where was I held?" Her voice shook on the last word.

Connor's expression softened. "Keep it simple. You were held somewhere in the woods, but with all the snow falling you have no idea where or for how long. They were holding you for ransom and wanted to blackmail your father into paying for your release. Since they wore masks the entire time, you have no idea who they are or what they look like. Plenty of people saw you being kidnapped at the hospital and you have no reason to lie to the cops. Since the men who actually took you are dead, the cops will eventually close your case as a cold one."

Kat looked at December with raised eyebrows. She seemed so unsure of herself it made December's heart ache. "What do you think?"

December nodded. "It's a believable story, and like he said, you have no reason to lie."

Kat lightly bit her bottom lip before turning back to Connor and Liam. Dropping December's hand, she stood, her expression resigned. "If Aiden's ready, I want to go now. I just want to get this over with."

Connor and Liam both stood, but only Connor led her out of the room. Once the front door shut behind them, Liam finally spoke, but he didn't sit back down or make a move to comfort her. "How is she?" His voice was ragged.

December had no answer. "I honestly don't know. She hasn't said much since she's been back. I think she's in a mild state of shock. Considering . . . whatever happened to her, I think she's holding up okay."

Liam let out a string of violent curses before meeting her gaze again. "I'm so sorry I dragged you into all this."

She frowned at him, not understanding why he was obviously keeping his distance from her. "This isn't your fault. None of it." It wasn't anyone's fault except that of some ignorant people so consumed with their own hatred they couldn't see anything clearly.

He shook his head sharply, as if she hadn't spoken at all. "After Kat was taken, I realized how selfish I've been. If I'd never forced my way into your life, you'd never be in danger. You'd never know"—he spread his hands out helplessly in front of him—"all this shit. Crazy people wouldn't be after you. You'd be safe."

Her heart rate sped up as she started to digest his words. The reason for his distance at the barn and now here at the house was suddenly all too clear. "So what are you saying?"

He cleared his throat almost nervously. "I think you need to leave town for a while. Maybe take a long vacation."

"Excuse me?" What the hell was the matter with him? They'd just taken care of the leader of the local APL group and now he wanted her to leave. Now, when her friend was in so much emotional pain it was practically a living thing inside her. And now when December needed him more than ever.

Liam nodded resolutely. "We've got a list of all APL members in the area now. There aren't many locals and with these guys dead ... I don't *think* you're going to have a problem anymore, but I want to be sure. You need to be far away from me."

Like hell she did. "I'm not running away from anything. Especially not my home. When I was seventeen, my brother and I packed up and ran away from our problems. I'm not doing that ever again. There will always be problems or violence. Leaving is not the answer."

He swallowed hard, his gaze haunted. "This time it is. You can't be associated with me anymore. It will only bring you pain and suffering."

"What the hell are you trying to say? Spit it out, Liam." She had a feeling she knew what he meant, but she wanted to hear it.

His expression completely shut down. "There can't be an 'us' anymore. I'm sorry, December." She might not be able to read his face, but he actually sounded like he was sorry. All pitiful and pathetic and it just pissed her off even more.

"You are a coward." She bit out each word. "You pursued me like there was no tomorrow and now that I've finally given you what you want—given us a chance—you think pushing me away makes sense?"

"It's the only way to keep you safe."

"Bullshit. It's the only way you can lock up whatever feelings you have for me and cling to some noble idea that you're protecting me. But you're only trying to protect yourself."

When he didn't respond, she wanted to scream. He simply stood there, his face impassive, as if he'd already made the decision and she had absolutely no say whatsoever in it.

"So you're not even trying to deny it?" she demanded.

"This has nothing to do with me. I want to protect *you*."

She gritted her teeth, fighting back the surging, bubbling anger coursing through her. Was he really going to do this? Kick her out of his life? "I can't believe you seriously believe the crap that's coming out of your mouth."

He said nothing.

Which only infuriated her even more. "Don't think you can come crawling back to me when you finally pull your head out of your ass!" Giving Liam one last lethal stare, she turned on her heel and stalked from the room. She'd be staying in the guesthouse tonight—technically this morning—but she doubted she'd get any sleep. Not when she was so wired. Despite the exhaustion overwhelming her and the lingering fear she had for Kat even though her mind knew her friend was safe, she felt ready for a fight. But if Liam wouldn't fight back, she couldn't make him. The only thing she knew for sure was that this conversation wasn't over. Not by a long shot. After he stewed on his asinine decision for a day or two, she'd confront him again and see how ready he was to shove her out of his life.

Chapter 20

Three days later

December steered into her driveway and automatically glanced in the rearview mirror. She'd been overly cautious of her surroundings lately. Sure enough, one of Liam's packmates had followed her home as Connor promised.

After talking to the police, Kat had insisted on leaving the ranch. She'd quit her job at the ski lodge and she didn't want to be anywhere near Jayce or anyone really, and even though Connor and Liam had fought her decision, Connor had eventually relented as long as Kat accepted protection from the pack. December didn't exactly like being home considering there were still possible APL threats out there, but right now her friend needed this and Kat didn't want to be at the ranch. If it would help Kat heal, December could deal with it, though. Considering there were pack members constantly watching the house and she had a new top-of-the-line security system courtesy of Liam, she wasn't losing much sleep at night over safety issues. Well, she was, but that was because of a certain pigheaded shifter who thought he could make decisions about their life because it suited him.

For all of Liam's crap about keeping his distance and staying out of her life, he sure had a dumb way of following through. She knew she'd seen him outside her place last night with a team of guys watching her and Kat. While she might appreciate that, she felt as if he'd ripped her heart out, then stomped it into tiny pieces. He wouldn't even return her calls. As if what they'd shared together meant so little to him. It might not be true, but it was what it felt like each time he ignored her.

Even though thoughts of him consumed her day, she had other things to worry about. Kat wouldn't leave the house or even talk about what happened. Her pain was obviously still fresh, and even if she wouldn't talk to December, she really wished her friend would talk to someone.

When December entered the house, the subtle scent of chili teased her nostrils. She pressed a hand to her stomach as bile rose in her throat. Normally she loved chili, but the smell made her nauseous.

Shrugging off her jacket, she hung it up, then headed for the kitchen. She found Kat at the stove, still in her pajamas. Her friend glanced over her shoulder at her. Her eyes were red and puffy, likely because she'd been crying most of the day.

"Hey," Kat murmured.

Pushing down the unexpected nausea, she stepped farther into the room. She'd planned to wait until later but decided to plunge ahead. "Hey . . . listen, I know it's not my business but I was thinking maybe it wouldn't hurt to talk to a professional. Maybe not in Fontana, but we can find a doctor in a nearby town and—"

"Forget it," Kat said as she shook her head. She put the wooden spoon down and turned to face her. Leaning against the counter, she crossed her arms over her chest defensively. "I don't want to talk to anyone about what happened. I know I've been moping around here—"

"I don't care about that. I just want you to get some help and maybe find some relief." She heard her friend crying late at night and it broke her heart. She'd tried to help, but it was hard when Kat wouldn't even talk. And normal conversation was out of the question. It was too forced and fake.

"I spoke to Aiden today and he's going to . . . help me."

She frowned, not understanding. "Help you?"

Her friend nodded as if the answer should be obvious. "Understand more about the changes I'm going through and teach me to fight."

"That's not the kind of help I was thinking about."

"Well, I'm not talking to some freaking shrink about my feelings or problems that they'll never understand. I just want to know how to defend myself . . . and control myself. I woke up this morning in wolf form and it freaked me out. He's going to help me figure everything out and teach me how to fight anyone who wants to hurt me."

"What about Jayce?" she asked softly. The enforcer had been by the house every day and he'd called too many times to count. While December might not have exactly liked the guy in the beginning, it was obvious he cared for Kat and would do anything for her.

Kat's eyes immediately shuttered. She shrugged jerkily. "What about him? He didn't want me before. Just because I'm like him now doesn't mean he gets a second chance." Her voice was distant yet somehow bitter.

December decided not to push the subject. Not now anyway. Kat had too much on her plate and she just wanted to be supportive of her friend. So she changed the subject. "You need help with anything?"

Kat shook her head. "Nah, chili's almost done and I've got French bread in the oven. Should be done in twenty minutes."

"Okay, I'm going to freshen up and . . ." She trailed off at the sound of the doorbell.

"I'm not available if it's Jayce." Kat turned back to the stove after that, effectively cutting off any argument.

Sighing, December headed for the front door. When she looked through the peephole and saw her brother, sweat blossomed across her forehead. Without wasting time, she slung open the door. She wanted to hug Parker but didn't know why he was here or if he'd even return the embrace. They hadn't talked since before he'd been shot, and she hadn't realized until that moment how much she ached to see and talk to him. No matter what his issues with shifters, he'd always be the big brother who'd bandaged her scrapes and checked her closet for monsters when she'd been a little girl.

Wearing jeans and a dark cashmere sweater, Parker stood on her front porch looking as nervous as she'd ever seen him. Part of a white bandage was visible from the top of his sweater, wrapping back around over his shoulder. "Hey."

"Hi." She'd never felt weird around her brother, but after calling him a hundred times and trying to see him over and over, she didn't know what to say and was a little afraid of his rejection. "Uh, do you want to come in? Kat made dinner."

He swallowed hard and nodded. "That'd be great."

Once inside they didn't make it past the foyer. He jerked to a sudden stop and wiped his hands on his pants. "I'm sorry for being such an asshole. You can date whoever you want. I had a lot of time in the hospital to think about what a jerk I've been. And Ana stopped by to see me and politely told me how stupid I was being to my little sister. A relative stranger shouldn't have been there reminding me that family sticks by one another. She didn't admit it, but I think the only reason she was there was at Liam's request?" It came out as a question.

When December gave a slight nod, he continued. "On an intellectual level I know Liam's pack had nothing to do with Brandon's death, but it doesn't make it any less hard for me. Every time I see Liam or any of his pack, I'm reminded about Brandon, but mainly I'm reminded of how I failed him. I should have gotten there faster that day." He swallowed hard, but all December could do was shake her head.

There was nothing either of them could have done differently. It had taken a long time for her to get to that realization, but eventually she'd had to bury the guilt. If not, she'd have drowned in it.

Parker scrubbed a hand over his face before continuing. "I know Liam's not a bad guy. He's saved your life multiple times and for that I'll always be grateful. I should have said it before, but whatever you do with him—marry him, mate him, whatever—as long as you're happy, you have my blessing. I still want you in my life . . . if you can forgive me."

She stood there a moment in stunned silence. That was the most she'd ever heard her brother say at once. The stark emotion in his voice tugged at her heartstrings. Shaking her head, she pulled her brother into a tight hug.

When he grunted as if in pain, she immediately stepped back. "Did I hurt you?"

Wincing, he shook his head. "Not really. I'm just sore.... Are we going to be okay?"

Her throat thick, she nodded. She'd been a wreck the past few days and she didn't want to start crying again. If she did, she'd never stop. "You're my family." It was as simple as that.

A relaxed smile broke out on his face. "The dinner offer still stand?"

Grinning, she nodded again. "Yeah, come on."

In the kitchen they found the table already set and Kat scooping chili into their bowls. From what December knew, Parker couldn't have been out of the hospital long, but she guessed he'd be up to date on the bodies the sheriff's department "discovered" a couple days ago. He wouldn't know about Kat, though. No one except the people who'd been there that night did.

"Hey, Parker, good to see you out of the hospital.... December, will you pour me a glass of wine?" Kat asked.

"Nice outfit, Kat. Little early to be in your pj's, isn't it?" he jokingly asked as he grabbed a beer from the fridge.

December tensed for a moment, but Kat just rolled her eyes, so she poured two glasses for them. Once they sat, he surprised her by talking about the ranch. "I don't know if it was from the Armstrong pack, but thanks to an anonymous tip we found a bunch of bodies buried a few miles south of that Dogwood House."

December immediately clutched her spoon tighter as she stilled. She didn't look at Kat but out of the corner of her eye watched her stiffen too.

"So you two did know about it?" Parker asked with

one eyebrow raised. When they didn't respond, he shook his head and took another bite of chili. "Good chili, Kat."

"What does this mean exactly?" December hedged.

He shrugged. "We're not sure. Some of those bodies have been there for a while. They've all got ties to a couple right-wing hate groups and they were all killed with the same knife. Looks like whoever owns that property— or lived there—killed and disposed of them there. Until we figure out where the owner is, we don't have much to go on."

December pushed out a short sigh of relief. As long as those deaths didn't get tied to Liam's pack and no one found out what had happened to Kat, she didn't care.

After her third bite, she put her spoon down again and pressed an unsteady hand to her stomach.

Kat reached out for her. "You okay? Is it the chili?"

Afraid to open her mouth, she shook her head and bolted from the seat. Knowing she wouldn't make it to her bathroom upstairs, she hurried to the one off the closest hallway. She'd barely flipped the toilet seat up when she violently emptied the contents of her stomach.

The heaving and retching seemed to go on forever. Her stomach muscles clenched and tightened in pain as she puked until finally she was just dry heaving.

A knock on the door made her wince. "You okay in there?" Parker asked.

After shutting the lid, she grabbed some toilet paper and wiped her mouth. "Fine," she gasped out even though she felt dizzy and unnaturally weak.

Reaching up, she tried to grasp on to the back of the toilet for support. Instead she knocked over the small vase on the back of it. It tumbled to the tile and shattered.

The door flew open. Parker stood in the doorway with Kat right behind him.

"I just got sick," she mumbled, trying to regain her focus.

Her brother reached down and tried to help her up. When he did, she pressed down with one hand to push herself up and was met with sharp shards of broken glass.

"Ah," she cried out, and immediately withdrew her hand. Her brother lifted her up until she was sitting on the closed lid.

"Hold out your hand," he ordered softly.

Still feeling woozy, she didn't fight him.

"I'll grab a broom and dustpan," Kat said before disappearing.

With each tiny shard he pulled out, she winced. Trickles of blood rolled across her open palm, but none of the cuts were particularly deep.

After he'd gotten them all out, he stretched her hand out toward the sink. "I'm just going to rinse this to get the blood and any tiny slivers off."

"Okay." As the water rushed over her, she stared in confusion as the blood washed away. Shaking her head, she blinked and looked at her hand. "Do you see that?" There was nothing there. No puncture marks or cuts. It was as if her hand had healed in seconds. And it didn't hurt anymore.

Parker looked at her curiously. "Did Liam bite you or mark you in any way during . . . ah . . ."

Feeling her cheeks heat up, she shook her head. "*No* . . . and let's not even go there." She stared at her open palm. "This is really weird." As she tried to think of what other options there might be, bile rose in her throat again. Sliding off the toilet, she flipped it open again and just dry heaved into it. Her throat and stomach ached, but she couldn't stop.

"Either you have food poisoning or you're pregnant."

Kat's voice from the doorway startled her into looking up.

Broom in hand, her friend stared at her knowingly. Pregnant? December couldn't even think about that right now. Unable to respond, she just shook her head and shooed them away. If she was going to do this, it was going to be in privacy.

A couple hours later, December munched on a plain unsalted cracker and stared at the small boxes on her coffee table.

"You've got to take it sometime. And I'm sorry but it's the one thing I can't do for you. Considering I put on clothes and went out in public for you, you're doing this tonight." Kat's voice was wry and slightly amused.

After her brother had left, Kat had gone to the local pharmacy and picked up a couple pregnancy tests. Well, more than a couple. She'd gotten every brand.

The thought that she was somehow pregnant was crazy. Liam had always used condoms and it should be too soon to tell anyway. Sighing, she set the packet of crackers down and grabbed the box on top. "Fine."

She wasn't pregnant. She just couldn't be.

Chapter 21

Liam scrubbed a hand over his face and collapsed onto the couch. Only ten minutes until the next pack meeting and he wished it were already over. After almost four entire days without talking to December, Liam was ready to hurt someone. Namely himself. This self-induced torture was killing him. It was as if liquid silver were slowly eating away at his flesh and his insides, but he just wouldn't die from the pain. Even though he'd been working with the pack chasing down leads on the APL in surrounding areas, all he'd been able to think about was her. What was she doing? Was she thinking about him? And if she was, just how pissed was she? This foreign, twisting ache in his chest was something he could do without. He'd assumed that after a couple of days the distance between them would be easier. But it had only gotten worse. He couldn't sleep and even shifting and running in his animal form brought him no pleasure.

He hated how they'd left things. Well, how he'd left things. She'd called him a coward and now he wondered if she was right. Not contacting her was the hardest thing he'd ever done. And it was obvious she wasn't going to leave town. Not that it was fair he'd ever asked her to in the first place. This was her home. She'd been here for a lot longer than he'd known her. On a logical, human level, he knew that. It was just that—

"Uncle Liam!" He turned at the sound of Vivian in the doorway. With a chocolate-covered cupcake in her hand, she smiled broadly and raced toward him. As the little she-cat started to dive for the couch, she froze, then climbed up next to him using her free hand. "Ana would *not* be happy if I got chocolate on her couch," she said seriously.

Liam bit back a grin. "You could probably blame it on me and get away with it." Vivian's dark eyes lit up and Liam shook his head. "Don't get any ideas, cub."

She crossed her legs and twisted on the couch to face him. "What are you doing here? I thought Ana said you were out patrolling."

"We have a pack meeting soon."

"Oh. That's probably why Noel made all those cookies. Where's your girlfriend? She's pretty. I thought she was going to start living with us. I know she owns a bookstore and I wanted to ask her something." Vivian shot words at him like machine-gun fire while staring intently.

Liam tried to wade through everything Vivian had just said. "She's not my girlfriend anymore."

"What did you do wrong?"

He smiled wryly at her assumption he'd done something wrong. Not wanting to have this conversation with a ten-year-old jaguar cub who would surely repeat every word to Ana, he cleared his throat. "Shouldn't you be in school?" While Vivian and Lucas, the other wolf cub who lived with their pack, didn't go to regular school, they were homeschooled by Esperanze, a sweet beta female recently mated to one of their warriors. Ryan used to homeschool them, but since they'd moved to the ranch, the beta female had taken over the duties, since she was more qualified and genuinely seemed to enjoy it more.

She rolled her eyes. "It's Saturday. *Duh.* So what did you do to make your girlfriend mad?"

"It's complicated."

Vivian snorted loudly in the same manner he'd seen Ana do when annoyed with her mate. The little she-cat was definitely taking after Ana.

He raised an eyebrow. "That's funny, cub?"

"Whenever Connor says something is complicated, Ana calls him a bad word. Well, I don't think it's really bad. It means a donkey's butt, but I'm still not allowed to say it. I tried once and Ana took away my horse-riding privileges for a *whole day*." She shuddered and scooted off the couch, cupcake still firmly in hand. "I hope you and your girlfriend work things out."

"Me too." As soon as he said the words, he realized he meant it. He couldn't live like this. Not without December. It was like living without a limb. Since it was obvious she wasn't going to leave town, staying apart didn't really make her any safer, and it drove him crazy worrying about her. He wanted to be the one protecting her instead of other wolves from his pack.

Vivian looked longingly at her cupcake, then at him, as if fighting a decision. Finally she shoved it in his direction. "It's the last one. You need it more than me." When he didn't take it, she sat it on his outstretched leg before running out and yelling for Noel that she needed a cookie.

Smiling, he picked it up and shook his head as Erin strolled into the room. Her eyes widened when she saw what he had. "Are there cupcakes?"

"Last one." He grinned and took a bite of it.

"Figures." Sighing, Erin sat on the love seat opposite him.

"I think there might be cookies in the kitchen." Before the words were out, she had jumped up and was heading in that direction.

Liam ate half the cupcake, then set it on the coffee table. It was good but it might as well have been cardboard going down his throat. As other pack members and Brianna, the fae warrior they'd found the same night as Kat, filed into the room, he grunted acknowledgments to them but otherwise didn't talk.

Even though he wanted to sulk in his own pathetic thoughts, he tried to shake visions of December and her last parting words from his head.

"You okay?" Brianna, the soft-spoken fae, surprised him with her question. She sat on the opposite couch next to Noah.

"Yeah." He managed a half smile for her, but by the way she drew back from him, it probably came off as a snarl.

He rubbed a hand over his face. Brianna had filled them in about her time with Adler and the other APL members and today they were supposed to get updates from her boss—or bosses—or whomever—on what their next step was. He knew they weren't happy she'd failed her mission to ferret out Adler's boss, but from what he could tell, she hadn't had much of a choice. What little he knew about the fae was that some of them had powerful psychic gifts, and her powers had been so drained from keeping that evil psycho Adler under her control that she'd passed out after killing him. And she couldn't have known she had backup in the form of shifters on the way.

The two other humans there could have killed her while she'd been unconscious. Since it had taken her almost an entire day to recover from her comalike trance after expending so much of her energy, she'd clearly been prepared to die for a stranger. It was hard to ignore that kind of bravery.

Liam and his brother had every reason in the world to hate the fae considering they'd killed their father and original pack, but if he and his brother lumped all of them into the same category, they'd be no better than the APL. And as far as Liam was concerned, Brianna had proved herself by risking her own life to try to save Kat. Because of that, she had the full protection of the pack until she decided to leave the area.

As everyone around him chatted, Liam tuned them out until he saw Ana in the doorway. "Connor's on his way," she murmured to him. Thanks to his extrasensory abilities he could hear her over the dull roar of conversation.

He nodded. "Thanks." At least the meeting would be starting soon. Maybe then he could tune out thoughts of a naked, writhing, willing December underneath him. Though he seriously doubted it. While he missed the sex, that wasn't the only thing he missed. He missed everything about her. Her calming spirit, her undying loyalty to those she cared about, even the way she fought with him. She wasn't afraid to stand up to him and he loved that. Hell, he loved everything about her. Now he was afraid he'd screwed everything up.

After a full night's sleep, December was only more pissed than she'd been last night. When her first pregnancy test had come back positive, she'd been sure it was a fluke.

Ten positive tests, however, were *not* a fluke.

Ready to face the inevitable, she steered her car up to the closed gate at the Armstrong ranch. A lock was in place, but she didn't let it stop her. Slamming her car door, she marched up to the fence and climbed it. As she dropped down onto the ground, she spotted Connor jogging across the yard toward her from the direction of the barn.

"December? Is everything okay?" He asked as he stopped in front of her.

"That's a loaded question," she muttered. "I need to see your brother."

"He's out on patrol right now."

She crossed her arms over her chest. "Fine. I'll wait for him."

"He's going to be gone for a while. I can tell him you stopped by." His voice was placating and annoying and she wasn't having any of it.

Behind her she heard another vehicle pull up. Without looking, she knew it was her shadow, one of Liam's packmates. She hadn't recognized him, but he was huge just like the rest of the Armstrong pack. And she hadn't been surprised when he'd started following her from her house to the ranch.

Reaching into her purse, she pulled out one of the many pregnancy tests she'd brought with her and held it out for Connor. When he looked at it, his entire face softened. "Shit." He winced, then met her gaze again. "Come on. Liam's at my place." He tried to place a gentle hand on her elbow, but she shrugged him off.

He'd just lied to her face when he'd told her Liam was on patrol, so he could shove it too. That knowledge only served to ratchet up her anger even more. The closer she got to the house, the more the rage burned through her.

Like fast-moving lava, it was eating up all her reasoning powers. She knew that it had taken two to get her pregnant, but right now she wanted Liam's head on a platter.

The man had pursued her relentlessly for over a month; then once she'd finally allowed herself to care for him, even at the cost of her brother, he'd turned his back on her. Now to find out she was pregnant, she didn't know what to feel. She just knew she was spitting mad and someone was going to feel her wrath.

Connor opened the front door and led her inside. "If you'll just wait here—"

"I don't think so." She stomped farther inside and headed for the living room, to where she heard voices. Liam sat around a coffee table with five other people. Three males and Erin and the blond woman from the other night.

When he saw her, he immediately stood. Concern was etched in every line of his handsome face. "Is everything all right?"

She didn't give a damn that they had an audience for this. Still holding the positive pregnancy test, she looked at it, then threw it at him. "You tell me!"

He caught it midair. When he looked at it, his eyes widened. He met her angry stare with confusion. "We used condoms. Lots of them. Maybe this is a mistake."

At the word "mistake" her heart cracked. She wasn't exactly sure what she was feeling right now, but the word "mistake" had never entered her mind. Gritting her teeth, she pulled out a handful of the other tests and threw those at him. They clattered to the floor at his feet. "Are these mistakes too? Your super sperm apparently has no problem battling mere condoms!"

At the word "sperm," the others in the room quickly scurried out. As she stared at him, she'd never felt more lost in her life. Her throat was thick and she couldn't help the small tremor that raced through her. "Aren't you going to say something?"

He swallowed hard but still didn't say anything. Instead of anger at his silence, a terrible hollowness filled her chest. Even when he hadn't returned her calls, she'd figured they still had a chance. He'd freaked out and emotions had been high, but this . . . nonresponsiveness was too much.

Fighting back the tears burning her eyes, she turned and ran out the door.

Liam stared at the plus sign on the white stick in his hand and tried to catch his breath. December had asked him something. She was looking at him expectantly, but he couldn't think straight. He was going to be a father. He didn't know how that was possible, but holy shit, it was true.

When December turned away from him, his entire body jerked to life. He couldn't let her go. Not again.

The past few days he hadn't been able to sleep. Had barely been able to eat. The whole pack had been following up on leads and checking into local APL members, but he'd been functioning on autopilot. Without December he was absolutely lost.

He still didn't understand how his brother had walked away from Ana all those years ago. The pain inside him right now was like tiny razors shredding away at his soul. If that's what his brother had gone through for all those years, then he was a better man than he. Liam was too selfish to walk away from December, no matter what he'd said to her days ago.

"December!" He caught up to her halfway across the yard. Damn, the woman was fast. Grabbing her arm, he pulled her to a stop.

When she turned to face him, her blue eyes were bright with unshed tears. The sight was like a punch to his gut. She looked down at where his hand still held her upper arm and jerked away from him.

He hated the pain he saw in her eyes and knew he had to make it right. "I'm sorry. You just took me by surprise."

"Whatever." She started to turn away from him, but he gently held her arm again.

"I don't know how this happened, but are you ... okay?" God, the question sounded lame to his own ears, but he didn't know what to say. Or even if there was a right thing to say in this situation.

"I don't know what I am. I cut myself last night and healed instantly. What's going on with me?"

Oh, shit. He'd heard of what happened when shifters got humans pregnant, but it had been centuries ago. If a woman was in heat, shifters stayed away. Or used protection. Which was exactly why he'd used condoms. It wasn't as if he could get any STDs or give them for that matter, so he hadn't even bothered to explain to her about all that. He'd used condoms because she'd been ovulating. He thought she'd been perfectly safe from pregnancy. He snorted at the word "safe." Lot of good that had done them.

"Is this funny to you?" she practically shrieked.

Shit. She was going to hate him even more when he told her the truth. "No! I don't know how you got pregnant. . . . Well, I know *how*, but I didn't think it was possible since we used protection. I never meant to do this to you, I swear. I'd heard about this happening, but it's been so long and—"

"Spit it out, Liam. I want details, not excuses." She crossed her arms over her chest as she continued to glare at him.

Why couldn't there be an easier way to explain this?
"When a human female becomes pregnant by a shifter,
she . . . her body adapts to that of her child. In shifter
terms it means we're mates."

"I thought you said I'd have to be your bondmate
to . . . change to be like you. I didn't think I could just
become your mate unless I was a shifter."

He nodded again. "Under any other circumstance, a
human can't become a shifter's mate. Well, technically I
guess she can, but her life span would still be that of a
human. To be a bondmate, I'd have to take you from
behind and sink my canines into your neck as we made
love under the full moon. I didn't even think *this* was
possible." He held out one of the sticks she'd thrown at
him.

For a moment she eyed him curiously. "That's how the
bonding process works? I thought . . ." She shook her
head angrily. "So I'm a shifter now? Does that mean I'll
live as long as you? And will my baby come out as . . . ?"

Feeling miserable and even guiltier, he nodded. "I
swear I never meant to do this to you. Your life span will
be substantially longer, like mine, but your—our baby
will be born human. I didn't shift for the first time until I
was four and that's pretty normal for most shifters."

When she wrapped her arms around herself, he
wanted to reach out and pull her into his arms. Tell her
everything would be okay. But he didn't know how to
voice that. He could smell the fear and confusion rolling
off her. Maybe she was afraid of what the town would
think. Or maybe she was afraid of him. That thought was
excruciating. He could deal with anything she threw at
him, but not her fear. "I promise that no matter what
happens, I'll make sure you and the baby are taken care

of. If you don't want to live here, that's fine. I'll work something out, buy you a place anywhere you want."

She stared at him for a moment, then shoved him in the chest. Hard. "I never thought I'd say this, Liam Armstrong, but you're a Grade A asshole." Then she spun around and headed for the gate.

He started to go after her but didn't know what to say. Or what he'd said wrong. He needed to figure some shit out first. Figure out how they were going to make this work. If she didn't want to move, would he live with her? Would she live at the ranch? And more important, he desperately needed to figure out how to knock down the walls between them. She was his and this divide between them was his fault.

The last few days without her had been the worst days of his life. Nothing could have prepared him for the ache that had settled inside him and spread bone deep.

"You just gonna let her go?" Erin's soft voice startled him as she sidled up next to him.

He hadn't even heard the she-wolf approach, which said a lot for how messed up he was. "She's angry."

"Duh. I don't blame her either. You're acting like an idiot." She shook her head disapprovingly.

He glared down at her. "What the hell do you know?"

"I know that December is one of the nicest, strongest humans I've ever met. I know that she gave up a lot to be with you. Then when *you* decided that you thought it would be best, you pulled away from her like an idiot. Then, after she's probably had the worst couple weeks of her life, including her brother being in the hospital and seeing her best friend bloody and standing at death's door, you barely touch her or console her afterward. Then you kick her out of your life. And now she's pregnant? So you, what, tell her you'll take care of her or find her someplace to live? Dumb, dumb, dumb."

"I *will* take care of her," he growled. Why the hell was the she-wolf eavesdropping anyway?

She shook her head again and this time a spark of undeniable annoyance popped off her as she turned away.

Gritting his teeth, he let her leave and turned back toward December, who was already heading back down the drive. As the weight of Erin's words sank in, he realized what he had to do.

Chapter 22

Wearing a long-sleeved pink and red striped pajama set, December savored the warmth of the thick flannel material. Curled up on her couch, she took another bite of rocky road ice cream while she waited for Kat to return.

They'd decided to have a girls' night complete with ice cream, movies, and wine. . . . Well, Kat was drinking. December wasn't.

Kat walked back into the living room carrying a bowl of popcorn and collapsed on the couch next to her. "Want some?"

December shook her head and took another cold bite. "No thanks." She planned to eat her weight in ice cream tonight. Liam was such a jackass and hadn't even tried to contact her all day. Even after her parents had died, she hadn't felt so abandoned and alone. Right now, it was as if her heart had been ripped out and she didn't know that things would ever be right in her world again. After everything they'd shared, she'd expected more from him. Especially now.

Looked like men were the same, no matter the species.

As she started to press play, the doorbell rang. Kat sat straight up against the couch and shot December a nervous glance. "It's Liam," she whispered.

December frowned. "How do you know?"

"I can smell him. Or—I think it's him. I'm still getting used to this heightened-senses stuff," she whispered again.

Gritting her teeth, December looked away from her friend and back at the television. Now that she concentrated, she could actually smell him too. Ana had called December after she'd left the ranch that morning, because she'd been worried about her—and the other woman had promised to come by tomorrow to answer all December's questions about the changes she was going through—but Ana had already explained that Kat had more noticeable abilities since she'd been bitten. Since December was pregnant by a shifter, she had heightened senses—which made her nausea even worse—but she wouldn't fully develop all her extrasensory abilities until after her baby was born. Ana had also explained that even though December's body had adapted to her child's, her strength level would remain human until later. It was all too much to digest right now. And seeing Liam would just make it that much harder after the way he'd acted earlier. Pretending not to notice the faint masculine scent that reminded her of the forest in spring subtly twining around her, she pressed play.

"What are you doing?" Kat sat her popcorn bowl down and started to get up.

"Do not answer that! I don't want to see him." She did, but not right now. Not when her head was so messed up. He'd ignored her all day. He could suffer too.

Her friend eyed her disbelievingly and sat back on the couch. "You're sure?"

"What if it was Jayce at the door?"

Nodding, she picked her bowl up and sat fully back. "Good point."

When the doorbell sounded again, she turned the volume up. After the way he'd tried to brush her off earlier, telling her he'd take care of her or move her out of town as if she were some shameful secret, she had a lot of things she wanted to tell him but knew all she'd do was cry if confronted now. Next time they met, she wanted a level head.

Next the banging started but she ignored that too. Rolling her eyes, she shoved the thick blanket off and headed for the kitchen. As she put the ice cream back in the freezer, she heard the movie stop; then the front door opened.

When she heard Kat and Liam talking, she wanted to scream. What the hell? A few seconds later Kat walked into the kitchen. "I want to watch the movie and we can't do that with all that racket. Just talk to him, please."

December knew Kat didn't give a crap about the movie. She started to respond when Liam stepped into the kitchen.

"And that's my cue to leave." Kat quickly disappeared, leaving her alone with Liam.

He had bags under his eyes. She'd noticed it at the ranch, but they seemed more pronounced now under the bright lights of her kitchen. Some perverse part of her was happy he wasn't sleeping well.

When he took a couple more steps inside, she moved back until she hit the counter. She wanted to curse herself for showing weakness, but the reaction was instinctive.

Liam stopped dead in his tracks and spread his hands out. "I'm so sorry, December."

"For what?"

"For everything."

She glared at him. "It's easy to say that. What are you sorry for?"

"For . . . abandoning you when you needed me most. I saw how messed up Jayce was when Kat got taken and I thought . . . I thought it'd be easier on you if I was out of your life. I've brought you nothing but pain since we've met. You never would have been a target if not for me. I thought . . ." He shook his head slowly.

"You thought you'd make a decision about *our* future without consulting me?"

He jerked back at her question. "It wasn't like that."

"It's *exactly* like that. Since we've met, you do things *you* think are right without asking me first." She took a few steps closer to him, needing to fill some of the gap. Needing to gain control.

When she did, he also took a few tentative steps toward her but didn't respond.

"So why are you here?" She tried to keep her voice cold but couldn't. It cracked on the last word. He still hadn't explained himself.

Taking her off guard, he fell to his knees in a completely submissive position. "To beg your forgiveness and ask you to take me back. When I said I'd take care of you and the baby, I meant it, but I think you misunderstood what I said. I didn't mean without me. Unless you want to live without me of course." When she didn't respond, he shoved his hands in his pockets and suddenly looked so lost and confused, it made her anger waver.

Hating to see him like this, she covered the distance

between them until they were inches apart. Grabbing his hands, she tugged on him so he'd stand.

His dark eyes instantly flared with undeniable lust and she smelled something . . . spicy, masculine. Maybe it was an effect of the pregnancy. Or maybe she was just scenting his lust. "Will I turn into a wolf now too?" she blurted. She hadn't had any weird animal urges and she'd been so angry earlier she'd forgotten to ask. When she'd spoken to Ana, her anger had faded, but by then she'd been too afraid of the answer, so she'd skirted the subject, figuring she'd find out when Ana came to see her.

Half smiling, he reached out and cupped her cheek gently. "Not while you're pregnant, but later you will. . . . Speaking of, you need to see a doctor soon. A shifter doctor. I found one in the next county who handles pregnancies."

Even though she was still confused about her feelings, she stepped closer into his embrace and wrapped her arms around his waist. The feel of all that raw strength brought back so many naked images, but she forced them away. They still needed to talk. "Why can't I go to mine? I thought you said the baby would be born . . . human."

He nodded. "He will, but . . . shifter pregnancies are shorter by about two months. That's probably why you got sick so fast. I don't really know, though. This is all new to me too. I was only eight when my father's pack . . . uh, well, when my first pack died. I don't have much experience with cubs."

"Wait, did you say *he*? You know something I don't?" Her eyebrows lifted.

"We're having a boy. I don't think I can deal with a girl." He actually looked terrified at the thought.

"Are you going to love this baby any less if it *is* a girl?"

"No! I just . . . I don't know what I'd do with a girl. And if she looked like you, I'd be screwed. You two would gang up on me and get your way with everything, I know it."

Clenching her jaw against a smile, she shook her head. "It'd serve you right to have a little girl." She chewed on her bottom lip for a moment when he didn't respond. "I'm still pretty mad at you."

"I'm still mad at myself." He tightened his arms around her.

From where they stood, she had a clear shot of the hallway that led to the front door. For the first time since he'd arrived, she noticed two big bags sat in the foyer. "What are those?"

"If you'll have me, I plan on staying here with you. I know living on the ranch would be too hard on you and—"

She stiffened slightly. "You assumed I'd forgive you?"

He winced and shook his head. "No, I just hoped."

"I need to know something, and you better not lie to me. If I wasn't pregnant, would you still be standing here in front of me?"

"Yes." His answer was immediate and soothing. He reached up and took her face between his big hands. The contact sent tingles scattering across her skin, and when she met his eyes, she saw the depth of his feelings for her. They were raw and primal and he wasn't holding anything back from her now. "I love you, December. The short time apart was enough to kill me. It made me realize I'm not strong enough to walk away from you. Life isn't going to be easy for you in the beginning. Not all people accept shifters and—"

"I don't care about that. And don't ever try to make a decision about our future or my life without consulting me first. I won't live like that." She *couldn't* live like that.

"I won't, but I probably will screw up from time to time. You bring out all my protective instincts." His deep voice enveloped her like a warm embrace. One she'd been desperately craving the past few days.

Smiling at his honesty, she leaned up on her tiptoes. "I love you too, Liam."

A low growl tore from him and those dark eyes of his went molten hot as he covered her mouth with his in a hungry, frantic dance. She couldn't help it. Tears sprang to her eyes and spilled down her cheeks. When he tasted the saltiness, he pulled back, uneasiness in his gaze.

"These are happy tears. I'm pregnant, I can't help it," she murmured.

Immediately he broke into a wide grin. "You're going to be a great mom."

The statement surprised her. She hadn't really thought about it. Except for the morning sickness, it almost didn't feel real. Her eyebrows pulled down as another thought occurred to her.

"What is it?"

"So what exactly . . . uh, do shifters get . . ." Crap, she didn't want to be the one to bring up marriage, but she didn't know if shifters even got married. She knew that bondmates stayed together forever. Or she thought they did. But if she understood correctly, mates could still leave each other. And he hadn't said anything else about bonding.

"Do you not think I'll be a good dad?" The question was asked with such raw honesty she jerked back. His dark eyes were filled with concern and uncertainty.

She shook her head. "No! I mean, of course I think

you'll be a wonderful dad. Probably too overprotective, but that's okay. I just wondered if shifters married or, uh, not that I think we should get married just because—"

His lips covered hers again. This time not so demanding. Just sweet, probing, and made her abdomen clench with need. No one could ever make her feel as good as this man.

When one of his hands grabbed her behind and pulled her flush against his erection, she moaned at the feel of him. But when he grabbed her left hand and slipped something onto her ring finger, she pulled back.

Staring, her eyes widened at the glittering diamond on her ring finger. The marquise cut was at least two carats. And damn near flawless. Her chest tightened for a moment, but she found her breath. "What the heck is this?"

"I think it's called an engagement ring. I spent most of the day trying to pick the perfect one, so I hope you like it," he said quietly.

"Is this . . . are you proposing?"

He tightly gripped her hand. "Marry me."

"Okay," she whispered.

That's all he needed to hear. His mouth sought hers out so quickly she barely had time to catch her breath. The man was so dominating and stubborn she knew this wouldn't be the last argument they ever had, but as long as he stayed by her side, she knew they could handle anything.

Chapter 23

One month later

Yawning, December stretched her arms above her head and rolled over to see her clock. The digital screen said six thirty. She'd been so tired lately, barely making it to work on time every morning. This was the first morning since she'd discovered she was pregnant she felt alert. Her doctor had told her she'd eventually get over her sluggishness and morning sickness, but she'd been hesitant to believe her when all she ever wanted to do was sleep.

Big, callused hands encircled her waist from behind and pulled her close. Liam nuzzled the back of her neck as his hand trailed from her still-flat belly to cover her mound. Idly, he rubbed her clit in slow, soothing strokes. "You too tired this morning?" he whispered.

Smiling, she shook her head. If he kept touching her like that, she'd climax before he ever got inside her. Despite the morning sickness, she'd been incredibly receptive to his touch the past month. Even more so than before.

Everything was heightened. More intense.

As she started to turn over, he held her still and entered her from behind. The abrupt intrusion made her gasp in pure pleasure. She was used to his size by now, but she hadn't been ready for him. Her inner walls flexed and clenched around him. Keeping still, he stayed buried deep inside her and kept strumming her sensitive bundle of nerves.

With his teeth, he raked over the skin under her ear. She shivered as he quickly covered the area with moist kisses.

The feel of him inside her drove her crazy. Her entire body was now tingling in awareness and she needed him to move. "Move or do something," she ordered.

Inside her he felt thick and so familiar, but she needed more if she wanted to find relief.

"So demanding this morning," he murmured, and rolled his hips against her once. "You don't think I should tease you?"

"It's too early for that." She half turned so he could kiss her mouth.

When his lips covered hers, she lightly moaned. Waking up to him every morning hadn't gotten old. If anything, she loved it more every day.

After he tore his mouth away, he nibbled lightly on her shoulder. "Tonight's a full moon." His voice was quiet, hesitant.

She understood why. They'd talked about officially bonding almost immediately after he'd placed that engagement ring on her finger. Even though they'd both wanted to, he'd insisted she think more about it. Bonding was different from being mated. When shifters bonded, it was for life. Unlike mated shifters who could leave or divorce each other, bonded mates couldn't. They were marked and linked until one of them died. No other wolf would touch a marked one. It went against their nature and laws.

And she desperately wanted that mark from him. "I don't need more time to think, Liam."

He growled softly and pulled out of her. Instantly her body mourned the loss, but he quickly turned her on her back. And just as quickly he settled between her open thighs and pushed into her again.

She could tell by his relaxed expression that this morning would be slow and gentle. Some days he got this wild, almost feral look and he'd often take her the moment she got home from work. Not now. When he took his time like this, it turned her inside out.

"I want you to be sure," he breathed against her cheek.

Running her fingers down the corded muscles of his back, she kept her stroking light until she reached his backside. Then she dug into his skin and held him deep in her.

"It seems like you're the one with the problem, so if you want to wait—"

He cut her off with a searing kiss. Inwardly she smiled because she knew her words hit their mark. As their tongues intertwined, both their movements increased.

He pushed into her harder and faster and she met him stroke for stroke. Rolling her hips against his, she savored the feel of his thick length filling her. The more he thrust, the faster her inner walls contracted. The past few days she'd been too tired to do anything, but now her body was primed and ready for release.

By the tense lines of his body, she could tell he was close, was holding back for her. Liam certainly had no problem with stamina, but if they went more than a day or two without making love, he was always slightly frantic the first time. She loved that she knew that about him. Knew all the little nuances of his body.

As her breasts rubbed against his hard chest, the extra stimulation against her nipples pushed her over the edge. Clutching on to his back, she arched her own and let the climax rush through her.

The wild sensation surged through her, sending tingles straight to all her nerve endings. He wasn't far behind her. As soon as she let go, he did too. With a groan, he clutched her hips and emptied himself inside her. His orgasm was longer than usual as he continued thrusting until finally his hips stilled and he laid his forehead against hers.

"I love you, December." His voice was quiet and completely sincere, and it pulled at her heartstrings.

"Me too," she whispered back as she tightened her grip around him.

Instead of moving off her, he stayed where he was and lazily kissed her until a knock at the door tore them apart.

"Uh, guys?" It was Kat and she likely had an idea they were awake or she wouldn't have knocked. "I'm sorry to, uh, bother you, but I think you need to come downstairs and see the news." Blatant concern laced her words.

December heard her hurry away from the door without waiting for their answer. In a few weeks they'd be moving out of the house and back to the ranch and she had a feeling Kat was more than ready for that. Kat had changed a lot over the past month, gotten a lot stronger, and when she'd made plans to move out of the house, December and Liam had decided to just move back to the ranch. That way Kat could stay here and December wouldn't have to worry about selling her home.

Liam spent most of his free time at the ranch and she knew how much he hated being away from his pack—her pack now too. That was still a weird thought. One she hadn't totally adjusted to. Since she couldn't shift yet, she didn't really feel like she was a shifter. It didn't matter that her healing abilities or her life span matched Liam's—the reality hadn't quite set in yet.

They quickly dressed and hurried downstairs. Kat sat perched on the edge of the couch with a coffee cup in hand. She nodded at the television, so December and Liam sat next to her. "This is a replay from earlier," Kat quickly said as Liam turned up the volume.

Wearing a green peacoat and white scarf, a pretty blond reporter stood in front of the Fontana sheriff's department, microphone in hand. *"Is there a cover-up going on in the Fontana Sheriff's Office? Some people think so. With the recent rash of animal attacks in the surrounding areas, some locals are crying foul play. Others are more insistent that Sheriff Parker McIntyre is covering up for the Armstrong pack because his sister is now married to one of their pack members. . . ."*

December felt the blood drain from her face as the woman continued talking. As the reporter spoke, Liam squeezed her thigh gently.

"This will pass. It's probably some APL members trying to stir up trouble," he murmured.

She gritted her teeth. "They do it because your Council doesn't do anything about it. They never speak out when these people talk trash. If we have no one to defend us, people are only going to hear one side. And now my brother's name has been brought into it. That reporter basically called him corrupt!" December and Parker and even Liam and Parker had gotten so much closer this past month, and she hated the thought of anything tearing

them apart. And she really hated the thought of anyone
targeting her brother because of a bullshit newscast.

"I'm going to call him." She pushed up and stalked
from the room before Liam could stop her.

After December disappeared into the kitchen, Liam
looked at Kat. "Did the newscast say anything else?"

She shook her head and bit her bottom lip. He knew
what was on her mind and he also knew it wasn't his
business, but he decided to plunge ahead anyway. "Jayce
gets back in town today."

Instantly she bristled. "So?"

He lifted an eyebrow. "Are you going to pretend you
don't care?"

She gritted her teeth and turned back to the television. "Things would never work between us."

Liam didn't know about that. "You've got to know
how he feels about you. When you were taken—"

"I don't *ever* want to talk about that," she snapped.

He shook his head and stood. Jayce had been gone
the past month taking care of business with the Council
and other packs, but would be returning in a few days for
indefinite leave while he trained Erin, the she-wolf Jayce
believed was an enforcer. Liam wasn't sure how or why
Jayce thought she was, but he did know that Jayce could
have demanded Erin move up north and undergo the
training there. He hadn't. Instead he'd opted to move to
Fontana on a semipermanent basis and everyone knew
why: to be close to Kat.

After everything Kat had been through, Liam had
now come to think of her as a sister and he just wanted
her to be happy. Even though she'd been getting stronger
and was now learning to protect herself, lately she'd been
acting strange. Disappearing at odd hours.

It wasn't his business how she handled her stress and

for all he knew, she had a new lover. Though he really doubted that, since he couldn't scent anyone on her. She wasn't causing the pack any problems, so he had no reason to bring it up to his brother, but he'd definitely noticed her absences.

When December stepped back into the room with a frown on her face, he shoved those thoughts away and hurried toward her. Wrapping his arms around her, he pulled her close. "What did he say?"

"He said the newscast is just a stupid way to increase ratings and that I need to stop worrying and let him handle it." She snorted softly. "Like that's going to happen."

Liam held her tight. "Your brother's right. I'll call him later and see if he knows more about who leaked this info to the press."

He'd thought their battle with the APL was over, but it looked like it had only been dormant for a while. If they thought they could start shit using the media as an outlet, they were in for a surprise. The past month his pack had been gathering intel on all known APL members in the surrounding areas and if they had to fight dirty to bring the organization down, they would.

December slipped the sheer black and pink baby-doll lingerie over her head. It barely touched the top of her thighs and the almost-transparent material left nothing to the imagination. But she liked the way it hugged her curves and made her feel sexy. Besides, while she could still fit into it, she was wearing it. Liam had told her wearing anything to bed was a waste of time when he'd just take it off, but she figured he'd like this tonight. He might say one thing, but whenever she wore sexy outfits to bed, he got this hungry look that drove her wild.

And tonight was very a big deal.

Thanks to nature she was officially a shifter—some-thing she was still trying to completely grasp—but she wanted so much more than that. She wanted to be bonded to Liam in the most special way for his kind—her kind now. He'd wanted her to think about it longer before making her decision, so she had. A month later, she hadn't changed her mind and she knew she wouldn't.

December paused when she heard the front door open, then close. Next she heard the beeping of the alarm being turned off, then immediately being rearmed into stay mode. Liam was positively ruthless in keeping the house armed. Not that she had any complaints. After everything that had happened, having an alarm on when he wasn't here made her feel better. And Kat had left an hour ago for the ranch to train with Aiden, so December and Liam had the house to themselves for a while.

Perfect for what they had planned.

"December? I brought dinner home. Ana sent some *polvorones* home and Vivian wanted to make sure you knew that she helped." His voice trailed up the stairs.

December smiled at the mention of Ana and Vivian. Ana had been sending food home with Liam every other day for the past month. When she wasn't inviting them to the ranch for dinner. The entire pack had embraced her so warmly and so quickly it still amazed her. She'd never had a big family, so it was taking some getting used to. She was still getting to know Ana, but her new sister-in-law was fast becoming someone December knew she could count on for anything. The fact that she could actu-ally cook only made December love her more.

"December?" Liam called again.

"Up here."

"You hungry?"

"Oh, yeah," she murmured, but didn't say anything

else. She wanted him to come find her. She'd lit a few candles around the room—not that it mattered with his extrasensory sight—but the atmosphere was sexy. Or she hoped it was. Liam hadn't told her much about the bonding process other than how it actually went down—biologically speaking—and she wanted to make it special.

"Come on, Red, I'm starving. What are you doing up there?" The sound of Liam's heavy footsteps pounding up the stairs made her grin.

On the end of their bed, she sat on her knees and waited. He'd see exactly what she was doing soon enough.

The moment he stepped into their room, he froze. Immediately his dark eyes glazed over as he drank her in. Yep, he definitely looked hungry. For her.

She pushed up on her knees and slightly slid her legs apart. "Still starving?"

He nodded and something akin to a growl rattled in his chest. It was dark, possessive, and totally hot.

Her nipples immediately hardened at the sound. When he got to the point when words were an afterthought, she knew they were in for a long night. And she couldn't wait.

Staring at her, he slid his boots off, then shrugged out of his long-sleeved sweater. His stomach muscles bunched under her scrutiny and she didn't need any extra senses to see and hear how turned on he was. His breathing was erratic and lust seemed to pour off him in scorching waves. A spicy, pure male scent filled the room, wrapping around her like a shroud.

She knew he'd be able to scent her desire too. There was definitely no mistaking it. She'd been thinking about this all day at the bookstore and even closed her shop early so she'd have time to come home and get ready.

As her gaze slid down his chest and muscled stomach, she smiled when she landed on the top of his jeans. Right now too much clothing separated them. Before she could tell him to move his butt, he'd covered the distance between them.

Sliding his hands down her arms, he stopped once he reached the tips of her fingers. Then he slowly slid those strong, callused hands up her waist and ribs, making her shiver. Lust and obvious love shone from his heated gaze. "You wore this to drive me crazy, didn't you?"

"Of course." She smiled as he slowly lowered his mouth to hers. His kisses were soft and gentle as he explored her mouth. Her entire body hummed with excitement and she felt as if she could combust at any moment.

As their tongues and mouths intertwined, one of his hands slid across her stomach, then dipped lower until he cupped her mound. Despite the lingerie she wore, she hadn't bothered with panties. Losing them was *always* a foregone conclusion.

When he began sliding his finger along her slick folds with deliberately unhurried strokes, she moaned into his mouth. She might not mind it slow—and loved when he gave her hours of foreplay—but tonight she ached for him so bad it was all she could do to stop herself from ripping his clothes off.

Actually, that wasn't a bad idea. Reaching for the top of his jeans, she unsnapped the button and reached into his pants. Holding on to his hard length, she smiled against his mouth when his hips jerked unsteadily toward hers. She couldn't explain it, even to herself, but she felt as if she'd been waiting for this moment forever. For him.

With one hand she began slowly caressing him, from

the bottom of his shaft to the top. She slid her other hand up his stomach and chest until she grasped on to his shoulder. He growled softly and when she started pumping him at a faster tempo, Liam suddenly broke the kiss and pulled his head back. His eyes were dilated and his canines had started to protrude.

He sucked in a sharp, raspy breath. "I need to be inside you."

The way he said it completely unraveled her. There was so much warmth and love in those few words, she just came undone.

Before he could move, she grasped the hem of her nightie and tugged it over her head. As she did, he stepped out of his jeans, which had only fallen halfway down his legs. The moment she was completely bare to him, he lowered his head to her breasts and sucked one hard nipple in his mouth. Lately she was much more sensitive there and each stroke sent a pulse of pleasure shooting straight to the moist heat between her legs.

Instinctively she arched her back, wanting him to take more of her in his mouth. He ran his tongue around her areola and varied between kissing her and blowing lightly against her moist skin. The feel of his hot breath on her spiked her desire even higher.

Alternating breasts, he continued teasing her and seemed content to do nothing else. Her knees weakened, so she held on to his shoulders for support. When her fingers dug into that hard muscle, he simultaneously grasped her hips and flipped her onto her hands and knees.

Tonight was definitely it.

Her heart pounded wildly at the knowledge. The electricity in the air crackled with enough pent-up lust to set the house on fire.

She turned to look at him over her shoulder when he ran his palm down her spine. In the dimness she could clearly see his expressive need for her and for the bonding.

"You're sure this is what you want?" he rasped out.

When December nodded and smiled seductively, Liam felt his entire world shift. He felt like he'd been waiting for this moment forever.

With her in front of him like this, so trusting and all his, he finally understood the significance of taking a bondmate. She was putting all her trust in him to make sure tonight went right, to treat her right and to always protect her. She wouldn't know this, but shifters were extremely superstitious when it came to the bonding process and he refused to screw this up.

The past month he'd secretly been waiting for something else to go wrong, but each day that passed, the more he grew to love her. Finally crossing this line . . . he shuddered. Nothing would ever keep them apart again. Not even his hardheadedness. Once they were bonded, they'd be linked forever.

Running his hand down her spine again, he didn't stop this time. From behind, he reached between her legs and tested her slickness. He inserted one finger, then two, into her tight sheath. She clenched around him and moaned. The sound was barely audible and he wanted more than that from her.

He wanted her twisting underneath him and shouting his name in pleasure.

The soft candlelight played against her ivory skin, giving her an ethereal quality. With that and the mass of her shiny red hair spilling down her back, she looked like a goddess in front of him. He wanted to tell her how much she meant to him, how beautiful she looked, but he couldn't find the words.

Instead, he'd show her. Grasping her hips, he slowly pushed into her. Her inner walls tightened and molded around him as if they were made for each other. The clamp of her body around his cock was almost too much for his self-control. When he pulled back out of her, she quietly whimpered in displeasure until he moved inside her again.

His. She was his, forever.

Over and over, he pushed into her, unable to control the growing need inside him. His canines protracted with each stroke, his most primal side needing to claim her. To mark her. And be marked in return. He wanted that so badly he shook from it.

When she clutched the sheet beneath her and arched her back, she let out a long, throaty moan. "I need more," she gasped.

God, yes. And he knew exactly what she needed now. Leaning forward, he slid his hands up her ribs and cupped her breasts as his mouth met her neck.

She turned her head to the side, letting her hair fall away and giving him perfect access to her neck.

A growl rose inside him as he raked his teeth against her skin. When he did, he felt her sheath tighten around his cock. So he did it again, still not breaking the skin. And her inner walls tightened again. Gripping him like hot silk. She didn't speak, but moaned her pleasure each time he licked and nuzzled her neck.

His balls pulled up painfully with the need for release. Even though he wanted to drag this out as long as he could, he couldn't hold back any longer.

He sank his teeth into her, breaking the skin.

"Liam!" she shouted, a tremor ripping through her. Instantly she started climaxing around him.

He hadn't expected it so fast, but she jerked and

pushed back against him as she shouted out his name again. After he drew blood, the taste of that sweet liquid against his lips tore a raw growl from him. He'd marked her. United them.

Though he didn't want to, he slightly pulled back and increased his movements inside her. They both needed that release. Her contractions, which had been small, surged with each thrust he made until she was whimpering and murmuring things he couldn't understand. As her climax subsided, his own hit him with startling intensity.

December was his *bondmate*. The knowledge floored him on the most basic level and allowed him to let go of all his control. Coming long and hard, he emptied himself inside her. His hands tightened around her hips with each push until he was blindly thrusting into her and had to force himself to stop.

The moment he began to pull out of her, he felt a sharp stinging on the side of his neck. Reaching up, he ran his finger over what he knew would be a tiny Celtic symbol. Likely a bonding knot of some sort, similar to his father's and his brother's. Just as he'd marked her with his teeth—the small puncture marks would remain on her skin forever—their unification left a permanent imprint on him also. Like a tattoo but more permanent. And with a deeper meaning.

Liam reached underneath December and turned her toward him as he stretched out on the bed. He wanted to feel her body against his, couldn't bear to be apart from her for even a second. Not after what they'd just shared. She stretched out until her entire body lay along the length of his. He loved the feel of her full weight on top of him.

Smiling, she kissed his chin, then all around his mouth

until she centered on his lips. Her kiss was lingering and sensuous. When she pulled back, her blue eyes seemed even brighter somehow. "That was amazing. . . ." She trailed off and tilted his head to the side with two of her fingers. "I wondered what your bonding mark would look like. Does it hurt?" she asked softly, letting her fingers drop.

"I think I should be the one asking you that." *How do you feel?* he projected with his mind, praying the link was complete.

Her eyes widened. *Holy crap. I can't believe that actually works. I know what you told me, but . . . wow.*

Wow, indeed. Returning her smile, he cupped her face between his hands and brought her mouth to his once again. There might be a lot of unknowns in their life, but at this moment, he couldn't believe he'd ever thought he could live without her.

She was his other half. Definitely his better half. And he planned to spend the rest of their lives showing her how much she meant to him.

Epilogue

Liam entered his brother's home and immediately headed for the living room. Connor sat on the longer couch and Ana was curled up in his lap. Despite the way his arm was casually wrapped around his mate's waist, Liam could see the slight tension lines bracketing Connor's mouth. He couldn't scent anything, though. As Alpha, Connor was better than most at concealing his emotions. But as his brother, Liam knew him better than anyone. Well, almost anyone.

"Congrats, Liam." Ana grinned at him as she jumped up to hug him.

He returned the tight hug, then embraced his brother, who also congratulated him. Even though he hadn't been to the ranch in two days—he and December hadn't left the bedroom since bonding—he'd let his brother know he'd officially taken her as his bondmate. Informing him had nothing to do with pack rules and everything to do with the fact that Connor was his older brother. He might be Liam's Alpha, but he'd always be his family and he'd been the first person Liam had told.

"How's your mate?" Ana asked.

"A little nauseous but good. We have a doctor's appointment in a couple hours." After he left here, he was picking her up from her bookstore for an early lunch, then heading to their appointment. Right now, pack business called. Not that he'd left her alone. Until things settled down, one of his pack members was always shadowing her if he couldn't.

"I can't wait to have another cub around the ranch." Ana's voice was excited as she and Connor sat back down.

"Where is everyone?" There were scents of Vivian and Noel in the house but not strong enough for them to be there. But he was referring to Noah and Aiden, since they'd been called to this informal meeting also.

"Should be here any minute," Connor said.

As his brother spoke, Liam heard the front door opening behind him. Aiden and Noah walked in. Most of the males and Erin were out patrolling—or watching December—but later they'd be informed of what had been discussed.

After receiving congratulatory hugs from the two males, Liam went to lean against the mantel by the fireplace. Noah joined him on the other end, looking tense as hell, while Aiden sat on the love seat.

"Where are Brianna and Jayce?" Aiden asked.

Upon the request of her warrior brethren, the Fianna, she'd returned to Ireland a week after they'd found her passed out in that barn. Her people had been in contact with their Council and she was supposed to be back by today because they wanted her to attempt to infiltrate the APL again. Something Liam knew because of Connor. He also knew Connor wasn't sold on the idea of Brianna trying to infiltrate them again. Liam wasn't sure where Jayce was, though; he'd expected him days ago.

"Both were delayed, but they'll be here in the next couple days." Connor didn't give any other details, something that didn't surprise Liam. Why they weren't there wasn't important. "The Council and the Fianna both want Brianna to infiltrate the APL again, since she has a successful track record. Once she arrives in town, she'll be living with us, but Liam's found a cheap apartment for her as a cover on the chance anyone does a background check on her."

"Which they will." Liam had no doubt of that. He wasn't sure what Brianna's plan was other than to befriend local APL members, but if they started another cell here, someone would be checking up on her.

"How do we know she hasn't been compromised?" Aiden asked.

"Everyone she worked with before is dead." Connor's voice was grim. "Right now everyone on the list we have is lying low, but after the recent news broadcasts, the Council is tense and so am I. Just because the APL isn't doing anything at the moment doesn't mean the threat is over."

Aiden straightened on the couch, his body tense and primed for battle. "That reporter went on air and cleared up that those animal attacks were just two isolated incidents."

A dog with rabies had attacked two humans, but the news had made it sound like shifters were behind the attacks and the sheriff's department was covering it up. "It doesn't matter," Liam said. "Her report stated the tone for the feeling in town. Since we moved here, December said she's noticed a distinctive change in the attitude toward shifters. Especially after Dr. Graham killed himself." While Ana's pack might have lived in Fontana the past thirty years, Liam and his brother's pack had joined them only a few months ago. New shifter males living in any area were cause for concern by humans even if they weren't a threat. And when a local, respected doctor—murdering son of a bitch that he was—committed suicide rather than go to jail for killing innocent shifters, including one of Ana's sisters, some people in Fontana weren't so convinced he'd been guilty. Liam was aware of all this only because of December and her brother. They had a better pulse on the town than any of them ever would.

Noah frowned and the tenseness in him seemed only to grow. "But December's one of us now. Wouldn't the humans be more willing to accept our presence?"

Liam's heart twisted for the remembered pain he'd seen in December's eyes a couple weeks ago. She'd come home from work and she hadn't wanted to tell him, but he'd eventually gotten out of her that a woman she'd been friends with for almost a decade had come into her store to tell her what an abomination she was. Instead of telling them all that, he simply shook his head. "December's lost some friends since she turned."

There was a brief silence before Connor spoke. "Right now the APL in our region might be inactive, but they're still here. And Adler had a boss. According to Brianna, he pulled all the strings during their operations here, but Adler kept his identity close to his chest. The boss had a son Adler killed, but she didn't know his last name. Adler was careful about keeping that secret." Whoever Adler's boss was had ordered the attempted kidnappings of December and successful kidnapping of Kat.

That knowledge made Liam's hands ball into tight fists. His skin pulled taut as his inner wolf instinctively primed for battle. The sharp scent of his own restrained rage was the only thing that allowed him to get his wolf under control. The time would come when that unknown bastard would feel his pack's wrath.

Connor's voice cut through his thoughts, completely silencing his beast. "For the time being we're going to watch and listen for any threats. We're going to keep our guard up and quietly ferret out as much information as we can. However, we won't be blindly attacking APL members." He glanced around the room.

Liam nodded even though his brother already knew he'd follow him into hell. If Connor didn't want them taking any physical action against the APL, he'd abide by that. For now. Aiden and Noah also nodded.

As they did, Connor continued. "I just got off the phone with Jayce about an hour ago and he has new intel. There's been a report of someone possibly dealing vamp blood to humans. The APL included."

Liam straightened against the mantel. "Where?"

"Out of Winston-Salem."

A little over two hours from where they lived. "How good is this intel?"

Connor shook his head, his expression grim and weighted down with all the responsibility of his pack. "Don't know yet. Jayce said he wanted to follow up on a lead once he got here, but if APL members are taking the stuff, it changes the playing field."

His brother didn't say what they all already knew. Humans who ingested vampire blood gained superstrength. The effects didn't last forever, but it gave them a shot of adrenaline and pleasure no manufactured drug ever could. It also dulled them to pain in a way that could become very dangerous. If APL members were taking the stuff, it put beta shifters—those weakest in the pack structure—at a much higher risk. It also put all shifters at a risk to underestimate their opponents. Liam had no doubt he could take on a handful of humans hopped up on vamp blood, but if there was a gang of them against one shifter, even a powerful one, the odds of survival slimmed. "Shit," he muttered.

The others in the room silently nodded in agreement. If humans were taking vamp blood, Liam was damn sure vampires weren't selling it to them. Which likely meant someone had captured a vampire and was siphoning the blood. Holding a vamp hostage was hard to do, but vampires weren't pack oriented like shifters. If one had gone missing, it was possible no one even noticed.

And this only created a new set of problems for shifters and all paranormal beings everywhere. As silence descended on the room, something icy settled in his chest, spreading slowly to all his nerve endings. Being newly bonded with a baby on the way ratcheted up his protective nature in a way he'd never thought possible.

That need to protect would never go away. It was so deeply ingrained in him it was part of who he was. Despite the fact that there was now one person—and soon two—in the world he couldn't live without, it was worth being tied to December in a way he'd never have with anyone else. Bonding with her made him feel intrinsically whole. He hadn't even known something had been missing until she'd filled that gap inside him. Whatever the future held, as long as she was by his side and he got to wake up to her face every morning, he knew there wasn't much they couldn't handle.

Almost as if she'd sensed his mood, December's soft voice cut through his thoughts using their bondmate link. *I love you, Liam.*

As his brother continued talking about their plans to follow and watch known APL members and keep an ear to the ground about vamp blood usage, Liam had to bite back a smile as he communicated with his mate. *Right back at you, Red.*

Acknowledgments

A great big thank-you to Jill Marsal for being a fantastic agent and sounding board! I'm so blessed to work with you. To my amazing editor, Danielle Perez, thank you for all your help in making the Moon Shifter world shine. To the rest of the team at NAL who work so hard: Michele Alpern, Rosalind Parry, Kathleen Cook, Erin Galloway, and the very talented designer Anthony Ramondo. Everything you do is so appreciated.

Thank you to Dara Edmondson and Kari Walker a million times over. You two are amazing and I don't know what I'd do without you. I'm lucky to call you my friends. Caridad Piñeiro, thank you so much for all your support. Laura Wright, you are the ultimate voice of reason. Our weekly phone calls keep me sane, and I treasure our friendship more than you know!

To my parents and sister, you guys are like anchors in a storm. I'm so blessed to always have your support. To my husband and son, I love you both more than anything and am so grateful for your never-ending patience when I'm on deadline.

For my readers, thank you for all your support of the Moon Shifter world! I wouldn't be here without you. And last but definitely not least, to God for all the opportunities he's given me.

Jayce Kazan parked his Harley in front of December McIntyre's house. The feisty pregnant redhead wouldn't be there because she now lived on the Armstrong ranch with her mate and the rest of the lupine shifter pack who made their home in Fontana, North Carolina.

But Kat would be home.

Or she should be. Even after December moved, Kat had stayed there instead of moving to the ranch. She'd been brutally attacked by the radical Antiparanormal League (APL) a month ago, and then had been turned into a lupine shifter. Just like him. The only difference between them was he'd been born that way almost five hundred years ago, and she'd been bitten and turned by one of the Armstrong pack members to save her life. Well, that wasn't the only difference. He was a crass, roughneck enforcer who'd killed more beings than he could ever hope to count and she was ... fucking perfection.

At least to him.

Right now she wasn't returning his calls. Not that he blamed her. He hadn't been there for her when she'd needed him most and he wanted to rip his own heart out because of it. At least then maybe he'd be able to assuage some of his guilt. She'd only had a one percent chance of surviving the change, and even though Jayce was grateful that Aiden had saved her, a dark part of him hated that bastard.

He hated the fact that he hadn't been the one to save her. That someone else had had the honor of taking what was his. His human side knew he'd never planned to change Kat—it would have turned her into a walking target overnight if anyone discovered how deep his feelings for her ran—but his animal side didn't give a shit. No one should have ever touched what was his.

Though she really wasn't his, was she? Not anymore anyway. Hadn't been for almost a year. At one time she had been. He'd kissed and teased every inch of her naked body and she'd done the same to him. Things had never been particularly *easy* between them—not with their strong personalities—but with the exception of his MIA brother, she was the only person on the planet he'd ever let his guard down around. She brought out the best in him. Hell, she also brought out his worst—his jealous, fiercely protective side. For over a month he'd exercised all his restraint, staying away from her while working for the Council.

After getting only an hour of sleep last night, he was edgy and ready to rip someone's head off. Maybe it hadn't been the smartest idea to roll up to see her the moment he'd gotten back into town, but he didn't care. He needed to see her.

Craved it so bad, his canines ached at the thought. She could slam the door on him for all he cared. He just needed to *see* her face.

As he swung his leg over the bike and straightened up, he glanced over when he noticed Ryan getting out of his truck parked across the street. Though he didn't want to be patient or polite, he waited while the other shifter strode toward him.

Ryan wore a thick down jacket and jeans and even though Jayce couldn't see an outline, he knew the guy was packing a few weapons. The chilly January weather wouldn't have affected Ryan like it would humans, so he knew the main reason the shifter was wearing a jacket was to hide guns and blades. "Hey, Jayce. What are you doing here?"

Jayce raised an eyebrow at the question. Why the hell wouldn't he be here?

Ryan's lips pulled into a thin line. "I didn't mean it like that. I didn't know you'd be back so early. Thought you were still on Council business or something."

He shrugged. As the enforcer for the North American Council of lupine shifters, Jayce didn't answer to anyone. Not Ryan. Not even Connor Armstrong, leader of the Armstrong pack and also Ryan's Alpha. *No one.* While he might work for the Council, he sure as hell didn't answer to them either. They needed him and he made damn sure they never forgot it. So even if he didn't have to answer the wolf in front of him, or that wolf's boss, he knew projecting his own bad mood wouldn't win him any friends, and right now he needed all the fucking friends he could get. "Caught an early flight and headed over here. Haven't called Connor to let him know I'm in town though, so . . ."

Ryan nodded. "I'll let you call him."

He cleared his throat. "Thanks." The word felt foreign on his lips. He should have called Connor the moment he arrived in town out of respect, but he had a lot to discuss with him and some of it needed to be done in person. He'd received information that someone was trafficking vampire blood in the next county. After settling in, he intended to search out some former contacts. Not to mention, he still planned to ferret out any possible dangerous APL members still in the area. But mainly, he just wanted to see Kat, and everything else had taken a backseat. "When did she get home?" Jayce didn't need to specify whom he was referring to.

Ryan shrugged. "Few hours ago. She was at the ranch with, uh . . . Aiden, *training*, but she still won't move there to live with the pack. Which is why we're still watching her in shifts."

Jayce already knew that. After her attack by those APL fuckers nearly killed her, she'd been fairly defiant in her demand that she live away from what was now her pack. Connor had jurisdiction over her since she technically lived in his territory, but considering she'd been turned into a shifter without the proper introduction to pack life and rules, Connor was giving her some leeway. But he was a fair Alpha, so Jayce wasn't exactly surprised. Even if he did hate the fact that Connor wouldn't force her to live on the ranch where she'd be protected at all times.

"You have a key to the house?" Jayce asked, though he was already fairly certain of the answer. Connor wouldn't have left anyone to watch the house without a way to get inside if necessary. Of course, they could break in, but cleaning up a mess was a hassle Jayce knew the Alpha wouldn't want to deal with.

Ryan paused but nodded. "Yeah. She's gonna be pissed if you just walk in there."

"I know." He held out his hand, not asking but silently demanding it.

Sighing, the other wolf dug a single key out of his pocket and handed it over. As he headed back to his vehicle, Ryan muttered something under his breath about Jayce taking his life into his own hands.

If he'd had more sleep or was in a better mood, he might have smiled at the statement. A pissed-off Kat was a sight to see. And he'd only seen her truly angry when she'd been human. He could only imagine her attitude as a shifter.

One of the last times he'd seen her as a lupine shifter had been directly after her transformation. She'd been healed after the change but covered in her own blood. And another wolf had been holding her.

Protecting her.

Comforting her.

Jayce still didn't know the details of what had happened to her during her hours of torture—she refused to tell anyone about it—but according to December she still had nightmares.

And no one was there to ease her pain. Jayce's hands balled into fists as he turned and headed up the stone walkway. Ever since they'd found Kat in that run-down barn, he'd been living in a state of hell. It was the feeling of helplessness that nearly undid him every time he thought of Kat. Which was practically every second of every day. The tall, gorgeous woman invaded his dreams when he was sleeping. He should have been there to save her. If he had, he'd have been the one to change her into a shifter.

The second he stepped into the house, he knew Kat wasn't there. Her scent was there, but he couldn't hear a heartbeat. She'd been gone maybe twenty minutes if he had to guess from her fading scent. Had ducked her guard just like he feared she'd do since Connor had let her live apart from the pack.

Jayce knew it wasn't the first time she'd done this either. December had become an unlikely source of information as she was worried about her friend and often called him with updates on Kat.

This kind of shit was going to stop. If she didn't care about her own safety, she needed to at least be concerned about the rest of the pack. And according to December, over the past week Kat had been disappearing for hours at a time. She wouldn't tell anyone what she was doing either. Jayce had heard she'd been having difficulty controlling her change from human to wolf, and that could be a very dangerous thing for all the local shifters.

Worry and possessiveness rose up inside him. His need to protect Kat was deep-seated and something he still didn't understand completely. He'd felt it the moment he'd met her and it jarred him every time he was near her. Or thought about her.

Inhaling, he followed the trail of her scent out the back door, through December's backyard, and on to the next street over. The distinctive scent of roses was so blatantly Kat, every time he smelled the damn flower he thought of her. But it was slightly different from the actual rose. The classic smell intermixed with something sweeter, purer, and all Kat. He'd recognize it anywhere.

She hadn't been gone long, so he hurried back to his bike and headed out. He didn't bother telling Ryan that Kat was gone either. No one was going after her except him. If anyone tried to interfere tonight, they'd probably get hurt. Including any shifters.

On his motorcycle it was easy to trail her in his human form. Hell, as an enforcer, he preferred his human form. He was much older than most shifters, and once he let his animal take over, it was always a struggle for control with his inner wolf. Right now, where Kat was concerned, it was important if not absolutely necessary to exert as much restraint as possible.

A short ride later he pulled into the parking lot of Kelly's Bar and Grill, a local Irish pub in the middle of downtown Fontana. The mountain town in North Carolina saw a lot of tourists in the winter months, and judging by the number of cars in the parking lot, the place was packed tonight.

He rolled his shoulders as he stepped off his bike. Being around too many people—humans or supernatural beings—always put him on edge. All those scents were overwhelming. He much rather preferred to be outdoors, far from civilization.

As he stepped inside, Kat's scent grew stronger. Even among the stench of perfumes, booze, and other body odors, her sweet rose aroma tickled his nose and wrapped around him, embracing him like a gentle caress.

"Would you like to be seated in our dining area or would you prefer to find a seat at the bar?" A bubbly blond female wearing black pants and a black T-shirt held a menu in her hand as she looked at him.

"Bar's fine," he said as he brushed past her.

A burst of annoyance rolled off the human, but right now all he cared about was tracking down Kat. After a quick lap around the place, he followed her trail out a side exit door.

Once he was outside in the crisp night air, the strong scent of roses entwined around him. She was close. Frowning, he looked around behind the restaurant. A Dumpster was to his left, which gave him cover as he scanned the small area. There were a few cars on the makeshift gravel parking lot. Employee vehicles, he guessed.

And that's when he spotted Kat.

She leaned against the passenger side of an extended cab truck with her back to him. Tall, lean, drop-dead gorgeous. Her long, dark hair was pulled up into a ponytail that hung halfway down her back. She wore formfitting jeans and a skintight long-sleeved black T-shirt. If she'd still been human she'd have needed a coat, but thanks to her transformation from human to shifter, she had a higher body temperature.

Sticking to the shadows, he moved behind the Dumpster and slid along the wall of the restaurant until he was at the edge of the building and twenty yards away from where Kat stood talking to some human male.

A growl rose inside him but he tamped it back down and listened to their conversation. As the human talked about heading back to his place to "party," Jayce nearly lost control of his beast. His inner wolf clawed at him with razor-sharp aggression, tearing and stripping away his insides, begging for freedom.

When the human opened the passenger door for Kat and she actually got inside, Jayce's claws extended and dug into his palms. The tearing of his flesh jerked him back to reality. Ducking back behind the Dumpster, he somehow managed to keep himself under control as the vehicle pulled out of the parking lot.

Just barely.

As they drove around the left side of the restaurant, Jayce raced back around the right side and headed straight for his bike in the front.

Whatever Kat thought she was doing with that guy tonight, she'd better think again.

Kat glanced over at the dark-haired guy with the buzz cut next to her. He shot her a quick look and winked as he steered his truck out of the parking lot of Kelly's Bar and Grill. She wasn't sure what she was doing with him and was tempted to tell him to stop, but something held her back.

He was one of the bartenders at Kelly's and had been getting off work right as she'd walked in. From the moment she'd sat down, he'd started flirting with her and buying her drinks. Too bad the alcohol couldn't numb the pain inside her.

Nothing could. For the past month, it had festered, growing like an out of control vine. It twisted and expanded with no regard for anything in its wake, least of all her heart or emotions. If she dwelled on the ways she'd been tortured a month ago, she tensed up and her inner wolf wanted out.

Aiden, her friend and the wolf who'd changed her into a shifter, had explained it was a protective thing. Her inner wolf didn't want her to suffer, so it tried to take over whether she wanted it to or not. Some kind of coping mechanism.

Taking a deep breath, she forced those thoughts from her mind. Tonight she was taking control of her life again. Maybe sleeping with a stranger wasn't the smartest way to go about it, but she needed to be in charge of *something*. It's not as if the guy next to her could hurt her. He was human, and sure, he had a sexy edge to him, but she was still a hundred times stronger.

She kept reminding herself of that. *She* was the one in control tonight.

"Surprised I haven't seen you in Kelly's before," the guy, Scott . . . something, said.

She'd been there before a few times when she'd been human. But usually she'd hung out at the bars at the ski lodge where she used to work up until a month ago. Shrugging, she smiled and shifted in her seat, crossing her legs in his direction. She didn't want to make bullshit small talk. That wasn't what tonight was about.

The man's dark gaze drifted down to her covered legs, then back up to her chest. Even though she was clothed, the way he looked at her made her feel practically naked. That should have been a good thing, she told herself. She needed to be exposed in front of another person in a way she hadn't been since that awful night. Maybe this would help with her nightmares. Anything to help her get rid of the nausea-inducing memories she couldn't seem to outrun.

So why did she feel so guilty being out with someone else? She and Jayce had broken up nearly a year ago. He'd made it perfectly clear she wasn't good enough for him. Oh, sure, he'd loved her in the bedroom, but that was all he'd been willing to give her. He hadn't been willing to make her his bondmate when she'd been human and she sure as hell wasn't going to give him a second chance now that she was like him. Not that he'd actually asked for one. He'd just been calling a lot since her attack.

Acting all concerned.

Well, he could take his concern and shove it. She didn't

need him or his help. She'd take care of her own problems the way she always had—by herself. Unfortunately, she couldn't seem to keep her head on straight. For a brief moment back in the parking lot, she'd thought she scented Jayce but knew it had to be a figment of her imagination.

"So how far from your place are we?" Self-loathing bubbled up inside her as she asked the question.

Scott's dark eyes glanced her way and he grinned before turning his gaze back to the road in front of him. "Not far, baby. Not far."

Baby? She hated that term. Before she could dwell on it, she sniffed the air. Something sensual rolled off him and it took her a moment to realize it was lust. She was still getting used to tapping into her extrasensory abilities and deciphering one smell from another. This was like a sweet wine, clean and refreshing.

It reminded her that even though she might not care about this guy or plan to see him again, he wasn't a bad person, which was why she'd chosen him tonight. Before she'd been turned into a shifter she'd been a human but also a seer. Just like her mom. Back then she'd only been able to see the true faces of supernatural beings. She'd been able to see the wolves or jaguars or whatever kind of animal lurked beneath the surface of shifters. And with vamps, she'd been able to see their teeth and hunger for blood. After being turned into a shifter she could also see the truth of humans' nature. It was a weird addition to her psychic abilities. With the ability to see the truth about people, she could see Scott's "real" face, and he was just a horny guy looking to get laid. No darker intentions or freaky sexual proclivities.

As they pulled into the driveway of a cottage-style house in a normal-looking middle-class neighborhood, she took another deep breath. She could do this. Couldn't she?

When he put the truck in park, she fought the growing dread inside her, moving like molasses, weighing her down and making it hard to breathe. With a numb hand she opened the door and slid out of the vehicle. The second her boots hit the pavement she knew she couldn't go through with this. Not if she wanted to be able to look at herself in the mirror in the morning. One-night stands weren't her style, and while she desperately needed control in her life, the thought of this guy's hands on her body made her nauseous. Not because he was bad-looking or gave her the wrong kind of vibes, but because she didn't want this from a stranger. Not truly. As she started to walk around the truck to Scott's side, she turned at the sound of a motorcycle pulling into the driveway behind them.

Fury popped inside her at the sight of Jayce. Well, fury and something else she refused to define. It might have been relief but she wasn't going to go there. Not tonight. Not when anger was so much easier.

Stalking toward Jayce, she tried to keep her eyes from trailing down to those incredibly muscular legs as he slid off the bike. Didn't matter that he was wearing jeans—she'd seen every inch of his naked body and the image was seared into her brain. He moved with such fluidity that it always amazed her.

Even now, when she wanted to pummel him for having the audacity to follow her, she still had to admire the strength and power he radiated. He'd never be called hand-some or even good-looking, but there was something dan-gerous about Jayce that was incredibly alluring. Without even trying, he exuded a raw sexuality that made women stand up and take notice. With his shaved head and a gener-ally dark disposition, he had . . . a presence that refused to be ignored. The scar that crisscrossed over his left eye only added to his edginess. And he was directing all of that at her with a *very* heated stare.

"What the hell are you doing here?" she practically shouted.

Before he could answer, Scott was next to her—in front of her actually—partially blocking her from Jayce. "Can I help you, buddy?"

Kat smiled haughtily at Jayce. At least Scott wasn't a to-tal wimp.

But then Jayce trained his gaze on the other man. Jayce was scary when he wanted to be, and as she watched his normally gunmetal gray eyes turn to black, she actually had to force herself to stand her ground. He growled low in his throat. "You can go inside your fucking house and leave us alone."

Scott cleared his throat nervously, then looked at her. "You, uh, know this guy?"

She could smell the pungent fear on him. Bitter and acidic, it stung her nostrils. So much for not being a wimp. Ignoring Scott, she turned back to Jayce and placed her hands on her hips. "Did you *follow* me here?"

"What do you think?" he practically purred as he took a step closer.

Now she scented something dark and rich, like chocolate. *Lust.* As a human she'd never had a clue that lust or desire actually had a smell, but this . . . was addicting. She inhaled and for a moment she felt light-headed. But when she saw the knowing look in Jayce's eyes, she snapped. "I think it's pathetic that you're following me around like a little puppy dog." She knew he still wanted her and the knowledge gave her power. Even if she was playing with fire by taunting him, it gave her perverse pleasure to see anger flare in that newly darkened gaze.

"Puppy dog?" His voice was low, a soft, menacing growl that made the hair on her arms stand straight up.

Next to her Scott actually took a step back, using her body to block his own. Oh, yeah, total wimp. "Should I, uh, call the cops?" His voice was a little higher pitched than it had been earlier.

"No. Just go inside and forget you met me." She didn't look at him and he didn't question her directive. She just heard him shuffle away, then fumble for his keys. They hit the pavement once; then seconds later she heard the front door slamming.

Jayce continued staring at her, his chest falling and rising erratically. Oh, yeah, she'd pissed him off really well.

"Get. On. My. Bike." The words tore from his chest with apparent difficulty.

She really should just have given in, especially when he was geared up like this. But she wasn't in the mood to be passive or appeasing. She'd much rather fight. "No." With her gaze still on him, her eyes mocking, she pulled her cell phone out of her pocket and flipped it open. Before she had a chance to call someone for a ride, Jayce plucked it from her hand and shoved it in his front jeans pocket.

Kat stepped toward him until they were inches apart, and held out a hand. "Give me my phone."

"If you want it, come get it." He lifted a dark eyebrow in challenge.

Swallowing hard, she looked at the front of his jeans where the bulge of her phone was. Yeah, that so wasn't happening. Glancing past him, she looked at the bike. She could be stubborn and walk home, but that thought wasn't appealing. So she ignored him and strode toward the bike. After sliding onto the back—no helmets for either of them apparently—she sat there and tried to ignore the heated stare he gave her.

A combination of red-hot fury and lust emanated off him, both of which she could have done without. She wasn't scared Jayce would hurt her, but she didn't want to deal with his anger. Despite her desire to fight with him, when they argued, things almost always ended up in the bedroom.

And she definitely couldn't handle that right now.

Too many things had happened since they'd been together and she had too much resentment toward him. She averted her gaze, purposefully ignoring him as he got on the bike in front of her. As he tore out of the driveway she grasped on to him.

Sliding her hands around his waist, she tried to ignore the feel of all that strength beneath her fingertips. His back was incredibly muscular and the feel of it pressing against her breasts was almost enough to take her back to when they'd been together. Back when they'd actually liked each other, not just physically wanted each other.

Nine months wasn't that long but it might as well have been a lifetime ago. She was a different person now even if he wasn't.

When he took another sharp turn she had no choice but to grip him tighter. Over the sound of the rushing wind, she thought she heard him laugh, but it was impossible to tell.

After what felt like an eternity they pulled up to December's house. Kat immediately jumped off and strode up the walkway. She could get her phone later and she certainly wasn't going to ask him for it again. Before she'd made it up the front steps, Jayce passed her and inserted a key into the front door.

Gritting her teeth, she hung back as he stepped inside without giving her a backward glance. "What do you think you're doing?"

He didn't bother to turn around as he flipped on a light in the foyer. "We're talking. Now."

For the first time since she'd seen him that night, she was beginning to second-guess her decision to bait him earlier. She should have just kept her mouth shut. Sighing, she stepped inside and shut the door behind her. But she didn't bother locking it. Jayce wouldn't be staying long.

Leaning against the closed door, she crossed her arms over her chest as he turned to face her. Under the small decorative chandelier in the entryway, his gray eyes almost seemed to glitter. She refused to look away but she was thankful for the door holding her up. "What do you want to talk about?"

He took a menacing step toward her. "You and your bullshit." Before she could lay into him, he continued. "You might not care about yourself, but every time you go out in public without telling anyone where you are, you put the entire pack in danger. You might be an adult but you have the skills of a cub. Until you learn to control your urges or your ability to shift, you need to use your fucking head." All his words were gravelly and filled with anger.

"I didn't ask for this life," she snapped.

"No. You didn't. But at least you're alive and it's time to stop feeling sorry for yourself." He covered the distance between them, and before she realized what he intended, he caged her against the door using his body and braced his hands on either side of her head.

Asshole. "I don't feel sorry for myself." Maybe she did but she wasn't going to admit it to him.

His snort told her he didn't believe a word she said, but he didn't contradict her. "If you have a need to find sexual release, you won't search it out with any other male but *me.*" The words rumbled up from his chest in a low growl that sounded more wolf than human.

The statement took her so off guard she dropped her

arms from their protective embrace around herself. "*Excuse me?*"

He leaned in closer until his entire body was a mere inch from hers and his mouth was next to her ear. His hot breath sent a tingle racing through her, searching out every nerve ending until her entire body practically trembled with the need to feel that mouth all over her. "If you go to another male, I will kill him. That human tonight is lucky he's alive."

"You wouldn't do that," she whispered, even though she knew the truth. Could hear it in his darkly murmured words. She'd known he still physically wanted her, but this . . . was unexpected. And a little insane. Why should he feel all possessive when he was the one who'd decided she wasn't good enough for him by lying to her about the bonding process? It had to be his animal side asserting dominance. That was all. Like a dog peeing on a freaking fire hydrant, he was just acting territorial because he could.

"Do you really want to find out if your *puppy* will bite?" Another low murmur against her skin.

He wasn't quite touching her, but she could feel the heat rolling off him and onto her nonetheless. She didn't answer, partially because she didn't trust her voice, but mainly because she knew the question was rhetorical. Jayce was a deadly warrior, not a freaking puppy dog as she'd said earlier. She knew he was reminding her of that.

As she stared at the spot where the curve of his neck met his shoulder, she fought the sensation that shimmied through her. The thought of going to bed with Jayce was tempting. Even thinking about it made her feel light-headed.

He'd said she could find sexual release with him, but that was all it would be to him. Even if he did care about her, he'd never give her what she wanted. Not that it mattered anymore. She was so messed up and broken, she had no hope of having anything normal in her life again. And she refused to go to him for any sort of sexual pleasure. Especially since it wouldn't be about control. With him, she'd lose it, not gain it. She could find control of her life in other places. Like revenge.

The word rang loudly in her head. *Revenge.* After what that APL bastard had done to her, she was going to make every single one of those radicals pay. And she didn't need Jayce interfering with those plans.

Ducking out from under his arms, she put a few feet of distance between them in the blink of an eye. Without his spicy, earthy scent overpowering her, she could breathe again. And think clearly. "Get out of here."

Jayce gave her a hard look before fishing her phone out of his pocket. Wordlessly he handed it to her, then opened the front door, but before he'd shut it, he paused and turned back around. "Don't test me, *Katarina*. I don't think you could live with the knowledge that you got someone killed."

As the door shut behind him she pushed out a long breath and grabbed on to the stair railing to brace herself. Somehow with him gone, the pain and loneliness eating at her was almost impossible to bear.

Which was stupid. She'd left him over nine months ago. Or almost a year, she reminded herself. It sounded better when she rounded up. Why, oh, why couldn't she get him out of her system? When she'd first met Jayce she'd been utterly entranced. Not because of his looks—though she loved the dark edge he had to him—but because of the raw, untamed power that practically rolled off him.

Growing up with an arms dealer for a father she'd never been intimidated by anyone. Until Jayce. Of course she hadn't let him see it. She'd called him a puppy even then, completely taunting him. He'd been so surprised. She would never forget the shocked look on his face as she'd teased him. He deserved it of course after saying something rude to her. She couldn't remember the exact phrase but he'd insinuated that he wanted to do something sexual to her and she'd laughed at him.

From that point on he'd chased her with a single-minded focus. Not that it had bothered her. Being on his radar had made her feel empowered and sexy in a way she hadn't imagined possible. Before Jayce men had been either too scared to approach her because of her father's shady dealings—and his violent reputation—or they'd wanted to get close to her *because* of her father. Not Jayce. He'd just wanted *her*. She'd made him wait six months before agreeing to go to lunch with him. At the time she'd thought she could drag out her teasing even longer, but they hadn't even made it to her parked car at that restaurant before he'd kissed her.

And, oh, what a kiss. He'd told her everything she'd needed to know in that one very long kiss. He was claiming her, making a statement that she was his. Or at least that's how she'd taken it. But it hadn't been a permanent thing. That knowledge made her stomach turn sour. She'd wanted to make a life with him, but when she'd broached the subject of their future he'd told her that the chance of a human turning into a shifter from a bite was one percent. What he'd failed to mention was the fact that if he'd taken her as his bondmate she would have changed into a shifter without any issues. He'd lied because he hadn't wanted her as his bondmate. He'd never actually admitted it to her, but what other reason could he have had for lying? Swallowing hard, she ignored the sudden sting of tears.

Instead of heading directly upstairs to her room, she made a beeline for the kitchen. Sleep had been elusive the past month, and even though she hadn't wanted to, she'd seen a doctor just to get a prescription. After taking two sleeping pills, she prayed she would finally get at least a few hours of uninterrupted sleep. Once in her room, she didn't bother to take off her clothes, just slipped off her boots and slid into bed.

The moment she closed her eyes Jayce's face appeared in her mind, mocking her. It made her want to scream. Or maybe cry. She turned on her side and curled into a ball as she squeezed her eyes shut. She would *not* think about him. She couldn't afford to give him any power over her when all she wanted was some control in her life. Well, control and revenge.